Praise for the novels of Brenda Joyce

The Perfect Bride

"Joyce's seventh de Warenne novel is another first-rate Regency, featuring multidimensional protagonists and sweeping drama…. Entirely fluff-free, Joyce's tight plot and vivid cast combine for a romance that's just about perfect."
—*Publishers Weekly*, starred review

"Joyce's latest is a piece of perfection as she meticulously crafts a tender and emotionally powerful love story. Passion and pain erupt from the pages and flow straight into your heart. You won't forget this beautifully rendered love story of lost souls and redemption."
—*Romantic Times BOOKreviews*

A Lady at Last

"A passionate, swashbuckling voyage. Romance veteran Joyce brings her keen sense of humor and storytelling prowess to bear on her witty, fully formed characters."
—*Publishers Weekly*

"A classic Pygmalion tale with an extra soupçon of eroticism."
—*Booklist*

"A warm, wonderfully sensual feast about the joys and pains of falling in love. Joyce breathes life into extraordinary characters—from her sprightly Cinderella heroine and roguish hero to everyone in between—then sets them in the glittering Regency, where anything can happen."
—*Romantic Times BOOKreviews*

The Stolen Bride

"A powerfully executed romance overflowing with the strength of prose, high degree of sensuality and emotional intensity we expect from Joyce. A 'keeper' for sure."
—*Romantic Times BOOKreviews*

"Joyce's characters carry considerable emotional weight, which keeps this hefty entry absorbing, and her fast-paced story keeps the pages turning."
—*Publishers Weekly*

Also by

BRENDA JOYCE

The de Warenne Dynasty
The Perfect Bride
A Lady at Last
The Stolen Bride
The Masquerade
The Prize

The Masters of Time
Dark Rival
Dark Seduction

Watch for
Dark Embrace
Coming September 2008

BRENDA JOYCE

A *Dangerous* LOVE

HQN™

ISBN-13: 978-0-373-77275-9
ISBN-10:   0-373-77275-0

A DANGEROUS LOVE

www.HQNBooks.com

Printed in U.S.A.

A *Dangerous*
LOVE

PROLOGUE

Derbyshire, 1820

HIS AGITATION KNEW no bounds. What the hell was taking the runner so long? He'd received Smith's letter the day before, but it had been brief, stating only that the runner would arrive on the morrow. Damn it! Had Smith succeeded in finding his son?

Edmund St Xavier paced the length of his great hall. It was a large room, centuries old like the house itself, but sparsely furnished and in need of a great deal of repair. The damask on the single sofa was badly faded and torn, a scarred trestle table demanded far more than wax and a shine, and the gold and ivory brocade that covered the chairs had long since turned that unpleasant shade of yellow that indicated aging and a serious lack of economy. Once, Woodland had been a great estate, compromising ten thousand acres, when Edmund's ancestors had proudly borne the title of viscount and had kept another splendid home in London. Now a thousand acres remained, and of the fifteen tenant farms scattered about, half were vacant. His stable consisted of four carriage horses and two hacks. His staff had dwindled to two manservants and a single housemaid. His wife had died in childbirth five years ago, and last winter, a terrible flu had taken their only child. There was only an impoverished estate, an empty house and the prestigious title, which was now in jeopardy.

Edmund's younger brother stared at him from across the hall, as smug and cocksure as always. John was certain the title would soon pass to him and his son, but Edmund was as determined that it would not. For there was another child, a bastard. *Surely Smith had found him.*

Edmund turned stiffly away. They'd been rivals growing up and they remained rivals now. His damned brother had made a small fortune in trade and owned a fine estate in Kent. He regularly appeared at Woodland in his six-in-hand, his wife awash in jewels. Every visit was the same. He would walk around the house, inspecting each crack in the wooden floors, each peeling patch of paint, every musty drapery and dusty portrait, his disgust clear. And then he would offer to pay his debts—with a sizable interest rate. Edmund could not wait until John departed—leaving behind his high-interest note, which he'd signed, having no other choice.

He'd die before seeing John's young son, Robert, inherit Woodland. But dear God, it wasn't going to come to that.

"Are you certain Mr. Smith found the boy?" John inquired, his words dripping condescension. "I cannot imagine how a Bow Street runner could locate a particular Gypsy tribe, much less the particular woman."

He bristled. John was enjoying himself. He scorned Edmund's affair with a Gypsy and believed the boy would be a savage. "They winter by the Glasgow shipyards," Edmund said. "In the spring they journey into the Borders to work in the fields. I doubt it was all that hard to find this caravan."

John walked to his wife, who sat sewing by the fire, and put his hand on her arm, as if to say, *I know this is a distressful topic for you. No lady should have to comprehend that my brother had a Gypsy lover.*

His perfect, pretty wife smiled at him and continued to sew.

Edmund couldn't help thinking of Raiza now. Ten years ago she'd appeared at Woodland with their son, her eyes ablaze with the pride and passion he still vividly remembered. He had been shocked to look at the child and see his own gray eyes reflected in that darkly complexioned face. The boy's hair had been a dark gold, while Raiza was as dark as the night. Edmund himself was fair. His wife, Catherine, was in the house, pregnant with their child. He'd insisted the bastard was not his—hating himself for doing so. But his affair with Raiza had been brief and he loved his wife. He could not ever let her know about the boy. He had offered Raiza what little coin he could, but she had cursed him and left.

As if reading his mind, John said, "How can you be certain the boy is even yours, no matter what the wench claimed?"

Edmund ignored him. He'd been at a house party in the Borders, hunting with a group of bachelor friends, when the Gypsies had first appeared, camping not far from the local village. He'd walked past Raiza in the town and when their eyes had met, he'd been so stricken that he had reversed direction, following her as if she were the Pied Piper. She had laughed at him, flirting. Smitten, he had eagerly pursued her. Their affair had begun that night. He'd stayed in the Borders for two weeks, spending most of that time in her bed.

He'd wanted to stay with her even longer, but he had a floundering estate to run. With tears of regret in her eyes, Raiza had whispered, *"Gadje gadjense."* He didn't understand her, but he thought she was in love with him, and he wasn't sure that he didn't love her, too. Not that it mattered, for they were from two completely different worlds. He hadn't expected to ever see her again.

A year later he had met Catherine, a woman as different from Raiza as night and day. The niece of his rector, she was proper, demure and impossibly sweet. She would never dance wildly to Gypsy music beneath a full moon, but he didn't care. He had fallen in love with her, married her and become her dearest friend. He missed her even now.

He intended to remarry, of course, because he hoped for more heirs. He could not risk the estate. But he had learned firsthand how capricious life was, how uncertain. And that was why he had decided to find his bastard son.

Edmund heard the sound of horses arriving outside in the rutted dirt drive.

He rushed to the front door, aware of John following him, and flung it open. The heavyset runner was alighting from the carriage, a single-horse curricle. The damned shades were pulled down. "Have you found him?" Edmund cried, aware of his desperation. "Have you found my son?"

Smith was a big man who clearly did not like to shave on a daily basis. He spit tobacco at him and grinned. "Aye, me lord, but ye might not want to thank me yet."

He had found the boy.

John came to stand beside him. He murmured, "I don't trust the Gypsy wench at all."

His gaze glued to the carriage, Edmund retorted, "I don't care what you think."

Smith strode to the carriage, pulling open the door. He reached inside and Edmund saw a lean boy in patched brown trousers and a loose, dirty shirt. Smith jerked him out and to the ground. "Come meet yer father, boy."

Horrified, Edmund saw that the boy's wrists were tightly bound with rope. "Untie him," he began, when he saw the chain and shackle on his ankle.

The boy jerked free of Smith, hatred on his pinched face. He spat at him.

Smith wiped the spittle from his cheek and glanced at Edmund. "He needs a whipping—but then, he's a Gypsy, ain't he? Flogging's what they understand, just like a rotten horse."

Edmund began to shake with outrage. "Why is he bound and shackled like a felon?"

"'Cause he's treacherous, he is. He's tried to escape a

dozen times since I found him in the north, an' I don't feel like being stabbed to death in me sleep," Smith said. He seized the boy by the shoulder and shook him. "Yer father," he said, gesturing at Edmund.

There was murderous rage in the boy's eyes, but he remained silent.

"He speaks English, just as good as you an' me." Smith spit more tobacco, this time on the boy's dirty bare feet. "Understands every word."

"Untie him, damn it," Edmund said, feeling helpless. He wanted to hold his son and tell him he was sorry, but this boy looked as dangerous as Smith claimed. He looked as if he hated Smith—and Edmund. "Son, welcome to Woodland. I am your father."

Cool gray eyes held his, filled with condescension. They belonged to an older man, a worldly man, not a young boy.

Smith said, "She gave him up without too much of a fuss."

Edmund could not look away from his son. "Did you give her my letter?"

Smith said, "Gypsies can't read, but I gave her the letter."

Had Raiza agreed that his raising their son was for the best? As an Englishman, a world of opportunity was open to him. And he was entitled to this estate, his title and all the privilege that came with it.

"But she wept like a woman dying," Smith said, unlocking the shackle on the boy's ankle. "I couldn't understand their Gypsy speech, but I didn't have to. She wanted him to go—and he didn't want to leave. He'll run off." Smith looked at Edmund in warning. "Ye'd better lock him up at night an' keep a guard on him by day." He seized his arm. "Boy, show respect to yer father—a great lord. If he speaks, ye answer."

"It's all right. This is a shock." Edmund smiled at his son. God, he was a beautiful boy—except for his eyes and coloring, he looked exactly like Raiza. So much warmth began, flooding his chest. He should have never turned Raiza away so many years ago, he thought. But surely they could get past what he had done. Surely they could get past this terrible beginning and their differences. "Emilian," he smiled. "Long ago, your mother brought you here and introduced us. I am Lord Edmund St Xavier."

The boy's expression did not change. He reminded Edmund of a deadly, darkly golden tiger, waiting for the precise moment to leap and maim.

Taken aback, Edmund reached for the ropes on his wrists. "Give me a knife," he said to Smith.

"Ye'll be sorry," Smith said, handing him a huge blade.

John murmured, "The boy is as feral as I expected."

Edmund ignored both comments, cutting the ties. "That must feel better." But the boy's wrists were lacerated. He was furious with the runner now.

The boy stared coldly. If his wrists hurt, he gave no sign—and Edmund knew he wouldn't.

"Better guard your horses," John murmured from behind them, a snicker in his tone.

Edmund did not need his smug brother's presence now. Getting past his son's hostility was going to be difficult enough. He couldn't begin to imagine how he'd turn him into an Englishman, much less become a real father to him.

The boy had become still, staring closely, his expression wary. Edmund almost felt as if he were looking at a wild animal, but John was wrong, because Gypsies weren't beasts and thieves—he knew that firsthand. "Can you speak English? Your mother could."

If the boy understood, he gave no sign.

"This is your life now," Edmund tried with a smile. "Long ago, your mother brought you here. I was a fool. I was afraid of what my wife would say, do. I turned you away—and for that, I will always be sorry. But Catherine is gone, God bless her. My son Edmund—your brother—is gone. Emilian, this is your home now. I am your father. I intend to give you the life you deserve. You are an Englishman, too. And one day, Woodland will be yours."

The boy made a harsh sound. He looked Edmund up and down with scorn and shook his head. "No. I have no father—and this is not my home."

His English was accented, but he could speak. "I know you need some time," Edmund cried, thrilled they were finally speaking. "But I am your father. I loved your mother, once."

Emilian stared at him, his face twisted as if with hatred.

"This has to be a difficult moment, meeting your father and accepting that you are my son. But Emilian, you are as much an Englishman as I am."

"No!" Emilian snarled. And he said proudly, head high, "No. I am *Rom*."

CHAPTER ONE

Derbyshire, the spring of 1838

SHE WAS SO ENGROSSED in the book she was reading that she didn't really hear the knocking on her door until it became pounding. Ariella started, curled up in a canopied four-poster bed, a book about Genghis Khan in her hands. For one more moment, visions of a thirteenth-century city danced in her mind, and she saw well-dressed upper-class men and women fleeing in panic amidst artisans and slaves, as the Mongol hordes galloped through the dusty streets on their warhorses.

"Ariella de Warenne!"

Ariella sighed. She had been able to smell the battle, as well as see it. She shook the last of her imaginings away. She was at Rose Hill, her parent's English country home; she had arrived last night. "Come in, Dianna," she called, setting the history aside.

Her half sister, Dianna, her junior by eight years, hurried in and stopped short. "You're not even dressed!" she exclaimed.

"I can't wear this gown to supper?" Ariella said with mock innocence. She didn't care about fashion, but she did know her family, and at supper the women wore evening dresses and jewels, the men dinner jackets.

Dianna's eyes popped. "You wore that dress to breakfast!"

Ariella slid to her feet, smiling. She still couldn't get over how much her little sister had matured. A year ago, Dianna had been more child than woman. Now it was hard to believe she was only sixteen, especially clad in the gown she was wearing. "Is it that late?" Vaguely, she glanced toward the windows of her bedroom and was surprised to see the sun hanging low in the sky. She had settled down with her tome hours ago.

"It is almost four and I *know* you know we are having company tonight."

Ariella did recall that Amanda, her stepmother, had mentioned something about supper guests. "Did you know that Genghis Khan never initiated an attack without warning? He always sent word to the countries' leaders and kings asking for their surrender first, instead of simply attacking and slaying everyone, as so many historians claim."

Dianna stared, bewildered. "Who is Genghis Khan? What are you talking about?"

Ariella beamed. "I am reading about the Mongols, Dianna. Their history is incredible. Under Genghis Khan, they formed an empire almost as large as that of Great Britain. Did you know that?"

"No, I did not. Ariella, Mother has invited Lord Montgomery and his brother—in your honor."

"Of course, today they inhabit a far smaller area," Ariella said, not having heard this last bit. "I want to go to the Central Steppes of Asia. The Mongols remain there today, Dianna. Their culture and way of life is almost unchanged since the days of Genghis Khan. Can you imagine?"

Dianna grimaced and walked to a closet, pushing through the hanging gowns there. "Lord Montgomery is your age and he came into his title last year. His brother is a bit younger. The title is an old one, the estates well run. I heard Mother and Aunt Lizzie talking about it." She pulled out a pale blue gown. "This is stunning! And it doesn't look as if you have worn it."

Ariella didn't want to give up on her sister yet. "If I give you this history to read, I am certain you will enjoy it. Maybe we can all go to the steppes together! We could even see the Great Wall of China!"

Dianna turned and stared.

Ariella saw that her little sister was losing patience. It was always hard to remember that no one, not even her father, shared her passion for learning. "No, I haven't worn the blue. The supper parties I attend in town are filled with academics and Whig reformers, and there are few gentry there. No one cares about fashion."

Holding the gown to her chest, Dianna shook her head. "That is a shame! I am not interested in Mongols, Ariella, and I cannot truly understand why you are. I am not going to the steppes with you—or to some Chinese wall. I love my life right here! The last time we spoke, you were in a tizzy about the Bedouins."

"I had just returned from Jerusalem and a guided tour of a Bedouin camp. Did you know that our army uses Bedouins as scouts and guides in Palestine and Egypt?"

Dianna marched to the bed and laid the gown there. "It's time you wore this lovely dress. With your golden complexion and hair and your infamous de Warenne blue eyes, you will turn heads in it."

Ariella stared, instantly wary. "Who did you say was coming?"

Dianna beamed. "Lord Montgomery—a great catch! They say he is also handsome."

Confused, Ariella folded her arms across her chest. "You're too young to be looking for a husband."

"But you're not," Dianna cried. "You didn't hear me, did you? Lord Montgomery has just come into his title, and he is very good-looking and well educated. I have heard all kinds of gossip that he is in a rush to wed."

Ariella turned away. She was twenty-four now, but

marriage was *not* on her mind. Ever since she was a small child, she had been consumed with a passion for knowledge. Books—and the information contained within them—had been her life for as long as she could remember. Given a choice between spending time in a library or at a ball, she would always choose the former.

Luckily, her father doted on her and encouraged her intellectual pursuits—and that was truly unheard of. Since turning twenty-one, she had resided mostly in London, where she could haunt the libraries and museums, and attend public debates on burning social issues by radicals like Francis Place and William Covett. But despite the freedoms, she wished for far more independence—she wanted to travel unchaperoned and see the places and people she had read about.

Ariella had been born in Barbary, her mother a Jewess enslaved by a Barbary prince. She had been executed shortly after Ariella's birth for having a fair-skinned child with blue eyes. Her father had managed to have Ariella smuggled out of the harem and she had been raised by him since infancy. Cliff de Warenne was now one of the greatest shipping magnates of the current era, but in those days, he had been more privateer than anything else. She had spent the first few years of her life in the West Indies, where her father had a home. When he met and married Amanda, they had moved to London. But her stepmother loved the sea as much as Cliff did, and by the time Ariella came of age, she had traveled from one end of the Mediterranean to the other, up and down the coast of the United States, and through the major cities of Europe. She had even been to Palestine, Hong Kong and the East Indies.

Last year there had been the three-month tour to Vienna, Budapest and then Athens. Her father had allowed her this trip, with the condition her half brother escort her. Alexi was following in their father's footsteps as a merchant adventurer, and he had been happy to chaperone her and briefly detour to Constantinople, upon her request.

Her favorite land was Palestine, her favorite city Jerusalem; her least favorite, Algiers—where her mother had been executed for her affair with Ariella's father.

Ariella knew she was fortunate to have traveled a good portion of the world. She knew she was fortunate to have lenient parents, who trusted her implicitly and were proud of her intellect. It was not the norm. Dianna was not educated; she only read the occasional romance novel. She spent the Season in London, the rest of the year in their country home in Ireland, living a life of leisure. Except for charity, her days were spent changing attire, attending lavish meals and teas, and calling on neighbors. It was usual for a well-bred young woman.

Soon, Dianna would be put on the marriage market, and she would hunt for the perfect husband. Ariella knew her beautiful sister, an heiress in her own right, would have no problem becoming wed. But Ariella wished for a far different life. She preferred independence, books and travel to marriage. Only a very unusual man would allow her the freedom she was accustomed to and she couldn't quite imagine answering to anyone, not when she had such independence now. Marriage had never seemed important to her, although she had grown up surrounded by great love, devotion and equality, exemplified in the marriages of her aunts, uncles and parents. If she ever did marry, she knew it would only be because she had found that great and unusual love, the kind for which the de Warenne men and women were renowned. Yet at twenty-four, it seemed to have escaped her—and she didn't feel lacking. How could she? She had thousands of books to read and places to see. She doubted she could accomplish all she wished to in a lifetime.

She slowly faced her sister.

Dianna smiled, but with anxiety. "I am so glad you are

home! I have missed you, Ariella." Her tone was now coaxing.

"I have missed you, too," Ariella said, not quite truthfully. A foreign land, where she was surrounded by exotic smells, sights and sounds, facing people she couldn't wait to understand, was far too exciting for nostalgia or any homesick emotion. Even in London, she could spend days and days in a museum and not notice the passage of time.

"I am so glad you have met us at Rose Hill," Dianna said. "Tonight will be so amusing. I met the younger Montgomery, and if his older brother is as charming, you might very well forget about Genghis Khan." She added, "I don't think you should mention the Mongols at supper, Ariella. No one will understand."

Ariella hesitated. "In truth, I wish it were just a family affair. I cannot bear an evening spent discussing the weather, Amanda's roses, the last hunt or the upcoming horse races."

"Why not?" Dianna asked. "Those are suitable topics for discussion. Will you promise not to speak of the Mongols and the steppes, or supper parties with academics and reformers?" She smiled, but uncertainly. "Everyone will think you're a radical—and far too independent."

Ariella balked. "Then I must be allowed absolute, ungracious silence."

"That is childish."

"A woman should be able to speak her mind. I speak my mind in town. And I *am* somewhat radical. There are terrible social conditions in the land. The penal code has hardly been changed, never mind the hoopla, and as for parliamentary reform—"

Dianna cut her off. "Of course you speak your mind in town—you aren't in polite company. You said so yourself!" Dianna stood, agitated. "I love you dearly. I am asking you as a beloved sister to attempt a proper discourse."

Ariella groused, "You have become so conservative. Fine.

I won't discuss any subject without your approval. I will look at you and wait for a wink. No, wait. Tug your left earlobe and I will know I am allowed to speak."

"Are you making a mockery of my sincere attempts to see you successfully wed?"

Ariella sat down, hard. Her little sister wished to see her wed so badly? It was simply stunning.

Dianna smiled coaxingly. "I also think you should not mention that Papa allows you to live alone in London."

"I'm rarely alone. There is a house full of servants, the earl and Aunt Lizzie are often in town, and Uncle Rex and Blanche are just a half hour away at Harrington Hall."

"No matter who comes and goes at Harmon House, you live like an independent woman. Our guests would be shocked—*Lord Montgomery* would be shocked!" She was firm. "Father really needs to come to his senses where you are concerned."

"I am not entirely independent. I receive moneys from my estates, but Father is the trustee." Ariella bit her lip. When had Dianna become so proper? When had she become exactly like everyone else her age and gender? Why couldn't she see that free thinking and independence were states to be coveted, not condemned?

Dianna smoothed the gown on the bed. "Father is so smitten with you, he can't see straight. There is some gossip, you know, about your residing in London without family." She looked up. "I love you. You are twenty-four. Father isn't inclined to rush a match, but you are of age. It is time, Ariella. I am looking out for your best interests."

Ariella was dismayed. It was time to set her sister straight about Lord Montgomery. "Dianna, please don't think to match me with Montgomery. I don't mind being unwed."

"If you don't marry, what will you do? What about children? If Father gives you your inheritance, will you travel the world? For how long? Will you travel at forty? At eighty?"

"I hope so," Ariella cried, excited by the notion.

Dianna shook her head. "That's madness!"

They were as different as night and day. "I don't want to get married," Ariella said firmly. "I will only marry if it is a true meeting of the minds. But I will be polite to Lord Montgomery. I promised you I won't speak of the matters I care about, and I won't—but dear God, cease and desist. I can think of nothing worse than a life of *submission* to some closed-minded, proper gentleman. I like my life just as it is."

Dianna was incredulous. "You're a woman, Ariella, and God intended for you to take a husband and bear his children—and yes, be submissive to him. What do you mean by a meeting of the minds? Who marries for such a union?"

Ariella was shocked that her sister would espouse such traditional views—even if almost all of society held them. "I do not know what God decreed for women—or for me," she managed. "*Men* have decreed that women must marry and bear children! Dianna, please try to understand. Most men would not let me roam Oxford, in the guise of a man, eavesdropping on the lectures of my favorite professors." Dianna gasped. "Most men would not *allow* me to spend entire days in the archives of the British Museum," Ariella continued firmly. "I refuse to succumb to a traditional marriage—if I ever succumb at all."

Dianna moaned. "I can see the future now—you will marry some radical socialist lawyer!"

"Perhaps I will. Can you truly see me as some proper gent's wife, staying at home, changing gowns throughout the day, a pretty, useless *ornament?* Except, of course, for the five, six or seven children I will have to bear, like a broodmare!"

"That is a terrible way to look at marriage and family," Dianna said, appearing stunned. "Is that what you think of me? Am I a pretty, useless ornament? Is my mother, is Aunt Lizzie, is our cousin Margery? And bearing children is a wonderful thing. You like children!"

How had this happened? Ariella wondered. "No, Dianna, I beg your pardon. I do not think of you in such terms. I adore you—you are my sister, and I am so proud of you. None of the women in our family are pretty, useless ornaments."

"I am not stupid," Dianna finally said. "I know you are brilliant. Everyone in this family says so. I know you are better read than just about every gentleman of our acquaintance. I know you think me foolish. But it isn't foolish to want a good marriage and children. To the contrary, it is admirable to want a home, a husband and children."

Ariella backed off. "Of course it is—because you genuinely want those things."

"And you don't. You want to be left alone to read book after book about strange people like the Mongols. It is very foolish to think of spending an entire lifetime consumed with the lives of foreigners and the dead! Unless, of course, you marry a gentleman for his *mind!* Has it ever occurred to you that one day you might regret such a choice?"

Ariella was surprised. "No, it hasn't." She realized her little sister had grown up. She sighed. "I am not ruling out marriage, Dianna. But I am not in a rush, and I cannot ever marry if it will compromise my happiness." She added, mostly to please her sister, "Perhaps one day I will find that once-in-a-lifetime love our family is so notorious for."

Dianna grumbled, "Well, if so, I hope you are the single de Warenne who will escape the scandal so often associated with our family."

Ariella smiled. "Please try to understand. I am very satisfied with my unfashionable status as an aging spinster."

Dianna stared grimly. "No one is calling you an old spinster yet. Thank God you have a fortune, and the prospects that come with it. I am afraid you will have a great many regrets if you continue on this way."

Ariella hugged her. "I won't. I swear it." She laughed a little. "You feel like the older sister now!"

"I am sending Roselyn to help you dress. We are having an early supper—I cannot recall why. I will lend you my aquamarines. And I know you will be more than pleasant with Montgomery." Her parting smile was firm, indicating that she had not changed her matrimonial schemes.

Ariella smiled back, her face plastered into a pleasant expression. She intended it to be the look she would wear for the entire evening, just to make Dianna happy.

EMILIAN ST XAVIER sat at his father's large, gilded desk in the library, unable to focus on the ledgers at hand. It was a rare moment, as his life was the estate. But an odd gnawing had begun earlier that day, a familiar restlessness. He hated such feelings, and was always determined to ignore them. But on days like this one, the house felt larger than ever, and even empty, although he kept a full staff.

He leaned back in his chair, objectively looking around the luxurious, high-ceilinged library. The room bore almost no resemblance to the room in which he had so often been chastised as a sullen boy, when he had been determined to cling to his differences with his father, pretending absolute indifference to Edmund's wishes and Woodland's affairs. But even when he had first arrived at the estate, his curiosity had been as strong as his wariness. He had never been inside an Englishman's home before, and Woodland had seemed palatial. Raiza had insisted he learn to read English, and he had stared at the books in the bookcase behind his father's head, wondering if he dared steal one so he could read it. Soon he had stolen book after book. In retrospect, he knew Edmund had known he was secretly reading philosophy, poetry and love stories in his bedroom.

Even though his mother had wanted him to leave the *kumpa'nia* and go to live with his father, he would never forget her tears and her grief. Edmund had broken her heart by taking him away from her, and he had hated Edmund for hurting Raiza. He had known that he would not be at Woodland if Edmund's firstborn, pure-blooded son had lived. His Rom pride, which was considerable, had demanded that he remain detached and indifferent to the life his father offered him.

His Rom blood had dictated suspicion and hostility. He had lived with *gadjo* hatred and prejudices his entire life. He knew his father had to be like all the other *gadjos*. But in truth, Edmund had been firm, but fair and compassionate, too. The adjustment to the English way of life had been so difficult that he couldn't see it. He'd run away several times, but Edmund had always found him. The last time he'd stolen a neighbor's horse, and he had been physically branded so that the world would see him as a horse thief before Edmund had appeared to take him home. He was hardly the first Rom to have a scarred right ear, and it was one of the reasons he wore his hair so long. Edmund had finally asked him to stay, telling him he would willingly let him leave when he turned sixteen, if that was what he still wished to do.

He had agreed—and in the end, decided on his own terms to stay. In the following years he had gone to Eton and then Oxford, excelling at both institutions. Yet their relationship had remained somewhat adversarial, as if Edmund never quite trusted his transformation into an Englishman. Emilian never quite trusted his father, either. Being Edmund's son and heir did not change the fact that his mother was Romany, and all of society knew it—including Edmund.

The condescension and scorn from his youth remained, but it was disguised now. To the *gadjos,* even those warming his bed, no amount of manners, education or wealth would ever change the "fact" that his inclination was to steal horses and cheat his neighbors. Every supper party and ball, every business affair, every paramour, had proven that—and proved it, still.

Edmund's death had been a tragic accident. Emilian had just graduated Oxford with the highest honors, and he had been traveling with the Roma. It had been his first visit to his mother, whom he hadn't seen since his father had taken him from her ten years before. Edmund's estate manager had written him. Upon learning of Edmund's sudden death in a hunting accident, Emilian had instantly rushed home.

Shocked that his father had died without his having had the chance to say goodbye, he had gone from his grave directly to his desk. All he could think of was the opportunities of the past—and that he hadn't ever thanked Edmund for a single one. He recalled his father teaching him how to ride, explaining every aspect of the estate to him, insisting that he receive the best possible education, and how Edmund had proudly taken him to every country affair, whether a tea, a supper party or a country ball, as if he was as English as anyone. He had sat down at his father's desk and begun poring over every account and ledger until his tears had made it impossible to read the pages. And in the end, a very English sense of duty had triumphed. He had been aware of his father's failures as the viscount; he had always known he could do far better. Now, he intended to set Woodland straight. Now, he intended to make Edmund proud of him.

And he had. In three years, he had managed to erase all debt from Woodland's accounts. The estate was currently making a handsome profit. There were new tenants, and their produce was being exported abroad, as well as sold at local markets. He was a partner in a freight company. There were profitable investments in a Birmingham mill and a national railway, but the coup de grâce was the St Xavier coal mine. The export of British coal grew in tonnage annually and he was cashing in on it. He was the wealthiest nobleman in

Derbyshire, with one exception—the shipping magnate, Cliff de Warenne.

Emilian pushed the ledgers aside.

He did not know de Warenne personally—how could he? He had scorned society ever since coming into the title and the estate. From his first advent into society as a boy at Edmund's side, they had whispered about him behind his back, and nothing had changed except that he now expected it. He preferred avoiding all social intercourse, as it was nothing but a dull pretense for everyone involved. When he did sit down to a meal with Englishmen and their wives, it was with men who were important to him—the managers of his mine, his partners in the freight company, those who wished for him to invest in other ventures.

"My lord, sir?" His butler, Hoode, paused on the library's threshold. "You have callers." Hoode handed him a small tray containing several cards.

Emilian was surprised. Callers were rare. His last visitor had been a widow with four sons whose family had blatantly informed him she was a good "breeder." Now, as he took the cards, he fought to avoid cringing. As wealthy as he was, it was inevitable that marriage prospects were pressed upon him from time to time. The candidates were all excessively unmarriageable daughters. The crème de la crème were sent elsewhere to look for blue-blooded English husbands. He didn't give a damn. He didn't want children. Childhood was synonymous with misery and fear—and therefore he had no need of a wife, English or not.

He glanced at the cards and became still. These cards were not from families seeking marriage. One card belonged to his cousin, Robert, the others from Robert's friends.

"This is rich," he murmured. There was only one reason why his cousin would call, as they could not stand each other. "Send Robert in, Hoode." He stood, stretching his tall, muscular frame. He intended to enjoy the ensuing encounter, very much the way a basset would enjoy being locked in a small room with a mouse.

Robert St Xavier appeared instantly, smiling obsequiously, hand outstretched. Blond and plump, he boomed, "Emil, my God, it is good to see you, eh?"

Emilian folded his arms across his chest, refusing any handshake. "Shall we cut to the chase, Rob?"

Robert's smile faltered and he dropped his hand. "We are passing through," Robert said in a jovial tone, "and I had hoped we could share a good bottle of wine. It has certainly been some time. And we are cousins!" He laughed, perhaps nervously or perhaps at the absurdity that any familial affection lay behind the claim. "We've taken rooms at the Buxton Inn. Will you join us?"

"How much do you want?" Emilian said coolly.

Robert's smile vanished. "This time I vow I will pay you back."

"Really?" He lifted a brow. Robert had inherited a fortune from his father. He had spent every penny within two years. His life was dissolute and irresponsible, to say the least. "Then it would be a first. How much, Rob, do you need this time?"

Robert hesitated. "Five hundred, perhaps?"

"And that will last for how long? Most gentlemen can live off that sum for a year."

"It will last a year, Emil, I swear it!"

"Don't bother swearing to me." Emilian bent and reached for his checking book. He should let him starve. Too well, he recalled how Robert and his father had scorned him as "that Gypsy boy." They had called him a dirty savage. But it was only *gadjo* money—and it was *his gadjo* money. He ripped the note from its pad and handed it to Robert.

"I can't thank you enough, Emil."

He looked at him with disdain. "Have no fear—I will never collect anything from you."

Robert's smile, plastered in place, never wavered. "Thank you," he said again. "And would you mind if we spent the night here? It will save us a few pounds—"

Emilian waved at him dismissively. He didn't care if the trio stayed, for there was plenty of room at Woodland, enough that their paths would hardly cross. He moved toward the French doors and stared past his gardens at the rolling wooded hills that etched into the gray, fading horizon. He had a terrible sense that something was about to happen…. But it must be his imagination, he thought. Still, he looked at the sky again. Not even a thunderstorm was rolling in.

He turned at the sound of new voices. Two of Robert's equally disreputable friends had joined him, and Robert was showing them the draft. His friends were laughing and slapping him on the back, as if he had just managed some terrific feat.

"It pays to have a rich cousin, eh? Even if he is half Gypsy." The man laughed.

"God only knows how he does it." Robert grinned. "It's his English blood, of course, that makes him so wealthy."

The third man leaned close. "Have you ever had a Gypsy wench?" He leered. "They're at Rose Hill—I heard it from a houseman."

Emilian stiffened in surprise. *There were Roma nearby.* Had he sensed them all this time?

And suddenly a young Rom, no more than fifteen or sixteen years old, stepped onto his flagstone terrace, staring at him through the French doors.

Emilian moved forward. "Wait!"

The young Rom whirled and started to run.

Emilian ran after him. "Don't go!" he cried. Then, in Roma, *"Na za!"*

The boy froze at the sharp command. Emilian hurried forward. Continuing to speak in the Romany language, he said, "I am Rom. I am Emilian St Xavier, son of Raiza Kadraiche."

The boy appeared relieved. "Emilian, Stevan sent me. He must speak with you. We are not far—an hour by horse or wagon."

Emilian was stunned. Stevan Kadraiche was his uncle, whom he had not seen in eight years. Raiza traveled with him, as did his half sister, Jaelle. But they never traveled farther south than the Borders. He could not imagine what this meant.

And then he knew. There was news—and it could not be good.

"Will you come?" the boy asked.

"I'll come," he said, lapsing into English. He steeled himself, but for what he did not know.

CHAPTER TWO

ARIELLA STOOD BY the fireplace, wishing she could leave the supper party and return to her room. She would much prefer curling up with her book for the evening. Pleasant greetings had been exchanged and the weather had been discussed, as had Amanda's famous rose gardens. Dianna, who was very pretty in her evening gown, was now mentioning her mother's upcoming ball, the first at Rose Hill in years. "I do hope you will attend, my lords," she said sweetly.

Ariella fixed a smile on her face and glanced at her father. Tall and handsome, in his midforties, he was still a man who caught the ladies' eyes. But he did not notice; he remained smitten with his wife, who was as passionate as her husband about the sea, and eccentric enough to stand on the quarterdeck with him even now. Yet Amanda also loved balls and dancing, which made no sense as far as Ariella was concerned. After supper, she decided she would approach her father and see if he might allow a very bold adventure into the heart of central Asia.

Lord Montgomery turned to her. "You do not seem to anticipate the Rose Hill ball." He spoke quietly, seriously.

She could not help herself. "I do not care for balls. I avoid them whenever I can."

Dianna rushed to her side. "Oh, that is so untrue," she scolded.

"I prefer travel," she added. She saw her father smile.

"I enjoy travel, too. Where have you been recently?"

"My last voyage was to Athens and Constantinople. I now wish to visit the steppes of central Asia."

Dianna paled.

Ariella sighed. She had promised her sister to avoid any discussion of the Mongols. She debated several topics and gave in to one that interested her. "What do you think about Owen's great experiments to help labor improve its position and place in the economy?"

Montgomery blinked. Then his gaze narrowed, as if with interest.

But the younger Montgomery stared at her in shock. Then he turned to her father and said, "An absolute disaster, of course, to consolidate labor like that. But what do you expect from a man like Robert Owens? He's a merchant's son."

Ariella bristled and said to his back. "He is brilliant!"

Cliff de Warenne came to stand beside her, putting his hand on her shoulder. He said pleasantly, "I have been impressed with Owen's experiments. I support the theory of consolidated labor interests."

The younger Montgomery had to face Ariella with Cliff now. "Good God, and what will be next? The Ten Hours Bill? Labor will certainly argue for that!" He gave Ariella a dark look that she had received many times. It said, *Ladies' opinions are not welcome.*

Ariella planted her hands on her hip, but she smiled sweetly. "It was a social and political travesty to allow the Ten Hours Bill to be trampled under industrial and trade interests. It is immoral! No woman or child should have to work more than ten hours a day!"

Paul Montgomery raised both pale brows, then turned aside dismissively. "As I was saying," he said to Cliff, "the business interests in this country will go under if unions are encouraged and allowed. No one will be foolish enough to so limit the hours of labor or to support consolidated labor."

"I disagree. It is only a matter of time before a more humane labor law is enacted," Cliff said calmly.

"This country will go under," the younger Montgomery warned, flushing. "We cannot afford higher wages and better work conditions!"

Amanda smiled and said, "On that note, perhaps we should all go in to dine? We can continue the fervent debate over supper."

A debate over supper, Ariella thought with excitement. She would hardly mind!

But then she caught her sister's eye. Dianna looked at her with an obvious plea. *Why are you doing this?* She mouthed, *You promised.*

"I am too much of a gentleman to debate a lady," the young Montgomery said stiffly, but he looked terribly put out.

His older brother chuckled, and so did Cliff. "Let's go in, as my wife has suggested."

Suddenly a terrific round of shouting could be heard, coming from the front hall of the house, as if a mob had invaded Rose Hill.

"What is that?" Cliff exclaimed, already leaving the salon. "Wait here," he ordered them all.

Ariella didn't even think about it—she followed him.

The front door was open. Rose Hill's butler was flushed, facing a good dozen men who seemed to wish to throng inside. When Cliff was seen, shouts began. "Captain de Warenne! Sir, we must have a word!"

"What is going on, Peterson?" Cliff demanded of the butler. "For God's sake, it's the mayor! Let him in."

Peterson rushed to open the door and the four foremost gentlemen rushed in. "Sir, Mayor Oswald, Mr. Hawks, Mr. Leeds, and your tenant, Squire Jones. We must speak with you. I am afraid there are Gypsies on the road."

Ariella started. *Gypsies?* She hadn't seen a Gypsy caravan

since she was a small girl. Maybe her time at Rose Hill would not be so uneventful after all. She knew nothing about the Gypsy people except for folklore. She vaguely recalled hearing their exotic music as a child and being intrigued by it.

"Not on the road, Captain. They are making camp on Rose Hill land—just down the hill from your house," the rotund mayor cried.

Everyone began to speak at once. Cliff held up both hands. "One at a time. Mayor Oswald, you have my undivided attention."

Oswald nodded, jowls shaking. "Must be fifty of them! They appeared this morning. We were hoping they wouldn't stop, but they have done just that, sir. And they are on your land."

"If one of my cows is stolen, just one, I'll hang the Gypsy thief myself," Squire Jones shouted.

The others started talking at once. Ariella flinched, as they began describing children vanishing, horses being stolen and traded back to the owners so disguised as to be recognizable, and dogs running wild. "No trinket in your home— or mine—will be safe," a man from outside the house cried.

"The young women were begging in the streets this afternoon!" a man said. "It is a disgrace."

"My sons are sixteen and eighteen," someone said as fiercely. "I won't have him being tempted by Gypsy trollops! They already had one girl read their hands!"

Ariella looked at her father, stunned by such bigotry and fear. But before she could tell the throng that their accusations were immensely unfair, Cliff held up both hands.

"I will take care of this," he said firmly. "But let me first say that no one will be murdered in their sleep, and no family will suffer the theft of children, horses, cows or sheep. I have encountered Gypsies from time to time, over the years. The reports of such crime and theft are grossly exaggerated."

Ariella almost relaxed. She knew nothing about Gypsies, but surely her father was right.

"Captain, sir. The best thing is to send them on, out of the parish. We don't need them here. They're Scot Gypsies, sir, from the Borders, up north."

Cliff called for silence again. "I will speak to their chief and make certain they mind their business and continue on their way. I doubt that they intend to linger. They never do. There is nothing to worry about." He turned and looked at Ariella, an invitation in his eyes.

She grinned. "Of course I am coming with you!"

"Do not tell your sister," he warned as they stepped past the crowd and out of the house.

Ariella fell into step with him, happy to have left the supper party behind. "Dianna has grown up. She is so proper."

Cliff chuckled. "She did not get that from me—or her mother," he said. Then he gave her a closer look as they strode down the driveway. "She adores you, Ariella. She has been chatting incessantly about your visit to Rose Hill. Try to be patient with her. I realize no two sisters could be more different."

Ariella felt terrible then. "I suppose I am a neglectful sister."

"I understand the lure of your passions," he said. "At your age, better the lure of passion than no lure at all."

Her father so understood her nature. Then her smile faded. The shell drive curved away from the house before sloping down to the public road. Below her, she saw an amazing sight. The sun was setting. Perhaps two dozen wagons, painted in bold jewel tones, sparkled in the fading daylight. Their horses were wandering about, children running and playing, and the Gypsies added to the kaleidoscope of color, colorfully dressed in hues of scarlet, gold and purple. The mayor had been right. There were at least two dozen wagons present, and the Gypsies may well have numbered closer to sixty or seventy.

"Did you mean what you said about the Gypsies?" she asked in an awed whisper as they paused. She felt as if she had been swept away into a foreign land. She heard their strange, guttural language and she smelled exotic scents, perhaps from incense. Someone was playing a lively, almost occidental melody on a guitar. But there was nothing foreign or strange about the children's happy laughter and the women's chatter.

Cliff's smile was gone. "I have met many Romany tribes over the years, mostly in Spain and Hungary. Many are honest, Ariella, but unfortunately, they are not open to outsiders. They distrust us with good cause, and it is rather common for them all to take great pride in swindling the *gadjo.*"

She was intrigued. "The *gadjo?*"

"We are *gadjos*—non-Gypsies."

"But you told the mayor and his cronies not to worry."

"Is there ever a reason to worry about the worst case? We do not know that they will linger, nor do we know that they will steal. On the other hand, the last time I encountered the Romany people, it was in Ireland. They stole my prized stud—and I never saw the animal again."

Ariella looked at Cliff carefully. He was reasonable now, but she saw the quiet resolve in his eyes. If any incident occurred, he would not hesitate to take action. "Are you certain a Gypsy stole the stallion?"

"It is the conclusion I drew. But if you are asking if I am one hundred percent positive, the answer is no." He laid his hand on her shoulder with a brief smile and they started forward.

They had reached the outermost line of wagons, which encircled a large clearing where several pits were being dug for fires. Ariella's smile faded. The children ran about barefoot with barking dogs, and their pets were thin and scrawny. Women were hauling buckets of water from the creek. The pails were clearly very heavy, but the men were busy pounding stakes and laying out the canvas for tents, hurrying to get the camp made before dark. She looked more closely at the women. Their faces were tanned, lined and weather-beaten. Their colorful skirts were carefully patched and mended. They wore their long, dark hair loose or in braids. The woman closest to them had an infant in a pouch on her back. She removed items from a wagon.

This was a hard life, Ariella thought, and now, she realized that all the laughter and conversation had ceased. Even the guitar player had stopped strumming.

The women paused and straightened to stare. Men turned, also staring. The children ran to the wagons and hid there, peeking out. An absolute silence fell, broken only by a yapping dog.

Ariella shivered, uneasy. These people did not seem pleased to see them.

A huge bear of a man, his hair dark and unkempt, stepped out from the center of the camp in front of the wagons, as if to bar their way. His red shirt was embroidered, and he wore a black-and-gold vest over it. Four younger men, as dark and as tall, came to stand with him. Their eyes were hostile and wary.

Hoofbeats sounded. Ariella turned as a rider on a fine gray stallion galloped up to the outermost wagons, another rider trailing farther behind. He leaped off the mount, striding toward the Gypsy men.

She felt the evening become still. He wore a plain white lawn shirt, fine doeskins breeches, and Hessians that were muddy. He did not wear a coat of any kind and his shirt was unbuttoned, almost to the navel. Clad as he was, he may as well have been naked. No Englishman would travel publicly in such a way. He was tall, broad-shouldered, powerfully built. He wasn't as dark as the other Gypsies, and his hair was brown, not black, glinting with red and gold in the setting sun. She couldn't see him more clearly from this distance, but oddly, her heart began to wildly race.

Cliff took her elbow and started forward. Ariella now heard the newcomer speaking to the Gypsies in their strange, Slavic-sounding tongue. His tone was one of command. Instantly Ariella knew he was their leader.

And then the Gypsy leader looked at them.

Cold gray eyes met hers and her breath caught. *He was so beautiful.* His piercing eyes were impossibly long lashed, and set over strikingly high, exotic cheekbones. His nose was straight, his jaw hard and strong. She had never seen such masculine perfection in her entire life.

Her father stepped forward. "I am Cliff de Warenne. Who is *vaida* here?"

There was a moment of silence, filled with hostility and tension. It gave her the opportunity to really look at the Gypsy chief. Of course he wasn't English. He was too dark, too immodestly dressed and his hair was far too long, brushing his shoulders. Tendrils were caught inside his open collar, as if sticking to his wet skin.

She flushed but couldn't stop staring. Her gaze drifted to a full but tense mouth. She glimpsed a gold cross he wore, against the dark, bronzed skin of his chest. Her color increased just as her heart sped more fully. She knew she should look away, but she simply couldn't manage to do so. In the fine silk shirt, she could even see his chest rising and falling, slow and rhythmic. Her glance went lower. The doeskin breeches clung to his thick, muscular thighs and narrow hips, delineating far too much male anatomy.

She felt his eyes on her; she looked up and met his gaze a second time.

Ariella flamed. Knowing she had been caught, she looked quickly away. *What was wrong with her?*

"I am Emilian. You will speak to me," he said, a slight accent hanging on his every word.

"I see you are already making camp. You are on my land," Cliff said, his tone hard.

Ariella looked up, but the gray-eyed Gypsy was intent on her father now. She didn't know why she was so flustered. She had never been as aware of anyone. Maybe it was because he was an enigma. He was dressed like an Englishman might in his boudoir—but he was not in the privacy of his home. His English seemed flawless, but he spoke the Gypsy tongue.

Emilian smiled unpleasantly. "Long ago," he said softly, "God gave the Rom the right to wander freely and to sleep where they wish."

Ariella flinched. She knew a gauntlet when it was thrown, and she also knew that while her father wished to discuss the situation, he had a dangerous side. There was a hint of ruthless savagery in Emilian's cold gray eyes.

Cliff's smile was equally unpleasant. "I am sure you think so. But recently, the government of England passed laws limiting the places vagabonds and Gypsies can stay."

Emilian's gray eyes flickered. "Ah, yes, the laws of your people—the laws that allow a man to hang simply because he travels in a wagon."

"This is the nineteenth century. We do not hang travelers."

A cold smile began. "But to be a Gypsy is to be a felon, and for such an unlawful life, the punishment is death. Those are *your* laws."

"I doubt you understand the law correctly. We do not hang men because they are Gypsies. None of that changes the fact that you are on my private land."

Emilian said softly, "Do not patronize me, de Warenne. I know the law. As for this camp, there are women and children here who are too tired to go on tonight. I am afraid we will stay."

Ariella tensed. Why did their leader have to be so belligerent? She knew her father had not intended to send them
away, not that night. But she now saw Cliff's eyes flicker
with real annoyance, and she sensed an impending battle.

"I did not ask you to leave," Cliff said flatly. "But you
must give me your word that there will be no mischief
tonight."

The gray-eyed Gypsy stared. "We will try not to steal the
lady's necklace while she sleeps," he said scornfully.

Her father tensed, his blue eyes flaring with anger. "The
lady is my daughter, *vaida*, and you will refer to her with
respect or not at all."

Ariella quickly stepped forward, uncertain if the men
might not come to blows. The air was drenched with their
male fury. She smiled at the Gypsy leader; his gaze narrowed.
"We are more than pleased to accommodate you, sir, for the
night. There is plenty of room to spare, as you can see. My
father is only concerned because the townspeople are in a
tizzy. That, of course, is due to their ignorance." She spoke
in a rush and was terribly aware of her nervousness.

He stared at her. Her smile wavered and vanished.

Cliff flushed. "Ariella, go back to the house."

She started. Her father hadn't ordered her about in years.
How had a simple reconnaissance mission turn into such hostility? She stepped closer to Cliff and lowered her voice.
"You will let the Gypsies stay the night, won't you?" It had
become terribly important to her. "I am sure their leader
doesn't mean to be so abrasive. Father, you know that their
ways are different from ours. He probably doesn't realize
how impolitic he is being. Please give him the benefit of the
doubt."

Cliff's expression eased ever so slightly. "You are too
kind for your own good. You may be assured he intends to
be rude. But I will give him the benefit of the doubt."

Relieved, she glanced at the Gypsy, about to smile at him,

but his expression was so intense and so speculative that her intention vanished. It made him seem savage and even predatory—as if he was thinking about her in very inappropriate ways. Ariella swallowed. It was impossible to look away.

"We are *Rom,*" Emilian said to her and her alone. "And I do not need you defending me and mine."

He had overheard her. In that moment, she forgot that her father stood beside her and that four Gypsies crowded behind Emilian. Suddenly it was as if they were alone. She became acutely aware of his pull, as if a charge of some kind sizzled and throbbed between them. Her heart beat thickly and swiftly, almost hurtfully, in her chest; she thought she heard his heavy, thudding heartbeat, as well, although they stood at least three yards apart. "I'm sorry," she whispered hoarsely. "Yes, you are Romany, I know that."

His lashes lowered slowly. She was certain he looked at her still, but it was almost impossible to tell. A frisson went through her, giving her the oddest feeling in her stomach. Her body ached with a new, terrible tension.

Cliff stepped forward. "Go back to the house, Ariella." He was sharp.

He was angry, and she knew it was because the Gypsy had looked at her so boldly. She said, "Why don't we both go back? It is late, and Amanda is delaying supper for us," she tried.

Cliff stared coldly at the Gypsy, ignoring her. "I have been kind enough to allow you a night's respite here. You may keep your eyes where they belong—on your own women."

The Gypsy shrugged. "Yes, you are so very *kind,*" he mocked. "Do not expect gratitude from me."

Why did he have to seek a battle? Did he have to be so hostile?

"I expect you to be gone in the morning," Cliff said, his face set. "Let's go."

She didn't want to leave, but there was no reason to stay. As Cliff turned away, she looked back helplessly. He stared at her, his silver gaze smoldering. No man had ever looked at her in such a way before. A terrible awareness of what it meant began.

That man was different. She wanted to pull free of her father and go back to him.

He almost smiled, as if he knew the effect he had on her.

Her father pulled on her arm and she turned to keep up with Cliff. As she did, a woman cried out loudly in pain.

Ariella turned back, alarmed. Their gazes locked again. She whispered, "What is that? Is someone hurt?"

He grasped her arm and murmured, "She does not need you, *gadji.*"

Ariella forgot to breathe. His hand was large, strong and burning hot. His breath feathered her cheek, and his knee bumped her thigh. Then he released her.

It had happened so quickly that Ariella was stunned. Emilian said harshly, "We take care of our own." He looked at Cliff, his face hard and set. "Take your princess daughter away. Tell her we do not like *gadjos*. We will leave in the morning."

Ariella trembled. "I can send for a doctor," she tried, but her father cut her off.

"My daughter is just that to you, *Rom*—a princess. Never lay a hand on her again," Cliff exploded.

"Father, stop!" Ariella cried, shaken and breathless, still feeling the Rom's touch. "He didn't want me intruding—that is all! The mistake was mine."

But Cliff ignored her, too upset to hear. "Make sure nothing and no one vanishes in the middle of the night. If one horse is stolen, one cow or a single sheep, I am holding *you* responsible, *vaida.*"

Emilian smiled tightly and did not speak.

Ariella could not believe her father would make such a threat. As she stumbled to keep up with Cliff, she looked back.

As still as a statue, the *vaida* was staring after her. Even from the distance separating them, she felt so much strength and disdain—and an intention she did not understand. He swept her a bow, as elegant as any courtier's, but his eyes were blazing, ruining the effect. Ariella inhaled and turned away.

What kind of man was that?

EMILIAN STARED after the *gadjo* and his beautiful daughter. His insides burned with dislike for de Warenne. The daughter's defense of his disrespectful behavior echoed in his mind. His body rippled with anger and tension. He didn't need her or any *gadjo* to defend him. She thought to be kind? He didn't care that she was kind.

His loins were full. To a man like him, she was so far above him she was a princess—the kind of beautiful, perfect, blue-blooded woman that no English matron would ever present to him. But in spite of the differences of class and blood between them, she had looked at him the way all the Englishwomen who wished to use him did—as if she couldn't wait to tear off his clothes and put her hands and mouth all over him.

He almost laughed, mirthlessly. He exchanged *gadji* lovers with almost the same frequency that he did his clothes. Those wives and widows used him strictly for carnal passion, and he used them for far more. There was a satisfaction to be had in sleeping with his neighbor's wife, when his neighbor looked down on him with so much condescension and scorn. He may have been raised English, but he was still *didikoi*—half blood—and *budjo* was ingrained in his soul. A man who mowed his neighbor's hay and sold it back to his neighbor was considered great. To take what belonged to someone else and reap a profit from it before returning it to its owner, perhaps for even more profit, was a great swindle. Every Rom was born with the need for *budjo* in his or her blood. *Budjo* was a Rom's last laugh—and it was his revenge for the injustice every Rom had ever faced in the world.

He could have de Warenne's daughter, if he wanted to bother. More blood filled him, hot and thick. She would be wet clay in his hands. He was well aware of his powers of persuasion. But he had little doubt that Cliff de Warenne would murder him if he ever found out.

The temptation was vast, because she was so beautiful. He knew she'd whisper about him behind his back after leaving his bed, like they all did. His paramours couldn't wait to discuss the sexual prowess of their Gypsy lover with their friends—as if he was a stud for hire. She was unmarried, but the way she'd looked at him told him she was experienced. It would be interesting, he decided, to take that one to bed.

Something niggled at him, bothering him—a sixth sense, warning him, but of what he could not decide.

"Emilian."

He whirled, relieved at the distraction. Then the relief vanished as he stared at his uncle's sober face. "The woman?"

Stevan made a sound. "The woman is my wife, and she is having your cousin."

A warmth began, unfurling within his chest. Stevan had several children, whom he had met eight years ago, but he didn't even know precisely how many cousins he had, nor could he recall their names. *And another was on the way.*

Suddenly he was overwhelmed. He felt moisture gather in his eyes. The warmth felt like joy. It had been so long since he had been with family. Robert did not count; Robert despised and scorned him. Stevan, his children, Raiza, Jaelle—they were his family. And although he was *didikoi*, these people accepted him in spite of his tainted blood, unlike the English, who had never really accepted him at all. Even Edmund had had his doubts. In that moment, he did not feel isolated or alone. He did not feel different. He was not an outsider.

Stevan clasped his shoulder. "You are a grown man now. Djordi tells me your home is rich."

"I have made it rich," Emilian said truthfully. He wiped his eyes. He could not remember Stevan's wife's name and that was truly shameful.

Stevan smiled. "A lot of *budjo,* eh?"

Emilian hesitated. He had made Woodland profitable through English work, not Gypsy *budjo*. He did not want to tell his uncle he had labored honestly and industriously, instead of using cunning for his gain. "A lot of *budjo,*" he lied.

Stevan nodded, but his smile faltered.

Emilian tensed. Knives seemed to have pierced his guts. He asked slowly, "Why have you come to find me?"

Stevan hesitated, but as he did so, a young Romni ran out from the wagons, her bright red skirts swirling. She paused, barefoot, not far from them. "Emilian," she whispered, flushing.

It took him a moment to see Raiza's beauty in her young, striking features. He gasped, realizing he was staring at his little half sister, except she wasn't twelve years old anymore—she was twenty.

She smiled beatifically and rushed into his arms.

He felt himself smile widely, the kind of smile he hadn't felt in years, one that began in his heart. He held her, hard, just for a moment, relishing the rare embrace—it was entirely different from holding a lover he did not care for. When he released her, he was still smiling. "Jaelle! You are a beautiful woman now. I am in shock!"

"Did you think I'd grow up ugly?" She laughed, tossing her dark mane of hair. He now realized it was tinged with deep red tones and her eyes were golden amber.

"Never!" he exclaimed. "Are you married?" He was almost afraid of her response.

She shook her head. "There is no one here that I want."

He wasn't sure if that answer pleased him or not.

Stevan said gruffly, "There have been good men who have asked for her. She has refused them all."

"I will know when I wish to marry, and I haven't wished to yet." She touched his face. "Look at you—a *gadjo* now! With so much wealth—Djordi said so. But can pounds replace the wide road and the shining stars?"

His smile faded. Although he had tried to run away many times when he had first been brought to Woodland, he had finally chosen to stay. And he hadn't thought twice about taking over the estate upon Edmund's death. What could he say? Just then, surrounded by true family, he was uncertain his choices had been the right ones. "I am half blood," he said, hoping to sound light. "Woodland is a good place, but I miss the open road and the night sky." And in that moment it was achingly true. He missed Jaelle, Raiza and his uncle. He hadn't realized it until then.

Jaelle tugged on his hand. "Then come with us, just for a while."

He hesitated. There was so much temptation.

Stevan seemed doubtful. "Jaelle, you have heard it before—half blood, half heart. I don't think our way will please your brother for long." Stevan looked at him. "He has been raised a *gadjo*. Our life is better—but he cannot know that."

His uncle's words filled him with tension. The lure of the open road was suddenly immense. But he had duties, responsibilities. He saw himself hunched over his desk, attending to papers until well into the next morning, or standing in a great hall, apart from the ladies and gentlemen present, there only to discuss a business affair. He recalled the previous evening, when he had been in bed with a neighbor's wife, giving them both rapture. How easily he could sum up his life—it consisted of Woodland's affairs and his sexual encounters and nothing more.

"Maybe your life is the better way," Emilian said slowly. That did not mean he could leave, however.

Jaelle seemed ready to hop up and down. But she teased, "Your accent is so strange! You don't sound Romany, Emilian!"

He flushed. He hadn't spoken the tongue in eight years.

Stevan took his arm. "Do you wish to speak with your sister now?"

Emilian glanced at Jaelle, who was bubbling with enthusiasm and happiness. He did not want to disappoint her. He hoped her good nature was always with her. It crossed his mind that he wished to show her Woodland at some point in time, before the *kumpa'nia* went north again. There was so much he could offer her now—except she preferred the Roma way.

He could see her in his *gadjo* home, in a *gadji's* dress, and he stiffened because that was completely wrong. He faced Stevan. "Jaelle and I have all night—and many nights to talk to one another." He sent her a smile. "Maybe I can find you your husband, *jel'enedra.*"

She made a face. "Thank you, but no. I will hunt on my own—and choose on my own."

"So independent!" he teased. "And is it a manhunt?"

She gave him a look that was far too arch; she was no naive, virginal, pampered English rose. "When he comes, I will hunt him." She stood on tiptoe to kiss his cheek and darted off.

Emilian stared after her.

"Do not worry," Stevan said. "She is far more innocent than she appears. She is playing the woman, that is all. I sometimes think of her as being fifteen."

"She isn't fifteen," he said tersely. Romany mores and ethics were entirely different from *gadjo* ones. It would be unusual if Jaelle was entirely innocent when it came to passion. "She should be married," he said abruptly. He did not wish for her to be used and tossed aside like their mother.

Stevan laughed. "Spoken like a true brother—a full-blood brother!"

Emilian didn't smile. He waited.

Stevan's smile faded. "Walk with me."

He did, with a terrible sense of dread. The night had settled with a thousand stars over them. The trees sighed as they walked by. "She's not here."

"No, she is not."

"Is she dead?"

Stevan paused, placing both of his hands on his shoulders. "Raiza is dead. I am sorry."

He wasn't a boy of twelve and he had no right to tears, but they filled his eyes. *His mother was dead.* Raiza was dead—and he hadn't been there with her. She was dead—and he'd last seen her eight long years ago. "Damn it," he cursed. "What happened?"

"What always happens, in the end, to the Romany?" Stevan asked simply.

"She was telling fortunes at a fair in Edinburgh. A lady was very displeased with her fortune, and when she came back, she did so with her nobleman. She accused Raiza of deceit and demanded the shilling back. Raiza refused. A crowd had gathered, and soon everyone was shouting at Raiza, accusing her of cheating, of begging, of stealing their coin. By the time I learned of this and had gone to her stall, the mob was stoning her. Raiza was hiding behind her table, using it like a shield, otherwise, she would have died then."

His world went still. He saw his mother, cowering behind a flimsy wood table, the kind used to play cards.

"I ran through the crowd and they began to stone me. I grabbed Raiza—she was hurt, Emilian, and bleeding from her head. I tried to protect her with my body and we started to run away. She tripped so hard I lost hold of her. I almost caught her—instead, she fell. She hit her head. She never woke up."

He wanted to nod, but he couldn't move. He saw her lying on a cobbled street, her eyes wide and sightless, her head bleeding.

Stevan embraced him. "She was a good woman and she loved you greatly. She was so proud of you! It was unjust, but God gave us cunning to make up for the *gadjo* ways. One day, the *gadjo* will pay. They always pay. We always make them pay. Fools." He spit suddenly. "I am glad you used *budjo* to cheat the *gadjos* and make yourself rich!" He spit again, for emphasis.

Emilian realized he was crying. He hadn't cried since that long-ago night when he'd first been torn from his Romany life. He'd been locked up by the Englishman who was sworn to take him south to his *gadjo* father. He'd been in chains like men he'd seen on their way to the gallows—some of them Rom. He'd cried in fear. He'd cried in loneliness. Ashamed, he'd managed to stop the tears before the ugly Englishman had returned. Now, his tears came from his broken heart. The grief felt as if it would rip him apart.

He hadn't been there to protect her, save her. He wiped his eyes. "When?"

"A month ago."

The grief made it impossible to breathe. *She was gone.* Guilt began.

A month ago he had been immersed in his *gadjo* affairs. A month ago he had been redesigning his *gadjo* gazebo. A month ago, he had been fucking his *gadjo* mistress night and day.

Because he had chosen to stay with Edmund, when he could have left him.

He had chosen his father over his mother—and now Raiza was dead.

"They always pay," Stevan said savagely.

He wanted the murderers to pay. He hated them all. Every single last one of them. More tears streamed. But there was no single murderer to hunt. Why hadn't he been there to save her? The guilt sickened him, the rage inflamed him. Damn the *gadjos,* he thought savagely. Damn them all.

And he thought of de Warenne and his daughter.

CHAPTER THREE

HE WANDERED along the perimeter of the encampment, head down, allowing the rage to build. He preferred the anger to the grief. Raiza's fear must have known no bounds. But the rage did not erase the guilt. His mother had been murdered by *gadjos* while he lived like one, and he would never forgive himself for having visited her just once in the past eighteen years.

"Emilian."

At the sound of Jaelle's voice, he halted, realizing how selfish his grief was. Stevan cared for his sister, but that was no substitute for her mother. Jaelle's father was a Scot who hadn't cared about his bastard Gypsy daughter, for he had a Scottish wife and a Scottish family. "Come here, *edra*," he said, forcing a smile.

Her expression was uncertain as she approached. She touched his arm. "I am sad, too. I am sad every day. But it is done." She shrugged. "One day, *I* will make the *gadjos* pay."

He stiffened. "You will do no such thing. You may leave vengeance to me. It is my right."

"It is my right, as well, even more!" She flared. "You hardly knew Raiza!"

"She was my mother. I did not ask to be taken from her."

She softened. "I am sorry, Emilian. Of course you didn't." She hesitated, her amber gaze searching. "When I was small, you came to us. Do you remember? It was a happy time."

"I remember," he said, aware of what she wished him to recall.

But she simply stared and he knew she was thinking about how he had come for a month—and abruptly left.

"What is it that you wish to know?"

"You are as rich as a king. You have no master. Why? Why haven't you come to us since that time? Why haven't you come to me? Do you prefer the *gadjo* to the Romany people? Do you prefer the *gadjo* life to our own? You came when I was a small child. But you did not stay!"

She was intense, and tears shimmered in her eyes. He understood how important this was to her—he understood that he had this small woman's loyalty and love. He took her hand. It was awkward to do so, but he did not release her palm. A few days ago, his answer would have been different, he realized. But their mother's death hovered over them, a dark, terrible shroud. The grief remained, bursting in his heart, overshadowed by guilt. The anger threatened to explode. "I left because I received word of my father's death," he said truthfully. "But I didn't join the *kumpa'nia* intending to stay. I had dreamed of traveling with the Rom, and I was young, so I came. It was an adventure, *jel'enedra*."

He recalled the boredom that had quickly arisen after the first few days of aimless travel. In the ensuing years, he had forgotten how disappointing the journey had been, for his memory had been tainted by the news of Edmund's death. But while on the road, he had wondered about the duties and responsibilities he'd eventually return to at Woodland. He hadn't really appreciated the journey, not then, but perhaps it was because he had been so young. And everything was different now.

"I don't know what I prefer now, or what I want," he said slowly. "I have lived as an Englishman for a very long time, but we both know I am *didikoi*." His heart thundered as he spoke. He was an outsider; he would always be an outsider.

Yet he had always known that—he had simply ignored it. "I do know I am gladdened to have such a sister."

Her eyes widened. "You don't know what you want? Everyone knows their heart!"

He laughed roughly. "Growing up, I dreamed of the *kumpa'nia*. Sometimes, in my bedroom, I played our songs on the guitar. Even though I chose to become a *gadjo,* as my father had asked me to do, I knew my people—our people— were out there somewhere, perhaps even waiting for me. But I had duties at Woodland. I accepted those duties. I know you cannot understand this confusion. I have never understood it, either. At times, I have felt like two completely different people."

"So you are confused now?" she asked uncertainly.

"No. Today, I knew you were near. Today, I yearned to come. Today, I am Rom. Today, this is what I want." He gestured at the camp. "Yesterday I sat in the library at Woodland with my steward and the mayor of the nearby village, discussing local affairs." He shook his head. It became hard to speak. "They call me *Gypsy* behind my back, but they wish for me to lead them anyway. There was a matter of law to be solved. They wished for my advice—no one in Derbyshire has the education I have received." It was so ironic. "I am not truly one of them, but long ago, I made my life Woodland. The estate is *mine.* It is a good place. I have no desire to wed, but if I ever have a son, it will be *his.* Can you understand that?" In that moment, he wasn't sure he understood it.

"How can I understand such affection for land? I do not care about land and I never will. The Romany who have homes are not true blood. You are more English than Rom." She wiped at her tears. "But I have known that for a long time. And our mother knew it, too." She turned away.

He seized her. "There is no place I would rather be than right here, right now. That is the truth, Jaelle."

She searched his eyes. "But for how long? And when we leave, you won't come with us, will you?"

He stared at her, seeing not Jaelle but Raiza, lying dead in a cobbled street, bleeding from the head, the crowd thronging her, viciously satisfied. His pulse exploded. Did he want to go back to his life at Woodland? He had so many duties there! But what about the life he had forsaken?

He owed Raiza far more than his respects, and he owed Jaelle.

The rich and melodious chords of a guitar strummed, slow and haunting. And suddenly the guitarist changed the beat, the tempo lively, joyous—celebratory. No sound could be more incongruous with his anger and despair—or with his profound confusion.

"We have a new cousin," Jaelle said softly. "And it is time to celebrate."

It was the Romany way. As she pulled him back toward the center of the camp, more guitars were played, as were a violin and cymbals. Laughter sounded, and he heard the men clapping in a strong rhythm to the music. His heart lurched and his body stirred.

Jaelle released him and ran into the center of the clearing, where four young Rom were dancing, arms folded, their heels pounding the ground in rhythm with the instruments. Jaelle lifted her skirts and whirled, legs flashing, hair streaming. He felt himself soften and smile as she raised her arms and began dancing in the midst of the men.

Everyone had gathered—men, women and children—and he saw Stevan with his wife, who reclined on blankets, nursing their newborn. Now he recalled her name—Simcha. The gathered crowd was clapping in tandem with the beating heels of the male dancers. The music began to fill his hollow, grieving body. He felt his veins pulse with each stomped foot. He felt his blood heat and race. This was the Rom life and it was simple and good.

It had been so long.

Raiza had been murdered and he would not allow the *gadjos* to simply walk away unscarred from her death. Sooner or later, he would have his revenge. This promise he made now. But the revenge would not come tonight.

Tonight they would celebrate a new life.

More men and women had joined the original dancers. A woman with ebony hair, her skirts purple and gold, twirled by him. Her stare was sultry and direct.

She was a handsome woman, full figured, close to his age, and there was no mistaking the invitation he had just received. He looked at her thighs as she lifted her skirts dangerously high. There was no lover like a Romni.

She dropped her skirts, sensually raised her arms high, and began to gyrate, her rhythm far slower than the music's rapid beat. She turned seductively away, but cast a glance over her shoulder at him. He smiled and stepped into the clearing.

The guitars, the violin, the cymbals, a tambourine and the beating of the earth washed through him. His heels found the ground, right, left, right, left, and he lifted his face to the moon, his arms to the stars. Fingers snapped. His hips thrust and undulated. He remained aware of the woman, who danced on his right, but in that moment, his body needed nothing but the music and the night.

The moon smiled. The stars gleamed. The trees stood sentinel, and the fires blazed. It was a night for celebration; it was a night for lovers.

He returned the woman's bold stare.

THE LAST OF THEIR GUESTS were gone. Ariella stood in the front hall, watching the Montgomery carriage leave as the family went upstairs to their rooms. A touch on her shoulder made her jump.

Cliff smiled at her. "I see you have survived our supper party."

"Was I so transparent?"

He laughed. "You were daydreaming, and it was obvious."

Gray eyes assailed her and she prayed her father would not guess at the subject of her musings. "I guess everyone is excited about Amanda's ball."

"Yes, they are, as it has been some time since there has been a lavish event at Rose Hill. Ariella, did you like Montgomery at all?"

She stiffened, incredulous. "I thought a match was Dianna's idea."

"It is. But she confided in her mother, who told me. You have no interest in him." It was not a question.

"I am sorry, I do not."

He sighed. "Ariella, when you were a small child, I worried about your future. At the time, I decided I would make certain to arrange the perfect marriage for you, when you came of age."

Ariella was in disbelief. "I had no idea!"

He smiled. "That was a long time ago. I realized when you became an independent young woman, of whom I am so extremely proud, that I would do no such thing. In many ways, you remind me of myself before I met Amanda."

Her relief knew no bounds. "Thank you. But Father, you were a privateer, not a bluestocking."

"I treasured my freedom, darling, as you do. However, I believe that one day you will come to me with stars shining in your eyes. You will tell me you wish to wed—and that you are madly in love."

Ariella smiled. "You do know that you are far more romantic than I am?"

Cliff laughed. "Am I?"

"I fear I am not like you, Father. My passion is for knowledge. I did try to explain earlier to Dianna that being unwed doesn't bother me at all. I do not think about handsome men or moon over them like other women my age." The moment she spoke, she quickly looked away, because she had been doing exactly that since meeting the Rom with the gray eyes.

"That's only because you have not yet met the man who is unique enough to stir your interest."

She continued hastily, afraid he might sense her distraction. "The men I meet are scholars and historians, and very few of them are noblemen."

He laughed. "And if you bring me a radical lawyer without means, I will approve—as long as he loves you in return."

Ariella did not reply. She had been thinking about Emilian throughout the evening, almost against her own will. There was something provocative and unsettling about him, although she couldn't quite identify what disturbed her.

"It may take you some time to realize that your heart has been captured, but the day will come, I have no doubts. You are too beautiful and intriguing to escape love. And when you ask me for my blessing, I will be pleased to give it, no matter whom you have chosen."

She smiled. "I hope you are not in the rush that Dianna seems to be in. I cannot settle, Father. I have no interest in a traditional marriage. Dianna should marry before I do."

"I won't allow you to settle for anything less than what you deserve." Cliff kissed her cheek. "I will never rush you. Now, I fear I must leave you stargazing by yourself. Good night."

Ariella watched him hurry upstairs. She became aware of an odd tension within her. Emilian's gray eyes seemed to be engraved permanently in her thoughts. She hadn't ever been so preoccupied with a man, not in her entire twenty-four years. She wasn't sure what her strange distraction meant, but their brief interaction had haunted her throughout the evening.

We are Rom.

She remained haunted, she realized, for she was standing alone in the front hall, in the night-darkened, eerily silent house, wondering about him. He was proud and hostile, and she couldn't comprehend why he was so defensive, or why he had seemed to dislike her and her father so much. But he had found her attractive. She was woman enough to understand the kind of look he'd given her. Gentlemen had been looking at her with some admiration since she had turned sixteen, but it had never made her think twice—until now.

Her heart was racing.

There was no reason to linger in the front hall, but Ariella stepped closer to the window and pressed her face to the cool glass pane. She thought she heard music.

Ariella realized she should not be surprised. The Romany Gypsies were renowned all over the world for their music.

She was swept with curiosity and excitement. She swiftly crossed the hall, stepping into the parlor, and then she opened the terrace doors. The moment she did, she heard the unfamiliar, exotic music.

She went still. She had heard similar melodies in the Middle East, but she had never heard music with so much passion and joy. And did she hear laughter, as well?

She realized she had crossed the terrace and stood by the railing, staring down the hill. It was a bright night, with a million stars overhead and a waxing moon, but she could see only the light of their fires and the ghostly shapes of the covered wagons. There was no doubt in her mind that the Roma Gypsies were having a celebration.

She wanted to go down the hill. She told herself she did not dare. It was highly improper—and even imprudent. A woman could not wander about the countryside after dark alone. She didn't care about the scandal, but it could be dangerous.

But no one need know. If she kept hidden, the Romany Gypsies wouldn't see her, and her family was soundly asleep for the night. If she was careful to avoid any encounters, there wouldn't be any danger to her person.

She trembled with excitement. When would she ever have this opportunity again? She hadn't seen Gypsies since she was a child. She might never come across such an encampment again. How could she ignore the music, the festivities? Stories abounded about the Gypsies, about nights filled with music, dance and love.

And what about their charismatic leader?

Ariella breathed hard, her pulse pounding. She knew she found him highly attractive, as well as enigmatic. She was curious about him, too. He seemed so well-spoken, as if educated. He was clearly used to giving commands, and he hadn't deferred to her father. What kind of man was he? Where had he come from?

The Roma would be gone in the morning.

He would be gone in the morning, too.

Her decision was made. She lifted her pale skirts and stepped down from the terrace onto the lawn. A moment later, she hurried across the drive, her pace increasing along with her excitement. She could identify more than guitars now, for she also heard at least one violin, and the rich song was punctuated with cymbals and clapping hands.

And she could finally see the wagons ahead. The blazing fires within their midst illuminated them. She heard more laughter and conversation, and she glimpsed the dancers, a flurry of movement and jewel tones.

She paused behind the closest wagon, breathing hard. The music was fierce and demanding now. It almost beat inside her, causing her stomach to churn. The tempo had escalated, as had her pulse. Gray eyes dominated her mind's eye.

Ariella crouched low beside the wagon, slipping around the front. Seeing the dancers, she stiffened in amazement.

In the center of the clearing, he danced alone. He held his arms high, fingers snapping, his white shirt unbuttoned to the waist. His chest gleamed in the firelight as he danced. The fabric of his breeches strained over his thighs and hips, and each step was impossibly seductive and sensual. Each step brought him a bit closer to where she stood. Her mouth became dry.

His eyes were closed. His dark lashes were fanned out on his high, flushed cheekbones. His expression was tight, one of sheer pleasure. A sheen of perspiration covered his face, too, and as he gyrated, she could see his navel. Ariella tugged at her bodice. Every solid inch of his anatomy was visible in that open shirt and those doeskin breeches and she was terribly, uncomfortably hot.

She swallowed. She could not look away and she did not care. She knew her thoughts had become more than improper. She was thinking about his masculinity, his virility and his barely leashed power. He was dancing alone, but somehow, it was terribly suggestive—as if he would soon take a lover to his bed.

She did not know what was happening to her. She had never thought about a man this way. What he might or might not do after dancing was not her concern.

His eyes suddenly opened. Although there were many people dancing now, and a few exotic women had surrounded him, his gaze swung directly across the dancers at her.

Had he known she was there? Her heart exploded in her chest. She knew she should duck, but somehow, she had risen to fully stand. She knew she should tear her attention away from his beautiful face, his bare chest, but that was impossible. She realized she no longer stood by the traces; somehow she had actually stepped forward.

His gray eyes caught hers and blazed.

Ariella could not look away.

His eyes were so fierce, she forgot to breathe. Their gazes locked, his arms lifted and he turned slowly for her. His arms swept toward her, and his hips slowed. Ariella felt as if his hands had just drifted down her body, as if his loins had just brushed across her belly. She did not have to be a woman of experience to know that he was dancing for her.

As if under a spell, all she could think of was his embrace and being pressed against his hard body.

He smiled seductively and his thick black lashes lowered, just as the music ceased.

Trembling, Ariella wondered if he would hear her slamming heartbeat.

He stood still, except for his chest, which rose and fell rapidly. His eyes lifted, male and intense, searing hers.

She should run away. If she stayed, something would happen—if she stayed, he was going to touch her, pull her close, against his hard body...somehow, she knew.

A hand seized her from behind. *"Kon nos? Gadje romense? Nay!"*

Ariella cried out.

A young man, perhaps sixteen, stared furiously at her. He shook her and spoke angrily in his language again. There was no music now, no laughter or conversation.

"I don't understand," she whispered.

The youth dragged her forward. Ariella stumbled and paused. The dancers surrounded them. Emilian strode forward, his eyes flashing, his body hot and wet. *"Dosta!"*

Ariella was released. Trembling, she hugged herself. Her savior was as angry as the young man. She looked at the crowd. Hostile stares were trained upon her. No one moved. Stances were belligerent. She wanted to vanish into the ground.

He spoke again, rapidly and firmly.

The young man looked at her. "I am sorry," he said in a heavy accent. He turned and walked away.

Ariella was incredulous. She looked at Emilian and he stared back at her, while the bearlike man from earlier that afternoon clapped his hands and spoke to the crowd. Someone began playing a guitar. Conversation resumed, but in lower tones and whispers, as everyone walked away. And they were alone.

Ariella was so dry she had to wet her lips. Worse, her focus had precipitously dropped to his bare, sweat-slickened chest. She couldn't help it; she stole a glance at the tight lines of his abdomen. She knew she did not dare look lower; she knew what she would see there. "What…" She wet her lips again. She sounded horribly breathless. "I wasn't spying."

His gaze narrowed.

"I swear." She breathed hard, shaking now. "I heard the music, I could not help myself."

His stare remained enigmatic. "And were you amused? Did our primitive way entertain you?"

She inhaled. "The music…the dancing…it is wonderful."

He made a sound. His attention slid to the edge of her bodice. "Isn't it late, Miss de Warenne, for a stroll across your lawns?"

He was too close. She could feel his heat and smell his scent. She could so easily touch him if she tried. Her anxiety escalated. "Yes. I should go. I am sorry to intrude." She started to rush past him.

He seized her wrist, restraining her. "But you are my guest."

Her entire arm, bare to the cap sleeve of her dress, was pressed against the hot, wet skin of his chest. She felt dizzy, faint. The hollow aching became acute. "Is that what you told them?"

"We do not like *gadjos* in our midst." Suddenly he smiled at her. "But you have become the exception to our rule."

Didn't he care that he was indecently dressed and practically naked? Didn't he know that he held her entire arm against his chest? Couldn't he feel her trembling with more than distress, with more than fear?

"Do you really want to go?" he murmured, his tone becoming a caress.

She stared into his warm eyes. She didn't want to leave and they both knew it.

"The evening has only begun."

"I don't know...I only came to investigate." The moment she spoke, she realized how bigoted that sounded.

"Most proper ladies would not dare such an investigation at such an hour," he said. He released her arm.

She could have moved farther away from him, but she didn't. Instead, she looked at his muscular chest where she'd just been so intimately pressed. His abdomen was concave. She reached up to touch her cheek—it was on fire. And her own body was perspiring almost as much as his.

He smiled again. He leaned close. "But an improper lady might venture out at such an hour. Can I help your *investigation?*"

"I didn't mean it that way."

"Of course you did. You want to compare." He sent her a rather cool smile and took her arm.

He tugged her to a small table near one of the wagons, farther from the dancers. He poured two glasses of wine from a hefty jug, handing one to her. Before she could refuse, he drank thirstily, as if the wine were water. His gaze moved down to the edge of her silk bodice.

Her nipples tightened. That look was as bold as if he'd reached inside her dress, past chemise and corset. "I didn't mean that I had come to investigate."

"Of course you did. Drink the wine. You will enjoy the night even more fully."

"I have already had wine with supper."

His white teeth gleamed. "But you are so nervous, as much as a schoolgirl or debutante. I do not bite, Miss de Warenne. Nor do I cheat or steal—or seduce unwilling ladies. It is Miss de Warenne, is it not?" His attention strayed to her left hand.

She came to her senses. "It is Miss de Warenne. I don't

believe in stereotyping. Of course you don't cheat or steal—or seduce unwilling women." She thought she flushed. This man had a way of making his every word seem sexually suggestive.

His brows lifted. "So you are the single *gadjo* without prejudice? How laudable."

"Bigotry is wrong and I am not a prejudiced person," she managed.

He turned aside, lashes lowering, but not before sending her a long glance.

Ariella raised her glass and took a gulp of the wine. Had that look meant what she thought it did? She gulped again. She had seen her father, her uncles, even her brother and cousins look at women that way. That look had one meaning. What should she do?

She should stay and let him kiss her.

Almost in disbelief, ready to wonder if this were a dream, she took another draft of the wine. She was an enlightened thinker. She didn't care about propriety and she had never been interested in a kiss before. There was no doubt about it—she was highly interested now.

As if he sensed her decision, he murmured, "If you did not come here to investigate, then I wish to do so." He laid his hand on her waist.

She tensed, but not with fear. Instead, her body hummed. "What do you mean?"

"I mean that I wish to understand why a beautiful, unwed and *proper* lady of your age is wandering into my encampment in the middle of the night."

"I am passionate," she whispered, "about knowledge. I want to know more about the Romany people."

"The Romany people—or me?"

She went still.

"Give up the pretense," he murmured. His hand moved up

her side, a shocking caress. "You didn't come for the music or for them. You came for me. I am your investigation."

Ariella couldn't speak. He was right.

His smile twisted as he pulled her closer. "You aren't the first Englishwoman to wish for a Romany lover."

She started to protest but he murmured, "Why else would you come to me, *gadji,* at such an hour?"

She had no answer to make. She stuttered, "I don't know… I wanted to come…I was drawn."

"Good. Be drawn. I wish for you to want me." His eyes smoldered. "We are open about our passions. Wait here."

Ariella stared after him, shaken, while he went back to the crowd. She saw him pause before the violinist, an older white-haired man. She realized she was hardly the only woman staring at him with yearning. The younger Romni women were beautiful, and a few of them were watching Emilian as closely as she was.

But he returned to Ariella, smiling and holding out his hand. "Dance with me."

Dancing had never interested her and she had two left feet. Did he think to have her whirl about like the Gypsy women? She would be a laughingstock. "I can't dance."

"All women can dance," he murmured again, very, very softly. Suddenly the strains of a waltz began, coming from the violin. "The music is for us."

She was surprised, but before she could finish an internal debate, he took her hand and reeled her slowly in. Suddenly they stood hip to hip, thigh to thigh. His hands closed on her shoulders, her back. He swayed his body, moving her with him. She had never known such a sensation of male strength and male promise.

Their bodies were almost fused. Her cheek had somehow found the bare skin of his chest. She shuddered. All she could think of was his soft breath on her ear, and his hard manhood, so obviously aroused, against her hip. This wasn't the waltz: this was a couple swaying to soft music, the brush of breast against chest, the rubbing of loins and hips. This was a prelude to passion.

He said against her ear, "This night is for lovers."

She didn't want to move her cheek from his wet skin, but she looked up. He had danced her over to the trees, where the night was heavy and dark.

"Can you feel the music in your body, against your skin?" he whispered. "Can you feel it in your blood?" His gaze was searing. "It is throbbing there, with need, with passion." His mouth twisted. "Do you want to kiss a Gypsy?"

They weren't moving now. They stood in an embrace and she felt her heart thundering—or was it his? And she felt herself nod. She thought she might die for his kiss.

"I thought so." He suddenly caught her face in his hands. "Be forewarned, I never do anything halfheartedly."

Ariella whispered, "Emilian."

His eyes blazed. He covered her mouth with his and Ariella stiffened, for his lips were hard, fierce and demanding. She gasped as the pressure became painful; he made a sound, and before she knew it, he had thrust his tongue deep inside her mouth. Alarm began. She pushed at his shoulders. This wasn't the kind of kiss she had expected—she wasn't sure it was a kiss at all. There was rage in his actions.

He went still.

She began to shake, frightened, for now she realized she was truly at his mercy. Her strength was no match for his.

He tore his mouth from hers. Ariella again tried to push away. *This had been a terrible mistake.* But he caught her and held her against his hard, trembling body, his arms a vise from which there was no escape. "Don't go."

She continued to shake in genuine alarm. But standing still, his body throbbing against hers, she felt her own pulse begin to surge and race. He hadn't hurt her, she reminded herself, but for one moment, she had sensed that an explosion of brutality was imminent, a violence for which she had been entirely unprepared.

His tone was soft. "I won't hurt you. I want to love you. Let me." She felt a shudder go through him as he looked down at her.

His eyes weren't cool or mocking, nor did they blaze with a heat that was almost angry. They were searching for permission from her.

That hollow feeling inside her became acute. Her breasts tightened impossibly. She became aware of his arousal between them. She shifted. Flames fired across her belly, between her thighs. He made a harsh sound.

And before she could even decide whether to allow him any further privileges, he caught her face in his large hands. She tensed but he only lowered his mouth to hers, slowly.

His lips brushed hers, just barely, like the touch of a feather. Her heart exploded, as did so much sensation that she ceased to think. He dragged his mouth across hers, again and again, and her eyes closed as she began to swim in the pleasure of heat and sensation. He rubbed his lips back and forth, testing and teasing, until her lips were soft, open.

He made a sound, rough laughter, and his tongue flicked the seam of her lips. Ariella gasped, seeking his tongue with her own. He deftly avoided her, this time closing his mouth over hers for a long, deep, endless kiss.

She spun. The fever in her body became a conflagration; she moaned and he sparred with her, tongue to tongue. She pressed against his huge hardness shamelessly now. He laughed again, clasping her buttocks through her skirts and petticoats, hard. He hiked her higher, against him.

She moaned, clinging, lips locked. Somehow he had positioned himself exactly where she needed him to be and she felt maddened with urgency now. She moved more frantically upon him.

The kiss raged on. Vaguely she felt his hand slipping up

her leg, inside her thigh, beneath her skirts and over her silk drawers. She gasped with more wild pleasure. Vaguely, she knew that this was far more than a simple kiss and she did not care.

Without hesitation, his fingers slid into the slit of her drawers, against her bare, wet skin. Ariella whimpered, tearing her mouth away, pressing her face to his hard, wet chest. She was blinded now. She wasn't sure what she wanted—other than more unbearable friction. She wept.

He spoke to her in his language, slid his entire hand inside her drawers, palming her, cupping her. She became dizzier. He spoke, rough and guttural, but in English now. "Come for me."

She didn't understand. Who cared? The trees whirled and she bit down hard, tasting his sweaty skin and his blood.

She was still spinning when she realized he had laid her down on the ground, in the wet grass. The terrible, wonderful spasms slowed and dulled. Her breathing remained labored. She felt his fingers on the bare skin of her back. She tried to understand the pleasure and passion she had just had. Now, she could comprehend why love was so highly coveted.

His fingers skimmed lower on her spine. Ariella blinked and opened her eyes. Emilian knelt beside her, his face strained with passion. He was attempting to divest her of her dress. She seized his wrist reflexively.

His smoldering gray eyes shot to hers. Surprise tainted the desire smoking there.

She breathed hard. "Wait."

His eyes narrowed. Suspicion began.

"What…what are you doing?" Her skirts were tangled around her waist and she lay sprawled like a ragged doll. She sat up, and some sense of modesty began. She jerked her skirts down. Her bodice slid downward, but she pulled it up and looked at him.

He sat back on his heels, dangerously annoyed. "You wish to stop now?" He spoke far too softly.

"I...I didn't come for this."

"Of course you did." Anger flared in his eyes. "You came for passion. You want to compare me to your English lovers. I am not satisfied," he added in a dark tone.

The top buttons of his breeches had come undone, as if they could not bear the strain of what lay beneath the fabric. She wanted to speak but couldn't.

"That pleasure is nothing compared to the pleasure we will have when I am buried inside your body." He reached out and stroked her face. "Let me make you cry out in pleasure another time. Let me cry out in pleasure, too."

She went still.

He began to smile. "We both know this is why you came to me." He reached for her bodice and gripped it.

She clung harder. It would be so easy to give in to this man. His words, his look, were mesmerizing. But a kiss was one thing. This was another. She wanted to go further, but she also wanted to keep him at bay until she could understand what was happening. "This is a misunderstanding," she whispered.

His eyes went wide.

"I didn't come to compare you to my other lovers." She held her bodice up fiercely now. "There are no other lovers."

He just stared at her, his expression so uncertain it was almost comical.

"I'm not even married," she whispered. Did she have to be more succinct? "No one my age has lovers. Women my age have husbands first."

A terrible silence fell.

She became nervous. How had he assumed she was a woman looking for an illicit affair?

"Do not tell me you are a virgin," he said. "Virgins do not

wander about at midnight, to rendezvous with and tease strange men."

She hesitated. He looked as savage as a lion awoken from a deep sleep while in its den. "I don't know why I came…to see you…. I only wanted a kiss."

CHAPTER FOUR

HIS STRIDES WERE SO LONG and hard that she had to run to keep up with him. Ariella stumbled. "Wait!"

He didn't answer her and he didn't pause. His profile was a taut mask of frustration and anger. He was heading up the hill, toward the sleeping house. Clearly he wished for her to return home and this was his manner of escorting her safely back.

"I am so sorry," she cried, racing to catch up to him. Of course he had expected a liaison—her behavior had been so bold. But why was he so angry now? "I didn't mean to mislead you."

He finally looked at her, halting so abruptly that she went past him. He caught her arm, dragging her back to his side. "If you don't wish to mislead a man, stay in your fine, fancy house, in your fine, fancy bed, where well-bred virgins belong at this hour!"

She trembled, dismayed. "My curiosity led me astray. I heard the music and it was so enchanting." She hesitated, because that was only half of the truth. She had been curious about *him*. He was clearly unmoved. "I meant to watch from a distance. I didn't mean to intrude. I didn't think anyone would notice me. I didn't mean for…anything…to happen."

His mouth curved, but not with mirth. "Didn't you?"

She tensed. "Of course not!"

"The way you looked at me this afternoon—and this

evening—left me with one inescapable conclusion." He spoke so softly she could barely discern his words.

"You are wrong," she tried, but he was right and they both knew it.

His expression hardened.

She hugged herself, flushing. "All right! I will admit that I was staring at you, but surely you are accustomed to ladies admiring you. I did not mean to be coy—I have never been coy in my life." She felt herself blushing. She would never admit she had started thinking about his hard, male body when she had seen him dancing—and even earlier, during his confrontation with her father.

"That," he said harshly, "I do not believe. I believe you know exactly how to use your blue eyes to inflame a man—and you did so with purpose." His eyes flickered. "You inflamed me."

She was already breathless. Her pulse surged wildly in response to his frank words. Too well, she recalled being in his arms, their mouths fused, their bodies on fire. She didn't want to leave, not yet. In fact, a new and wanton part of her wished to explore what they had begun.

His laughter was harsh, as if he knew what she was thinking and feeling. "You need to go, before my baser nature defeats my sense of honor. It is getting light out. You have a reputation to maintain and I am not inclined to maintain it for you."

The sky was beginning to gray, but she did not move. They couldn't part company this way, especially when he was leaving Rose Hill shortly. "Why are you so angry? I am sorry—I have already said so, twice. Will you accept my apology?"

"Why should I? I do not like being played, Miss de Warenne."

Her heart slammed. He was not going to accept an apology from her, even after she had explained her intentions.

He laughed harshly. "Am I the first man that will not do as you wish when you flutter your lashes at him?"

"I am not a flirt," she said.

"Good night." He nodded abruptly at the house, clearly wishing her to go.

Ariella took a deep breath, determined. "We have gotten off to a terrible start." She smiled at him. "Obviously a third apology will not soothe you, so I won't offer it. But can we start over again? We hardly know one another. I should like to further our acquaintance, if at all possible."

His eyes widened and then narrowed, gleaming. "Really? How odd. Proper ladies—proper *virgins*—do not have Gypsy acquaintances. In fact, the ladies who wish for my acquaintance want one thing and one thing only—which you have clearly refused."

"I will not believe that," she whispered, aghast. Surely he was exaggerating!

He shrugged. "I do not care what you believe. Now that our ill-fated liaison is over, I do not care about you at all, *Miss* de Warenne."

His words actually hurt. After what they had just shared, she could not believe he meant them. "I think you have *decided* to dislike me, although I cannot comprehend why. I think you decided to dislike me this afternoon, almost at first sight, even though I was trying to help you convince my father to let you stay the night here. Yet you liked me well enough a moment ago."

He stared. Finally he said, every muscle in his face tensing, "Spoken with so much naiveté, I might actually believe you."

"I am hardly naive," Ariella said.

"I did not ask for this," he continued roughly. "I did not ask for a beautiful fairy-tale princess to appear in my life, offering me a temptation I can barely refuse. You are a noblewoman, an heiress. You will clearly wed some English

Prince Charming one day—and he will take your innocence in an ivory tower. Go home, Miss de Warenne, where you belong." He turned to go.

She was finally angry and she seized his arm. She wasn't strong enough to detain him, but he faced her, his eyes as cold and turbulent as a winter storm. "If I refuse to judge you, why do you insist on judging me? You know nothing about me. I am not like other women of my class and age, desperate for a proper husband and home, and while it might appear I am like those ladies who wish for your attentions, I am not like them, either. I did not seek you out for a love affair!"

"No, but you did seek me out." He folded his arms across his chest. "Let us cut to the chase. What do you want from me, Miss de Warenne?"

She inhaled. Although she instantly recalled his torrid kisses and his shockingly sensual touch, she did not hesitate. "I want to be friends."

He laughed. "Impossible."

"Why? Why is it impossible? I know you are leaving tomorrow, but we can exchange letters. We could even meet a few times before you leave Derbyshire."

He choked. "Exchange letters? Meet?" He looked at her as if she were mad.

"I am interested in getting to know you, and letters are the perfect way to further our acquaintance. As for meeting, why is that suggestion so shocking? Surely you like to converse."

"You wish to meet and converse?"

"That is what friends do." She smiled at him. She thought her plan a capital one.

"We are not friends," he said harshly. "I have no friends—nor do I want any!"

She was in disbelief. "Everyone has friends."

"You do not want friendship and we both know it." He

pointed at her. His hand shook. "You are a de Warenne heiress! Your *friends* are tony!"

"I have all kinds of eccentric friends in town!"

"When I demanded you cut to the chase, I was merely curious as to how you would respond—and with how much subterfuge. I know why you came to the camp tonight. You sought me out for *passion*, Miss de Warenne, not friendship. I caught your interest and you wished to be in my arms, although not my bed. You wish to *exchange letters?* You wish to *converse?* I think not. In fact, I don't think you very different from my *gadji* lovers. The difference is you only want safe kisses." His eyes blazed. "And the kind of pleasure I so recently gave you."

Ariella stared, taken aback, but not by his candor. He was partly right—after what had just happened, how could she not yearn to be in his arms? But why didn't he believe that she was interested in friendship, too? She was eager to know what he thought of the world!

"I have been a sexual object for the ladies of the ton, and now, I am an object of sexual *fascination* for a virgin princess." He seemed disgusted.

Ariella wasn't quite sure what his statement meant, precisely, but she would think about it later. "I can't possibly forget our kiss," she said slowly. "How could I? I had no idea a kiss could be so wonderful. But I do want to be friends, Emilian. I always say what I mean. I have many unusual friends in town. If you truly have no friends—and I pray you are dissembling—then I will be the first."

"What the hell did you mean, that you had no idea a kiss could be so wonderful?" he demanded. "I do hope you are not going to tell me that was your first kiss."

"Why would that distress you?"

His eyes widened impossibly. "No one has ever kissed you before?"

"No, no one ever has. You gave me my first kiss. And I have no regrets—not a single one," she cried, flushing.

He snarled, "Then I have enough regrets for the two of us."

She inhaled. "You don't mean that!"

"Go home and wait for Prince Charming. And stay there—with your *unusual* friends."

He was rejecting her offer of friendship. Ariella was in disbelief. "But you are leaving in the morning! We can't part this way."

"Why not?"

She wet her lips, her heart thundering. "It isn't right," she floundered. "We just shared passion, Emilian."

"We shared a simple kiss, one you will soon forget."

She shook her head. "No. I won't forget it. Please consider an exchange of letters!" she cried.

"Just *go*," he roared.

She flinched but couldn't tell her feet to move. How could this be happening?

He turned furiously, strode down the hill, and did not look back a single time.

As IF A SPIDER caught in her web, he was drawn back to the bottom of the hill. He stared up at the house.

The sun had risen over an hour ago, but the camp was hardly stirring, due to the celebration the night before. He had not slept. He had not even thought to try. Emilian stared up at the de Warenne mansion. He did not want to lust after Ariella de Warenne, especially not now. He did not quite trust himself with his lust. There was too much rage.

He whirled and started back to the camp. He hoped to never encounter her again. Mariko could take care of his needs, as could a dozen well-bred Derbyshire wives. He had meant his every word. That morning had been goodbye. There would not be an exchange of letters or a flurry of meetings. He hadn't asked for a woman like that to appear in his life, especially not now, when he was grieving and enraged.

She was the kind of young lady that no one had ever presented to him—and no one ever would—because of his tainted blood. She was beautiful, wealthy, well-bred and undoubtedly accomplished. She was even, somehow, innocent, in spite of her passionate nature—and her nature *was* passionate, he had uncovered that. He was deemed worthy of the fat, the aged, the infirm, the ugly—those rejected by everyone else. A lady like Miss de Warenne would never be presented to a man who had Gypsy blood running in his veins, no matter his wealth, his title. One day, Miss de Warenne would be presented to a genuine Englishman, one as blue-blooded and properly English as she. Her suitor would take one look at her and be smitten. Any sane man would instantly conclude that the beautiful and genteel Miss de Warenne would make the perfect wife.

No other man had ever kissed her before.

It was unbelievable.

He had given her pleasure for the first time. Too well, he recalled her cries. Even now, his skin was abraded from her nails and teeth.

He had wanted her attentions when he had first seen her, in spite of the fact that he had surmised she wasn't married. He never chased unmarried women, but she was beautiful, English and above him. Perhaps because of her father, he had deliberately looked at her with sexual interest. He hadn't been surprised when she had come to him last night. She could claim that she had drifted to their camp to hear the music, but she had come because of him. But he had assumed she was a woman of experience, a woman with lovers.

Young unwed ladies were meant to lounge in the drawing rooms of their mansions, sipping tea in the latest London fashions, awaiting their callers and suitors. She claimed she was different. Obviously, she was clinging to propriety, and he wondered if she would manage to continue to do so until her wedding night. Suddenly he hated the idea of an Englishman being the one to fully show her passion.

He could have had her; why hadn't he taken her?

Because he was more English than Rom. As a gentleman, he had a strong sense of honor. The English valued innocence, the Roma did not. He had never dallied with a virgin, not even during his traipse with the Romany across Scotland eight years ago. It was not just because he preferred experienced women in his bed. The Englishman he had become, the man who was Woodland's viscount and Edmund's son, could not take or destroy a woman's innocence. It was that simple.

Just then, he did not feel particularly English.

And he hadn't felt English at all last night.

He had reached the outermost wagons. A baby was crying; it might have been his newborn cousin. His head was pounding so badly he thought it might split in two. His body was pulsing as terribly, a combination of desire and rage. He wasn't even certain that he wanted to be English anymore. He only knew that he wanted to avenge Raiza, and, if he was brutally honest, a part of him was now regretting not taking the *gadji* princess to his bed.

But he kept thinking about her wide blue eyes, not her face or her body. Her eyes disturbed him, because she had looked into his as if she might find some ancient truth about him there.

He shook himself free of the fanciful notion. She claimed she wanted to be his *friend*. He laughed out loud.

He had no friends. He had brothers—every Rom in the *kumpa'nia* was his brother. He had family—Stevan, his cousins, Jaelle. Even Robert, no matter how much he despised him and was despised by him, was family. He had enemies—almost every *gadjo* and *gadji* on the street could be thrust into that category. But he did not have friends. He wasn't even sure what a friend really was or why anyone would want one.

What was wrong with her? He slept with women; he didn't befriend them.

Maybe she *was* different from the *gadjis* he took to his bed. She claimed she did not judge him the way all the *gadjos* did. But she had sought him out for passion, just as his lovers did. Had she been married, he was certain she would have leaped into his bed. That made her no different, after all. And one day, he would turn his back and overhear her speaking of him with condescension and scorn. He had not a single doubt.

His fury escalated. He hated the *gadjos,* every single last one of them—even her.

"You look ready to break someone apart."

Emilian breathed, hoping to relax his tight muscles, and turned to face Stevan. "Do I?"

"Before I ever told you about Raiza, I saw the dark clouds in your eyes. Do you want to tell me your troubles?" Stevan asked quietly.

"I have worries at Woodland," he lied. "All *gadjo* nonsense, really."

Stevan smiled, clearly not believing him.

"But I want to speak with you," Emilian said. His chest throbbed with pain. "I must go to Raiza's grave."

"That is proper," Stevan agreed. "She is buried at Trabbochburn, not far from where you were born. When will you go?"

There had been no time to grieve and no time to think. Just as he had learned of Raiza's murder, the celebration over the birth of his cousin had begun. And then Ariella de Warenne had appeared, distracting him. There was no question of his duty—he must go to his mother's grave and pay his respects. But now he regarded his uncle, thinking of his young sister, who needed a guardian and a brother. Raiza would want him to take care of Jaelle. "I think I would like to join you when you travel north," he said slowly.

Stevan was surprised. "Your grief is speaking, is it not?"

"Maybe." But the idea had so much appeal. By choosing to stay with Edmund when he was only twelve years old, he had forsaken the Roma people and their way of life. He had been so young to make such a choice. Shouldn't he attempt to understand the Roma way—especially when the Rom part of him was burning with hatred of the English and the need for revenge?

And he could get to know his little sister, who needed him.

"You know you are always welcome. But Emilian, why not take your fine *gadjo* carriage and your many servants with you? Why travel like a Rom, when you left us so long ago to become English?"

Emilian spoke with care, trying to make sense of the urgings in his heart, his soul. "I have forgotten what it means to be Rom. I feel that I owe Raiza far more than I could ever have given her—and far more than paying my respects at her grave. Everything has changed, Stevan. I am enraged with the *gadjos*."

"You are her son—you should be enraged. I do not think you know what you want. But you are merely speaking of a visit with us, are you not?"

Emilian stared. "I am as much Rom as I am English."

"Really? Because I see an Englishman standing before me—even if you dance like a Rom." Stevan smiled, but Emilian could not smile back. "My sister was proud of the man you have become. She wanted you to have a fine life, with a fine house filled with servants. She would not ask you, if she were alive, to give up your English life for the Roma way."

"What am I giving up?" Emilian cried. "I know she wanted more for me than the life of the Rom. I remember very well that she wished for me to live with my father—but she grieved over my loss, as well. I made the choice to stay at Woodland when I was too young to understand it. Did I make the right choice? My neighbors scorn me, Stevan, just as fully as they scorn you."

Stevan was thoughtful. "I think I begin to understand. For half your blood is Romany and nothing will ever change that. But I still think you will tire quickly of the life. There have been too many changes made over too many years."

"Maybe you are right. Maybe you are wrong. Maybe, after a month or two, I will spit upon the *gadjos* and their way and never wish to return home." He trembled with his rage and his attention strayed back up the hill, toward the huge de Warenne mansion.

Stevan looked at him and Emilian flushed. He had just called Woodland home.

"I think we both know that the day the *gadjo* took you away from Raiza, your *baxt* was made."

Emilian stiffened. "I do not believe in fate."

"Then you are very much a *gadjo*, Emilian."

Emilian thought about how he had surrendered far more than his body to the intense, evocative Roma music last night. Briefly, he had been so consumed with the fiery passion of the dance, it had been as if the gap of eighteen years had ceased to exist. It had been as if he had never left the Romany people. "Last night I was Rom."

Stevan clasped his shoulder. "Yes, you were. When will you be ready to leave?"

"I need a week, maybe more," Emilian said. The lure of the open road beckoned, not just in his mind's eye, but in his heart. He could not wait—he felt as if the moment the caravan left Derbyshire, he would be free. "I must hire an estate manager, a man I can trust. Can you linger that long? The *kumpa'nia* will be welcome on my estate."

"We will wait as long as is necessary," Stevan said, smiling. "I am very pleased you will come with us."

Emilian was suddenly certain that, this time, the choice he was making was the right one.

Because now, with the road lying in wait for him, he could look at his English life and question it. He was tired of the parade of *gadji* women who ogled him as if he was an exotic specimen of manhood, and who expected him to be insatiable because he was a Gypsy. If he became bored after an hour or two, his lovers were affronted. They all expected him to be hugely endowed, and couldn't wait to see if Gypsies really were built unnaturally. He had even seen his lovers checking their jewelry in the morning, to see if he had stolen anything from them.

And every *gadjo* he did business with expected to be cheated. He had never cheated anyone but he toyed with the newcomers ruthlessly; those with whom he'd conducted his affairs for years understood that he was an honest man.

He had never been a hateful man. He expected bigotry, for he had grown up with it. He could not recall the last time the words "dirty Gypsy" had really hurt him—maybe when he was a young boy, or maybe when he had first been forced to Woodland. Long ago, his heart had turned to stone. He was different from them, and he had always known that and accepted it. He might sit at their supper tables, or even, once in a great while, dance at their balls, but he was an outsider. Their scorn meant little when he was richer and more powerful than most of them, when he needed no one but himself.

Their differences had now become glaring. His life was a pretense that was no longer tolerable. He would not accept the bigotry now.

Their scorn and hatred had killed Raiza.

There had to be revenge.

He was staring up at the de Warenne house. The de Warenne woman was innocent, but she was one of them. In fact, she epitomized English society, with her beauty, heritage and wealth. She had sent him a sexual invitation, even if she hadn't known it. He remained English enough to have refused her, but the Rom part of him could not help but calculate the seduction and envision the conquest. To take a virgin like Ariella de Warenne, use her and return her used, sending her to her betrothed that way, was more than *budjo*—it was revenge.

It would be so easy....

The English part of him was horrified.

ARIELLA SAT in the window seat of the bay window. The lush lawns and blooming gardens extended below, but she saw neither. She stared instead at the Gypsy encampment, which she could see clearly from where she sat.

Their horses were loose, grazing at will. Colorful wagons remained where they had been left last night. There was no sign of preparations for their departure.

She hugged her knees to her chest. She hadn't slept at all; she hadn't even tried. She had changed her clothes and slipped into her current position, vibrating with tension. She was worried. Emilian was a stranger, but last night she had danced in his arms and he had given her a glimpse of passion. She had never been attracted to any man before, and now she was drawn, like a moth to the flame. Wasn't he drawn, too?

He intended to leave with the Romany—to simply walk away, as if nothing had happened between them.

It hurt. Even if society thought her odd, her stature as a de Warenne heiress guaranteed her acceptance wherever she went. Proper gentlemen both desired and feared her, but Emilian had rejected her.

How could she convince him to change his mind and begin a friendship with her? Her heart raced at the thought. She was beyond distraction, really, and not just because of his kiss. Ariella was uncertain of many things regarding Emilian, but one thing she knew without question: she couldn't walk away from him, not yet.

And she couldn't let him walk out of her life as abruptly as he'd appeared in it, no matter what he intended.

What was happening to her? Could she have fallen in love at first sight? There were quite a few de Warenne men and women who had instantly fallen in love, or so family myth claimed. The de Warennes were notorious for falling wildly and absolutely in love—once and forever.

"Ariella!" Dianna pounded on her door. "Can I come in? Are you awake? Alexi is here. He came with Aunt Lizzie and Margery!"

Before she could respond, Dianna came inside. "Wake up, sleepy..." She stopped. "You are up! Oh, of course you are. You are usually the first one up in the house." Her smile faded and she stared closely.

Ariella knew then that her tension and excitement showed. She forced a smile. All she could think was that Alexi would discover her new secret if she wasn't careful.

He was her half brother and her elder by two years. His Russian mother, a countess, had handed him off to their father at birth, as neither she nor her husband cared to have her bastard son remain in their family. They had grown up together with their father on Jamaica Island, and he was far closer to her than any full sibling could be. He was her dearest friend, her brother, her protector. He would take one look at her and demand to know what was wrong.

Panic arose. *If he ever learned of her tryst with Emilian, he would try to kill him.* He was that protective of her.

"What is wrong? Are you ill?" Dianna asked, coming close and touching her cheek.

"I couldn't sleep," Ariella said truthfully. "I doubt I slept at all last night."

For one moment, Dianna stared as if she knew the truth. "It was their music, wasn't it?" she said, low. "I heard it, too. It took me a while to fall asleep. There must have been dancing."

Ariella thought there was innuendo in her sister's words, but surely that was not the case. "I don't know."

Dianna sat down on a blue-and-white-striped ottoman. "They say that is what they do—dance and sing all night long."

"I don't think we should accept rumors as fact," Ariella said. The moment she spoke, she heard how cross she sounded. She stood, hoping Dianna had not noticed her harsh tone.

"My, you are a grouch today. Are you coming downstairs to see Alexi?"

Ariella prayed she could pretend that all was as it should be now. "Of course." But as she followed Dianna down the wide, central staircase, the steps covered with a red and gold Persian runner, she heard her brother's voice. His tone was hard.

"I cannot believe Father would allow them to stay on our property."

Ariella tensed. Alexi was obviously speaking about the Romany. He traveled the world extensively, as he had global shipping interests, and he spoke often about cultures different from their own with interest, not suspicion or prejudice. She was taken aback by his words and tone.

He whirled, smiling. "There she is!" His white teeth flashed in his handsome, swarthy face. Tall and broad-shouldered, his eyes were the brilliant blue shared by so many de Warenne men. Like his male cousins, he had been a notorious rakehell before his marriage—unlike his male cousins, he remained a notorious rakehell even after marriage. Five years ago, he had wed their childhood friend, Elysse O'Neil, to save her from scandal—and had abandoned her at the altar immediately after taking his vows. Needless to say, that had caused an even greater scandal. As far as Ariella knew, neither husband nor wife had set eyes upon each other since.

He strode to her, but before he could embrace her, his smile faded and his stare became searching. "What is wrong?" he asked instantly.

"Is Elysse with you?" she queried, hoping to distract him. Besides, she loved Elysse as a sister and wished she were happily married to Alexi.

His face hardened. "Do not start."

Nothing had changed. Whatever had happened, Alexi would never forgive Elysse and never forget. She sighed and hugged him, standing on tiptoe to do so. "You are such an impossible man. I love you, anyway." She finally smiled, and it was almost genuine. "You promised to be in London for my birthday, but instead, you sent that impossible gift!" He'd sent her a music box inlaid with semiprecious stones and filigreed with gold from Istanbul. It must have cost him a small fortune.

He set her at arm's length. "I am sorry I missed your birthday, but I explained in my note that we were becalmed. You look unhappy."

Ariella moved past him. She glimpsed her Aunt Lizzie, the Countess of Adare, in an adjacent room, chatting happily with Amanda. Her cousin, Margery, smiled at her and they hugged. "I am so happy to see you," Margery said. Like her mother, she was a pretty, buxom strawberry blonde. "Even though it's only been a few weeks, there is so much to catch up on."

Margery spent a great deal of the year in London, too. "How was your trip? You have arrived so early!" Ariella said.

"We had an easy journey, thanks to the new rail," she replied. "You do look a bit peaked, Ariella. Are you all right?"

"I couldn't sleep a wink last night," Ariella said. She was afraid to look at Alexi. He was scrutinizing her far too closely.

"The Gypsy music kept her awake," Dianna said. "I had a bit of a problem falling asleep, as well."

Ariella felt her cheeks warm. She stole a glance at her brother, but he had strode to the terrace doors. He stared across the lawns toward the brightly painted wagons of the caravan.

"A Gypsy woman came to the door at Harmon House a year or so ago," Margery said. "I was the only one at home and I happened to notice how shabbily she was dressed before our doorman could send her away. She begged to tell my fortune. I only wanted to give her a meal, but she read my palm."

"And did her fortune come true?" Dianna asked.

"Well, as she predicted a terribly handsome man as dark as the night riding in on a white charger, no." Margery laughed. "How unfortunate."

Alexi turned. "She was hustling you, obviously."

"She was too proud to accept a meal without offering a service," Ariella refuted. Her tone must have been strong, because everyone stared.

Alexi's interest had become intense. Ariella said, "I went to their camp with Father. I haven't seen Romany people since I was a child. That was in Ireland, Alexi, do you recall?"

"Yes, I do. Father's stallion was stolen and he was furious for a week."

She crossed her arms and stiffened. "It was unfortunate," she began.

"It was a felony," he said grimly.

She walked over to him, her temper flaring dangerously. She knew she should control it—she never lost her temper and everyone would know something was afoot. But she couldn't hold it at bay. "So *all* Gypsies are horse thieves, fortune-tellers, hustlers and criminals?"

He towered over her. "I did not say any such thing. I have encountered Romany all over the world. They are great musicians—in Russia, the Crown has a Romany choir, as do many of the great nobles. In Hungary, Romany musicians are the rage and they play in the greatest homes, and on the stage. Many of them earn an honest living. They are tinkers, smiths, basket makers, chair menders. But," he said very emphatically, "they are nomadic, and a disproportionate number prefer any activity other than one that brings in an honest wage."

She knew she must back down. "I cannot believe that there are more thieves amongst the Romany than amongst the English."

"That is not what I said."

"Their music is strange, but very enjoyable," Dianna said swiftly, clearly wanting to intervene. She smiled anxiously at them both. "It is exotic but filled with passion, like an opera might be."

Ariella ignored her, as did Alexi. He said softly, "Since when have you become the defender of the Romany tribes?"

Ariella debated several placating answers. "Since I went with Father to their camp and saw mothers caring for their children and preparing supper for their families, just as we do!"

"Their culture is vastly different from ours." He was firm. "I do not like them camping here."

"Why not?" she cried.

His gaze shot to hers. "There will be trouble."

She could not believe he had become so bigoted. "Their leader swore that there would be no horse stealing or cattle rustling."

"Really? How odd. Theirs is more of a brotherhood than anything else. I doubt their *vaida* could speak honestly for his brothers. You have become enamored of the Romany!"

Ariella's heart had stopped. For one moment, she had thought he had been about to say she was enamored of their leader. She breathed, trembling. "Yes, I have. I want to study their ways and learn all I can about them."

"Last night you were going on and on about the Mongols," Dianna exclaimed.

She had the perfect excuse to seek Emilian out now, she realized, but her anxiety did not ease. "I have had enough of the Mongols. When I saw the Romany camp with Father, I became fascinated with them. I want to know what is folklore and what is fact." She glanced at Alexi to see if he believed her.

He groaned, but then he smiled. "I should have known! So it has been the Mongols...until now? Well, look at the bright side. You have a *kumpa'nia* right at Rose Hill. You can do research in the field." He pulled her close and gave her a brief kiss on the cheek. "You, my dear, shall be well swindled before this day is done." He laughed and walked out.

Ariella felt her knees buckle. She moved to the closest chair and sat.

"What did he mean?" Dianna asked.

Ariella could barely believe her turn of good luck. Her family would now think her interest in Emilian no different from her recent passion for Genghis Khan.

"He meant, dear, that your older sister is very naive, too much so her for age and intelligence, and she is about to be hustled." Margery smiled. "Unless, of course, we can dissuade her from her newest obsession."

"That will never happen," Dianna said, smiling, as well. "Ariella is not dissuadable, not when she is smitten with a new subject."

"I, for one, think their wagons are works of art. Do you want to take a stroll down to their camp? We can admire their craftsmanship and decoration firsthand." Margery's eyes twinkled.

Ariella shot to her feet. "That is a wonderful idea."

"I thought you might like it." Margery winked at Dianna. "Maybe we can save her from a dangerous Gypsy."

CHAPTER FIVE

WHILE MARGERY AND DIANNA paused to exclaim over a wagon painted fantastically red, green and blue and decorated with a carved horse head in a wreath, Ariella stood on tiptoe and searched the entire camp for Emilian.

Horses had been gathered, and a few were being brought into their traces, a sign that the Romany were preparing to leave. Then Ariella saw him.

He stood by a fire, just a short distance away. With long tongs, he held a horseshoe in the flames. A black horse was tied to the wagon a short distance from him.

In the light of day, his hair was really a rich brown, shot through with amber and gold. He did not wear a shirt and, although he was motionless, his biceps bulged as he held the iron tongs. His profile was as classic and noble as any man's could be. His shoulders were broad and strong, and as he shifted his weight, his back rippled with muscle.

"Oh," Dianna gasped.

"Oh…well…my," Margery murmured.

Ariella jerked and faced them. "I think the sun will come out. It should be a beautiful afternoon!" He was even more beautiful than she had remembered.

Margery stared at her while Dianna stared with wide eyes at Emilian. Ariella knew that her cousin was thinking about Ariella's sudden passion for the Romany people—and the man standing a few paces from them.

"You'd think he'd wear a shirt. There are women and children everywhere," Dianna whispered, her tone hoarse.

Margery's focus remained on Ariella, filled with speculation.

Ariella tore her regard away. Dianna was bright pink and she seemed transfixed by Emilian, who had just removed the horseshoe from the fire. He turned and laid it on a low stump, and this profile revealed his full, hard chest and the flat, tight planes of his abdomen. But Ariella saw only the scratches on his right shoulder.

Had she done that?

He placed one foot on the stump and began swinging the hammer. His arms and back bulged. The muscles in his raised thigh swelled, even through the breeches.

Dianna choked.

Ariella glanced at her and realized her proper sister was hardly a prude.

"*That* is a handsome man," Margery said in a factual tone.

Ariella knew her face flamed. "Who? Oh, you mean the smith?" Her tone was far too high.

"We should go," Dianna said nervously. "How can he be so immodest?"

"We can't go," Margery said. She gestured at the basket of breads, cake, cookies and muffins they had brought with them. It had been Margery's idea to bring treats for the children. "We need to leave this with one of the adults." She glanced at Emilian. "My good man!" she called, her tone authoritative but not brusque.

Emilian laid down the hammer and turned. He glanced indifferently at Margery, and then his eyes slammed upon Ariella. They widened.

Maybe this had not been the best idea, she thought frantically.

"Sir? I am Lady de Warenne. We have brought some bread

and muffins for the children," Margery said with a pleasant smile.

Emilian's gaze had not wavered from Ariella. She saw his eyes fill with anger.

But he nodded at Margery. "I beg your pardon," he said. As he reached for a shirt, Ariella saw the mark on his upper chest, which gleamed with perspiration. She closed her eyes, recalling biting him accidentally in the heat of the most extreme moment.

"I don't blame you," Dianna whispered.

Ariella looked at her with panic. Did she now guess the truth, too?

"I am undone, too."

Ariella could barely believe Dianna, but the conversation taking place between her cousin and Emilian drew her attention, instead.

"That is very generous of you, Lady de Warenne," Emilian said, buttoning his shirt halfway. He reached for a dark green brocade vest, embroidered with silver and gold. The item would not pass as a waistcoat; it was far too exotic in design. He shrugged it on. "You may leave the basket with me. I am sure the children will enjoy the fare."

"I hope so." Margery smiled. "Your wagons are beautiful, sir. I have never seen one up close before. The craftsmanship is superb."

His smile began, reluctant and wry and so stunning. "Unfortunately, we cannot take credit for the workmanship. Our wagon makers are Englishmen."

"But obviously someone has designed them so fantastically," Margery said. She turned. "I believe you have met my cousin, Miss Ariella de Warenne."

Ariella tensed as his gaze swept over her, his smile vanishing. She felt disrobed by the glance. She touched her silk skirts reflexively, hoping all was in order, wishing she had chosen something prettier to wear than a simple, long-sleeved day dress.

He shocked her by inclining his head. "I am afraid I have not had the pleasure."

She breathed in relief.

Margery introduced Dianna. "I see some wagons being readied. Are you taking to the road so soon?" Margery asked.

He gave Margery his attention again. "I am afraid we have been denied permission to linger."

"Really? Captain de Warenne is a very generous and accommodating man. I am surprised."

Emilian chose to remain silent now.

Ariella could not believe how polite and respectful he was being to her cousin. He had not treated her so cordially, not even from the first. He had spoken to her suggestively before there had ever been an introduction. He had turned his glittering eyes upon her, as if a magician capable of enchantment, and she had fallen instantly under his spell.

He did not seem to wish to enthrall Margery. She was relieved, for she felt fairly certain he was a ladies' man. But just then, he was behaving like a well-born, noble and proper gentleman.

Margery wished him a safe journey. She turned. "Shall we return to the house? I have yet to chat with your stepmother, Ariella. And then I think I am going to rest before supper."

Ariella looked at Emilian.

He sent her a cold glance. Using the tongs, he took the horseshoe, which had cooled, and returned it to the fire.

He wanted her to leave. Ariella swallowed. "I think," she said quietly, "I will stay a while."

He did not look up, but he stiffened.

"I was hoping to converse with some of the women before they leave and I may never have such a chance again."

Margery's eyes danced. "Field research?" she said teasingly.

"It is an amazing opportunity," Ariella said. He was intent on the burning shoe, which was the color of hot coals now. It didn't matter. She knew he was listening to their every word.

"Very well, but I think you should rest this afternoon, too. The Simmonses are having their May Day country ball tonight, remember?"

Before Ariella could respond, Dianna said, "No, it was moved—it is at the end of the week."

"I suppose I misunderstood. Dianna?"

Dianna gave her arm, and the two women walked off.

Ariella did not move.

Emilian took the horseshoe from the coals and laid it on the stump. He tossed the tongs aside, jerked his shirt open and lifted the hammer. He slammed it into the shoe. "Come closer," he said, "and you will get burned."

Ariella was fairly certain that he did not refer to the fire at his feet.

"Nervous, Miss de Warenne?" he mocked, finally leveling a cold gray stare at her.

"Yes, I am terribly nervous." She had no intention of dissembling now.

"You have come back, so I can only assume you wish to be burned. I must warn you, linger and you will suffer the consequences."

"I believe that you are more bark than bite," she managed. "In spite of what could have happened last night, you were a gentleman when you realized my position."

He made a harsh sound, his eyes diamond hard. "You clearly know nothing about the Rom, and as clearly, you know nothing about me."

"You're right." She hesitated. "I was hoping that, in the light of a new day, we might be able to discuss everything more calmly."

"There is nothing to discuss." He turned away.

He was going to reject her again? Hadn't he felt what she'd felt last night? Didn't he feel that interest and attraction now? She bit her lip. "I was hoping to learn about your culture," she tried. "I was glad to see that you haven't left yet."

He stiffened, staring at the horseshoe. Then he slowly faced her. His mouth tightened. "I will not be a part of your *field research,* Miss de Warenne."

She tensed. "That is not fair, as you have no idea what Margery meant."

"I think she meant exactly what she said."

"I won't deny my curiosity. I would like to know more about your way of life. But...I came back because we argued last night." She stared and their gazes locked. "I don't wish to argue with you."

"You mean this morning." He gave her a direct look, both scathing and male, and turned away. He retrieved the shoe with gloves. A black mare was tied to the wagon and he went to her, stroking her rump once. He lifted her hind hoof and placed the shoe there, checking the fit.

"You know what I mean," Ariella said to his back. He did not look up. "I was hoping your temper might have improved with a few hours of sleep. But I see I have been hoping in vain."

He straightened and faced her, his gaze now deeply penetrating. "I did not sleep, Miss de Warenne. My temper has never been as foul."

She was certain their encounter was the reason he hadn't been able to sleep, either, and that thrilled her. He could claim indifference, but he was affected by her, too. "Then that makes two of us," she murmured.

His face hardened. "Are you trying to provoke me? Was last night not enough provocation? Or is this a virgin's seduction?"

She was surprised. "You make it sound as if I wanted to

lead you a merry chase, when I had no such plans! I wouldn't even know where to begin a seduction!"

He ripped off the gloves. "Last night, you wanted me to pursue you—do not dare deny it. You wanted me to take you into my arms and you wanted my kisses. I know when a woman sends such an invitation, Miss de Warenne. I did not mistake your desires last night. I have little doubt you were born a seductress."

She was amazed that he thought her seductive, when all of society found her too independent, too intelligent, too educated. "You are the first man, Emilian, who has ever made me think of kisses," she said slowly, "and the first man to make me feel passion. You are the only man I have ever wanted to kiss. I never understood what the fuss was about, or why my brother and male cousins are such rakes, going from conquest to conquest. I don't think I even knew what I was doing last night. But when we met, something happened to me—I won't deny it. And it is wonderful!" she cried passionately.

A silence fell.

She trembled. "I was hoping we could start over this morning."

"Oh, yes, I had forgotten, you want more than my kisses. You wish to know me better—as friends! You may rendezvous with me tonight at our next camp, but though you will claim it is to converse, we both know there will be little conversation."

His temper hadn't improved, she realized, not at all. He was as set against her now as he had been when he'd learned of her innocence. "But there is so much to speak of! We could gossip and debate. We could share stories. I grew up in the West Indies—I have many stories to tell! I am sure you have many stories to tell, too, as you have traveled even more extensively. Just because I have been dreaming of your kisses—and perhaps, you have been dreaming of mine—doesn't mean we have to act on our desire!" But she flushed, because she wished to do just that.

He choked. "Ladies do not admit to such feelings…just as ladies do not tryst with Gypsies and wish to become their friends."

Ariella breathed deeply, wondering if a question was contained in his words. "Emilian, I am outspoken and considered eccentric by society. I am also an honest person. Can't we discuss this with honesty? Don't I deserve that much, after the passion we shared last night? You were kind and respectful to Margery, my cousin."

"I am not lusting for your cousin," he said flatly. "We shared a simple kiss, nothing more."

Her heart slammed. "It was far more than a kiss, Emilian."

"For you, a woman without experience."

"That's right. I have no experience when it comes to kisses and lovemaking. What happened last night was hugely important to me. I am hoping it was important to you, too."

His eyes were dark and unhappy.

She breathed, "Were you awake last night because of me?"

"Stay longer, and you will find out."

She thrilled in spite of the terrible tension and enmity coming from him. "What can I do to form a truce between us, so we might have a real beginning?" She smiled hopefully.

"Leave. Forget last night and find someone else to satisfy your newly awakened desires. If you want to bed a Gypsy, it can be arranged—there are many lusty men in the *kumpa'nia*."

"You can't mean that!"

"I do. I have never meant anything more." He turned away from her, his face dark with anger, reaching for some nails. He stroked the mare once and lifted her hind leg, but there was tension in the gesture. Ariella watched him nailing the shoe. She could not understand him. He was a stranger from a different culture, and she did not know a single hope or dream he harbored. She didn't know why he was so angry.

Yesterday he had been angry before she'd even said a word, as if he disliked everyone—or at least, all Englishmen.

She hoped that was not the case. But if he was truly set against her, if he really wished to end their relationship, there was little she could do. She had already pursued him shamelessly. Ladies did not pursue gentlemen.

But she wasn't like Margery or Dianna or anyone else. Her every instinct told her not to let him slip away. Her heart demanded she pursue him, even if that meant she was shameless. She wanted to soothe his anger—and she wanted to understand it.

Hadn't the women in her family always fought tooth and nail for the men they loved?

She became still. A man and woman could fall in love at first sight; the event certainly abounded in her family. She was beginning to feel as if it had happened to her, for she seemed to care that much. "I am going to miss you when you leave. I know it's absurd, but it's how I feel," she finally whispered.

He ignored her, nailing the shoe.

"Do you believe in fate?"

He kept nailing the shoe.

"Although I am well-read and I consider myself fairly rational, I believe in fate. I never come to Rose Hill. I haven't been to Derbyshire in years. But my first night here, we met."

"This is hardly fate," he said. He paused, bent over and, breathing harshly, lifted the hammer.

She spoke softly. "Do you believe in love at first sight?"

The hammer glanced off the shoe, hitting his thumb, and he cried out. Dropping the mare's leg and the hammer, he straightened. His expression was one of shock and dismay.

She realized she was hugging herself. "I know it's madness, because we've only just met. But it's a bit of a family tradition and I may be following in my ancestors' footsteps."

He strode toward her, seizing her shoulders. "You are *not* falling in love with me. One day, you will fall in love with some charming, well-off aristocrat. What you feel is *lust,* Ariella, and nothing else! You don't even *know* me."

"I so want to know you, but you are refusing my very sincere overtures!" she cried.

"You are a romantic fool," he said, releasing her. "Have you not noticed our differences?"

"I don't care. My best friends, after my brother, sister and cousins, are university professors, scholars, lawyers and a radical writer! None of them are nobly born."

He shook his head. "None of them are Rom, either. What woman even makes such a confession? Have you no pride? I am Rom, Ariella, *Rom.*"

She held up her chin. "I have great pride. I am proud of the fact that I am not like any of the other women of my class and upbringing. And I don't care that you are Rom." She touched his cheek. "Is this why you are refusing my offer of friendship? Because a friendship between us is forbidden?"

He jerked away and folded his arms. "Who I am matters vastly. The fact that you are late to sexually awaken, and you dare to wander out alone at night, hardly makes you different enough. It doesn't change that you are a *gadji princess.*"

She bristled. "I am hardly royalty. Yes, I am well-off—so what? I live in London very independently by choice. I am well-read. I spend most of my time reading. I speak four—" She suddenly stopped. What was she doing? He was not going to be impressed by her obsession with history, biographies and philosophy, her advocacy of social change and reform, or her unusual education. The women who were admired and pursued did not read anything but romance novels and literature on travel. They did not live independently, and they had, at best, an elementary-school education. The women gentlemen pursued and loved excelled at sewing and needlepoint and were passionate about fashion; they desired only a husband and a family.

"Pray, do continue," he mocked. "You live independently and you read and therefore you are suited to be the paramour of a Gypsy?"

"I prefer London to the country and as my aunt and uncle are often in town, I spend most of the year with them. I read a lot. I read…romance novels. And travels guides," she said lamely. She was glancing aside now.

"Yes, that makes you very original."

His scorn was so hurtful. "I hate balls and teas," she flared. That much was the truth. "I hate idle, frivolous chitchat about croquet and steeplechases. I *am* suited to be your friend— and perhaps even your lover, if a natural progression leads us that far."

His eyes widened impossibly.

She had never been so determined. "You see, I am very different from other young ladies. I have not ruled out a love affair with you."

"You are mad! How you have maintained your innocence thus far is beyond me!"

"I told you, I have never desired any other man. But a friendship must come first, Emilian." She trembled, because in a way, she had just made a very shocking proposal.

"If a *natural progression* leads you to my bed, you will be filled with regrets," he said harshly, eyes ablaze.

"To the contrary," she whispered. "I will probably be very satisfied."

He choked again.

She felt her insides churn with the yearning that had become, overnight, so familiar now. "I am becoming used to your threats," she whispered. "You no longer frighten me, Emilian."

"Really? Then come to me tonight. Because you will be frightened, I am sure of it, and on the morrow, you will have regrets."

Ariella stared, refusing to believe him.

His chest heaved. "When will you understand? You are a terrible temptation, one I don't even wish to resist. *I want to ruin you!* But I will not give you love when I take your innocence. We will not be friends…we will never be friends. I will give you nothing but passion, pleasure—and then it will be goodbye."

She shivered. In that moment, she realized he believed his every word. Was it possible that he had never had a friend? Was it possible that his lovers were only that? He had made a terrible comment about being used by women. "Why are you afraid to give a friendship between us a chance?"

"I am not afraid. I am trying to make you run far from me. I am trying to protect you, not from yourself, but from me!" He whirled and began untying the black mare.

Ariella realized tears had begun to fill her eyes. She swiped at them. "So I will never see you again."

The mare's lead in his hand, he faced her. "We will be at Woodland tonight. If you come, I will ruthlessly seduce you and take you to bed. If you come, there will not be conversation or *friendship*. If you are falling in love, I suggest you come to your senses immediately. If you join me for a night of passion and pleasure, it will only be that. You will be no different from the *gadji ladies* who so often join me in my bed. So think long and hard if you wish to become one of them. Oh! And in case I am not clear, when the sun comes up and you leave my bed, I will not recall your name." He gave her a harsh look and walked away with the horse.

Ariella cried out and sank down on the ground. She pulled her knees up high and hugged them to her chest, shaken to the core of her being. She felt as if she had offered a wonderful gift to someone and had it thrown back in her face.

But wasn't that what had happened?

Would he really take her innocence and forget her afterward?

Was it possible he was such a cold man?

Her heart screamed at her in protest now. She didn't want to believe he would ever be so crude and ignoble. He had said very clearly that he wished to scare her away. He was trying to protect her. That was noble. And last night he had accepted her decision, instead of ruining her. That was noble, too. Clearly, he had a conscience. As clearly, taming the beast would not be easy—if she ever dared go near him again.

Ariella didn't think she could stay away. She had never been to Woodland, but she knew of the estate. It was about an hour's drive from Rose Hill. How long would the Roma stay there? If she went, was his threat to seduce her only intended to scare her away, or did he mean it?

About to get to her feet, she froze. Emilian was talking to a beautiful young Romni woman. They were both smiling, and their affection was obvious. Jealousy consumed her, startling her with its intensity, but there was also uncertainty and fear.

Emilian left and the Gypsy woman started purposefully toward her. Ariella stood. If this woman was a rival, she was far too attractive. She was young, perhaps twenty, with auburn hair and amber eyes. She wore bold purple skirts and a pale green blouse with a gold sash that framed a tiny waist. She was petite, but her figure was lush. Ariella was dismayed. She hadn't even considered that a man like Emilian would surely have a lover or a mistress. Dear God, this woman could even be his wife.

The woman paused. Her gaze was curious, not hostile. "I am Jaelle. I saw you here with my brother last night."

Relief flooded her. "I am Ariella de Warenne." This pretty woman was his *sister.* "Jaelle is a beautiful name."

Jaelle was wry. "As beautiful as Emilian?"

Ariella started. "His name is beautiful, too," she said carefully. Was Jaelle a potential friend—or would she be set against Ariella, like her brother seemed to be?

"Everyone saw you with him last night. My brother is strong, handsome and rich as a king. Many women want him. They would be fools not to. They are jealous of you today."

Ariella was surprised. "But we only just met. We barely know one another."

"A man doesn't need to know a woman to want her," Jaelle smiled. "Emilian chose you last night over everyone else."

"I'm not sure if I should be flattered."

"You should be very pleased."

Ariella began to relax. "He wasn't very friendly a moment ago."

Jaelle laughed. "You refused him! He had to go to bed alone. Of course he is angry with you. No man likes being teased."

Ariella gaped.

"The Rom like *gadji* women and Emilian is half blood." She shrugged. "I would not be surprised if one day he chooses a *gadji* wife over a Romni one." She glanced up the hill at the house. "You live like a queen."

Ariella took a breath and tried to appear calm. "I am not a queen," she said, aware that Jaelle had made the same kind of reference to royalty that Emilian had. "Is he thinking about marriage?" Ariella asked cautiously.

"I don't know. All men marry, sooner or later." She became sly. "Would you marry him, Ariella? Would you marry a Rom?"

"If we decided to marry, I would not care that he is a Romany man." She blushed. "We just met. He doesn't even wish to be friends—and he is leaving soon."

Jaelle smiled, puzzled. "What does friendship have to do with my brother? He wants a woman in his bed, not a friend."

Ariella shook her head. "I don't know why both are not possible."

Jaelle touched her. "Do you love him already?" she asked softly. "Because I saw him watching you as if you *are* a queen. And you look at him as if he were a prince."

Ariella looked at her and did not hesitate. "I have never felt this way before. I think I am falling in love."

Jaelle said instantly, "You must not refuse him for too much longer. The Rom like their women in their beds well before the wedding vows are spoken."

Ariella felt her insides hollow at the thought. Her pulse increased.

Jaelle said, "We are going to Woodland now. We may be there for a week. My uncle Stevan had a son, his first." She pointed to a large man Ariella recognized from the night before. "A first son is cause to celebrate for many nights. You should come to Woodland."

Ariella imagined Emilian dancing passionately beneath the stars, his every movement a sensual invitation, his every step suggesting far too much raw and masculine virility. She tensed. Tonight other women would be dancing with him—other women would be trying to attract him to their beds. She *hated* the notion.

Did she dare go to Woodland?

How could she not?

"I am glad we met," Ariella said. "Have a safe journey, Jaelle."

Jaelle smiled. *"D'bika t'maya."*

EMILIAN LEFT the caravan far behind, galloping his Thoroughbred across the fields and jumping the occasional stone hedge. As hard as he ran the horse, he could not shake her words. *Do you believe in love at first sight?*

She had mistaken her desire for love, which merely

proved how inexperienced she was. And she was far too inexperienced for him. He must never forget that.

Would she come to Woodland?

He hoped to never see her again. If she came to him tonight or tomorrow or the next day, he would lose his English conscience and make good his threats. And he would enjoy using her. He would be ruthless. It would be *budjo* and it would be revenge.

She did not deserve to be used that way.

He slowed his mount to a walk, hoping she would stay far away from him. And there was the proof that he was far more English than Rom.

The road to Woodland led through the village of Kenilworth. He began passing whitewashed homes with slate roofs, an old Norman chapel in ruins, and a newer Anglican church made of pale stone. The main street, where a dozen shops, two inns and a pub were located, was two short blocks. A few carts and carriages were on the street, and several shopkeepers were sweeping their porches and tending their flowering window boxes. Otherwise, there were just a handful of pedestrians, and he saw a group of men coming down the block.

Suddenly he pulled his mount to an abrupt halt, the horse flinging up his head in protest. He stared at the sign on the haberdashery. *No Gypsies Here.*

He was in disbelief. Then he saw that, next door, the milliner had the same sign in his front window. He whirled the gray to face the opposite street where the White Stag Inn was. Hanging on the dark green door was the same sign, but in even bolder and larger letters—NO GYPSIES HERE.

At Morgan's Alehouse, he saw the words painted boldly in red on another sign. He spurred the horse up to Hawks' Fine Goods. The abominable warning was posted on every door and in every window, on each and every public shop, as far as he could see.

He whirled and galloped back to the handsome stone church where, once in a while, he attended services, usually on Christmas Eve or Easter Sunday. NO GYPSIES HERE.

Rage suffused him.

Those signs had not been present the last time he was in the village, just a few days ago. For a moment, he was so distressed, he simply sat his mount, staring at the church doors. Ariella de Warenne's pretty image came to mind, and he hoped she was foolish enough to seek him out at Woodland.

The English part of him was dead.

He spurred his gray into a canter and went right up the stone walk to the church's front door. He reached out and tore the sign from the door. Then he whirled the horse so cruelly it reared. He galloped toward the inn.

This time he flung himself off his mount and reached the door in one stride. As he tore the sign off, he cursed the *gadjos* for their snobbery, their bigotry and their hatred. Then he felt the stares.

"As Gypsy as the rest of them."

He turned slowly and saw five village men standing on the opposite sidewalk. They instantly looked away and started walking rapidly toward the town's center. He didn't know who had whispered the slur with such scorn.

But he'd overheard that exact remark a hundred times.

He breathed hard, needing control. He could rip off every sign, but it wouldn't erase the prejudice and hatred, and the signs would reappear—until Stevan and the *kumpa'nia* were gone. But he couldn't just walk away, either.

He led his mount over to Hawks' Fine Goods. The emporium carried exotic merchandise like Far Eastern spices, letter openers made from ivory tusks and American tobacco, as well as furniture from the finest cabinetmakers, clocks and watches, leather desktops, writing sets, urns and vases, lamps and candlesticks. Over the years, he had purchased many expensive items from the merchant.

He looked at the sign as he seized the door handle, feeling sick now, deep in his soul. Then he stepped into the large, glass-fronted store.

Inside, it was dimly lit. He glanced around at the merchandise, aware of the boiling rage he needed to mask at all costs.

"Didn't you see the sign? No Gypsies are allowed here!"

He was still wearing the emerald-green, brilliantly embroidered vest. He slowly turned and faced Hawks's pompous son.

Edgar Hawks paled. "My lord St Xavier," he cried, bowing. "I do beg your pardon."

Emilian spoke. "I will take those two crystal vases. They are handblown, are they not?"

"Yes, they are Waterford, sir, the finest Ireland has to offer—"

Emilian cut him off. "Those rugs, the pair."

"They are Turkish, my lord, and very costly. Do you wish for me to unroll them?"

"No, I do not." He walked over to a chest that had clearly been imported from Spain. "I will take that."

"Let me get my ledger," Edgar said, his tone rough with anxiety. He vanished toward the back of the store.

Emilian stood still, despising the plump shopkeeper, and Ariella de Warenne came to mind again. *Do you believe in love at first sight?*

He cursed. The sooner he found a suitable estate manager, the sooner he and the caravan could leave Derbyshire.

Edgar ran back to him, huffing. His even more portly father was with him. "Lord St Xavier, I am so pleased to see you, sir. You haven't shopped with us since last winter," Jonathon Hawks cried. His smile was ingratiating.

He glanced up at the ceiling, ignoring the remark. A crystal chandelier hung there, and he knew it was a part of the store's décor. "I will take that, as well."

"It is not for sale," Edgar began, sweat shining on his brow.

Emilian looked at him, wishing he could put his hands around his throat and squeeze.

Edgar paled. Jonathon exclaimed, "Of course we will sell it to you."

"Very good. That is all for now. You may put the sum on my account."

"Of course," the elder said. "It will take me a moment to add up the amount of your purchases."

Emilian smiled coldly. "I so enjoy shopping in your emporium."

"I am pleased, my lord," Jonathon began.

"Really? For I should so hate to have to take my business to Sheffield's in Manchester."

Jonathon stared.

Emilian stared back. A long silence ensued. "I suggest you take the sign down. I also suggest you encourage your neighbors to remove their signs, as well."

Jonathon paled. His color now matched that of his son. "I think the sign has been a vast misunderstanding," he finally said.

"Good." Emilian stalked out.

CHAPTER SIX

As EMILIAN STRODE into his home, he heard his cousin's voice and that of his two bachelor friends. They were in the great room and could not be avoided. He almost hoped they would taunt him. He had behaved politely at Hawks' Emporium, exercising great self-control, and he would not be restrained now. One gibe and he would explode. He needed but a single excuse...

But the moment he entered his great room, he paused, uncertain. He had refurbished the room at great expense over the past few years, and it was the luxurious hall of an Englishman. New sofas, chairs, occasional tables and lamps filled the room. The hall's one stone wall, in which a huge hearth resided, contained the family coat of arms and the portraits of his St Xavier ancestors. Swords that Edmund claimed had been carried into the Civil Wars were crossed above that plaster mantel. An antique table, with two high-backed chairs, its leather cracking, was at the hall's far end. According to Edmund, that table had been in the house since its construction in the late sixteenth century.

This was his home, and he had spent years turning it into a fine estate. But this was an Englishman's home, and he didn't want to be English—not anymore.

NO GYPSIES HERE.

He saw the hateful signs in his mind's eye, and he envisioned Raiza as she lay battered on a cobbled Edinburgh street. He breathed hard, all uncertainty vanishing. The need for revenge burned as brightly as before.

He stared at his cousin coldly. Robert had despised him and scorned him with an Englishman's prejudice from the moment of his arrival at Woodland, when he was only twelve years old. He would never forget his history with his cousin. Even then, Robert had been a pompous, bigoted ass. When Robert's taunts had caused Emilian to come to blows with him, their fathers had torn them apart. Edmund had defended him, while Robert's father had been as condescending and as obnoxious as his son.

"He's Gypsy scum!" Robert had shouted. "Whip him for what he's done!"

Emilian had bloodied Robert's nose. He didn't say a word as Edmund restrained him. Robert had started it by calling him names in front of the servants and the very pretty daughter of the cook.

"He assaulted my son!" John exclaimed. "He's a wild, savage animal! He should be locked up! Better yet, he should be sent back to his Gypsy mother!"

Emilian trembled, hating them both. "No one will be whipped or locked up," Edmund said firmly. He added quietly, so only he could hear, "Are you all right?"

He had the urge to cry. He fought it, nodding.

In that moment, although he'd been at Woodland for months, he wished he was with the kumpa'nia, traveling the Borders. He was so homesick. And he knew he would never fit into the life Edmund intended for him—the life he had agreed to.

Robert and his friends sat at the table, two wine bottles there, one empty. They were playing cards. It was three in the afternoon and far too early for cards and drink, but then, not one of the gentlemen understood anything about responsibility or duty. He was disgusted. Robert's friends were wastrels and the sons of noblemen without means.

The abominable signs danced in his mind's eye. Robert was the kind of man to put up signs like that, or encourage others to do so. In fact, he and his scurvy friends could easily be behind the acts of hatred and bigotry.

Robert saw him and stood. "Emil!" he cried, smiling widely. "You have returned." But he took in Emilian's billowing yellow shirt, a gift from Jaelle, and the green vest, a gift from Stevan's wife.

Emilian fervently hoped one of them would dare to scorn him now. "Of course I have returned," he said softly. "This is my home." Even as he spoke, an image of the *kumpa'nia* flashed in his mind, followed by the damned signs—and Ariella de Warenne.

"It's a good thing," Robert said, his smile strained. "Your housekeeper and another servant have left their employment, and there seems to be chaos among the staff."

His temper escalated dangerously. "I have been gone for a single night," he said softly. "Did you abuse my staff? Which servant left with Mrs. Dodd? Oh, let me guess—her daughter, the redhead?"

Robert flushed.

Instantly he knew that his brother and his friends had made advances toward Mrs. Dodd's daughter, who was only sixteen. He trembled. "I have just given you a tidy sum to see you though the year, yet you abuse my staff behind my back?"

Robert blanched. "I beg your pardon, Emil! The wench jumped into my bed on her own, and somehow her mother found us!"

Emilian thrust his arm across the table, striking the wine bottles, glasses and cards from it. Robert's friends jumped up and leaped away, cowards that they were. He felt like going after each and every one of them, in turn.

"Are you also behind the present mischief in town?" he asked coldly.

"We have not been to town," Robert cried anxiously. "I do not know what mischief you refer to."

He breathed hard. "You may pack your bags," he said, "while I try to make amends to Mrs. Dodd. Get off these premises within the hour." Before his cousin could respond, he stalked into the library and slammed the door closed, hard.

It reverberated.

He had wanted to smash Robert's nose. He stood motionless, fighting for control. As he did so, he recalled the night before. The music had claimed him body and soul—the Romany had claimed him, and it had felt good. He had lost the Englishman when he had begun to dance. In the dance, there had only been a Rom. There had been so much freedom....

He did not need this life, and he intended to prove it to Raiza's memory—and to himself. Now, too late, he realized that in becoming so English, he had lost the most important part of himself. He had lost more than his identity—he had lost his Rom soul.

But he would recover it.

WE WILL BE AT WOODLAND tonight.

Ariella sat beside Margery and Dianna in the carriage, Alexi facing them, but she did not see the passing countryside as they raced through it. She only saw Emilian, his face strained with the anger she still could not understand.

Come to Woodland tonight and I will seduce you...

She inhaled. Of course she couldn't go. It would be terribly hard to steal out after midnight and not be caught. On the other hand, it would be easy enough to hire a driver from the closest village and pay him handsomely for his silence. Dear God, was she really considering meeting Emilian at Woodland, after he had told her to run from him? When he had so boldly stated his intentions?

I will give you nothing but passion, pleasure—and then it will be goodbye.

She refused to believe he would make love to her and walk away. He had spoken cruelly and harshly, but that was because he wished to push her away—he had even admitted that. He was not ruthless. She would never be attracted to such a man.

The Rom like their women in their bed well before they make their wedding vows.

Did she dare begin a love affair with him? It was not the English way, but it was the Romany way. And while he seemed to think a friendship was impossible, she believed a love affair and a friendship were not exclusive.

What if the Romany left on the morrow, even though Jaelle thought they'd be there for a few days?

"What is wrong with you today?"

She started. She had been so immersed in her thoughts of Emilian she had forgotten where she was. She quickly smiled at her brother. The village was in the near distance. Spotted cows grazed alongside the road. "I am thinking," she said.

"Dianna asked you three times what you will wear to the Simmonses' ball," he said, staring closely. "I know you don't care what you wear, but you are very distracted. Is something bothering you?"

She smiled widely. "What could be bothering me? I am with my brother, whom I adore and whom I have dearly missed. My little sister, who I have also sorely missed, is here, too, and Margery is with us! The afternoon is perfect."

Now Margery and Dianna stared. Alexi frowned. "Now I know you are bothered by something or someone. You hate shopping. We usually have to drag you from the library for an outing. Today, you came without a word. You do know the ladies wish to make some purchases at Hawks', don't you?"

She kept her smile in place. "Of course I do."

"You are lying," Alexi said flatly. "And you are terrible at it." He sent her a dangerous smile. "Something is wrong. I intend to find out what that is."

"Nothing is wrong," Ariella cried in real dismay. "Can't I enjoy my family?"

Dianna said softly, "It's just the Gypsy."

Ariella's heart turned over, hard. With dread, she looked at her sister. But Dianna shrugged at Alexi, clearly unaware of the havoc she could wreck.

Alexi's blue eyes became brilliant. "I beg your pardon?"

Dianna blushed. "They have a very handsome smith. Margery chatted with him. I was agog—so was Ariella."

Alexi looked at her.

Ariella felt her cheeks turn red.

Her mind sped. She must make light of it. She said quickly, "Dianna is correct. The smith was very handsome. We couldn't help but ogle him while Margery asked where to leave some treats for the children."

"You are dreaming about a Rom?" Alexi demanded.

Ariella wished her color would fade. She sat up straighter. "I am actually thinking about the conversation I had with a young Gypsy woman—it was very edifying and educating."

The Romany men like their women in their beds...

Ariella quickly glanced out of the open carriage at the small farm they were passing. The homes on the outskirts of the village were just ahead. She was always disappointed when Alexi left on his various affairs, which usually took him to distant ports. Now, she hoped he would be off very soon, before her interest in Emilian was discovered.

"What will you wear to the Simmonses'? They are calling it a 'country' ball." Margery touched her hand.

"I haven't thought about it. I was hoping to beg off," Ariella said honestly.

"Ah, now I have my sister back," Alexi said, smiling.

Then his glance strayed past her and widened. His face hardened.

Ariella knew something was amiss. She looked in the same direction and saw a placard on the front door of the livery, but she couldn't read the sign.

Alexi looked at her. "I didn't need a crystal ball to know there would be trouble, and this is another step in that direction."

"What are you talking of?" Ariella asked, but now, she saw a sign on the front door of one of the village's two public inns. *No Gypsies Here*. She cried out loudly. "That is terrible!"

"Oh, dear," Margery murmured. "How rude."

"Look," Dianna said.

Everyone followed her gaze. Two Gypsy boys stood on a street corner, one playing a fiddle, the other with his hat turned upside down on the ground. The hat was empty. The pedestrians passing by were ignoring them, even though the older boy played beautifully. The younger boy kept trotting up to the passing villagers, asking for a coin. Ariella saw one heavyset gentleman actually elbow the child away, as if he had leprosy or another disease.

"Stop this carriage immediately," she cried furiously.

Their coachman braked the coach.

Alexi seized her arm. "What do you intend?" he demanded.

She tried to wrench free. "Let me go. I wish to pay for the music—it is beautiful."

He stared into her eyes and released her. "Fine." He jumped to the ground and held out his hand.

Ariella stumbled from the carriage with his help, Margery and Dianna following. She hurried over to the boys, holding her skirts to move swiftly. She recognized the dark-haired young man from the night before. He was the one who had been so angered by her intrusion, until Emilian had claimed her as his guest.

She smiled at him, out of breath. "You play beautifully."

He didn't smile back. He was a handsome lad, with very dark hair and eyes.

Ariella smiled again. She dug into her reticule and intended to empty all of her coin in the hat. Alexi muttered, "They are proud," and it was a warning.

She thought of Emilian. Alexi was right. She put a shilling in the hat.

"Thank you," the older boy said gruffly.

"You are very welcome," she said. She was thrilled when Alexi put a shilling in, as well. "What is your name?"

"Djordi."

"I am Ariella de Warenne, and this is my brother, Alexi de Warenne, my sister, Miss Dianna, and Lady Margery de Warenne."

The boy looked wary and said nothing.

"I didn't bring any coin with me," Dianna whispered.

"I'll put enough in his hat for us both," Margery said, doing just that. "Shall we walk over to Hawks'? It is just across the street. When we're done, we can take tea at a private room in the inn."

Ariella bristled and turned. The placard with the grotesque words remained at the inn's door. She breathed hard, fighting her outrage, then gave up. She strode to the inn's front doors and pulled at the sign with both hands. It didn't give.

Frustration mingled with her rage. She pulled harder. Splinters caught in her gloves. Alexi caught her wrists. "Let me," he said quietly.

She backed away, wiping the tears from her eyes. He ripped the nailed sign down and flung it into the street. She hugged herself. Djordi and the younger boy simply stared at them as if they were mad.

Alexi turned. "Are we going to remove all the signs? I can see a half-dozen from here."

She hugged him. "Yes, we are—you are. Thank you! I love you!"

He grinned, a devilish expression that Ariella had seen very proper ladies fight amongst themselves for. "Does that mean you will confess your secret to me?"

She stepped back. "I have no secret. But this is obscene. And the boys are right there."

"I am not sure they can read English, but I am sure they know exactly what the signs mean."

Ariella stared at him.

"What are you trying to tell me? That the Romany know they are not wanted?"

"Yes. They know they are scorned, and even despised."

Instantly, she thought of Emilian. She was sickened. She could imagine what he must feel when confronted with this kind of bigotry and hatred. No man was prouder. Her outrage would pale in comparison to his.

The boys, standing a short distance from her, didn't seem to care about the signs. Then again, Emilian would likely pretend disinterest if he came to the village, too. But he would care—deeply—and those boys had to care, as well.

"Not only will we remove every sign, we will make our displeasure with each and every merchant known. We will make it abundantly clear that, in the future, the Romany are to be tolerated when they pass through Kenilworth." She exhaled. "And I am not stepping one foot in that inn. I am far too offended."

"It is too bad a woman cannot be the town mayor," Alexi said with a smile.

"Women have ruled crowns, thrones and great estates," Ariella said grimly, thinking of great women like Queen Elizabeth and Eleanor of Aquitaine.

"Women often rule men from their beds."

Ariella looked at him.

"Every single day," he added with a shrug. "But you wouldn't know that, would you? No one has turned your head yet."

Ariella heard him, but her mind was racing with sudden comprehension. Her father, a great, powerful man, was on bended knee around Amanda. Her uncle, the earl, was the same way with the countess. And Lady Harrington most definitely ruled her husband, Ariella's Uncle Rex, although gently.

She looked at her brother. "Maybe it is through love that these women rule."

He chuckled. "Oh, no. They wield their power from their beds."

The Romany men did not value virginity and chastity at all. Emilian's image flashed. *Come to Woodland tonight and I will seduce you...*

"While you debate the great and original subject of women in power, Dianna and I are going into Hawks'," Margery said. She smiled at Ariella. "We'll take tea elsewhere or at Rose Hill."

Ariella hugged her. "Thank you." But Margery gave her an odd look before she left with Dianna, heading toward the fine goods emporium. Ariella was relieved when she saw no sign on that door.

Alexi plucked her sleeve. "Well?"

"We have some signs to remove, and some merchants to speak with," Ariella said firmly.

But before she could take a step toward the next offending sign, he grasped her arm. "Is your heart intact, little sister?"

Her eyes widened. How could he possibly guess?

"Are you finally mooning over someone?" His gaze narrowed.

Her heart thundered. "If I liked someone, I would bring

him home," Ariella said. She was horrified at how hoarse her tone sounded.

And Alexi knew he had been right and that she was obfuscating, because his eyes widened in surprise. Too late, she realized he had merely been fishing.

"Who is he?" he asked quietly.

He could never know. He was very protective of her, and unless Emilian wished to court her with marriage on his mind, Alexi would never approve. Ariella was suddenly sober. No matter how open-minded her family, a Rom suitor was hardly what anyone was expecting—and Emilian was not even a suitor. She would have to convince everyone that this was a grand, once-in-a-lifetime, *fated* de Warenne love.

But was it?

"You are mistaken," Ariella began. But the front door of the inn opened, slamming against the wall, and a woman came running out. As she stumbled past them, Ariella glimpsed her frightened face, her long, auburn hair and bright purple skirts. *Jaelle.* Alexi seized her arm to keep her from falling headfirst to the ground.

But Jaelle wrenched free and leaped into the street.

A carriage was coming and she was about to be run over. Ariella screamed at her, horrified. "Jaelle!"

But Jaelle somehow ran past the oncoming horse, so narrowly that her skirts whipped its knees. The driver braked abruptly, the gray rearing. Ariella was certain the horse would trample Jaelle as it came down, but she escaped its hooves, never breaking stride, fleeing across the street.

"Good Lord!" Alexi exclaimed, horrified.

Two men burst from the inn, shoving past them both.

Jaelle had paused, panting, almost doubled over. She saw the men and whirled, running into an alley between a house and the church.

"Go behind the church. I'll follow the cheating bitch," one

of the men said. The heavyset speaker started to follow Jaelle across the street, while the other man ran toward the church.

Alexi leaped forward and seized the second man from behind, so hard he caused the man to stumble. "Care to think twice about pursuing a lady?" he asked softly.

The man straightened and flushed. "That's no lady," he snapped. Then his eyes widened as he realized from Alexi's stature and dress that he was a nobleman. "Beggin' yer pardon, sir."

"It is Captain de Warenne," Alexi said. He flung him back toward the inn. "I suggest you keep your hands to yourself."

Ariella wanted to applaud, but the first man had vanished into the alley, just moments after Jaelle. Alexi was already leaping onto a horse tied outside the inn. Ariella knew her brother would rescue Jaelle. "Hurry," she told him.

He didn't answer, galloping across the street and into the alley.

Ariella jumped into the coach. "Follow them, Henry," she ordered.

The coachman whipped the chestnut mare and she broke into a madcap gallop, veering into the alley so wildly that the curricle came off one wheel entirely and Ariella was thrown across the backseat. As the gig came down and she straightened herself, she saw that the heavy-set man was in the courtyard behind the church, panting and furious but alone. Alexi sat the borrowed horse, whirling it about, clearly looking for Jaelle. High stone walls enclosed three sides of the yard, making it a dead end. Her coach halted. She did not see Jaelle, but there was no way she could have escaped.

"Is she in a tree, damn it?" the white-haired man cried, peering up at the two tall elms that grew along the back wall.

Alexi walked his prancing mount toward him.

The fellow suddenly stiffened. Clearly recognizing him, he doffed his cap. "Captain de Warenne!"

Alexi smiled and it was ruthless. "How manly you are, Tollman, to chase a small, helpless woman."

"There's nothing helpless about the Gypsy bitch. She asked if she could tell her fortunes to my customers, and I agreed. But all she's done is cheat the men, one by one."

"She's a woman," Alexi said softly-dangerously.

"She's a Gypsy! They're no better than wild animals!" Tollman cried.

Ariella saw that her brother's temper was explosive. He said even more softly, "I suggest you leave her alone. I find it impossible not to defend a beautiful woman, and I do not think you wish to make me your rival, Jack."

Tollman glanced behind him, as if wishing for his friend, who did not appear. He nodded, backing away, then finally turned and started down the alley, past Ariella's coach. Ariella could clearly see his face. He was furious and muttering to himself. She heard the words *Gypsy, whore* and *de Warenne.*

What had Jaelle really done?

Ariella glanced at the two elms. There was no way a small woman could reach the first branch to climb either tree. She glanced at the back door of the church. Alexi said, "It's locked."

Then he slipped from the horse and turned to the wall. "You can come out now. We won't hurt you."

Ariella's eyes widened. There was a very small drainage grate built low into the wall. Her brother knelt and tore the grate from the wall. Then he held out his hand.

Ariella saw a small dirty hand reach her brother's extended one, and then Alexi pulled Jaelle out.

She was a ragged, muddy mess, but she straightened to her full height, flung her hair back and stared at him as if she were a queen. Then she looked down the alley and it was the wary, watchful look of someone being hunted.

"They're gone," Alexi said quietly.

Jaelle gave him a wary look. Then she began brushing off her skirts. As proud as she was attempting to be, Ariella saw that her hands were shaking. Her compassion soared.

Alexi touched her arm. She flinched. His tone kind, he said, "Why don't you sit down with my sister for a moment?"

She smiled at him scornfully. "And then what? You will ask your sister to leave so you can be repaid for *rescuing* me?"

He stiffened. "I hardly expect to be repaid for anything— and not in the way you suggest."

She tossed her hair. "All *gadjos* are the same." She looked at Ariella now, ignoring Alexi.

Ariella slid from the coach. "Are you all right, Jaelle?"

"Of course," she said.

Alexi started, surprised that she knew her. Ariella said quickly, "I meant it when I said I had interviewed a young woman at the Romany camp." She turned back to Jaelle, concerned. Her arms were bleeding. "They didn't do that, did they?"

"No, the scratches came from being in there." She gestured at the drainage hole.

Ariella looked very closely into her eyes. She was trying to be proud, but she was distraught. Ariella thought her incredibly strong and brave. Any other woman would be weeping now—and probably in her gallant rescuer's arms.

"Those cuts should be cleaned," Ariella said. "Why don't you come back to Rose Hill with me, so we can take care of those abrasions?"

Jaelle stood like a soldier. "I am going to Woodland."

A silence fell. Ariella was about to offer her a coach when Alexi stepped forward, directly in front of her. Although she refused to look up at him, he said, "My sister wishes to take you to the house to clean your cuts. Why would you refuse?"

Jaelle slowly lifted her amber gaze, and Ariella realized she was valiantly fighting to keep her composure.

Alexi's face was so hard that Ariella almost didn't recognize him. "Did they hurt you?" he asked bluntly.

"No," Jaelle said.

He stared, his expression doubtful.

"They wanted to." Her eyes darkened. A single tear finally slipped free. "You know what they wanted."

Alexi turned away. Ariella knew he was enraged. "Take her to Rose Hill," he ordered. "Then make certain she gets to Woodland."

Ariella was alarmed. "Alexi, what are you going to do?"

"She is a woman!" he exclaimed furiously. "Those lechers need a lesson in good manners." He vaulted onto the horse and spurred it into a canter.

Ariella turned to Jaelle. "What happened?"

"I only wanted to read their palms." She added, "But they all wanted more—they all thought I'd read their palms and warm their beds!" She wiped another tear furiously from her face. "The fat one grabbed me. Bastard! He grabbed me and started kissing me—I struggled and got away. I hate them all!"

Ariella put her arms around her, appalled. She hoped Alexi beat them soundly. "Well, thank goodness it is over." She smiled brightly. "Come home with me so we can clean those cuts, and I will make sure you have a carriage to take you to Woodland."

Jaelle met her gaze. "You are a good woman. I am glad we are friends." Then she pulled free. "But I don't need your help."

"Jaelle!" Ariella objected, but it was too late.

Jaelle hurried from the courtyard.

EMILIAN FINISHED the letter to his solicitor, asking him to locate several prospective estate managers. He had indicated that the matter was urgent. He sealed the envelope with wax, and then stared at the family crest that was the seal. He would not be using that seal again for some time. Maybe he would never use it again.

He refused to think about Edmund now.

His temples pounded. He stood, walked to the console and poured himself a brandy, feeling even more dissatisfied than before. There was no way to avoid the fact that a part of him was attached to the estate. He had begun to worry about his tenants, his business partners and several important contracts. But he had decided to go to Raiza's grave with the *kumpa'nia* and find his Rom soul, and nothing would change his mind.

An image of the de Warenne woman filled his head.

He had been thinking about her often. He lusted for her, and the lust kept interfering with his grief and mingling with his rage. Lust was acceptable—he was a man—but he had never given his previous lovers any thought outside of the bedroom. She was different, after all.

I am suited to be your friend—and perhaps even your lover, if a natural progression leads us that far.

None of his paramours were interested in friendship. They wanted one thing from him—and he wanted the exact same thing in return. Why did she want his friendship? It was strange, it was odd, it was inexplicable!

He was beginning to see how she could be considered eccentric by society. She wanted a natural progression; he wanted sex and revenge for all the injustices the Roma had suffered. He hoped she stayed far away from him, as he had warned her to do. He knew, with every fiber of his being, she could not withstand his vengeance.

He also knew she was an innocent in this tragedy, and he should find a better target for his revenge. And that signified just how English he remained. It was unacceptable.

He drained the brandy, torn and frustrated, and felt a presence behind him. He whirled and saw Jaelle. Instantly, he saw that her nose was red, as if she had been crying.

"Are you all right?" he asked in concern, striding to her. She smiled brightly. "I am fine. Can I come in?"

"Of course you can come in," he said. Warmth filled him and it felt so good—and unfamiliar. He looked more closely at her and thought her eyes were filled with shadows. Was he imagining it? He wished he knew her better. "Are you certain you are fine?"

"Very," she said archly. "What a grand home. Maybe you are too *gadjo* to come north with us."

His smile vanished. "That is not the case."

She gave him a considering look, now walking the room, trailing her hand along the fine tables, stroking the vases, the candlesticks, the tiny painted boxes, all items collected by Edmund's wife.

"Are you too Rom to stay here at Woodland with me, until we leave?" he asked.

She sent him a beautiful smile. "I cannot sleep in a *gadjo's* bed." Her smile faltered and she stared at the bookcase. "You can read, can't you?"

"Yes. Do you want me to teach you?"

"I read English." She turned to him. "I am clever. It would be stupid not to read the language of the place we live." She glanced at the decanters on the console. "Is your *gadjo* whiskey better than ours?"

He didn't hesitate. "Yes."

She went to the sideboard and started to pour a drink.

"Absolutely not," he said, stepping to her. He reached for the glass but she took it before he could do so.

"I am a grown woman, Emilian, of twenty years." She saluted him with the glass.

She had been wearing a long-sleeved coat over her shirt and skirt. The sleeves fell back to her elbows as she raised the glass and he saw the raw abrasions on her arms. His world went still.

A terrible calm began. Someone had done this to her—someone would pay.

She paled, realizing what he had seen.

Very quietly, he said, "What happened? Who did that to you?"

"It is nothing," she said quickly.

"The wounds need to be cleaned and they need salve. What happened?"

She was mute, clearly refusing to answer.

"I know what happened." A ruthless determination began and he paced away from her. "*Gadjos*. You're too pretty. No, too beautiful, too tempting. *Gadjos* did this to you, somehow. Tell me." He faced her, staring.

"I am fine."

"I will decide if you are fine or not."

She held her chin high. "I was reading palms. You are right. It was *gadjos*. They wanted more." She shrugged dismissively.

He had thought his temper tightly controlled. Now rage threatened. He shoved it aside. "They tied you? Those cuts were made with ropes?"

"No! I ran away and hid under a stone wall. The stones scraped me. Another *gadjo* sent them away." She flushed. "But I hate them all."

He put his arm around her. It felt awkward. "Which *gadjos* tried to force you to bed, Jaelle?"

He saw the reluctance in her eyes. "I am here to protect you now. I will find out, whether you tell me or not."

"You're *didikoi*. If you hunt an Englishman, they will send the sheriffs and the high lords after you!"

"Nothing will happen to me," he lied smoothly. To convince her, he smiled. "I am a lord here, Jaelle. I am viscount."

She hesitated. "It was the innkeeper from the White Stag, and a fat *gadjo* with brown hair named Bill."

"Let's clean those scrapes," he said. And finally, he allowed his hatred and rage to boil.

He could not wait for his revenge.

He would take it out on the first Englishman—or Englishwoman—who dared to cross his path.

CHAPTER SEVEN

THE BOOK LAY OPEN on her bed unattended. She had tried to read, but she could not see the words, which danced and blurred like the flames in the bedroom's hearth.

Something had happened to her.

Emilian had happened to her.

Still clad in a cream-colored silk and chiffon evening gown, with small, off-the-shoulder sleeves, wearing pearls and diamonds and her hair curled and pinned up, Ariella stood by an open bedroom window, her pulse racing frantically. She was hot when the night air was cold. The tendrils that curled around her face were wet.

The driver she had secretly hired that afternoon was waiting for her just beyond Rose Hill's front gates. She hadn't decided to go to Emilian. She would prefer to get to know him better and gently segue into a love affair, but she had hired the driver just in case.

The decision she was poised to make seemed monumental and life altering. He had threatened her, warned her, told her forthrightly not to come. *You are a temptation I do not even wish to resist. I want to ruin you!*

Of course he did. He was a virile man. Every male in her family had been a notorious rake until wed. He was as insanely attracted to her as she was to him. But it wasn't just physical—there was an almost magnetic charge between them. It could not be one-sided. In the de Warenne family, that was the beginning of love. But Emilian couldn't know that.

How could she *not* go to him when she felt this way? When she was almost certain they would fall in love, or were even falling in love already? When she was coming to believe that he was the man meant for her?

She stared out the open window, tugging at her bodice, which was sticking to her skin. Her heart thundered. She gazed past the stars, seeing not their bright light but the campfires of the night before. She strained to hear. She imagined that if she tried hard enough, she could hear their soulful guitars all the way from Woodland.

But they were an hour's drive away. All she heard was an owl hooting—and the echo of last night's memory.

And it wasn't the music she needed. Oh, she knew that now. She closed her eyes and almost felt his hands on her warm, wet skin.

She could see him standing by a fire, staring toward the east, and she was certain he was thinking about her, too. *He was at Woodland, waiting for her, just as hot and feverish as she was.*

Ariella went to the bed and sat down. She was falling in love with a complete stranger, a man from a different culture. She had to fight for him, for them. This had to be a beginning, not just an interlude and an ending. She had to make certain that, when the Romany left, he stayed.

It was the Romany way to take lovers.

She shivered. Did she dare? Why not? She was not like Margery or Dianna, who would never dream of such a thing. She meant for them to be friends, as well as lovers. After the afternoon in the village, she began to understand his life. The Romany suffered every day of their existence. Her mother's people had suffered that way, too. There seemed to be amazing and terribly tragic similarities between the Romany history and that of the Jews.

He was so proud and strong, but what lay beneath that hard exterior? It had been hard enough that afternoon, watching the two young Romany boys behaving with such indifference to the terrible signs and the bigoted passersby. No one could be unaffected by such hatred and prejudice.

But I will not give you love when I take your innocence. We will not be friends…we will never be friends. I will give you nothing but passion, pleasure—and then it will be goodbye.

He was wrong. A night together would change everything, if they dared become lovers. Hadn't Alexi even said that women ruled men from their beds? If she became his lover, he would soften toward her. It would be the beginning she yearned for. He might soften completely—the way her father had with Amanda, the way her uncle Ty had with Lizzie. From this one night, there might be so much love. From this night, there could be a future.

Her mind was made up. She strode to the closet and opened the door, taking out a wrapper and placing it over her dress. If anyone caught her sneaking through the house, she would claim she was looking for a sweet in the kitchens. After tonight, he would not want to leave the county—he would not want to leave *her.*

ARIELLA RAPPED on the glass window that was between her and the coachman and he halted the single-horse carriage.

The moon was full and shining silver in a night sky shimmering with bright stars. Woodland was a dark gray shadow, situated at the end of a long, pale drive, with a number of outbuildings closer to the public road. Just ahead she saw the bright fires of the Romany encampment. She heard their guitars and violins. The music was more sensual than she recalled and even more enchanting.

Ariella breathed hard. Once she stepped out of the coach and let the coachman leave, there was no turning back. But she had no intention of turning back now. She was going forward—with Emilian.

She pushed open the carriage door and stepped down, trembling. In spite of her determination, she had never been more nervous and anxious. The stakes felt huge.

She barely smiled at the driver, her attention already moving to the perimeter of the camp and the fires blazing within. *He was close by, waiting for her.* She was certain. "Thank you."

He leered and said, "Want me to wait, miss?"

She hadn't given her name for a reason. Ariella was fairly certain that, if he had any intelligence, he would realize who she was, but she hoped he thought her just a visiting guest. If he did realize her identity, what was left of her reputation was now in shreds, as there was only one reason a lady would secretively be out and about at such an hour. She didn't care very much, but her parents would be devastated if they ever heard of her affair.

She would worry about them later. She somehow shook her head.

He grinned again and lifted the reins and the gig moved away.

Ariella's heart was pounding so fiercely now she let her shawl slip. Perspiration had gathered between her breasts. Her body seemed to hum with tension. Breathless, she started across the road, stumbling in her narrow slippers with their dainty heels, but it didn't matter. What mattered was this new beginning.

Her strides lengthened. She started to run. She crossed the foot of the drive. Veering across the fields toward the outermost wagons, the light of the fires intensified, allowing her to see the ground more clearly.

The Romany's grazing horses drifted out of her way. She reached the first wagon and hurried past. As she came closer to the circle of light from their fires, it did not occur to her to hide. She halted abruptly, breathing hard, and saw a half dozen dancers now. Emilian was not with them.

The music was more exotic, subdued and sensual than the night before, the tempo slower—like two familiar lovers slowly and sensually touching and caressing one another, a prelude to the storm of their love.

And then she saw him. From across the clearing, he stared. *She had known he was waiting for her.*

His eyes silver and hot, their gazes locked.

She forgot to breathe at all. He started toward her, leaving the camp behind.

The music seemed to stop. His strides were long with purpose, but somehow, he did not seem to rush. The seductive smile she had dreamed of began. There was so much promise, all of it was sensual.

She remembered to take in some air. Now, she studied him. He wore a red shirt with full sleeves, narrow black trousers and a black sash. The red shirt had a tie at the throat that had been left open. As he moved, it fell away from his skin, revealing the cleft between the two bulging planes of his chest.

A terrible urgency began. So much heat gathered and she felt moisture trickle beneath her undergarments. She was no longer shocked.

He paused before her and she smelled musk, whiskey, citrus, man. Although their bodies did not touch, she felt the heat coming from him in waves. His thick heavy lashes lowered slowly. "So you took the bait," he murmured.

She wasn't sure she could speak. "I was afraid…you might be gone…in the morning."

His lashes lifted. Hot silver scorched her. "Did you even consider my warnings, my sweet?" He lifted his hand and drifted his fingers across her cheek.

Pleasure jumped like sparks from nerve to nerve, from her

face to her neck, to her breasts. Her nipples stiffened. A reply became impossible.

He knew. He let one blunt forefinger slide down her throat. Her pulse slammed beneath it.

"I wanted you to come," he whispered.

She wet her lips, swallowed. "I can't let you leave."

"Tonight, I am not going anywhere without you."

That wasn't what she had meant, but it didn't really matter. "Did you know I would come here tonight?"

He caressed her cheek. "Yes."

She turned her mouth to his palm and pressed her lips there.

"Beautiful," he whispered, "brave...and bold."

She closed her eyes, the skin of his palm salty against her tongue. She was feeling faint. So much desire had gathered, consuming her. It was hard to think, to speak. "I have never been bold before." She looked at him as he dropped his hand, only to lay it on her throat and collarbone.

"I know." His fingers played. "May I teach you how to be very bold before this night is through?"

"You may teach me anything you wish," she breathed.

The beautiful smile reformed while his silver eyes glittered. He took her hand and lifted it. His mouth caressed the edges of her fingers and more delicious pleasure sparked and the flames fanned. "An invitation I could never refuse."

She went still as he rubbed his lips sensually over the inside of her palm. He slowly straightened and pulled her gently forward. One arm went around her back; his palm moved over her breast, above her clothes, but the glancing touch was like fire. His fingers brushed her throat; she inhaled. He pulled a hairpin from her hair and smiled at her. Then he removed another one.

He was taking her hair down. She trembled.

He pulled more pins out and tossed them aside. "In one night, I can only do so much," he murmured, his smile filled with secrets she didn't understand. "But in one night, I will teach you what I can." He tugged more hairpins loose, scattering them. "I hope you are prepared for endless pleasure." His hands moved into her curls.

She hollowed and gave in to the stabbing need. His huge hands were in her hair, fanning it out, parting the tight curls, loosening them, but every time he brushed her head, her face, her shoulders, the tension tightened. Her flesh throbbed with growing urgency now. Her knees felt weak and maybe they buckled, because he caught her.

"Then one night will not be enough," she whispered, acutely aware of his hands splayed out on her lower back. He didn't press her close but it didn't quite matter. The heat coming from him was searing.

"You may be right," he said, but there was soft, sensual laughter in his tone. "One night might not be enough for us, princess."

"Are you going to kiss me?" she cried, her pulse explosive.

He laughed. "The first thing you will learn is patience." His smile vanished. "I think I might be able to give you pleasure, right now. Shall we find out?"

She stared, uncertain whether to be dismayed or not.

He grasped her waist, pulled her against him, and the skirts between them no longer mattered. He moved his mouth against her neck. Ariella closed her eyes and trembled violently. Pleasure fanned.

His hands lowered. He caught her buttocks, pulled her high and hard and she felt herself spasm against his rock hardness. She gasped.

His tongue stroked over her throat as his fingers dug into her waist. His arousal thrust into her skirts. And then his mouth moved over hers.

She threw her arms around his neck and felt him grunt in satisfaction. Pleasure blinded her; she wrapped one leg around his waist and he tore her skirts from between them, spinning her. Her back found something hard—a wagon. And then his bulging loins thrust against hers. With his fingers, he tore open the slit in her drawers, ripping them, fabric tearing loudly.

She wept with pleasure as he ground against her and caressed her. The spasms slowed. Her racing heart slowed. She felt almost boneless. He slid her down his body, her skin inflamed and firing, until her feet touched the ground. And for one moment, he held her that way.

Sanity began to return and she felt his hot, hard body, throbbing restlessly against hers. But she was still aching, too. "Oh," she whispered.

His eyes blazed and he lifted her into his arms. "That is only the beginning," he said thickly, but as if in warning. He started away from the encampment, toward the house. His strides were long, hard and rapid; Ariella's grasp tightened. "It's too late now to change your mind," he said swiftly, glancing down at her.

He had misunderstood her gesture. "I am not changing my mind," she said. Something flickered in his eyes. It might have been relief—and it might have been dismay. She ignored her thoughts. "Where are we going?"

He gave her a burning look. "I am going to make love to you in a bed."

Her heart somersaulted at his choice of words, even as some small alarm began. "We can't just go inside and claim a room," she said.

He now sent her the most promising smile any woman could ever receive. "Why not? The master of Woodland is gone for the evening."

She was becoming light-headed again, while her body was heavy and hot. He knew his effect—he smiled with satisfaction, his strides increasing. She turned her face so she could kiss his chest. She felt him tense in surprise.

The skin there was salty, too. She kissed the underside of one hard chest muscle. She let her lips linger there and play. Then she rubbed her face there. She wanted to rub her face over every possible inch of him before the night was through.

He was breathing harshly now. He walked up a set of stairs and onto a terrace. "Are you certain you are not without some experience?"

Ariella kissed his nipple, which was hard and tight. "I don't want to talk." She tasted it with her tongue.

More tension filled his body, as he shoved open a door with his shoulder. "I can walk," she said softly, whispering so no one would discover them.

"I like you exactly where you are," he said firmly, not bothering to lower his voice. His grasp on her tightened.

He didn't seem to care about being caught. Ariella managed to think about the fact that he knew the house quite well, but she didn't dare ask him how. She was afraid to speak again in case they were overheard. She saw the shadowy form of a bookcase and realized they were crossing the library.

They stepped into a well-lit hall. He did not hesitate, but turned right. A moment later he was using his knee to push open a door. "Now you may stand—but briefly," he murmured, and he slid her to the floor.

Ariella found herself standing in a well-appointed bedroom. She glanced at the big, four-poster bed. His mouth curved as he reached behind her, locking the door.

"Shall I make a fire?" he asked, staring boldly at her.

She slowly shook her head. "No. I'm already warm."

His nostrils flared. She was surprised when he pulled her damp silk bodice from her sticky skin, the proof to her words. His red shirt was sticking to his torso, too.

She trembled, aware of his chest rising and falling beneath the red shirt. In the light cast from the single lamp, his skin was the color of copper. Her gaze drifted lower. She inhaled at the sight. The black trousers contained such a terrific bulge that the fabric caught the light. "I have never seen a man naked," she whispered, aware of her cheeks heating. "But I've seen statues."

His beautiful smile appeared. "You will not be regarding a statue tonight, or touching a statue...."

All the air vanished from her lungs. "I want to touch you, Emilian, very much."

"I know you do." His face hardened.

"Emilian, no more games." She almost added, *hurry*.

"But this isn't a game," he whispered, slowly reaching around her for the buttons on the back of her dress. "It is foreplay, darling." His mouth drifted across her nape.

Anticipation made her light-headed. He was deftly unbuttoning the dress, so expertly that she knew he'd done so for dozens of lovers. She hated the thought. Had he called his other lovers *darling* and *princess*, too? But it didn't matter, not with his fingers skimming her spine.

As if a mind reader, he said thickly, "You don't want a green boy in your bed." The bodice of her dress collapsed to her waist.

He studied her breasts, thrust out over the boned corset, clearly visible through her thin silk chemise. His fingers lay still on her bare shoulders. Not looking up, he grasped her shoulders, and his mouth covered hers. His lips were firm, urging her to respond but with surprising restraint. Instantly she opened and let him in. There was no other choice; she didn't want another choice. She wanted him.

His tongue thrust deep, slowly. He threaded his fingers into her hair and moved her against the wall. She moaned with pleasure and then the fires conflagrated as she felt his arousal through her skirts. He began a rhythmic movement there.

She became dizzy; every inch of her body became hollow. She wanted more than kisses now.

His mouth left hers. "So much passion, *gadji*," he whispered.

Ariella glanced up and tensed. His tone was soft and seductive, but his eyes were so fierce they were almost maniacal. She knew another frisson of sudden confusion.

Was she being ruthlessly seduced?

But before she could consider that unpleasant notion, his mouth brushed hers with urgency. "No," he said softly, kissing her, and suddenly her skirts fell between them, pooling at their feet. "There will be no escape." His mouth stroked along the pounding pulse there, down to her collarbone.

So much pleasure ignited. She forgot the sudden doubt and ran her hands over his muscular arms, realizing he had tossed his shirt aside while kissing her. Before she could explore the hard, rippling planes of his back, he feathered each nipple with his mouth, then moved lower, dropping to his knees while anchoring her hips to the wall.

Ariella went still, realizing what he intended, her heart rioting. And then he moved his face closer, and she felt his breath through the torn opening in her drawers, a silky caress that made her shiver with pleasure. He touched his cheek to her pulsing flesh and her mind shut down. She seized his shoulders, hard.

She felt him smile and then his mouth brushed her. She cried out. As her legs became weak and useless, his lips pressed more firmly to her hot, wet skin. "Come for me," he said roughly, and his tongue crept against her.

She whimpered desperately, and could barely stand the exquisite sensation. She had never imagined such an act. He softened, stroking perfectly, exquisitely, over her swollen lips, many times, and rapture blinded her.

She was falling now, back to reality and the room, as he stood, palming her with his hand. For one moment he held her, whispering to her in his native tongue, words she could not understand but knew were a sensual endearment. And then his mouth covered hers, the kiss deep and hot. His body shuddered while he kissed her.

He pulled away and swept her into his arms, carrying her to the bed. "You are such a beautiful *gadji*, the princess of a man's dreams," he whispered, their eyes meeting as he laid her down.

Ariella tensed, uncertain. His stare was cold, his expression hard. "Emilian?"

He sat beside her, smiling, lashes lowering over his eyes, one hand on each side of her shoulders, kissing her now. "Don't think…this is what you have come for."

She hesitated. She had come for a new beginning—one of friendship and passion, of love. A nagging doubt raised itself, but he slid her undergarments off her, his mouth moving sensually in the path of his hands. She embraced him, still uncertain. He stood, reaching for his sash.

Ariella realized she was naked, while he was still partially dressed. He pulled the sash off and tossed it aside, but his eyes were on her nude body. Instead of reaching for a cover, Ariella went still. "Make love to me, Emilian," she whispered.

He seemed to flinch. He glanced away and shed his boots and trousers. "I never hurry in bed."

She couldn't speak; all she could do was ogle his hard, perfect body. *He was too beautiful, too magnificent, for words.* "I don't mind."

His smile seemed amused. "You may stare until your heart's desire is met," he said, "although I do have other plans."

His tone was so calm and his eyes were so ruthless again. For one moment, he had the look of a man going into battle, not the look of a lover going to bed. Where was that seductive smile, one filled with sensual promise? Why wasn't he shaking with the same terrible urgency consuming her?

I will not give you love when I take your innocence.

Ariella felt a moment of panic.

His hands settled on her. His expression changed, hot and soft at once. His smile faltered, vanished. "Don't doubt that I need you," he said suddenly.

That bewildering look was gone. His regard was raw, hungry. She touched his cheek. "I need you, too," she whispered, relieved by his confession.

His stare intensified impossibly. "I am trying to control myself. I want to ravage you," he whispered. "I meant it when I said you are the princess of a man's dreams."

More relief came. He wasn't ruthlessly using her.

"You may change your mind—but you must do so now."

She was so surprised, it took a moment to realize he was offering her a way out. Ariella's heart exploded. She somehow smiled, touched his cheek, then ran her hand down his hard, heaving chest to his belly, which tensed. Ariella brushed his huge, throbbing length with her fingertips.

His eyes blazed silver. Making a hard sound, he put his arms tightly around her, pushing her down into the soft mattress and pillows. Fluidly, his body followed hers, and before she even realized it he was mounted above her. Ariella heard herself whimper.

For one instant their eyes met before his lashes lowered. Braced above her, he began stroking the huge tip of his erection over her. He was wet and slick and terribly hot. The friction was shocking, exhilarating. So much wet heat pooled. She felt very faint. She didn't know how much longer she could stand this.

He kissed her, but this time, he was frenzied. Ariella threw her arms around him and held on hard. She arched for him and whimpered his name. She thought she begged. He seized her hips so she couldn't move them and murmured to her in his Roma tongue.

She didn't know what he was saying, but he was cajoling her now. It didn't matter.

His mouth covered hers frantically. The heat between them was explosive. She started to sob, choking on the urgency coming from her loins and his huge manhood pressed into her. Ariella instinctively tensed.

"No," he said hoarsely, lifting his head. "Let me inside, Ariella."

Wildly she looked at him. His eyes were searching, intent. He was asking for permission. She nodded, aware of tears falling. She would never deny him.

He made a harsh sound and then he moved abruptly, deep.

He groaned. The pleasure was so intense she barely felt the pain as he sank into her. She spun, her body clenching at his.

He was watching her; she did not care. The pressure was incredible, impossible, escalating. She gave over to it and she was flung into the universe, shattering apart. She was aware of him moving fast and hard now, his groans filling the room. He cried out. She glimpsed his face. The passion…somehow savage, somehow gentle…the triumph….the need…. He was so beautiful…it was so beautiful. "I love you," she whispered, kissing his cheek and holding him tightly.

He held her, his tremors easing, his face buried against her cheek. If he heard her, he gave no sign. Ariella stroked his long, brownish gold hair, floating in happiness.

He moved to his side.

She turned to look at and enjoy his beautiful smile, but she met only his profile as he stared at the ceiling. He didn't look happy—not at all.

Alarm began.

Instantly he rolled over to face her. "Did I hurt you?" he asked harshly.

How could he not be ecstatic? Did she see guilt reflected in his eyes? "No. It was wonderful." A smile formed, coming from her heart. She reached out to stroke his cheek and, for one instant, thought he would flinch and pull away. Instead, his lashes lowered, hiding his eyes.

"Emilian, I am fine. I am too happy for words," she whispered.

She wished she knew what he was thinking. At first, she thought he might not respond, but he caught her hand and brought it to his mouth. He lifted his lashes and smiled at her.

A spark ignited, even though his smile seemed strained. She was about to ask him what was wrong, when he laid her hand on his massive chest, rubbed it there, and moved it a bit lower. Then he finally looked at her.

It was hard to think when his hot, tight skin was beneath her palm, but no message could be clearer. Her eyes widened. "We aren't finished?"

He smiled that beautiful seductive smile she would always love. "We have only just begun. Or have I tired you already?" His eyes gleamed.

She dared to move her hand down his abdomen, and as she did so, his body tensed and his manhood strained for her. She forgot her worry, her question. She forgot her alarm.

"Some Englishwomen are very passionate, too, just as passionate as the Rom."

He moved onto his back and lay very still. "Then this is a test," he said softly, sending her a long look. "A test of your passion—and mine."

CHAPTER EIGHT

ARIELLA AWOKE cocooned in heat. She blinked, feeling as if she had been drugged, her body sluggish and somewhat sore, and then she was wide awake.

She lay naked in Emilian's arms, in a guest room at Woodland. Their bodies were entwined, one of her legs caught between his. His arms were around her, her face pressed to the hard upper ribs just below his chest. Instantly she recalled his making love to her slowly, deliberately and exquisitely.

She had never been so happy, she thought, a thrill beginning. She noticed the pale gray dawn was filtering into the bedroom. Although delicious sensation was building, real alarm began. But before she could sit, his grasp tightened. She turned and realized he was awake and watching her closely.

She smiled, but he did not smile back. Instead, his gray, watchful eyes moved over her face, her hair, her breasts. "I have to go," she whispered, realizing that he was ready to make love to her another time.

A smile finally flickered. "Do you?" He pulled her closer, moving over her.

Oh, she did not want to ever leave! "Emilian," she began, images flashing. The sun would soon come up and she had to be at Rose Hill, in her own bed, as if she had spent the night there. She could see the staff beginning their day's chores. Her parents were early risers. So was Alexi. "I have to get home."

He kneed her thighs apart, while nuzzling her throat. "How can you leave me now, like this?" he murmured in a most seductive tone.

He hadn't even finished speaking when she felt him entering her.

Her body responded instantly, urgently—he had taught her so well. She felt him smile against her neck as he stroked deeply into her swelling flesh. She had to go…but the warm waves of sensation held her back, threatening to become unbearable. She looped her hands around his neck. "Make love to me," she whispered fiercely.

His silver eyes hot, his mouth claimed hers.

BRIGHT SUNLIGHT AWOKE HER.

She was so tired. She didn't want to awaken, and she groaned, covering her eyes with her hand. The movement hurt her arm. She began to awaken anyway, and she became aware of how utterly exhausted she was. She felt swollen and sore in unmentionable places and she suddenly recalled the evening before. She opened her eyes, but the other side of the bed was empty.

The sunlight flooding the room indicated that it was midmorning, at least. She sat up, dismayed. Why hadn't Emilian awakened her?

Memories of the night before began, flooding her. No wonder she was sore. Emilian was a superb and insatiable lover—but she had been rather insatiable, herself. She blushed.

She sat very still, her heart racing, her tired body trembling, thinking of all that they had done. They were lovers now. This was the beginning of the rest of their lives. Wasn't it? She wanted to smile. Her heart was trying to sing its way out of her breast, she was so deeply in love.

Where was he? Why had he let her sleep so late?

Ariella now saw her torn underclothes on the floor. Her dress lay there, too, in such a wrinkled state that she inhaled. How could she go home in that? What if someone saw her?

She looked up. A large Baroque mirror was above the bureau on the adjacent wall and she saw a stranger in the glass.

She could not look like that. She was naked in the rumpled bed. Her body was lush and flushed. Her disheveled hair streamed past her shoulders and over her breasts. Her blue eyes were far too bright, her mouth swollen and red.

She looked like a woman who had spent the night in her lover's arms.

A chair creaked.

Ariella looked past the bureau. Her eyes widened. Emilian sat in a green velvet chair in the shadows by the closet, staring silently at her.

She smiled, about to greet him, but he did not smile back. His expression was distant, hard and watchful.

Unease made her heart lurch. She felt her smile fade. She summoned it back. Reflexively, she reached for a sheet and pulled it over her chest. "Good morning. Emilian?"

"Good morning." He rose from the chair. His impassive expression, impossible to decipher, never changed. He was fully dressed, but not in the clothes he'd worn the night before. He wore a plain white shirt and his breeches and riding boots.

Her heart clenched, beginning to hurt in her chest. Why wasn't he smiling at her? "What are you doing?"

He simply stared. "I was watching you."

"Watching me? Why did you let me sleep? I have to get home! What time is it?"

He folded his arms, stepping to the foot of the bed. His focus moved from her eyes to her mouth, then to her hair. "It is half-past ten," he said flatly.

She cried out in dismay but did not move from the bed. "I have to get home! God, they will find me out! Emilian... you are making me uncertain about you—about us. Have I done something to anger you?"

"How could you anger me? We have passed an excellent night."

Hurt began, piercing through her chest. Thus far, his tone mirrored his expressionless face. "We have passed an excellent night?" she echoed.

"You learn quickly," he said with a negligent shrug. "I knew you would be an extraordinary lover."

He wasn't speaking like a man in love—or even like man who cared. But he could not consider her an object he had used—he could not compare her to others!

"Last night was wonderful," she began nervously, dread arising. "It was wonderful, wasn't it?"

"I have arranged for one of Woodland's carriages to take you to Rose Hill. It is waiting out front."

Her eyes widened. When his expression did not change, she cried, "You know I can't go home with my hair like this, in those clothes! What is happening? Why aren't you smiling? Why are you speaking as if you are dismissing me—and us?"

"It is very late. You should leave...Miss de Warenne."

She gasped. "It is Ariella!" She realized he had called her by name exactly once the entire night, when they had first consummated their relationship. "We had a wonderful night—it is a wonderful beginning," she cried—and she heard the desperation in her tone.

His face hardened. For the first time, she saw the anger in his eyes. "What beginning to do you refer to?"

She was reeling. "I thought...that after last night..." She could not continue.

"If you are suggesting that we continue the affair—" he shrugged "—that can be arranged."

She choked. "That isn't what I meant! You know what I meant! I didn't come to your bed for an affair! I came—" She stopped. She was becoming sick at heart. He couldn't mean his words. He could not be so cruel.

"I told you what would happen if you came to me last night."

"You did not ruthlessly seduce me. We made love!"

"I seduced you, coldly and callously. We had *sex*."

She cried out and stumbled from the bed, forgetting the sheets. "Why are you doing this?"

He folded his arms across his chest and a ruthless look entered his eyes. "Exactly what am I doing, Miss de Warenne? You threw yourself at me. I accepted your offer of sex. You were well pleased last night—eight times, I believe. I enjoyed myself, as well. Now you should hurry to dress, otherwise you will never make it home undetected by your family. They must be distraught by now." Finally, he smiled.

She trembled with shock, with hurt. "We made *love*."

"And how would you know that?"

She recoiled.

He turned his back and started for the door, without any sign of being in a hurry. There he paused. "I'll see if I can find you a maid."

She covered her mouth with her hands but could not stop the choked sob of anguish. "Do you *want* to ruin me?" And too late, she recalled his terrible words.

He whirled. "I did not make you a single promise!" His eyes blazed with anger. "I was blatantly honest with you. I am sorry if you had absurd expectations. I told you to *run!*" His voice had risen to a shout.

"But I thought…I thought you felt the same way about me as I do for you!" she begged. She realized tears were falling.

His face tightened. "You thought wrong. I wanted an enjoyable evening, nothing more—and I never indicated otherwise." He left.

She had made a terrible mistake. Emilian had meant his warnings. She should have believed him. He had no feelings for her. He had coldly and ruthlessly used her.

She felt her legs give way. She didn't care. She dropped to the floor, knocking over a table as she did so, landing hard on her shoulder. Pain exploded, but she welcomed it. He had to have heard the bric-a-brac shattering, but he did not come back.

She curled up into a ball.

HE CAREFULLY CLOSED the door to his library and leaned against it. His heart thundered; he could not breathe.

He would never forget the look on Ariella's face.

He had wanted *budjo,* a Gypsy's best revenge for all of the world's ills. As a boy, he'd stolen a cow, painted its face and sold it back to the original owner. Stevan had praised him and Raiza had been proud. He had enjoyed the swindle, and the fact that the *gadjo* cow owner had refused to allow them a night on his farm had only made the hustle better. The farmer had deserved *budjo.*

He had wanted Ariella de Warenne to be *budjo.* He had wanted her to be revenge for Raiza, and even for Jaelle. He had known it would be easy to take her and then return her to the *gadjos,* tainted and used. A fool would marry her, not knowing she was used by a Gypsy lover.

But she did not deserve to be *budjo,* and he damn well knew it.

Last night, he had played her like his violin. Last night, she had told him that she loved him. He had pretended not to hear.

He didn't want her love. Why couldn't she have been a different woman, a woman of experience, a woman who only wanted to have sex? Why did she have to have those huge blue eyes, which could look into a man's empty soul and find something bright and light? He knew that she was confused; she was mistaking desire for love. He did not believe in love at first sight.

Why did he have to be her first? Why did she have to claim that she loved him?

He reached for the floor-to-ceiling bookcase. Using all of his rage and strength, he tore it from the wall. Wood thundered as it fell; it cracked and splintered loudly, books flying everywhere, thudding like dropping stones. And then he stood in the havoc of the room, a terrible silence falling.

He had only wished to use her and return her that way to the *gadjos*. Had she been a different woman, one with experience, the *budjo* would have been simple and she would not have suffered very much. Instead, he had crushed her.

Too late, he realized he hadn't considered all the consequences of his actions. Too late, he knew he hadn't really meant to use, abuse and hurt such a woman.

Finding air was impossible. It was as if he suffered with her. And then he heard the piano.

He stiffened. He had never heard such beautiful yet soulful music. He often played by ear, according to his mood. He could not imagine who played now, especially a melody so deeply sad and haunting. It was filled with yearning.

He recognized the depth of the pain he was hearing and for one moment, he was still.

And then the melody changed. It became light, lively, filled with hope and joy.

He thrust the door open and raced to the music room. He halted, both doors open, and he saw Jaelle seated at the piano, engrossed, her fingers moving deftly over the keys. She was smiling, but tears streaked her face.

He closed his eyes. She had found joy in this moment, but her life was one of pain.

All Rom lived that way.

He had done the right thing using the de Warenne woman.

"OH, GOD! What happened?" Margery cried.

"Shut the door," Ariella whispered, seated on the window bench, wrapped in a sheet. She was numb now. She supposed she was in shock. She had managed to send word for Margery, but had done nothing but sit and stare since.

Margery closed the door, a parcel in her arms. Her eyes were huge, taking in the rumpled bed and Ariella's clothes scattered on the floor. Her regard moved back to Ariella's face. "Who did this to you?"

Ariella looked at her distraught cousin. "I am fine," she choked. It was a lie. She had been grossly abused, and she would never be fine again.

His image flashed as she had last seen him, cold and impassive and ruthlessly set against her.

More pain stabbed through her.

Too late, she realized she was a romantic fool.

Margery set the parcel down and ran to her. Ariella stood and her cousin wrapped her in her arms. She had no tears left, even though she wished to weep in Margery's arms. But the pain remained, burning in her chest. Maybe one day she could hate him, except he had told her exactly what would happen if she trysted with him.

"Darling." Margery stepped back but held her shoulders. *"Who did this?"* She looked at the bed. It was obvious her innocence was gone.

Ariella couldn't answer. As horrible as Emilian was, she was reluctant to name him, even to Margery, whom she could trust with such a terrible secret.

Margery clearly fought for calm. "Why aren't you telling me what happened and who did this to you?"

She tensed. "I came here for a tryst. I thought I was in love and that he loved me, too. I was wrong," she managed.

Margery gasped. "When did you fall in love with St Xavier? For that matter, when did you meet?"

Ariella felt the grief rising. Her love had been one-sided.

She couldn't possibly love him now. It was hard to analyze her emotions, as she was so consumed with hurt. "It's almost noon. Will you please help me get home without discovery?"

"Without discovery? Ariella, your father will make certain St Xavier marries you!"

"I don't want to marry him. It wasn't St Xavier!" Ariella cried in return, her composure fragile. "It was the Rom!"

Margery gasped. "The Gypsy?"

Ariella walked over to the parcel, clutching the sheet tightly to her body. She felt battered all over, physically, as well as emotionally. "Yes, it was Emilian."

Margery followed. She took the parcel and opened it, laying the items not on the bed, which she now fastidiously ignored, but on the small sofa. She said tersely, "I am not certain how you could think yourself in love with a man you met the other day."

Ariella wiped her eyes. "Everyone in our family falls in love suddenly, sooner or later. I am no exception to that rule, obviously."

"You are in love with Emilian," Margery said slowly, paler than before.

"I thought I was!" Ariella cried.

Margery took her into her arms. "Oh, Ariella, I don't know what to say! You have gone too far…but your father can force him to the altar!"

"I have never been so drawn to anyone before. The moment I laid eyes on Emilian, I was smitten." She inhaled. "I suppose he was right. He told me it was desire, not love. He warned me to stay away from him. In fact, I dismissed his every warning. He told me if we made love, he'd walk away the next day." She trembled. Why hadn't she listened? "Apparently I have not fallen in love after all. Apparently I was simply stricken with desire."

Margery's eyes were huge. A terrible pause ensued. "He

warned you away and you came to him anyway?" she finally asked in disbelief.

"I made a terrible mistake." Ariella bit her lip. "How simple hindsight is. He is leaving soon. I kept thinking that if I came to Woodland, an affair would be the beginning for us."

Margery rubbed her face. Then she spoke briskly. "He is a terrible rogue, reprehensible, truly, but at least he told you his intentions, as dishonorable as they were. He seemed to wish for you to stay away. Any other woman would have heeded his word!"

Ariella closed her eyes briefly, in pain. How well she knew that.

"Well, mistakes are made every day and it is not the end of the world. Let's get you dressed and home and we will consider the situation then together. We *will* save your reputation," she added firmly.

Ariella wasn't sure she cared about her reputation, but her parents would care very much. "Thank you," she whispered.

Margery helped her pull on a chemise, petticoats and a blue dress. "Would you marry him?"

Ariella looked at her. Her mind went blank.

"I meant what I said before. If you go to your father, he will bring Emilian to the altar and you know it."

Her heart began shrieking at her. She didn't understand its turmoil. She covered her breast with her hand. "I am confused, Margery. An hour ago, I woke up in joy and so wildly in love."

Margery became even paler.

"He was so cold, so calm. He was *cruel.*"

Margery rushed to her to hold her again.

Ariella pushed her away. "No. I am a fool. I thought I had found what everyone else in this family has—true love that will last forever. But instead, I walked into a sordid affair. I am so hurt I cannot think straight."

"I am utterly tired of that family myth," Margery said with heat. "Do you know when the Gypsies are leaving Derbyshire?"

Ariella realized Margery was considering a forced marriage for her sake, but it would be impossible to accomplish if Emilian vanished with the Romany and couldn't be found. "I don't know when the Roma will leave. I don't think Emilian can be forced to do anything, not even by my father." Suddenly her knees buckled and she felt faint. Her entire plan had failed. He was leaving anyway.

"Last night I made love to him," she gasped, light-headed and crying. "I told him I loved him. But he didn't make love to me. I can't marry a man who doesn't love me." She wanted Margery to understand. "Could you?"

"No," Margery said grimly. "I could not."

Ariella inhaled. "I have never wanted a proper marriage, anyway." But as hurt and distraught as she was, she knew there would be nothing ordinary and proper about marriage to a man like Emilian.

"You deserve true love, Ariella—and you will find it, because you are the most extraordinary woman in this family!" Margery exclaimed. "You are brilliant, educated and kind. You have never been mean to anyone. That man will suffer for what he has done! You deserve a gentleman, Ariella, not a cad."

Ariella shook her head. "He probably suffers every single day of his life."

Margery's eyes widened.

"You were in the village yesterday. He is hated, despised. There are shops and inns which refuse him admittance. You should have seen the mayor and his cronies at Rose Hill before you arrived. They were in a frenzy to chase the Gypsies away."

"Please, do not allow yourself any compassion for him now."

"If you are telling me to hate him, I cannot. He is hated enough as it is." She realized, in that moment, she had spoken an absolute truth.

"Ariella," Margery cried. "Your compassion is dangerous! What if he takes advantage of it?"

"Don't worry. I am never going near him again. I am never joining him in bed again. I have learned my lesson. It is far too painful to ignore." She would stay away from him now. Her compassion wasn't dangerous; *he* was dangerous.

Margery began buttoning up the back of her dress. "We need a plan. For the life of me, I do not know how we will return to Rose Hill. Your disappearance has been noted. When I left, Amanda said you must have taken a book and were curled up somewhere, reading."

As she often disappeared for hours upon hours with a book, it was not unusual. "I have a plan, but it isn't a good one." She picked up a hairbrush. "I am going to tell half of the truth and then I am going to lie."

Margery turned and their gazes locked. "When have you ever lied, much less to your parents, your family?"

"I have no choice," Ariella said firmly. "If I don't lie, my father will kill him."

EMILIAN HALTED his gray stallion in front of the White Stag Inn. The sign with the hated words remained. Red rage filled him as he slid from the horse, and an image of his sister at the piano, tears ruining her smile, assailed him. He tied the stallion to the post and barged inside.

The common room was dank, dark and smoke filled. About a dozen men were at several tables and the bar. Heads turned his way and conversation ceased. He glanced at the bar, where the innkeeper, Jack Tollman, was serving ale. He smiled, relishing the likelihood that someone would point out that he was a half blood and must be put out. *Let them try.*

Instead, Jack beamed at him. "Welcome to the White

Stag, my lord," he said. "'Tis a fine afternoon fer a mug. Aye, boys?"

The two men seated at the bar nodded, smiling in welcome, obsequiously.

Emilian knew that when he turned his back, they would whisper about him. They would slur him and *his kind*. He slowly moved, his eyes on Jack. "Where is the palm reader, Tollman?" he asked coolly.

Jack's smile faltered. "Haven't seen her, my lord. She was here yesterday. But she cheated the customers and I sent her packing."

He leaned on the bar, uncomfortably close to Jack, who stiffened. The man's breath was sour from imbibing. "The reader cheated no one," he said softly.

"I beg yer pardon," Jack said with obvious unease. "O' course, we made a mistake about the Gypsy wench."

"The Gypsy wench is my *sister*."

Jack blanched.

Emilian seized him by throat and tightened his fingers. Jack choked. Emilian imagined Jaelle being groped; he saw her running from these men. He increased the pressure with pleasure.

"S-stop!" Jack Tollman begged.

"You touched her, hurt her!" he roared. He wanted to kill this man for what he had done.

Hands grasped him from behind. He ignored them, dragging Tollman over the bar while his customers frantically tried to pull him away. As the innkeeper's eyes bulged in fear and panic, he heard them shouting at him to stop. Hands pulled at his shoulders, his arms, his wrists. He refused to release Tollman, aware that every man in the room was trying to get him off of the innkeeper now. *Let them try.* Tollman would pay for what he had tried to do to Jaelle and he would watch him slowly die.

He was about to commit murder.

The knowledge wafted through his mind. A distant part of him was horrified.

But Raiza's sightless eyes came to mind, as she lay broken on a cobbled Edinburgh street, murdered by the *gadjos*.

I love you, Emilian.

He heard Ariella's passionate declaration, but saw her as he had left her, hurt and pale, her eyes filled with tears of pain.

Don't do this, Emilian.

It was as if Ariella stood there beside him, he heard her that clearly.

He hesitated, his grip easing. Suddenly he was wrestled away from Tollman, a blow landing on his jaw. He was pushed hard across the room. He stumbled to the floor, swiftly rising. As he did, he saw Tollman collapsing, choking.

"Tried to kill Jack!"

"Murdering Romany swine!"

He straightened, aware now that the mob was ready to come after him. Braced for an attack, he silently dared the assembled crowd to say another word about him. A silence fell. Every stare directed at him was hostile; every man was poised to rush him.

"No one touches her again," he said, fingering his bloodied lip. "Or you will answer to me." As he strode to the door, he heard them muttering about Gypsies and thieves. He felt the crowd moving behind him like wolves, following him with predatory intent.

He knew if he ran, they'd set chase. He knew they wanted to tear him apart. He pushed outside, into daylight, brushing past a gentleman entering the inn. They followed him to the threshold.

"What is going on?" the dark man demanded, turning around.

Emilian paused by the hitching post, breathing hard,

shaken by his own actions. He had never been filled with such murderous violence before.

"He tried to murder Jack, Captain de Warenne," someone cried.

He started, glancing at the gentleman. As the man looked at him grimly, he recognized his blue eyes and guessed that this man was Ariella's brother. A new tension began.

"This is over," the gentleman said. "Go back inside," he ordered the crowd. Grumbling, they obeyed, except for Jack Tollman, who appeared in the doorway.

"I will fight my own battles," Emilian told de Warenne.

De Warenne looked at him as if he was an idiot. "Really? You were about to be beaten and, considering the odds, I think you might have wound up dead." His demeanor was cool. "I am Alexi de Warenne."

Emilian had no intention of introducing himself. He didn't need help from Alexi de Warenne or anyone.

"He assaulted me," Tollman gasped furiously. "I want him locked up. I want him charged with murder!"

The insane urge to do violence swiftly arose. Emilian stepped forward and he smiled. "Good. Charge me. And you will be charged with the attempted rape of my sister."

Tollman paled.

Alexi de Warenne looked from one to the other as Tollman said, "I didn't know she was your sister! There was no attempt at anything—she read the hands of a few customers, that is all!"

Emilian breathed hard. He wiped more blood from his mouth. "She was *running* from you. You wished to force her to bed. That is attempted *rape.*"

"That's not true," Tollman began. "Tell him what happened, Captain!"

Emilian started.

Alexi said grimly, "I was there. I saw the pursuit. And I ended it before your sister was genuinely hurt."

"You ended it?" Emilian was stunned.

"Yes." Alexi's eyes darkened with anger. "I would never allow a woman to be abused. I had hoped Jaelle would go with my sister to Rose Hill, but she ran off before Ariella could tend to her wounds."

Emilian was in disbelief. *"You helped my sister."*

"Of course I did. I would help any woman in distress."

He turned away, the disbelief becoming horror. Alexi de Warenne had saved Jaelle from ruin. And in return, he had ruined Alexi's sister.

He was violently ill. The dizziness returned. He reached for the post and wondered if he would vomit. He *hated* himself.

Alexi de Warenne turned. "No one is charging anyone with anything…yet," he said to Tollman. "Leave the Roma alone, Tollman. Leave their women alone. We do not need this kind of hatred and violence in Derbyshire. They will be departing shortly—I assure you of that."

The nausea passed, but not the new, terrible tension. Emilian turned his back on the younger man, walking over to his horse. His behavior was beyond dishonor. He should have chosen anyone other than Ariella for *budjo* and revenge.

Emilian felt de Warenne walk up behind him. He sought control, and finally turned. "I can fight my own battles, but I am grateful you aided my sister."

Alexi shrugged. "It is what a gentleman does. You need some advice. I don't blame you for your fury—I would do the same for my sister—but I am not a Rom. Confronting Tollman in his inn was foolish. What did you think to gain? If you had murdered him, you would hang."

He looked at him and saw Ariella instead. Her brother would kill him if he ever knew what had happened between them—and he would have every right. "I'll try to remember your wisdom in the future." He turned to go.

De Warenne seized him. "I am trying to help."

"I don't need your help," he said sharply.

Alexi de Warenne stared for a moment. "You need to take your people and leave," he said firmly. "The sooner, the better. The townspeople are angry. They are suspicious. They are filled with hatred and fear. This won't end until you go."

"And you are not filled with hatred?" Emilian stared closely.

Alexi's eyes narrowed. "No, I am not filled with hatred."

Like brother, like sister, he thought. He took his reins and mounted, ignoring the other man now. But he could not ignore the guilt.

CHAPTER NINE

"YOU SPENT THE NIGHT at the Romany encampment?" Cliff de Warenne asked in disbelief.

Ariella faced her father, Margery by her side, standing very straight and still, her pulse pounded with alarming force. She had never been so dismayed and uncomfortable. Cliff de Warenne adored her; in his eyes, she could do no wrong. She was acutely aware of the fact that he would be crushed by what she had done. Worse, he would kill Emilian.

"One of the women invited me," she said, trying to smile.

He was disbelieving and briefly speechless. Amanda stood beside him, as surprised, and she glanced with worry at her husband.

"You have gone too far!" Cliff exclaimed. "How did you get there? Wait—you knew I would not allow it so you stole from this house? The Roma do not like outsiders, yet one of their women invited you?"

He was suspicious. Ariella tensed. Their relationship had always been one of absolute trust. She had never done anything to violate his trust before. "Yes." She wet her lips. "Yesterday Alexi and I helped Jaelle in the village. She was in a predicament with several men. And I spoke to her earlier, as well, when we brought some sweets to their children. We are becoming friends."

He stared, his expression searching.

"You know I have very eccentric friends in town," she

said breathlessly. She tried to smile calmly but she simply couldn't.

Her father smiled at her so dangerously she stiffened. "What happened, Ariella?"

Amanda touched his arm in warning. He ignored her.

"It was a festive evening." She felt her cheeks heat. "They played guitars and violins, men and women danced, there was singing."

He began shaking his head. "It was a festive evening," he echoed.

She didn't think he had ever been angry like this with her. "Father, it was field research. I am very interested in the Romany culture. When will I ever have this kind of opportunity again?"

His face tightened. "Were you approached?"

"Approached?"

"Where was their chief last night, Ariella? The half-blood *vaida,* Emilian?" he asked softly.

She trembled. She couldn't lie to him—but she couldn't tell him the truth, either. "He was there, but we only spoke briefly."

He stared and she hoped she was not red. "Really," he said, his tone filled with skepticism.

"We spoke very briefly," she repeated. She flushed. "Truthfully, I had hoped we could have a serious conversation, because he is an unusual man—I have never met a *vaida* before, and I am sure he has many interesting stories to tell. After all, he is probably as well traveled as you are! But he was not interested in furthering my acquaintance. Shortly after I arrived he left the encampment."

"If you think to befriend him, I am telling you it is a very unwise idea. You should stay away from him. And you cannot simply walk out of the house in the middle of the night to investigate your latest passion," he said sternly.

Ariella held her tongue. She'd had many rousing debates

with her father—and every other family member—as she loved a lively difference of opinion. Now was not the time to point out that in London she attended radical assemblies that went well past midnight without reporting her actions to anyone other than her driver.

He seemed calmer now, but his blue eyes were piercing. "I heard what happened in town. I am sorry for the woman, and I am glad you and your brother were there to help her. And I am not surprised that you would feel so much empathy for the Romany people, especially after the assault on Jaelle. Your mother's people suffered the same persecution and hatred. But you are taking your interest and compassion too far. You could have been accosted on the highway or at the Roma camp. You are a single, young, vastly inexperienced woman. I do not care how much of the world you have seen, I have made a point of sheltering you as if you are a rare gem. You are my daughter, Ariella, and until you are wed, it is my duty to protect you in every possible way. You cannot leave this house at such an unacceptable hour without my permission—and without a proper escort."

She had no intention of arguing, not when she was about to escape their confrontation unscathed. "Father." She smiled and touched his sleeve. "My judgment was lacking and I will be the first to admit it." She somehow smiled again, but she was acutely aware that her heart remained a gaping wound in her chest. "I am very sorry."

"No more midnight research, Ariella." He turned to his wife and kissed her briefly. "I will see you later," he said, and left.

Ariella shared a glance with Margery, whose look was incredulous. Ariella knew she had escaped discovery by a single chin hair.

Amanda took her arm. "It must have been quite the evening," she said.

Her stepmother's green eyes were questioning. "It was very educational."

"You seem exhausted."

A response escaped her.

"And you seem sad." Amanda smiled gently. "If something is wrong, you know you can come to me."

Ariella nodded, but did not mean it. She loved her stepmother. She had never known her own mother, and her father had met Amanda when Ariella was six years old. Amanda was her mother in every possible way. But she was madly in love with Cliff, even all these years later. Ariella knew they had no secrets. If Amanda ever learned the truth, she would feel obliged to go to Cliff.

Amanda kissed her cheek and left the salon.

Ariella was about to collapse into the closest chair when she saw Alexi standing on the threshold of the adjacent room. She stiffened.

His face hard and tight with suspicion, he folded his arms across his chest. "What, exactly, were you doing last night?"

EMILIAN WALKED down the hall. Several days had passed and he was glad he hadn't killed Jack Tollman. He was many things, but he was not a murderer. However, he had almost lost all discipline that day. He must never allow himself such free rein again. It was simply too dangerous. Revenge was one thing, murder quite another.

As he reached for the pair of closed library doors, his temples began a slight throbbing. Going to his library each and every day had become a difficult feat. He was acutely aware of the bedroom door that was farther down the hall and what had transpired there.

But bypassing the bedroom did not erase his thoughts, nor did it vanquish his memories or change the facts. He stepped into his library. Ignoring that room could not change what he had done.

I love you, Emilian.

He cursed as he went to his desk and pulled forward his mail. He knew he was never going to forget what he had done. There should have been triumph, but there was only anger and guilt and too much regret. He rifled through the pile, finding the letter from his solicitor. As he slit it with an ivory-handled letter opener, Ariella's face, hurt and accusing, appeared in his mind.

At least she did not love him now. He reminded himself that she hadn't even loved him then. He had been her first lover; that was all.

He forced himself to focus on his lawyer's letter. Brian O'Leary had several candidates for the position of estate manager, all highly recommended. He would send one or all of the gentlemen to Woodland for interviews, pending knowledge of the most convenient dates.

Emilian shifted restlessly and scrawled a reply. But as he dated the letter, he became still.

It was May 22. Why did that date cause some nagging alarm?

He stood and went to the door. "Hoode!"

A moment passed before his majordomo came running. "My lord?"

"What is significant about this day?" he demanded brusquely.

"I am uncertain, sir."

"It is May 22. The date is ringing a bell," he said, feeling irate.

Hoode raised his pale brows. "The only significance I can attach to this day, sir, is that tonight is the Simmonses' country ball."

Emilian felt himself still. He heard Ariella's cousin as clear as day, saying something about the country ball. Her family would be there—everyone would be there—*she* would be there.

His heart exploded, racing hard and fast.

And he knew very well what that reaction signified—it was excitement.

"Thank you, Hoode," he said, turning away. She continued to excite him, but there would be no hunt and no conquest. He had done enough. He had hurt her, and that had not been his intention. He should have chosen someone else for *budjo*. He owed her brother now.

She was going to the ball.

He almost smiled. She was a poor dancer, but he suddenly imagined her in a ball gown and jewels, gracefully gliding about in a waltz in some gentleman's arms. And then he realized that the gent was himself. His tension escalated wildly.

He had been thinking about her for days, ever since his calculated seduction. He didn't want to keep thinking about her, not her smile or her eyes, and certainly not about her passion, and he didn't want to envision her waltzing with anyone, much less him. But she was like a bright beacon in a dark, dangerous harbor. She was impossible to miss in person, and apparently impossible to dismiss, even in his most private thoughts.

He leaned against the wall. She was very beautiful, and somehow more enticing than any woman he'd ever met, but then, she had been eccentric enough to meet him at Woodland. She was a rare woman, he knew that now.

He knew he must not consider her very passionate nature. It was his nature to enjoy the women he found desirable, but he had never pursued an innocent unwed woman before— Ariella had been the first and his intent had been revenge. She might not be a virgin now, but she was still naive and inexperienced. She had been abused by him. He must never abuse her again. Pursuing her was out of the question.

If he ever had the opportunity to bed her again, he might lose himself completely while in her arms.

He intended to finish his reply to O'Leary, but his pulse pounded and her image danced in his mind as if she was seducing him from afar with her eyes, her innocence, her smile. He did not know how she had fared since their encounter. She probably hated him now.

He hoped she hated him. Then there would never be any chance of her approaching him to finish what they had begun. Especially as he hadn't meant to begin anything with her.

On the other hand, what if she did not hate him?

He slowly turned, filled with tension. He would not analyze his motives now. "Hoode, ready my evening clothes."

This time, he was the one who could not stay away.

THERE WAS A PERFECT crescent moon in a star-bright night sky. He stepped out of his coach, which had halted in front of the Simmons mansion. Three dozen vehicles lined the semicircular drive, in the center of which was a fountain. As he paused before the wide limestone steps leading to the front door, he tugged on his stock. He rarely went out in the evening, much less to an affair. The length of the tails of his coat bothered him. The stock felt suffocating, and he preferred his Hessians to his shoes. He loosened the black silk tie again. He felt warm, and he damned well knew why.

He started up the steps. He had never been to the Simmonses' home before, although they had invited him dozens of times. He never even looked at the social invitations he received, he simply discarded them. As Hoode had helped him dress, his servant had carefully informed him that he had not been invited to this ball. Emilian had briefly been dismayed, but his mind was now made up and he would go anyway. He could no longer deny that he wished for a glimpse of Miss de Warenne, but not to pursue her. He wanted to determine that she had recovered from his rude abuse. And he owed her an apology, one he intended to discreetly make.

He also wanted to know if she hated him.

"Sir, they will be thrilled to receive you," Hoode had insisted. "I have no doubt you were not invited because they have given up your ever accepting an invitation."

Emilian hoped Hoode was right. The words *No Gypsies Here* drifted through his mind. But he had been invited by all the great Derbyshire families to their fetes on many occasions. Hoode was probably right—he would be well received tonight.

The doormen bowed as he walked past them. He was late by perhaps forty minutes, and as he was ushered toward the ballroom, he heard the many guests conversing, along with a piano and a harp. The moment he was left on the threshold of the ballroom, in spite of the glittering, colorful crowd, he saw her.

She was on the dance floor, in another man's arms. She was so beautiful, and the memories were so terrible, that his heart lurched.

It crossed his mind that he was in some trouble, to have such a vast reaction to her after only five days.

But he didn't move. His heart thundered. He stared.

She wore a pastel green gown, one with a low V-neck and small sleeves which bared her shoulders. She wore her hair in the English style he found so unattractive, tightly curled and pinned up, with several thick curls hanging about her face. It didn't matter. Her beauty could not be diminished by any hairstyle—and he hoped her spirit had not been diminished by what he had done to her. He realized she was beaming at her partner.

A dangerous anger uncoiled as they turned. She hardly belonged in his arms, so he could not be jealous. Then his anger vanished, for she was dancing with her brother.

Though relieved, he realized he was too intent to relax. His blood was too hot. One night of seduction had not been enough.

He watched them move across the dance floor in the waltz, a dance he thought elegant but far too staid. Her brother was a good dancer, but she was not. She had just tripped over her brother's foot. He felt his lips curve. She was laughing about the error, too.

She was happy, and he was oddly glad. He watched them whirl about, her steps distinctly awkward, as if she was counting them. How could she dance so stiffly, when in bed she was so sensual?

His heart slowed dangerously, but every pulsing beat was heavy. He was recalling her body sliding beneath his, and he almost felt her sweaty, silken skin. If she allowed herself to feel the music the way she had felt him, she could dance superbly.

"My lord St Xavier," a man boomed.

He turned. He did not recognize the gentleman holding out his hand, his smile wide and fixed. He inclined his head and took the proffered hand.

"A great pleasure to see you, sir," the man said, pumping it.

Behind his back, he heard a man say in total disbelief, "St Xavier is here?"

He knew that whispers were beginning and that they contained more than speculation—they contained slurs.

"My lord, good evening." A beautiful brunette smiled at him, her shorter, balding husband with her. She held out her gloved hand, and her eyes were warm with a far too familiar invitation.

Jane Addison had been in his bed every single afternoon in the month of April, but he hadn't seen her in at least three weeks—nor did he wish to enjoy her favors again. He took her hand and bowed indifferently over it.

"My lord, sir, this is a great pleasure!" her husband cried, beaming.

Emilian smiled briefly at her husband. He had seen the

man in passing over the years, but had no intercourse with him. He nodded, and as he did, he overheard someone say, "I can't believe he's come out."

The tone was vitriolic.

He looked at his ex-lover's husband without guilt or remorse. He was hardly Jane's first adulterous affair, and he would not be her last. Besides, he hadn't been thinking of any insult while mounting Jane on the floor, or atop his desk, or against the door. He glimpsed several women he'd enjoyed in the room. But their husbands had unknowingly paid a high price for their scorn and condescension.

"Is it really true?" a woman whispered.

He knew, without doubt, that they were discussing his Romany heritage. Annoyed, he turned. Three very pretty young women stood with his cousin, Robert, and his two ne'er-do-well friends. All the women flushed. Robert grinned at him, and he knew his cousin, in particular, had been enjoying the subject of his heritage.

"I see you've stepped out, finally." Robert took his hand and shook it as if they were close. "May I introduce the ladies, Emil? Miss Hamlin, Miss Cutty, and Lady Haverford."

Amidst blushes and giggles, they curtsied and simpered. They were so silly, and he had forgotten how annoying young virgins could be. He glanced across the dance floor. The music had ended and Ariella was slipping out of her brother's embrace. His heart slowed dangerously again.

She was not annoying.

She was proud, intelligent, direct.

What if she didn't hate him?

He realized the three young ladies were chattering at once, but he didn't bother to look at them. He scanned the crowd. A dozen gentlemen were watching Ariella. He wasn't the only one to desire her—of course not. More tension arose and he welcomed it, preferring to be distracted by potential rivals.

"Sir, sir, my lord!" One of the debutantes tugged on his sleeve. "Does this mean you will now come out with us? We should so love your company at the June fête!"

He didn't look at the young woman speaking but restrained himself from flinching at her touch. *There were no rivals.* He shouldn't have come, because he wanted to pursue her. Worse, he wished the company would vanish so he could watch her openly, in pure enjoyment.

He wouldn't mind teaching her how to dance.

He shook himself. Dancing with her would be impossible now, after the night they had shared.

She was crossing the dance floor, her brother handing her off to her cousin and sister so he could join a group of men, most of whom were boldly staring at her. He folded his arms. He should leave. He wanted her back in his bed, and that was simply unacceptable. Tonight he intended to behave with honor. But maybe he would stay the entire night—just to see which buck thought to make inroads with her.

Ariella, her profile to him, stiffened. He knew she had felt his stare.

Slowly she turned, her expression bewildered. Her face went starkly white. Margery seized her arm. Then her cousin also saw him, and her expression turned incredulous.

Ariella's hand covered her bare décolletage, where her heart obviously raced. Her distress was clear and he did not blame her. He despised himself.

Ariella turned and hurried from the room with her cousin. He saw them slip outside onto an apparent terrace or backyard.

"Do you know Miss de Warenne?" Robert asked blandly.

ARIELLA HURRIED across the dark courtyard, leaning heavily on Margery. She could not breathe. She had spent the past five days trying to forget him, but now he had appeared at the dance—dressed as an Englishman.

"You must sit down!" Margery cried.

Ariella fought for air, her heart pounding, as Margery led her to the edge of a low fountain. Ariella sat gratefully, but she was disbelieving. "What is he doing here?"

Margery sat beside her, putting her arm around her. "I don't know! I will make sure he leaves," she said fiercely.

Ariella felt her heart cracking apart. She covered it again with her hand. "I have tried to forget what happened. I have tried to forget him! I have been determined to be sensible. I have been reading about the Mongols!" she cried.

"I know," Margery whispered.

But Margery didn't know that the words on the written page blurred, and all she saw was Emilian looming over her, his eyes blazing with desire. Or she saw him seated in that chair, staring at her watchfully, distantly, already done with her. Margery could not know that the memories were so vivid, she could almost feel his hands on her and hear his soft voice, encouraging her—or his cold tone, abusing her. She had not been successful at holding the memories at bay. Even worse, the memories of their passion stirred her body, when she did not want any passion, ever again. The memories of his ruthless dismissal continued to hurt her.

She could tell herself a thousand times that they were both at fault and that she was the fool, but the memories were inescapable. She could pretend her heart wasn't broken, but it was a very fragile pretense, indeed.

The stone scraped. Ariella tensed as the door she had come through opened. Emilian stepped onto the flagstone and into the courtyard.

Margery leaped to her feet. "Be gone!"

Ariella fought to breathe as she stood. She was so dizzy. What did he want? Why was he doing this? She had fallen in love. He did not return her feelings, but she might still be in love—as stupid as that was—because her heart was racing. She could not look away as he stood there, moonlight spilling over his perfect face.

"I'd like to speak to Miss de Warenne," he said quietly.

Margery marched forward. "I think not!"

Emilian didn't look at her. He stared at Ariella, his demeanor grim, awaiting her response.

Did he wish to twist the knife of his indifference into her already bleeding heart? Ariella began to shake. "Leave us," she said to her cousin hoarsely.

Margery whirled. "Ariella," she began in protest.

"No, leave us." The anger appeared out of nowhere. It was huge and it stunned her. In the past five days since their affair, she hadn't been angry, not once. Instead, she had done her best to rationalize the hurt away and try to forget the entire affair. But Emilian was not the kind of man a woman could easily forget.

Margery slowly turned to Emilian. "You may not hurt her again," she warned. "I do not like this."

He finally glanced at her. "I only wish a word. Your charge is safe for the moment."

His tone was derisive, but directed, Ariella thought, at himself. She couldn't comprehend why.

Margery walked past Emilian and slipped into the house.

Ariella didn't think. She strode up to him and struck his face as hard as she possibly could. He didn't flinch, but the smack rang out loudly and she gasped, tears of pain instantly arising. She hugged her throbbing wrist to her breast.

"Damn it, you could break your wrist!" He took her wrist in his hands and held it tightly.

She looked up, aware of shaking wildly. Her wrist hurt so badly the tears streamed. "Let go! Don't touch me! I can't bear your touch!" But it wasn't true. His grasp was shocking, yet somehow comforting.

They stood so closely her skirts covered his shoes. She

could see his face clearly, and something flickered in his eyes. He released her and stepped back.

Her words had hurt him. She wasn't normally vindictive and she almost regretted what she had said.

"You need ice on your wrist and it needs to be tightly wrapped." He was firm. "Let me help you…Ariella."

She stared at his face now, acutely aware that he had used her name. He had only called her by her name one time, when he had first pushed his hard body into hers, at the precise moment of their union. Slowly, she looked into his gray eyes, but there was nothing suggestive about the light there.

"I believe you have helped me enough," she said thickly. He had hurt her, used her. She was angry, but she had never been as aware of anyone as she was of him. They must not prolong this encounter, she thought.

He was flushed. "You wrist is probably sprained."

"I don't want to talk about my wrist."

His eyes were bright but impossible to read. "I don't blame you for hating me."

She stared at him. She didn't hate him, but she had no intention of telling him so.

"I am sorry," he said roughly.

She felt the world stop turning. "What?"

"I said, I am sorry. I came here to apologize. I am filled with regret."

She was stunned.

He seemed uncomfortable now. He tugged on his stock, which was already too loose.

She took a breath. It was almost calming. "I don't understand. What has brought this change of heart on?"

"I did not intend to hurt you."

She thought about his skilled lovemaking, and her exuberant responses. She thought about awaking that morning, and being devastated by his coldness. "No. You only intended a pleasurable evening. You only intended for us to enjoy one another physically—and to quickly forget my name."

His face tightened. "Yes. That was a part of it."

Ariella knew she should walk away. His admission hurt, even though it was nothing new. But walking away was impossible. "I have realized how foolish I was. A more experienced woman of a different nature than mine would have enjoyed the encounter and escaped unscathed."

His chest rose and fell. "Yes, that is true. But I knew your nature. I should have refused your offer. Instead, I seduced you. I realize you will not accept my apology, but I am resolved to make it."

She certainly wasn't ready to forgive him. "Was some small kindness the next morning impossible?"

His eyes flashed. "Yes. It was impossible."

She shuddered. "So I have misjudged you. You are cruel, ruthless even."

He did not answer.

Her logical mind turned this development over now. "Yet you have donned an Englishman's clothes and entered an Englishman's home, in order to apologize to me." She could not make sense of him. His efforts to apologize were in utter contradiction to his behavior the morning after their affair.

He spoke slowly. "I have never seduced an innocent, unwed woman before. I have never thought of myself as cruel, yet obviously I am. But I came here tonight to make certain you had recovered somewhat from our encounter and to tender my apologies and regrets, even being certain you would reject them."

She folded her arms. "Your actions indicate you are not entirely ruthless."

"You may think what you wish," he said, appearing angry. "I did not come to argue over my character. I realize you are inclined to think the best of everyone, instead of the worst." He shrugged. "It is a mistake."

Hugging herself, she stared at him and saw only pain and regret in his eyes.

"I did not expect you to accept my apologies." He inclined his head and whirled away.

She seized his elbow from behind, astonishing them both.

He slowly faced her. "What are you doing?"

For one instant, in disbelief, she stared at her small, pale hand on his larger arm. Then she dropped it, inhaling. She did not know what she was doing! "We have all made mistakes," she began.

How could she not accept his regrets? She had thrown herself at him—in spite of his warnings. She had wanted to go to his bed. "Thank you for your apology. It is accepted."

His eyes widened.

She breathed hard. "I am not one to hold grudges."

He choked. "We are not discussing a game of cards or a business affair! I took your *virginity*."

She no longer hesitated. "I have thought long and hard about us. I was the foolish one, to harbor romantic feelings when you warned me this was not about romance. I refused to heed your warnings." She felt herself flush. "I was compelled to go to you."

His eyes locked with hers and she wondered if he really understood what she meant. Nothing could have kept her away from him—and his bed—that night. He said firmly, "The blame is all mine. I know how to look at a woman, Ariella. I am no stranger to pursuit and seduction."

"I am aware that you have seduced dozens of women. I don't want to hear about it."

He hesitated as they searched each other's faces. "It was unfair of me to play someone so innocent and romantic."

"Yes, it was. But you are forgiven anyway," she said thickly.

His eyes flickered. After a thoughtful pause, he said, "The

truth is, your generosity and kindness does not surprise me. Are you ever mean-spirited?"

Were they really conversing without hostility? Without rancor? "I am not petty by nature and I am never mean." She realized her heart was thundering. Where could such a dialogue lead? But, he had dared to come to the Simmonses' ball, simply to apologize to her. She wanted to smile but the smile didn't come, for her heart was too afraid to allow it out. The stakes had been returned to the table, and her heart knew how high they were.

He suddenly added softly, "I saw you dancing with your brother. I was pleased to see you smiling." Then he shrugged. "Clearly, you were not in love with me after all. Your passion was awakened, but not your heart." His regard slid back to hers.

She trembled. He was so wrong, but she would not correct him. Because she was in a whirlwind of emotion, confusion and even hope mesmerized her once again.

Why did he care if she was enjoying herself at the ball?

Did he wish for her to be happy?

She suddenly recalled the way he had urged her to take pleasure from him, time and again, while he waited for her. She turned away, hugging herself. That was different, she told herself. Wasn't it?

So much warmth arose. She did not want or need those memories now, not until she comprehended Emilian exactly.

She felt him staring at her back. The night had shifted. Her anger had vanished, and that left bare the current that always seemed to charge and pulse between them. It was there now, hot, hard and tangible.

She slowly faced him. "Alexi is a good dancer. I always enjoy dancing with him, as he doesn't care if I tread all over his feet."

He smiled. Her heart stopped and then raced wildly.

Instantly his smile vanished. The entire time they had

been speaking, he had stared into her eyes, as if he wished to know her innermost thoughts and feelings. Now, finally, slowly, he looked at her mouth.

Her heart began a slow, thudding, dangerous dance. He looked up, his eyes silver and bright. His magnetism was inescapable—and it was entirely sexual.

What should she do?

A small voice in her head urged her to run.

Her heart simply beat out its new cadence, waiting and patient. *If she continued to converse with him, the heat between them would ignite.*

But she could never withstand the kind of rejection she had already suffered. No matter the heat his proximity generated, she must ignore it—mustn't she?

Recalling his mouth on her throat, his powerful body deep within hers, she said, "You took a chance, coming here."

It was a moment before he responded. "Although I was not invited to this ball, I have been invited to this house many times," he said softly. "I expected a warm welcome."

Confusion reared. "I do not understand."

"It is hardly a secret," he said, his eyes moving now to the lowest point of her bodice. "While my mother was Romni, my father was St Xavier."

She gasped, recalling now his familiarity with Woodland and his utter arrogance in taking her into the house as if it was his. "You are a member of the St Xavier family?" Comprehension dawned—his aura of authority, his impeccable manners and speech. Her attention shot to his hand and she saw the emerald signet ring. "*You* are St Xavier?"

He bowed. "The Viscount St Xavier, at your service."

She gaped at him, her mind racing, trying to make sense of this. "But you appeared to be with the *kumpa'nia.*"

At her use of the Roma word, his eyes gentled and his mouth curved. "Yes, I did. They came for me, to share news. When we met, I had just arrived at their camp."

"I should have guessed—your English is too flawless!"
She walked away, shaken. Her brain was screaming, trying
to tell her something.

Everyone knew St Xavier was odd.

No Gypsies Here.

She whirled to face him.

"What is it?"

She was briefly speechless and she shook her head, trying
to analyze the scrambled data in her mind. All she said was,
"Are you an Englishman, or are you Rom?"

His easy expression vanished. "I see. You wished for a
Gypsy lover and you are sorely disappointed."

She flared. "No, I wished for you to be my lover—and my
love." And she wished she hadn't spoken that last truth. "But
we are now agreed, I confused love and desire."

His lashes dropped, hooding his eyes.

She stared at him, dismissing the painful topic. If one did
not know the facts, one would assume him an English nobleman. But she had seen him dancing beneath the stars, as Rom
as any of them. What did it all mean? "Emilian?" she asked.

He started and looked up.

"Were you raised here?"

"My father needed an heir. He hired runners to find my
mother and brought me to Woodland when I was twelve," he
said matter-of-factly.

Her heart softened like melted butter. "And your mother?"

He gave her a glance. "She was Rom, Ariella. She stayed
with the *kumpa'nia.*"

She paused before him, trying to imagine being a Romany
boy, taken from his mother, his people, to learn a new way
of life, to love a new, foreign family. "Was your father kind?"

His eyes widened. "He did not beat me," he said, "if that
is what you are asking. He treated me fairly and with affection."

She stared into his eyes, which were open and direct, and

neither bold with desire nor hot with anger. It was a rare moment.

He shifted. "Why are you staring? Why are you looking at me as if I were a wounded creature in some cage?"

She knew so little about the Gypsies. *No Gypsies Here.* "It was hard, wasn't it, painful even, to make the adjustment from one life to another?"

"Why are we discussing my childhood?" he asked with annoyance.

"It must have been very much like being a wild creature forced into a cage." She spoke her thoughts slowly, aloud.

Tension caused his entire body to ripple. "It was difficult. I hated Edmund and I hated all the *gadjos,* at first. That was then. This is now."

He had called her *gadji* a dozen times that night, and she had the terrible inkling that it was not an endearment.

"What?" he asked harshly.

"Did you mean to insult me by calling me *gadji?*"

He inhaled. "You are a *gadji,* Ariella, and nothing will ever change that. It is a fact I am acutely aware of—whether we are in bed or not."

"Your answer is no answer at all."

His mouth almost curved. "And what if I tell you that you are the most beautiful *gadji* in the land?"

She had to smile in spite of her humming pulse. "Then I will tell you that you need spectacles." She touched his jaw impulsively.

He stood very still, not pulling away. And in that moment, as the heat filled his eyes, the transition became complete. She had hoped to avoid a deeper intimacy, and any further entanglement, but she felt herself whirling in the dance that could only lead to one place. She had forgiven him and she wished to be friends, but he was too seductive, too virile and too attractive for a simple friendship. And they had a history now.

None of it mattered.

She knew that she should remove her hand from his jaw. He was enjoying her touch too much and she wanted, desperately, to caress far more than his face. She should have walked away from him when he had first stepped outside, but she hadn't. She should drop her hand now, but she did not.

His large chest lifted, lowered. He turned his face very slightly and slid his mouth over her palm. "I never said," he said softly, his every word a warm caress, "that I no longer desired you. It is time for you to go."

It was hard to think when he had just kissed the sensitive flesh in the center of her palm. *I am not immune to this man,* she thought, *and I never will be.* Nor did she want to be. For better or for worse, they were entangled.

She had her beginning, after all.

The door opened. He instantly turned, so that she could barely look past him.

Margery stood there. "Your father is asking where you are, Ariella."

He faced her. "Run now," he murmured, "before it is too late." And his silver eyes gleamed with heat.

She felt herself shake her head. "I am not running away."

"Ariella. I hurt you once. It was enough. I came tonight to apologize, but clearly, I should not have come at all." He breathed hard. "I do not trust myself now."

She smiled. "I trust you."

"A dangerous idea."

She moved past him, paused. "Emilian? In case you haven't realized, I don't hate you—and I never will."

CHAPTER TEN

ALEXI STRODE toward Margery as she stood on the threshold of a back courtyard. She seemed very tense. "Where is my sister?" he asked, instantly aware that some female conspiracy was being formed. He was amused. He had suffered female conspiracies with his sisters and cousins his entire life. However, Cliff had asked him directly to go look after Ariella, so he would tolerate them.

Margery actually stepped in front of him. "Ariella has a migraine. She is coming in, but I daresay she will wish to go home."

Suddenly he was suspicious. "She has been avoiding me all week, when she usually spends her time annoying me with her historical obsessions and her latest political questions. She usually makes my ears ring!" He did not add that she mostly hounded him about Elysse, but she had only brought that painful subject up once this visit. "I have hardly seen her since I arrived. Now she has a migraine? Excuse me." He stepped past his cousin. His sister never had headaches. His sister never failed to attempt to pry into his personal life. Something was bothering her.

Ariella was coming forward. He took one look at her smile, saw her flushed cheeks, and he understood. Real alarm began. He scanned the courtyard but saw no one.

"Will you dance with me again?" She smiled at him.

He took her arm. "You hate dancing. You hate balls. Why are you smiling like that?"

Her smile vanished, then returned. "I do not *hate* dancing. I do not *hate* balls. I usually have better things to do, that is all."

He was perusing the shadows of the courtyard again. He turned to her. "If I did not know better, I would say you have just had a tryst."

Her color increased.

He had been right! He was in absolute disbelief, for his bluestocking sister was the least passionate, least romantic woman he knew.

"You are mad," she said, and she slipped past him, going inside with Margery. He stared after them and watched them put their heads together.

Very intently, he walked into the center of the courtyard. A low stone wall divided it from the lawns behind the house. He saw no one slipping across the lawns.

Maybe he had been wrong. He was relieved. His sister was too intelligent for her own good, and terribly sensible when it came to political matters and social issues, but she had no experience with men. He was hoping that one day, she would fall for a good, kind, honorable man—a marrying man—someone steady and understanding from a good family, perhaps even with some means.

Until that happened, it was his duty to keep the rakes at bay.

ARIELLA SAW her father standing by a column, waiting for her. Emilian had vanished across the lawn, but she did not know if he was leaving the Simmonses', or merely returning to the ball through another entrance. Still, it was hard not to look behind her, just to make certain he was not standing there.

Cliff came over to her. Women looked at him in the hopes of catching his attention as he crossed the room, but he did not seem to notice. "Where have you been?" he asked with concern. "Are you all right?"

She smiled at him. "You know I do not care for balls. I decided to go outside and enjoy the stars."

"I looked for you in the library," he said. "This is the first time that I can recall you slipping away to go outside—you always manage to find some rare volume to read."

Ariella hesitated. "I was looking for the library," she began, when Margery stepped forward.

"I asked her to step outside, Uncle Cliff. I needed her advice on a rather personal matter."

Seemingly satisfied, Cliff smiled and excused himself. Ariella shared a glance with Margery, who sent her an *are you mad?* look. Ariella decided not to defend her actions.

"It is shocking…St Xavier."

Ariella heard the phrase and Emilian's name, disdainfully spoken by a man standing behind her. She turned and saw two men and two ladies huddled together. She hoped she had mistaken the condescension in the speaker's tone.

Margery seized her arm and tried to pull her away. Ariella glared at her and mouthed, *Hush!* She intended to eavesdrop.

"He wasn't invited," a pretty blonde said eagerly. "Lady Simmons told me so herself. She is livid, truly livid, for he has refused every single invitation she has ever sent. Now, he appears uninvited—and he hasn't even said hello to her and Lord Simmons!"

"That's the savage in him, Belle," one man said. "You can dress anyone up, but you cannot teach good manners. You cannot purchase good breeding."

Ariella was aghast.

"I have never seen him before," the redhead said. She was flushed. "Are all Gypsies so stunning?"

The gentlemen stared at her, then the first speaker said coldly, "Letitia, surely you are not considering him for your second husband? Your children will be tainted with Gypsy blood and you will be scorned."

"I heard he will marry Widow Leeds." The other man laughed. "She is close to forty, but she has four healthy sons and claims she can have a few more. That is the best he can do."

"I was not considering him as a suitor," Letitia huffed. "I simply have never seen a Gypsy man before. You must admit, he looks like a Russian prince."

The blonde leaned close. "He is notorious for his affairs, Lettie." They exchanged fascinated looks.

"He has returned. Shall we introduce ourselves? You may not find him so stunning when you hear his accent and realize his well-tailored clothes disguise the lowest class of humanity," the heavy gentleman said with a snort.

Ariella shook with anger. She saw the quartet actually walking toward him, clearly wishing to be amused at his expense. The ladies curtsied and the men smiled broadly, falsely, shaking his hand. Ariella knew it was all an absolute pretense. Did he know they despised him, scorned him— slurred him?

His focus moved past the foursome and found her.

She bit her lip and shook her head, hoping he would understand that they were a treacherous lot. Across the room, she saw him start, as he realized she was trying to communicate with him. From his expression, she saw he did not understand her.

The first speaker, whom she truly abhorred, was now talking to him. Ariella could not stand it. She would not allow those jackals to use Emilian as a form of entertainment. She moved fiercely toward him.

The women were staring raptly at him. She saw that he was indifferent to them. She was even more pleased when he sensed her and turned. His expression became warm and interested as she approached. "Hello, my lord. It is a pleasure to see you here." She ignored the ensemble, curtsying for him alone. She was aware of being rude, but she did not care. She didn't know them and would be damned before being introduced. "May I have a word with you, my lord?"

His smile began, impossibly slow and seductive. "An offer I cannot refuse." He finally glanced at both women and nodded politely. He was dismissive to the men. He stepped aside and they left the hateful group behind, carefully not touching each other.

She stole a glance at his profile. His stance was so stiff and so correct, so set. He held his head with vast pride. He knew they whispered behind his back. Her heart ached for him.

No Gypsies Here.

"What are you doing?" he asked frankly, as they paused by a column.

"Saving you." She smiled.

And for the first time, she saw him smile with amusement. "I hardly need saving."

"I beg to differ—you did need rescuing from them. They were grossly obnoxious," Ariella insisted, her heart filled with sudden happiness. She loved seeing him smile. If only he would smile more often!

"Just as you wished to defend me the first time we met?" he asked.

It took her a moment to recall that incident. "I refuse to condemn anyone without facts," she said firmly.

His tone changed. "Miss de Warenne, it is a pleasure to properly meet." His smile had vanished and he bowed soberly.

She jerked and saw her father approaching. Her pulse skittered. She felt as if they had been caught in a tryst. "Father, there has been an amazing turn of events," she said. Her cheeks had become hot. "The *vaida* we met at Rose Hill is St Xavier."

"I have just realized that," Cliff said, and he did not appear pleased. Suspicion flickered in his eyes. "I believe a proper introduction is in order."

Emilian inclined his head and looked at Cliff with evident disdain. Ariella became alarmed. He did not need to be belligerent now!

But Emilian's smile was arrogant. "The viscount St Xavier. The pleasure is mine...*Captain.*"

Ariella somehow stopped herself from moaning. Emilian had just shoved his title in her father's face. She knew Cliff didn't care about titles, but her father loved a challenge, all the de Warenne men did. Could Emilian not behave properly, for once?

"How odd," Cliff said, "that you failed to make your identity known when you were pretending to be a Gypsy at Rose Hill."

"My mother is a Romni," Emilian returned. "I am half blood. There was no pretense."

"I had heard the gossip about you. I should have made the connection," Cliff said. "I have also heard you never attend social affairs. What brings you to the Simmonses'—or need I even ask?" His gaze never left Emilian's set face.

He guessed a part of the truth, Ariella thought. He sensed that Emilian had come to the ball to see her. She trembled. "Father? You and St Xavier are neighbors. I think it is wonderful that you have finally met. Hopefully this will begin a dear acquaintance."

Both men ignored her. "If you think, for one moment, I will explain myself to you, Captain, you are deluded," Emilian said softly. "I go where I wish, when I wish."

"So you are incapable of a polite response? Of course you are. You believe yourself above the need to explain yourself. I think you are young, hotheaded and overly ready to battle anyone who steps into your path. That is foolish, St Xavier,"

Cliff said tersely. "Ariella, Lord Montgomery wishes a dance." He eyed Emilian. "Good evening."

Ariella wrung her hands at the pointed dismissal, but Emilian flashed his white teeth. It was feral and unpleasant. "Yes, how could I manage such a faux pas as to speak with your daughter? Miss de Warenne is too blue-blooded to withstand my presence."

Cliff had been about to turn; he stiffened. "My daughter is a lady and she deserves a gentleman's attentions, not a scoundrel's. She will only accept suitors with honorable intentions," Cliff shot. "What are your intentions, St Xavier? Can you bother to answer that?"

Emilian did not look bothered. "I happen to agree, de Warenne. Your princess should be pursued by honorable gentlemen. As for my intentions?" He shrugged. "I have none. However, we were merely conversing, and that is not a crime—not even for a Gypsy." His eyes flashed and he walked off.

Ariella trembled wildly, beyond relief that the hostile encounter was over. Then she whirled on Cliff. "He suffers enough as it is! Did you have to attack him that way? Can't you see how they treat him?"

Her father was startled. "I did not attack him, but he needed a warning, Ariella. That man is a rogue—he is arrogant, hotheaded and far too appealing to your gender. Look! Half the ladies in this room are trying to attract him! I am sorry to be so crude, but I have no doubt he will take one of them to his bed tonight—and damn it, it will not be you."

Ariella gasped, flushing. "We were only speaking," she managed, aware of the terrible lie. "Father, have you heard the horrible things they are saying behind his back? They smile to his face and scorn him when he turns away. It is unfair and cruel!"

Cliff's blazing eyes mellowed. "Yes, it is, but damn it, it

is not your concern. He will take advantage of your kind heart. Please, do not think to take on his cause. No good can come of it." He smiled. "I did fabricate that part about Montgomery, but why don't you greet him? Perhaps he will ask you to dance."

"First, I do not want to dance with Montgomery. Second, I don't give a fig about suitors and you know it!" She closed her eyes, and then gave in. "Frankly, I wish to be St Xavier's friend. He is in need of one."

Her father paled. "You are so naive. A man like that does not have female friends. A friendship will lead to one place. In this instance, you must trust my experience."

She stiffened. "Will you now tell me who I am allowed to be friends with?"

He became still. "Of course not."

"Thank you. I am aware of his reputation," she added. It would be so much easier to discuss Emilian if she hadn't already betrayed Cliff's trust. "I will be careful."

"Darling." Amanda appeared at Cliff's side, smiling, but her green eyes were wide with concern. They darted between father and daughter. "How can you be arguing on such a beautiful night? Come dance with me."

"In a moment, Amanda," he replied. "Ariella, please heed this one warning. He doesn't want friendship from you—and I am certain he is dangerous. You will be in over your head."

She shivered. She was already in far more deeply than she had ever imagined. "I promise to be prudent and cautious."

Grimacing, Cliff started away with his wife. Ariella sagged with relief, watching as her stepmother took his hand and tugged him to the dance floor. She hated deceiving her family, but she couldn't regret what had happened.

Feeling his stare, she glanced across the room.

Emilian stood amidst the crowd, yet he was obviously alone and utterly apart from everyone. Their gazes instantly locked. She wanted to tell him that these people were hateful, that her father was only protecting her, and that she was his friend, no matter what, but she didn't dare go over to him.

"Would you care to dance?"

She turned to face a portly, pale blond man, a few years older than herself. It was hard to smile. "I am sorry, I have two left feet. You truly do not wish to dance with me...sir."

He bowed. "To the contrary, Miss de Warenne, it would be an honor to dance with the loveliest lady in the room."

His regard was piercing, but it was not sensual or bold. She was about to insist that she could not dance, and offer up another excuse, when he smiled and said, "How remiss of me. I have not introduced myself. Robert St Xavier." He bowed.

Her pulse sped. Was this Emilian's brother? He was close to Emilian's age, but they did not share any resemblance. She smiled. "I would love to dance—if you will ignore me when I tread upon you." She held out her hand.

He laughed. "It is impossible to ignore a beautiful woman."

He led her onto the floor and she turned into his embrace. She was certain he did not find her very attractive; his words were spoken as if by routine. Bemused, Ariella said, "You dance well, sir."

"As do you." He smiled, studying her closely.

"Do you also reside at Woodland?" Too late, she hoped she had not given anything away.

"I reside in London, Miss de Warenne. My cousin, the viscount, resides at Woodland. As he comes to town so infrequently, I find myself in Derbyshire often. Otherwise, we should lose our close familial affection."

He insisted he was close to Emilian, yet somehow, his words made her want to pause and carefully consider them. She was uncertain—he gave her an odd feeling. "I have just met the viscount. Your cousin is very charming."

Robert laughed. "Yes, all the ladies find him quite gallant, although I have never understood his charm. But he is available and Woodland is a fine estate."

She tensed. "I found him charming, sir, that is all."

"So you know him well?"

"Not at all. We only just met."

Robert smiled, and somehow, the expression was smug.

EMILIAN WAS TIRED of playing games with the *gadjos*. He was already sick of their whispers, but he was oddly reluctant to go. There was one reason—she had, miraculously, forgiven him for what he had done to her. There hadn't been any hysterics or accusations. Instead, she thought to be friends; she had even tried to rescue him from the *gadjos*. It was stunning. He turned to look at her one last time before leaving.

Ariella was in his cousin's arms.

The alarm he felt was quickly replaced by rage. Robert was a scoundrel, a worthless rake. He was his rival. And now he was pursuing Ariella? Did he wish to thwart Emilian as he had tried to do time and again for the past twenty years? It did not truly matter. The dance they were sharing was unacceptable and he would not have it.

As he approached them, images flashed from that night, of her crying out in rapture as he moved within her. The images changed and he could see her being kissed by his cousin. He shook off the horrid fantasy. Ariella was no fool. She would never allow Robert to seduce her. *He* would never allow it.

But Robert was entirely English. He came from old stock, a good name, and he would be an acceptable suitor, just as Emilian would not ever be such a candidate. De Warenne would surely approve of him, at least socially.

That fueled his rage.

He moved, his strides stiff and hard. He saw her polite smile and Robert's affected one. Were they enjoying dancing together? It didn't matter. He would tear them apart.

She started when she saw him. Robert glanced at him blandly, and Emilian knew he relished the moment.

"I am cutting in," he said curtly, taking his cousin's arm and pulling it away from her waist.

Robert released her and stepped aside. "Of course you wish to dance with the most beautiful woman in the room." He bowed gallantly. "Miss de Warenne, another time."

She managed a smile. "Of course."

Emilian seethed, swiftly taking her into his arms. It was hard to think clearly now.

The black mare was the most beautiful horse he had ever seen. It was his thirteenth birthday present, given to him by his father shortly after he had agreed to stay voluntarily at Woodland and explore the opportunities Edmund wished to give him. That first night, he had slept in her stall with her, refusing to come out. He had ridden her every day and the horse had been a great joy in his new and still-frightening life. He had fallen in love with the mare and she had loved him in return. And then Edmund had taken him to London for the day.

When they had returned to Woodland, he had instantly gone to his horse to give her treats. He had found the mare hot and wet and lame, her forelegs swollen, whip marks on her haunches and neck. Robert had taken her and ridden her into the ground....

Near tears, he had meant to kill his cousin but his father had broken them up. The mare had survived and healed and Robert had gotten away with his crime. But that was only the beginning.

Robert had made certain to take whatever he could, if he thought Emilian had wanted it....

"What are you thinking?" Ariella asked. "You look ready to commit murder!"

He heard her and focused, but with difficulty. It took another moment to forget the black mare and Robert's treat-

ment. How often had he heard Robert complaining to his
father that Woodland should belong to him, and not Emilian?

Those complaints had ceased, of course, with Edmund's
death, but Emilian knew he lusted after the estate, the title,
and Emilian's wealth and possessions. Now he lusted after
Ariella.

"Emilian," she cried.

He looked down at her and met her wide, searching blue
eyes. The moment he did so, he became aware that she was
in his embrace.

He held her very closely, the way a man would hold his
lover or his wife, but not a dance partner. He held her as if
it were the other night. He recalled the extent of the passion
that had consumed her, and he thought about the passion that
would consume him if he allowed it. In that moment, he
realized he wanted her even more than he had before arriving
at the ball.

He glanced past her and saw Robert watching them. He
took a breath as he put a proper distance between them. "You
will dance with others, but not with me?" he asked, but he
could not force levity into his tone.

"That isn't fair, Emilian. Of course I will dance with you."

Her eyes had softened. She was so easy to play. She was
too naive and kind for her own good. He had learned how
kind she was that night. De Warenne had every right to
protect her from rogues and scoundrels—he had every right
to protect her from him. He whirled her on the dance floor
and immediately, she tripped. He steadied her and murmured, "Dancing should be easy for you. It is a pleasure,
Ariella." His mood had finally eased.

Her eyes warmed. "It is not easy for me. But I am glad,"
she whispered, "that you insisted we dance."

His hand tightened and he pulled her closer. His own loins
were entirely full now. He let the heavy, hot feeling mesmer-
ize him, just for a moment. Why were they denying the at-

traction that surged between them? He had never been this
tempted by any woman before.

"We are being watched," she said breathlessly.

He reminded himself that she deserved better and he had
already wreaked havoc on her life. She deserved her Prince
Charming, not a *didikoi* viscount. Besides, he was leaving.

He saw Robert then, continuing to stare openly at them.
"Did you enjoy dancing with Robert?"

"No, I did not. Generally I do not like dancing."

"Then I must change that, must I not?"

She smiled and he saw warmth and trust in her face.
"Maybe you already have," she said—and stepped on his
foot.

He thought he heard himself laugh. "Follow my lead…as
you did the other night…and you will dance superbly."

"Emilian," she whispered, and he felt her body melt
against his.

He gave over to the moment and the woman in his arms.
She was soft and she trembled with tension, and so did he.
He murmured, moving his cheek against her hair, thinking
about sharing her bed, "Do you hate dancing now?"

"No."

Their eyes locked again. *It would be so easy to renew the
affair. They both wanted it. She wouldn't look at Robert
twice, not when she was sharing his bed, day in and day out.
He could never let Robert have her. She wasn't innocent
now and she was smiling…she was smiling at him.*

Instantly, he put a distance between them.

"What is wrong?" she asked softly, and he felt her fingers
graze the nape of his neck.

He stared down at her. He must not allow his desire to best
him. She wasn't indifferent or nonchalant. She claimed she
wanted to be friends, and that meant she wanted a part of him
he would never give. She couldn't love him now, not after
his seduction, but the look in her eyes told him she cared

more than she should. She deserved better than a meaningless, carnal affair. She deserved a friend, he realized, if that was what she wished her lover to be. He would hurt her, no matter what she claimed, because he could only give her a night or two.

"Is it Robert? Or did someone else say something?"

He whirled her forward, not wanting to discuss his cousin.

"Do you dislike your cousin?" she probed.

He sighed. A conversation about Robert would be the nail in the coffin of the desire thrumming between them. "I hate him." He halted but tightened his hand on her waist.

"How can you hate your own flesh and blood? You can't mean that!"

"We are not all as fortunate as you, to have kind and caring relations."

"Robert says you are close," she insisted.

He realized they stood in the center of the dancing crowd, and more stares were being directed their way. He pulled her back into the dance, but without any feeling now. He kept her carefully at arm's length. "Stevan, Jaelle, Simcha and my cousins are my family. The *kumpa'nia* is my family. Robert is barely a relation. He is heartless. Stay far from him."

She was the one to halt abruptly. "I have no intention of going near him. But I am sorry you dislike your own cousin so."

"Do not feel pity for me," he warned.

"I do not feel pity for you," she said. "I am sorry you have no emotional connection to your father's family, which must make you feel isolated, indeed."

The dance was a mistake. She was a mistake. He stiffened. "And what would you suggest? That I pretend to care for my cousin? Or better yet, I pretend to be an Englishman?"

She cocked her head at him, "You could have fooled me tonight."

He knew she was teasing, that she wished to defuse the

moment, but he was annoyed. Worse, he felt like crushing her in his arms, and kissing her senseless, until she stopped caring about him. Maybe, if they had an affair she would learn to hate him and then it would be over. "I am afraid it is late and I must go."

"Coward."

He was stunned by the slur.

She stared back very boldly.

"I beg your pardon?"

"You heard me."

"And why, pray tell, do you think me cowardly?"

"Because you are afraid to face the truth about a great many things, perhaps even about me." She flushed, glancing around. "We should finish this discussion aside from the dance floor."

"What's wrong? Do the stares and whispers bother you?" he snapped.

She glared. "Yes, they do, just as they must surely bother you!"

He whirled, intent on leaving her standing there by herself, but that was despicable. He turned back to face her. "I have never met a more annoying woman! My concerns are mine, not yours! Why do you meddle? Oh, wait, of course, how foolish of me. You wish to be my *friend!*"

"I am your friend, no matter how rude you try to be. And you need someone to share your concerns with. That has become glaringly obvious tonight."

He was incredulous.

She smiled. "And, as annoying as I am, you can be insufferable. That is what makes us well suited."

He did not smile back. She was daring to presume upon him, as if they were really friends. He was truly angry, but she was laughing at him. Did she think to have the upper hand? "We are very well suited." He leaned close. "In exactly one place—my bed."

Her smile faded but did not fail entirely.

"Whatever you think you know about me, you are *wrong*."

She stiffened, unsmiling now. Quietly she said, "I know you are not heartless. I know it is a facade. I understand now, after this night, why your bark is so terrible and why you threaten to bite. But you won't bite. Not me, anyway."

"You know nothing." He was livid with her, although he didn't quite know why. He bowed like a courtier. "I am afraid I must end this dance prematurely."

She seized his arm. "I know you are lonely." She released him.

It took him a moment to recover from the accusation. He would not even deign to respond. "Thank you for the dance. Good night."

"You're welcome...Emilian."

Didn't she care about being exposed? He was aware that parts of their conversation had been overheard. Pretending not to hear, forcing himself not to look back, he strode from the dance floor. But all he could think of was the small woman standing behind him on the dance floor, feeling sorry for him. She thought him *lonely*.

But at the door he did look back.

She stood where he had left her, as if a beautiful statue, her face as pale as alabaster. Several gentlemen had come up to her, perhaps to ask her to dance. One of them was Robert. She shook her head—but she was staring only at him.

Her eyes were soft, shining.

In that moment, he knew he must stay as far from her as possible. Her allure—and her faith—were simply too immense. Shaken, he hurried out.

CHAPTER ELEVEN

ARIELLA TENSED as her carriage paused in the circular drive at Woodland. Another carriage, hardly as grand as her own, was also parked before the estate's paneled front doors. Emilian had callers.

It was the afternoon after the ball. No matter how loudly he barked at her, they were friends now—even if it was a strained and odd friendship. Last night, she had seen how desperately he needed her friendship. It was a bit forward to call, but as he would never call on her, she had no choice. She had briefly attempted to come up with an excuse for the visit, but then she had given up trying. She hated pretense.

How did he live the way that he did? She couldn't imagine having so much malicious gossip aimed at his back. Was that why he preferred his Romany relations to his English ones? Was Robert as bad as he thought? She had overheard the gossips mentioning that he had never been to the Simmonses before. Was the gossip why he avoided society?

Ariella's nervousness increased as she was ushered into Woodland's front hall. Last time she'd been at Emilian's home, she had entered from a terrace through the library. She looked carefully around, very curious now. The hall was entirely English, from the ancestral portraits on the walls to the ancient armor standing in one corner of the room. The chairs, placed against the walls, were faded and worn. The tables were centuries' old. Everything in the hall had undoubtedly been in his father's family for years.

She recalled their first two unforgettable meetings, when he had been as exotic and different from an Englishman as a Rom could be.

"Miss de Warenne, please follow me," the butler said, having read her calling card.

Ariella started. "Surely you wish to inform his lordship that I am here first?"

The butler, who was a small, thin man with bright eyes, smiled. "The viscount cannot stand formality, Miss de Warenne. And I am certain he will be pleased by your call."

Ariella grinned. The servant was unusually garrulous. "My good man, *I* am certain he will be in a snarl when he sees me."

"We shall see, won't we?"

Ariella followed him into a corridor, glancing at a central staircase that swept upstairs. "What is your name?"

"It is Hoode, Miss de Warenne."

"Have you known the viscount for many years?"

"I was employed by the previous viscount when his lordship first came to Woodland as a boy."

Ariella took his arm. "Hoode, I am intrigued!"

He stared at her, surprised by her enthusiasm.

She flushed. "He told me he was twelve years old when his father brought him here. I am aware that he spent the first years of his life living with his Romni mother. I am so curious about his life." She knew she was entirely transparent.

"The viscount is not a loquacious man," Hoode said, eyebrows furrowed. "I am surprised he would reveal so much," he added. "Although perhaps I am not surprised at all."

Ariella didn't comprehend that, but she knew this was an opportunity she must grasp. "What was the previous viscount like?"

Hoode smiled. "He was a proud and honorable man— very much like his son. However, unlike the current viscount, he was not adept at managing the estate, and he left it in a state of ruin. Matters continued to worsen. It wasn't until the present viscount came home from Oxford that Woodland was revived from its state of disrepair and indebtedness."

He had gone to Oxford and he had salvaged the estate. She was astonished by the former and impressed by the latter.

"Edmund St Xavier was still alive, but he let young Emil have a free hand with the accounts, the tenants, the repairs and the debt. Emil quickly realized the value of coal, and there is abundance here. All matters were quickly put in order."

"He must have been very conscientious," Ariella said slowly. "To turn this estate around, at such a young age—and so quickly."

"The viscount does little else other than attend to the estate," Hoode said. "I was shocked that he chose to go out last night."

Ariella glanced aside, a small thrill unfurling.

"May I assume he wished to make your acquaintance at the ball?"

She smiled at him. "You are bold, Hoode. But we did dance." She blushed anew. "However, we met earlier."

Hoode seemed pleased. "Ah, so he went to the ball to pursue you."

She did not respond to that, but asked, "He was a good student, wasn't he?" She had not a doubt that his intellect was outstanding.

"The viscount graduated with the highest possible honors."

She tried to hide a smile and failed. Emilian was highly educated and very responsible. She was thrilled. Then she sobered. He thought her the avid reader of romance novels. She had lied because very few men would find an intellectual woman attractive. But Emilian was different from every man she knew. Hopefully, he would not hold her unusual education against her. She would have to tell him the truth—soon.

"Do you wish to go inside?" Hoode nodded at the closed door.

She wanted to know more, but she wanted to see Emilian, too. Although it had only been a few hours since she had last seen him, it felt like days, even weeks. "I will go in." Then she grasped Hoode's arm. "How irascible is he today?"

Hoode chuckled. "Foul, my young lady, his temper is foul."

She thought about their parting argument. She couldn't be certain if that was the cause for his mood, or if it was the terrible tension that had been between them during the ball. She nodded and Hoode opened the door.

Emilian was as elegant as he had been last night. He wore a dark, custom-cut frock coat and tan trousers, white shirt and stock, and his arms were folded across his chest. But his face was set with resignation as he listened to two matrons and their daughters. They were seated before him and chattering away, going on and on about the fine Derbyshire weather. Ariella instantly saw that Emilian was miserable.

A true boor would have booted them out. Instead, he was trying to politely smile and nod, but his lips were pursed together rather grimly, and his head was oddly bobbing.

"Tell his lordship about our May Day picnic, Emily, dear," the matron, dressed in pink-striped satin, was saying.

A tall, thin, blond girl looked up, her cheeks turning red. She was perhaps eighteen. "It was very pleasant, my lord." Before she'd finished mumbling, she looked down at her hands, clasped in her lap.

Emilian grimaced.

"It was a perfect day for a picnic," her mother cried enthusiastically. "The Farrows, the Chathams, the Golds and of course, my dear friend, Mrs. Harris and Mr. Harris were all there! You should have joined us, as we are all neighbors."

Emilian smiled tightly. "I believe I was out of town."

Ariella realized she was becoming indignant. Emily was

not nearly clever enough for Emilian. She now looked at the other debutante. She was a plump, overly voluptuous brunette, seated by the other matron. She was staring at a plate of cookies as if smitten by them. Her mother patted her plump thigh. "Lydia made the tart. The apple tart was exceptional, was it not, Cynthia?"

Any alarm Ariella might have over their pursuit of Emilian vanished. There was only outrage. Emilian deserved the princess he talked about, a woman of pride and courage and intellect, someone absolutely outstanding—as outstanding as he. These women were too shy, too plain and too ordinary for him.

Emilian saw Ariella and his eyes widened.

"My lord, Miss de Warenne," said Hoode.

He flushed, his embarrassment obvious. "Miss de Warenne," he said stiffly. "Please, join the merry crowd."

Both matrons were on their feet, crying out in delight while greeting her. Ariella vaguely recalled seeing them the night before. She hurt for him once again, even if the wounds being inflicted were so slight. But it was shameful to try to match him up with such ordinary women. She sent him a look. He stared back at her grimly.

"Miss de Warenne, how lovely to see you again!"

She managed a smile as she went inside. They hadn't been introduced and she did not know their names.

Emilian tugged at his stock. "Hoode, more refreshments, please." He seemed to be strangling.

"I am Lady Deane and this is my dear friend, Mrs. Harris. Emily, come meet Miss de Warenne. Lydia, do not take another sweet! Come here!"

Ariella greeted both women and their daughters. The blonde seemed incapable of speech, and the brunette had chocolate on her dress and the corner of her mouth. "I do hope I am not intruding. I was hoping to discuss some matters with the viscount. I am breeding a prized mare to one of his stallions." The lie had instantly formed. Emilian now stood by the French doors, staring yearningly outside. In that moment, he looked like a young boy caught in the schoolroom, wishing desperately to be allowed to go out and play. He glanced at her with some surprise.

"Oh, this is so delightful. We had so hoped to meet you. You reside in London, is that true?" Mrs. Harris cried.

Ariella responded, noting that the brunette had taken a cookie anyway and the blonde was simply twiddling her thumbs. She smiled at the latter. "Did you enjoy the ball last night, Miss Deane?"

Emily Deane looked at her as if she had spoken Chinese. Then she flushed scarlet and mumbled a reply, casting her eyes down. Ariella had no clue as to what she had said and she heard Emilian sigh.

"Emily loves balls," her mother said. "She has been to fourteen this year alone. I so admired your dress, Miss de Warenne! You must give me the name of your seamstress, and I shall use her for the next season. It is a Parisian couturier, is it not?"

"I have no idea," Ariella said.

Emilian met her gaze and his face finally softened.

She sent him a warm smile. *I am so sorry,* she thought. *How awkward this must be for you!*

He turned away.

"Oh, dear, it is half past one and we have two more calls to make. The girls must get out, you know! Emily, take your leave of his lordship. You, too, Lydia."

A moment later, the quartet was gone. Ariella watched as Emilian tore off his stock, shrugged off his handsome frock coat and went to the console, pouring a brandy. He was red faced. He drained half the glass.

"Was it that bad?" she asked, coming up to stand behind him.

He finished the glass. "Good God!" he exploded, facing

her, "I go to one damned affair and I must entertain chatter-boxes and dimwits!"

"You were exceedingly polite," she said, trying to keep a straight face.

He glared at her. "Why are you amused? Are you pleased to see me set down?"

Her light mood vanished. "Absolutely not. Those debutantes were inappropriate for you. They should be cast upon your cousin, perhaps. You deserve a princess." She managed to glance aside. He had called her a *gadji* princess several times.

He folded his arms across his silver brocade waistcoat and stared. She had not a doubt he was thinking about her choice of words.

"Your behavior was exceptionally correct. How long did they linger?"

"Too long," he snapped.

"You could have made an excuse."

"I was about to do so when you walked in. I doubt they were here for more than twenty minutes—which is twenty-one minutes too long."

"Bark away—I am becoming quite accustomed to it."

His smile formed, and it was dangerous. "I am in an exceedingly poor temper."

That was becoming obvious. "But you were so valiant, and trying so hard to be a perfect gentleman. Surely I have not set you off?"

His mouth curled. "I will take the hook. You always set me off." He turned his back on her and poured another drink.

She debated objecting and decided not to interfere. She doubted he drank this way every day. "You are never so polite with me. Is that why?"

He whirled. "You are not stupid, and I had no desire to bed either one of them!"

She went still. "So you are rude to me because of some impossible attraction?"

He gave her a long, hard look. "It is very annoying," he said slowly, "to still want you, yet to have decided, at all costs, to behave with English honor. In fact, I grow increasingly tired of the mere concept of honor. I am tired of all games and all pretenses, yet you come here."

"My calling isn't a game or a pretense. I know you will bark and growl, but we found a new ground last night." She hesitated.

He didn't smile. "So that is what this is? A new ground?"

His silver eyes were gleaming, and only partly with suspicion. She said, "I am pursuing our friendship."

He laughed. "Our friendship…or me?"

She felt her heart explode. "I am pursuing our friendship, Emilian." She tried to be firm and not think about their love affair. "Last night changed everything for me."

"Oh, yes, of course it did. You have decided I am lonely!" His eyes blazed.

"You are so irascible today! You stood alone at that ball, with no friends and gossips behind your back. It was horrid! Why would you resist my offer of friendship? You need me!"

He pointed at the couch. "Yes, I do need you—there. That is where we will go, and that has nothing to do with friendship. I hurt you once, and I am very close to not caring if I hurt you again."

She trembled. "But you do care. Otherwise you would take me in your arms right now. I feel an impossible attraction, too. I know you know it. I don't think I could resist you for very long if you decided to seduce me—especially after last night."

"Do you have to be so direct, so candid? I don't want to know how you feel, not about me!"

Her heart was thundering. She had never felt more tension

coming from him, so potent and so male. She wet her lips. "But I *have* thought about it—about us—all night."

He inhaled.

"We have begun a friendship, and that leads to all kinds of wonderful possibilities." His eyes widened. "When I next share your bed, it will be when I am certain that the following morning will be filled with kindness and smiles, perhaps even affection and laughter." She smiled but she trembled nervously. She had never meant her words more.

"The next time you share my bed," he repeated.

She tensed. "I believe it inevitable."

"You are aware, are you not, that you are waving a red flag at me?" He started toward her.

She backed up instinctively. "That is not my intention! At least, not consciously!"

"I am glad you realize the inevitability of our next encounter. I give in. I give up." He paused as her back hit the bookcase.

"You do? What does that mean?" It had become difficult to think clearly.

His smile began. He looked at her mouth. "It means I am past all temptation. I want you as a lover. Not tomorrow or the day after that. And we both know that you want me, too."

Her eyes widened and her heart thundered. He was right. The problem was, in spite of her best intentions, he was impossibly seductive and, after last night, she wasn't all that certain she wished to entirely resist him, even though she knew she should.

He laid one hand above her shoulder, on the bookcase. "I want to make love to you repeatedly. But I do not want to hurt you and I will not utter false declarations."

"I do not want false declarations," she said.

His face hardened. "I think you want some deep affection from me. I even wonder if, somehow, you are still in love with me, or believe that you are. You will be hurt by any lack of affection on my part, so I will be blunt. I want to take you to bed. But there will be nothing more—not even friendship," he warned. "And I am *not* lonely."

Ariella knew one thing—the last statement was a lie. He was the loneliest man she had ever met. Because of that, she had never been more resolved to be his friend through thick and thin. He was somehow hers, no matter what he said. He had hurt her terribly, but they were on new ground now. She wasn't all that convinced that he would be cold and indifferent the next morning if she did accept his offer.

She breathed hard, very, very tempted. "I am not insulted by your proposition."

His face tensed. "I am not trying to insult you."

"I know you're not. However, I do think we should allow our friendship to blossom. Therefore, as difficult as it is, I must decline." She bit her lip, her pulse exploding. In truth, she almost regretted her determination.

His eyes flickered. "I thought you would."

He had deliberately maneuvered her into a refusal. "You are so clever, Emilian," she said. "But I am not giving up on our friendship." She added, "I look forward to the day when you admit to some small affection for me."

He flushed. "It is not affection, it is interest."

Ariella smiled. "Very well. Today I can accept a declaration of interest."

"Are you laughing at me?" And then his other hand came up on the bookcase on the other side of her head, trapping her.

She knew he was thinking about kissing her and she nodded at him. A kiss was acceptable. She would so enjoy a kiss...or two.

His mouth covered hers.

She gasped, thrilled. The onslaught was fierce and determined. He was as hungry for this kiss as she was. And then his mouth softened and stilled against hers. Her heart hammering, their lips pressed against each other, she waited desperately. And then his lips moved over hers again, brushing and gentle, seductive and sensual. She knew there was affection in his kiss. She could not be mistaken.

A tear of joy welled, but it was overshadowed now by the wet heat of desire. She opened and his tongue filled her instantly. She reached for his shoulders, desire exploding like fireworks in her breast. Briefly, he pulled back and looked at her, and in spite of the heat, there was something gentle in his searching gaze.

She cupped his rough jaw. "Emilian," she whispered hoarsely.

His gray eyes blazed silver and he leaned his hard, stiff body against hers, claiming her mouth. More tears fell. She kissed him back frantically. His loins felt so full against her that she began to think of the obvious conclusion to their kiss. In spite of her resolve, she wanted to be in his arms, in his bed, his world. Nothing else would do; nothing else could be as right.

He tore his mouth away, panting. "You need to leave—or we need to find a bedroom."

She stared, trembling. She knew what would happen if they left the library. He was going to make love to her. There would be tender looks and caresses and so much wild passion. But then he was going to push her away. It was all tangled up in his denial of any need for love and friendship. She was beginning to understand him now. She could *almost* manage such a rejection, but she would be hurt, even understanding how complicated he was. As tempted as she was, she had to deny their passion—for now.

She touched his cheek. "I care for you, Emilian, and I will fight for this friendship. I will fight for you, too, against all those hateful *gadjos.*"

His gray eyes were watchful, wary.

"And when we go to bed again, the next morning you are

going to tell me that you care." She wanted to smile but couldn't.

He pushed himself away from the bookcase. "I hope you are not counting on that."

Ariella decided not to tell him that she was very hopeful. She smiled at him. His gaze narrowed.

A knock sounded on the door. Ariella turned as Hoode showed Emilian's uncle in.

"Stevan?" Emilian asked sharply. From his tone, she knew something was wrong at the Romany camp.

"I was hoping you had some laudanum, Emilian. We have none and there has been an accident."

Ariella stepped forward as Emilian said, "Yes, I do have laudanum. What happened?"

"Nicu fell on a nail. I have to take it out, but he is in some pain and whiskey is not enough."

Ariella seized Emilian's sleeve. "We should summon the surgeon."

He gave her a dismissive look. "He won't come. I'd like to look at the wound. I'll get the laudanum." He left the library with his uncle.

For one moment, Ariella stared after them, hoping the nail was not old and rusty. The accident did not sound life threatening itself, but an infection certainly was. Then she hurried into the hall. "Hoode?"

He appeared instantly. "Miss de Warenne?"

"Will you please send a reliable servant to Kenilworth in search of the surgeon? Use my carriage and tell him that Miss de Warenne has sent for him. And tell him he should rush—it might be an emergency."

Hoode nodded and hurried off.

Ariella hoped that it was not serious. She didn't even know if there was a good surgeon in Kenilworth, and Manchester was several hours away. Then she lifted her skirts and hurried from the house to the Romany encampment.

ARIELLA SAT on the damp grass, her back against the wheel of one of the Romany wagons. She hugged her knees to her chest. The surgeon hadn't come.

She was disbelieving that the village surgeon had refused to attend the Romany boy. Nicu was inside a tent, sleeping off the laudanum. Stevan had removed a nail from his hand and sewn up the wound—Jaelle had told her that Stevan had been tending to his people as if a surgeon for most of his adult life. No one had expected the surgeon to come. No one had even thought to call for a surgeon, except for her.

She laid her face on her knees.

A shadow fell over her.

Ariella knew it was Emilian before she even looked up. "How is he?"

"He's comfortable now."

She hugged her knees more tightly to her chest. Emilian's face was expressionless. Surely he was dismayed and enraged with the surgeon. Or was he so accustomed to such treatment that he no longer cared about the injustice?

"It must be close to five. You did not have to stay. You should go home now." He held out his hand.

Ariella took it and stood. She didn't release his hand. "I would like a brandy," she said unsteadily.

She had no desire to go home, not now. She wanted to talk about what had happened. She wanted Emilian to explain how he could live with such bigotry.

He headed for the house. Ariella let him go but walked beside him in a tense silence, acutely aware of him. "Do you know Nicu well?"

"Not at all." He ushered her ahead of him and they stepped into the front hall. "But Jaelle is distraught. They are the same age, and they are more like brother and sister."

"I am so sorry."

His serious regard met hers. "I did not doubt it for a moment."

A silence fell, huge and potent, and their stares remained locked.

Hoode materialized. "My lord, what may I serve you and Miss de Warenne?"

Emilian looked at her. Ariella shook her head. He said, "We are fine, Hoode. You may tell my chef I doubt I will be eating supper tonight."

"I will have a tray left out, sir," Hoode said.

Ariella hugged herself as she followed Emilian into the library. So he was upset, after all. She paused before the hearth, grateful someone had lit the fire, as she was chilled to her very soul. His back to her, Emilian poured two brandies.

"Hoode is a fine servant."

"Yes, he is." Emilian approached and handed her a glass. "Most ladies do not enjoy brandy."

She smiled slightly. "I have been drinking brandy with my father for years." His eyebrows lifted slightly. "We sometimes stay up late after supper, discussing the latest successes and failures of men like Owens, Shaftesbury and Place, or the characters of those who manage our government, or even the latest developments in India." She paused. "I am so sorry that the surgeon did not come."

He made a harsh sound. "I knew he wouldn't." He turned away and she saw his body ripple with tension. "It doesn't matter. Stevan is probably far more skilled with a knife and needle than a village surgeon."

She breathed hard, staring at his set back. "It matters."

"It doesn't matter," he said, and suddenly he threw his drink furiously at the wall. The glass shattered. Brandy streaked the fine green-and-gold fabric that covered the wall.

She closed her eyes, hurting for him—hurting for them all.

He kept his back to her. "I am sorry. Please go, Ariella. I cannot entertain tonight."

He could claim he didn't care about the surgeon's hateful

refusal to attend Nicu, but he did. How did he manage to live like this, with one foot in two disparate worlds? She didn't think twice. Putting her drink down, she walked up to stand behind him. She wrapped her arms around him and laid her cheek on his back.

He stiffened. "What are you doing?"

She hugged him for one more moment, allowing the tears to finally fall. Then she stepped back.

He turned, eyes wide, and his expression hardened. "You are making a mistake, Ariella," he warned. "I am not feeling noble—or English—now."

"No," she shook her head. "I am not." She took his hand. "I cannot leave you now, like this."

His gray gaze blazed.

She said, "I have changed my mind, Emilian. I want to be your lover."

CHAPTER TWELVE

HE SHOOK HIS HEAD. "I do not want your pity, Ariella."

She touched his face again. "I do not pity you. I am filled with compassion."

He breathed deeply. "Come back tomorrow, or the following day, when you have come to your senses—and when I have returned to mine. But you do not want my attentions now."

She tensed but stood her ground. "I can comfort you," she whispered. "I want to comfort you, Emilian."

"I hardly need comfort!" he exclaimed. He turned and walked across the room. She stiffened, thinking he meant to leave, but at the door he paused, holding it wide for her. "Good night."

She did not move. She would not leave him alone, not after what had happened.

And he slammed it closed, so hard the door shuddered. He faced her, eyes hard and hot. "You are one of them," he warned. "And I do not feel particularly *friendly*."

She almost cringed. "No! That is unfair. I am not a Romany woman, but I am as different from those *gadjos* as you are! I am on your side, Emilian."

"Very well, you are different. But there will be no extra affection, and no damned friendship! Why would you even think to stay with me now?"

"Because I can't bear seeing you like this…because I have begun to understand your life."

"You understand nothing!"

"I understand your anger. I am angry, too," she said.

"Of course you are, because you are so damned kind!" Frustration erupted on his face. "You are too good for this."

She recalled him standing in misery with his afternoon callers, just a few hours ago, his appearance that of an English gentleman. She remembered him at the ball last night in his tuxedo, standing within the crowd yet so apart from everyone. She saw Nicu lying in the tent, being attended by Stevan, Emilian hovering over them. She saw Jaelle as she fled the White Stag Inn, her face filled with fear. And she saw him as he had danced fiercely beneath the stars, so passionately Rom.

He was a man torn between two very different worlds. In spite of that, he had salvaged Woodland from ruin, had received the highest education, and chose to comport himself with dignity and honor in the face of bigotry. But he suffered every single day of his life, in one way or another. This day was just one of many filled with fear, hatred and scorn.

She started toward him. His eyes widened and he went still. She paused and laid her hands on his shoulders. "I am not too good for this," she whispered. "I am not too good for you."

Beneath her hands, she felt him shudder. "This is not a good idea," he said roughly. "I am very angry. You will be badly hurt if we go forward now."

She stood on tiptoe and leaned into him, feathering her mouth against his. "It will be all right," she breathed.

Instantly he pressed her impossibly closer, holding her tightly. "You are not the one I wish to hurt," he said hoarsely. "Yet you are the one in my path."

"I know. I want to be in your path."

"Do you really mean it?"

She nodded.

His thick lashes lowered. She thought she saw relief

etched on the high planes of his face. His hands closed on her shoulders. "Then I accept *your* offer," he said thickly. "Even though we will both regret it."

Before she could protest, he brushed his cheek against hers, slowly, sensually, his big body trembling. Instantly her blood heated.

"Ariella." As if afraid to let her go, he lowered his face, his eyes closed, seeking her mouth. Ariella went still as he brushed his mouth across hers. Pleasure sparked deep within the core of her body and swelled her flesh as she gripped him. She allowed her eyes to close and he prodded her lips, asking her to admit him. She did.

He made a choked sound, harsh and almost soblike, and crushed her frantically in his arms. His mouth tore at hers, frenzied, and he whirled her closer to the couch. The explosion of desire blended with anger and frustration stunned her, but she wished to be trapped in that whirlwind of emotion with him. Before she could think further, he pushed her down, moving on top of her, fusing their mouths.

She kissed him wildly back, sliding her hands beneath his shirt, her nails scraping across his chest. He grunted, his rock-hard thighs pressing hers apart. He reached for her skirts, jerking them up, and Ariella cried out as he palmed her wet, throbbing flesh.

His kiss became deeper and more frantic. She clung, faint with her impending climax. He began a slow and heated entry.

Slick friction began, escalated. The pleasure ignited and she threw her arms around his neck to hold on tight while she sought a wonderful release. He broke the kiss, gasping with the same pleasure, and she felt him smile as he paused deep within her. He lifted his head.

She was about to implode. But she saw so much desire, and so much anguish, too.

His lashes fell and he moved. She could not withstand the growing pressure now. *"Emilian."*

He reached between them as he moved, a single, perfect caress. She gasped, spinning into a thousand rapturous pieces. He made a harsh sound, holding her legs tightly to his waist now. She wept.

He gasped and cried out, straining above her.

When it was over, she floated, dreamlike, in his arms. *Emilian had made love to her.* She opened her eyes, love filling her chest. He was staring closely at her. She touched his cheek and smiled at him. *They were lovers now.*

He did not smile back. His lashes lowered again in that habitual way he had, a means of hiding his feelings from her. She so disliked it.

She became aware of their surroundings. They were on the uncomfortably small sofa in the library. A servant could interrupt them at any time. In fact, if someone had come in a moment ago, neither one of them would have even noticed. She entertained the terrible thought, but there was no denying how wonderful being with Emilian was. She stroked his back through his shirt. Now she felt as if she were resting on a cloud of love. There were no regrets. He tensed beneath her hand, and within her, he stirred.

And because she knew how insatiable he was and how much stamina he had, she expected him to begin making love to her all over again. But they should probably steal away to a bedroom. Discovery was too dangerous.

"Do you feel better now?" she murmured, teasing him, her fingers in the long hair that just reached his shoulders.

He shifted away from her and sat up. "Yes."

Instantly, she reached for her skirts and curled her legs beneath them. She touched his arm, concerned. His tone had been remote.

He sent her a rather grim look. "It is half-past five."

She was dismayed. What was she thinking? She could

hardly linger with him this way in the late afternoon as if a courtesan. She was expected at home. There was no time for smiles, laughter and affection.

"If you leave immediately, you will be at Rose Hill in time for supper."

Ariella started. Emilian was avoiding looking at her. She reminded herself that they were on a distinctly charted path now. They were not strangers, as they had been before. He hadn't used her. She had chosen to comfort him in a very timeless way.

"We are lovers now," she said, but she heard the question in her tone.

He stood, turning away, and adjusted his clothing. "Do you wish to openly carry on?" he asked as if discussing the weather. He still refused to look at her.

She tensed. "Of course not. My family would be devastated. My father, Alexi, and numerous uncles and cousins would likely attempt to murder you." She stood, truly alarmed. "Why would you suggest such a thing?"

"I was making a point. If you linger, we will be discovered. Discretion is the better part of valor, don't you think?"

She tried to comprehend his meaning.

He started for the door. "You need to repair your hair before you step out of this room. I will send a maid with a brush and mirror and give you a moment."

He was withdrawing from her. There could not be any other possible explanation for his cool and distant behavior. "Wait," she cried.

He hesitated but faced her.

"I hate it when you place a waxlike mask of absolute indifference on your face!" she exclaimed. "Please, don't do this."

He folded his arms. "You have to go home. I am going to check on Nicu."

She had almost forgotten the young man lying hurt in the encampment. "I'll wait. I want to know how he is faring."

"You cannot wait," he said calmly. "You are expected at home."

She breathed. "Are you pushing me away?"

"Why would I do that?" he asked, his tone mocking and angry. "Why would I push away my beautiful *gadji* lover? Am I a fool? We have decided on an affair. An unusual one, but nevertheless, it is an affair. Affairs are rather sordid—not that you could know."

Leaving like this, after a few moments on his couch, was beyond sordid. A small kindness would take some of the bitter aftermath away, but he had warned her that there would be no affection. She had wished to go forward anyway. Once again, she simply hadn't believed him. The man standing in the midst of the room—her lover—was not displaying one iota of affection. Didn't he care?

"You deserve far more than a brief coupling on my sofa," he said flatly, "and we both know it." He went to the door and paused. "I am staying below at the camp, but I'll send someone up with word of Nicu, if that will ease your mind."

She hugged herself.

He glanced warily at her. "Will you come back?"

She hesitated.

"I thought so. You do not have the licentious nature requisite for a casual affair."

There was nothing casual about the affair for her; how could it be casual for him?

"We should have left things the way they were last night," he said. He reached for the door and added, "I don't hold your wish to end this against you."

She stared as he walked out.

WHAT HAD SHE BEEN THINKING?

It was the day after Nicu's accident; the day after she had

tried to comfort Emilian in Woodland's library. Ariella stared out of her carriage window, seated beside her cousin. A small sign hung in front of a barber shop: James Stone, Barber and Surgeon.

"Why are we stopping here?" Margery asked. "For that matter, why have we come to town if we are not shopping or taking tea?"

Ariella didn't move, only vaguely hearing her cousin. She felt ill, thinking not of Nicu or the surgeon but of Emilian, when he had left her alone in the library yesterday after their liaison. Being with him hadn't felt sordid at the time, but it felt sordid now, looking back, even if she loved him.

It was too late, but she realized he had been right again. They should have left things as they'd been the night of the Simmonses' ball. She should have stayed out of his arms, pursuing only a friendship with him. She was not the kind of woman to call on him at Woodland in order to spend an hour or so in his bed. She wasn't cut out for an unattached, sensual affair. She simply couldn't do so, not when she cared so much. She had assumed that the intimacy that had begun at the ball would continue and deepen, but he did not want intimacy. That had become so clear.

And she was hurt all over again.

"What do you want with the surgeon?" Margery touched her.

Ariella inhaled. "There was an accident yesterday at the Romany encampment."

"It was all you spoke of when you came in late for supper yesterday. You were as distressed then as you are now. But I do not think you are grieving for a young Romany stranger."

She tensed. "Did I mention that the surgeon refused to come?"

"A dozen times." Margery's stare was searching. "And when your father offered to take you with him to London, you refused. We all know you love town and languish of boredom in the country. The Ariella of old would have jumped at the chance to leave Rose Hill for a few days. What is wrong with you? And what do you want with the surgeon?"

"I have a few choice words for him," Ariella said, reaching for the door. She paused. "Does everyone think I am behaving oddly?"

"Yes, everyone does. When you retired early, you were the object of vast speculation."

Ariella stared in dismay.

Margery seized her hand. "I do not think that you spent the afternoon with that girl, Jaelle, in their camp. I think you went to Woodland to see St Xavier."

"Does everyone think that?"

"I don't know. But Dianna mentioned how handsome the two of you looked dancing and your father abruptly left the room. I think he went to brood on the matter."

Ariella realized it was a fortunate turn that Cliff had gone to town with Alexi to take care of some business affairs. She did not want Emilian clashing with him again.

"He has hurt you again, hasn't he?" Margery accused. "Why else would you be behaving so morosely?"

"I went to see him yesterday."

"What are you thinking?" Margery cried.

"I am still in love with him—more so than ever, now that I understand the life he lives."

Margery seemed ready to cry. "I have never met anyone as smooth and charming, when he wishes to be. It must have been so easy for him to seduce you. You are the most trusting person I know. You may be well-read, but you have no experience with men! I know you have made up an incredible story about him, one you believe, but I have grave doubts about his character!" She was incredulous. "What kind of man takes a gentlewoman's innocence and simply walks away?"

Ariella tensed. "He is so deeply wounded, Margery. He

is like a wild animal, forced into a cage. Of course, when you reach inside to give the animal affection, it bites. It simply doesn't know better. It is expecting cruelty and abuse. Please, do not condemn him."

"You are mad! The man is wealthy and powerful. Even if they whisper about his heritage, so what? That doesn't give him the right to toy with you. And this analogy to a wild animal in a cage? Do you think to win his love by being kind and sharing his bed? You are sharing his bed, aren't you?"

Ariella had never seen her usually placid cousin so fiercely aroused and angry. She hesitated and Margery cried out, realizing the truth. "So you would settle for crumbs! I have half a mind to urge your father to force St Xavier to the altar!"

Ariella gripped her hand. "Do not think to make this right. Forcing him to marry me will accomplish nothing. I would only marry him if he loved me in return."

"Can I convince you to stay away from him before you are ruined in name, as well as spirit and body?" Margery asked.

Ariella faced her. "He needs me. I cannot turn away from him, now or ever."

"You are too good for him!" Margery cried, flushed.

Ariella did not want to argue any further. "I trust you to keep my secrets." When Margery didn't answer, she opened the carriage door and stepped outside, staring at the door to the barbershop. She could see through the storefront window that Stone had no customers.

Aware of Margery coming to stand beside her, she entered the surgeon's, the doorbells jingling. Stone, a tall stout man, came out from a back room, smiling obsequiously at them both.

Ariella did not smile back. "Mr. Stone, I required your services at Woodland yesterday but you sent my coachman back, refusing to come."

His eyes widened. "Miss de Warenne, I was busy with a patient. Your coachman apparently did not explain correctly."

"Jackson was very clear," Ariella trembled with anger. "You refused to come. I believe your exact words were that you would not treat a lice-ridden Gypsy."

He stared at her, no longer smiling. "I don't treat Gypsies, Miss de Warenne, just like I don't treat Jews or Africans."

She inhaled. "You are despicable."

He shrugged. "I have been to Rose Hill several times, miss, and I have always admired your father greatly. Go home, where you belong. And when you need my services at Rose Hill, I will gladly come."

"Your services will never be required by my family ever again!" Ariella cried.

Margery seized her arm. "We should go."

"No! My mother was a Jewess, Mr. Stone. You have insulted not just me, but my father, as well."

"No wonder you're a Gypsy lover," he spat.

Margery stepped forward, between them. "You will pay for that remark!" She pulled Ariella from the shop, ashen. Outside, they stared at each other, horrified. Ariella could not recall every being spoken to in such a way.

Ariella breathed hard. "That is what Emilian lives with every single day of his life."

THE MOMENT HE SAW the de Warenne seal, he knew the letter was from Ariella.

A tension he had never before experienced filled him as he slit the envelope. He was seated at his desk in the library, his hands shaking slightly. After their last encounter, she hadn't come back to Woodland. He had not been surprised.

Three days had passed since their tryst—three endless days in which he had roamed his home, filled with regret and guilt, torment and concern. He had been very busy with his business affairs in preparation for his departure, but she remained on his mind, impossibly. He had been resolved to deny his interest, attraction and desire. He knew such denial was best for her, yet in the end, he had so quickly succumbed to passion. Each and every day since the affair, he had wondered if she would ever call again, his insides churning with his tension. It was best that she did not come; it was best that she hated him now. But Ariella was so entirely unpredictable.

He was sorry he could not be someone else, a proper suitor, the kind of nobleman who could give her the friendship she craved. He was sorry he had been so aloof after their encounter, but what did she expect? The guilt had exploded the moment they were done. And he'd never had a lover who wanted anything except his prowess in bed.

Did she finally hate him?

Aware of fearing her rejection when he should covet it, he opened her letter and began to read.

Dear Emilian,

I hope this letter finds you in good spirits and good health. I have been concerned about Nicu's condition. How is he faring? I thought you might like to know that I set down the surgeon quite boldly, although I doubt my actions will affect his behavior in the future. He is truly a base fellow with no concept of proper humanity.

He was disbelieving. She had gone to the surgeon and confronted him? Was she mad? He could barely imagine the debate Ariella must have engendered. He read on.

My father and brother have gone off to London for a few days, leaving the ladies to their own devices. I am very much enjoying the company of the females in my family, especially my little sister, Dianna, whom I simply do not spend enough time with. I am hoping to convert them all to my latest cause, a trip to the steppes of Mongolia and China's Great Wall.

He laughed.

Then he stopped, shocked by the sound that reverberated in the library. *What had just happened to him?*

He inhaled and finished the brief letter.

Alas, Dianna's interest is in a husband and fashion, and Margery, ever the dutiful daughter, claims she cannot leave her family for such a great length of time. My stepmother, however, is an adventuress and has said she would dearly love to go. I shall begin lobbying my father the moment he returns.

Cliff de Warenne would surely refuse his daughter such an insane journey. Emilian had never traveled that far east, but he didn't have to in order to know it would not be safe for her and her stepmother. Neither land was civilized, to the best of his knowledge.

I would like to know you are always welcome at Rose Hill. The next time you are in the vicinity, I would be pleased to receive you.

He reread the last two lines five times.

She wanted him to call.

He tossed the page across his desk, suddenly as furious as he was incredulous. When would she lose faith in him? Why couldn't she understand that no matter how kind and resilient she was, she was a *gadji* princess and he was a half-blood Rom? He was not a suitor! He did not wish to be a suitor! *What did those last lines mean?* Did she still think a friendship between them possible? If so, she was deluded—their tryst had proved that!

He leaned hard on the desk. He had expected anything but an invitation to Rose Hill. Of course he would never accept.

Did she even know that he was leaving with the *kumpa'nia* in a few more days? He couldn't recall if he had ever mentioned his plans.

He was eager to go. He had begun to feel that he couldn't stand being in his own skin at Woodland—or was it being in an Englishman's skin? Her haunting him did not help, nor did his guilt and concern. This letter had suddenly made the pretense of his life even worse. He was almost certain that, once on the road, he would forget his entire past, including Ariella. And that would be best for them both.

ARIELLA SAT in the chaise by her bedroom window, trying to read a copy of Francis Place's latest program of social change, the People's Charter. She should be fascinated, but she could not make heads or tails of what he was saying. She missed Emilian and thought about him constantly. Almost a week had passed since she had last seen him. She wanted to pursue the friendship he was refusing her, but to call on him again felt very forward now. Besides, he might misconstrue such a call as a very improper advance. As she had already made very improper advances—which he had accepted—she wouldn't blame him if he misunderstood her this time.

However, if she did not encourage their friendship, she was fairly certain he never would. She had finally sent him a friendly note, casually ending the brief missive with the polite suggestion that he stop by Rose Hill when he was next in the vicinity. Not only had he failed to do so, he hadn't even penned a reply.

The past few days felt like an eternity.

It was beginning to appear that she must call on him after all, or at least call on Jaelle at the Roma camp and use his sister to her personal advantage.

"Ariella!"

Ariella was relieved to put down the pamphlet, even if Margery sounded distraught. She took one look at her, standing at the door, and saw that something was very wrong. "What is it?"

Margery was pale and stiff. "You have a caller—one I am more than prepared to send away."

So much disbelief began. *Emilian had come.* "Don't you dare refuse to admit him!" she cried, leaping to her feet.

Margery didn't move as Ariella rushed to the mirror over her bureau. She wore a pale short-sleeved dress and she quickly adjusted the bodice. *It was so plain.* She opened the jewelry box on the bureau and chose a pair of pearl drop earrings, which she hooked onto her ears. She added a pearl cameo on a dark ribbon, aware of her hands trembling. *That was better.* She dabbed perfume between her breasts. Then she started pulling pins from her hair. *He liked her hair down.*

"What are you doing?" Margery exclaimed. "You can't receive a caller with half your hair down!"

She had let the back half-down and she began combing the tight curls. Finished, she turned. "I am starting a new fashion. How do I look?"

"You look like a woman in love—or one about to meet her lover."

Ariella went to her and hugged her. "I don't know what he wants. I sent him a note, but I was certain he would not respond. I am afraid to hope!"

"I am dearly afraid, too," Margery said, following her from the room.

Ariella ran down the stairs, her skirts held ankle high. She took a breath, slowed her charge into a sedate walk, squared her shoulders and tried to manage a calm, serene smile.

Ahead, she saw him standing in the blue receiving room, a top hat in his hands. He saw her at the very same time.

He looked so English in a dark green hunting coat with a waistcoat beneath, even with his too-long hair, and he was the handsomest man she had ever laid eyes on. He took her breath away.

He inclined his head. "Miss de Warenne," he said politely. He straightened but did not smile. His gaze was searching, his demeanor far too solemn.

"Emilian," she said. Impossible tension filled her. She was always so terribly aware of this man. "This is such a surprise—a very pleasant one." Was something wrong?

His gaze flickered past her. "I received your invitation." She realized Margery stood on the threshold, intent upon chaperoning them.

Ariella turned. "Can you give us a moment alone?"

Margery was clearly displeased, but she departed, leaving the door widely open. Ariella faced him breathlessly again.

He seemed to peruse every feature of her face before he slowly spoke, as if choosing his words with care. "Your letter was a surprise. I did not think you would ever wish to receive me."

She was surprised. "I will always receive you."

His expression hardened into severe lines. "That is far too generous, even for you."

Ariella hated this formal pretense. She went to the doors and closed them, then faced him. "Nothing has changed. I remain your steadfast friend, Emilian. What happened recently was as much my fault as yours."

His stare did not waver. "I beg to differ with you. Nicu is better."

"I am so glad!" she cried, beaming.

His mouth seemed to lift before it firmed. "I was in some

disbelief when I read that you went to the surgeon to berate him."

"He deserved it, Emilian. It was a bit awkward, but I did what I thought right."

He stared. "I cannot imagine any encounter being awkward for you."

She smiled. "That is high praise, indeed."

"It was meant to be." His eyes held hers, dark and intense. "I do not wish for you to fight my battles, Ariella."

Her eyes widened. "I fight many battles, all of the time. I am proud of being an independent thinker. I consider myself somewhat radical."

"Yes, you are an independent thinker, a radical, as well as an eccentric." His faint smile faded. "But you were distressed at the ball, and then with the surgeon. You do not need to be a part of a world of bigotry and hatred."

Ariella shook her head. "Now I beg to differ with you. I am a part of *this* world, Emilian, this *entire* world, even the shadows we do not care for—shadows most men and women pretend are not there."

Silence simmered between them as if charged, like the sky before a storm.

"I am so glad you have called. I do not think I could have held out for too much longer," she whispered, wishing suddenly she were in his arms. She wanted to reach out and stroke his cares away, but did not dare.

"I should not have accepted your advances, Ariella," he said abruptly. "And I am filled with even more regret than previously."

She was dismayed. "I have no regrets! Not one!"

"Then we are at an impasse." His expression tightened. "Surely you have not decided you wish for a casual and sordid affair."

"No! Of course not. You were right. An affair without

friendship or love is far too base for my nature." She wondered if he could hear her heart thundering.

"I have come here for several reasons. One is to apologize. You may not be sorry, but I am." His face almost softened. "I do not wish for you to be the one in my path, Ariella."

"There is nothing to forgive, Emilian," she said, meaning it. "You speak as if you are a hurricane!"

He tensed and their eyes locked. "It feels as if that is exactly what I have become—and you are the carnage I leave in my wake."

This was not the call she had expected. It felt dangerously like an ending. "Something is wrong, isn't it? Why have you really come?"

"I came to say goodbye."

And the moment he spoke, she knew he was leaving for a very long time. "What do you mean?"

"I am going north with the *kumpa'nia*. We'll go to the Borders, where I was born. I don't know when I am returning," he said, "or if I ever will."

She went still. *"What?"* He could not leave! What about their friendship, their affair? "But you are the viscount St Xavier! What about Woodland?" she cried, shocked and filled with dread.

"I hired an estate manager. He started his duties today. I have been English for too long," he said flatly.

She was in disbelief. "You *are* half-English, Emilian!"

"Edmund took me from my mother, rather forcibly. Although I chose to stay with him, I have begun to have grave doubts that my choice was the right one."

"Grave doubts!" she echoed, horrified. He was going to walk away from his father's heritage, from his estate, from his title, his life—from *her*—to become a Gypsy?

She recalled seeing him that very first night, when she had mistaken him for the *vaida*. He had been dancing under the stars with the kind of passionate fervor that only a true Rom could have. Their music had been in his blood, in his soul, because he was as much a Rom as an Englishman.

They were his people, too.

But to leave his entire life behind?

Ariella sank into a chair. He could not be leaving forever. "You have to come back," she gasped, and pain exploded in her heart. He had to come back to her.

"Isn't this for the best for everyone?" he asked gravely. "Look at the damage I have already done. You will find your Prince Charming, Ariella."

"You are my Prince Charming," she cried, her sight blurring with tears. Panic overcame her and she leaped to her feet, reaching for his arms.

"I know you believe that." He did not pull away. "One day you will see that you were wrong. In fact, the day will come where you will not even remember me."

She would never forget him. "When will I see you again?"

He shook his head. "I do not know."

She clung to his powerful arms. "How can this be happening? I love you!"

"Don't," he said harshly, twisting away.

She barely heard him. Her mind raced wildly in confusion. "Are you leaving now?"

"We leave shortly after sunrise tomorrow."

"Spend the night with me."

His eyes widened.

She clasped his face. "I can feel that you still want me. Make love to me tonight, Emilian. Give me something to hold on to until you return."

He went still, breathing hard. "What good can come of that kind of evening?"

She had shocked him. "I need to be with you another time. I don't want you to leave. You must let me have memories I can cherish!"

She felt the male heat blazing in him and his eyes smoldered, but he began shaking his head. "You deserve a great love and that friendship you are always speaking of. You do not deserve another ill-fated liaison."

She couldn't speak. He was leaving Derbyshire. He was leaving her. Why couldn't he see that they had begun a precious and fateful journey together?

"Don't cry," he said roughly. "Please."

She choked on a sob and moved into his arms, which opened to admit her. She clung, wishing she could do so forever. His huge body was stiff and hard against hers, and he was trembling, too.

"I am hurting you again," he said.

Ariella could not speak.

He held her for one more moment, his grasp on her tightening, before stepping back from her. He glanced at the salon's closed doors. "Your cousin is probably pacing in the hall."

She didn't care. If only she had the courage to go with him. But that would require the loss of all pride. Besides, she knew he would send her back.

"Ariella?" he asked.

She couldn't move. He turned grimly and went to open the doors. The moment he did so, he stiffened. Ariella saw past him, into the front hall.

Margery stood there, speaking with Jack Tollman, the owner of the White Stag Inn.

She hurried to Emilian and saw his face change. His expression hard and dangerous, he said, "What is he doing here?"

"I don't know. I am sure he has a valid reason," she said uncertainly.

"He is here for me." He started forward determinedly and she ran to keep up. What was Emilian talking about?

Tollman saw them and he smiled unpleasantly at Emilian. "Your butler said you'd be here."

Something was terribly, dangerously wrong.

"Why are you looking for me?" Emilian demanded.

Tollman grinned. "'Cause we thought you'd like to watch us hang a horse thief."

CHAPTER THIRTEEN

EMILIAN'S DISBELIEF TURNED to fury. "Like hell!" He snarled.

Ariella rushed to step in front of him, horrified by the unfolding events but determined to prevent a full-scale battle. Emilian gave her a darkly incredulous look. "This is Tollman's idea of revenge."

"What is happening?" Ariella gasped.

"This is no game, St Xavier," Tollman spat. "One of the Gypsy boys stole Pitt's roan and he got caught red-handed, selling it to Pitt's neighbor!"

Ariella was about to point out that horse thieves were not hanged when Emilian said, "Is there proof? Or have you cleverly laid the blame on some innocent Rom?"

This was going to explode into something terrible! Why did these two men hate each other?

"There are no innocent Gypsies."

Ariella began to protest, but Emilian glared furiously at her and she decided not to speak. "Whom do you accuse?" Emilian demanded.

"Djordi."

Ariella covered her mouth, her alarm increasing. Djordi was the young man who had first espied her intruding upon the Romany camp. He was sixteen, if that. "We do not hang thieves in this day and age," she managed. "I will send for my father. He will straighten out this entire affair."

Ignoring her, Emilian strode from the house. Tollman made a sound and followed. Ariella did so, as well. "Emilian!

I am coming with you! Mr. Tollman, please, let us wait on my father. You know how just he is."

Emilian leaped onto a gray stallion. Tollman was climbing into a gig. "Miss de Warenne, do not bother your pretty head with such matters." He reached for the whip. "A hanging is no place for ladies."

"Dare you break the law?" Ariella cried, aghast.

"An example must be set. No more Gypsies will dare to come here and swindle us," Tollman said firmly. "Gadup!"

Ariella did not watch as the gig careened down the drive, for Emilian rode his gray right up to her, causing her to jump frantically out of the way. He sawed on the gray's reins and it reared. "You stay at Rose Hill," he shot. Then he spurred the horse forward, and it charged away, kicking up dirt and gravel.

Ariella looked at Margery, shocked by the unfolding events. Margery said, ashen, "It will take five minutes to ready the coach."

ARIELLA CLUNG to the safety straps as their carriage careened toward the village square, the four horses in a mad gallop. She and Margery were thrown back and forth across the cab's interior with every rut hole and sharp turn. A crowd had gathered in the square. Women and children were present, and she heard shouts and catcalls. Then she glimpsed Stevan and some other Romany men, too. In disbelief she saw that they had been herded into one tight group. Two of the villagers had rifles and would not let them pass.

In the center of the square was a huge elm tree. A noose already hung from its branches, drifting in a breeze, and beneath it was a horseless wagon. Djordi stood on the flatbed, his hands tied behind his back. The noose dangled just behind his shoulders. His face was belligerent, but he was pale with fear.

And now, Ariella saw Jaelle near Stevan, her face tight and white, too.

"Oh, dear God," Margery whispered. "We must stop this."

Ariella jumped from the coach before it came to a full stop. Lifting her skirts, she ran frantically toward the crowd. Now she saw Emilian standing by the wagon, facing Tollman and Mayor Oswald. Not far from the mayor, Robert St Xavier stood, arms folded, with two other gentlemen his own age. His peers were smirking.

She shoved brusquely through the men, women and children, ignoring their mutters of annoyance and surprised gasps. A few of them, realizing whom she was, instantly stepped out of her way.

"St Xavier, there must be justice," Oswald was saying, his cheeks crimson, as she rushed up. But he seemed uncertain.

"You will *not* hang him," Emilian returned, his eyes blazing. He saw her and his stare turned incredulous, but his focus moved back to the mayor. He said to Oswald, "Hanging is unlawful in this case. There will be no more incidents—you have my word. We are leaving in the morning."

Oswald wrung his hands and looked at Tollman for help.

"The word of a half blood?" Tollman mocked. "That is no word at all!"

Emilian snarled at him. "Do you listen to an innkeeper, or the viscount of Woodland?"

"The whole town wants justice," Tollman snapped. "The whole town wants the damned Gypsies gone!"

"Mayor Oswald!" Ariella cried breathlessly. "You must not let hot tempers dictate here!" She glanced at Robert pleadingly, waiting for him to come forward to help resolve the crisis.

But Robert simply stood near the mayor, his expression somber. He looked away from her.

Emilian whirled toward her. "I told you to stay at Rose Hill."

She ignored him. "We have sent word to my father in town. He'll be back by nightfall, I am sure. Please, let us put this matter in his hands."

Before the mayor could respond, Emilian seized her. "Do not interfere."

"I will not stand idly by and watch a terrible miscarriage of justice."

He jerked her toward Margery. "Lady de Warenne, neither one of you should be present. You both need to return to your carriage and go home."

Margery came forward, as white as a sheet. "Ariella is right. Captain de Warenne can adjudicate this matter—or my father, the Earl of Adare."

But her mention of the powerful earl did not ease matters. Tollman said, "He hangs."

Oswald wrung his hands. "Hanging is unlawful, Jack," he began.

Tollman was furious. "You can't let him go," he shouted. "More of the scum will come and steal our horses and cows! They'll seduce our sisters and daughters! They will sell us rotten wheels!"

The crowd muttered in agreement with him.

"Then what will we do?" Oswald was sweating and pale. "We are all lawful Englishmen here."

The surgeon stepped forth from the crowd. "Give him a good whipping and send him back to the north. Let him know that if he comes back, it is on pain of death." Stone had hardly finished when the crowd began supporting his plan with avid cheers.

"Whipping a young man is barbaric!" Ariella cried, stunned. "Surely we can wait a few more hours to resolve this!"

Tollman spoke to the mayor but never took his burning gaze from Emilian. "He stole the horse and he is guilty.

There has to be justice. I can go along with flogging and banishment."

Emilian stared at Tollman with hatred, and Tollman stared back as hatefully.

"Why can't we wait until my father returns?" she cried loudly.

Oswald looked at her, clearly uncertain.

"She's a Gypsy lover," James Stone said. "Her father would probably think as we do. Everyone's agreed—the Gypsy will be whipped and sent away."

Ariella trembled. "My father would never approve of a flogging," she said. "He would follow the law."

Margery took her hand tightly. Stone, Tollman and Oswald now put their heads together and began a hushed and hurried discussion. The mayor listened, not speaking.

Emilian spoke to her, silver eyes like ice. "Get into the carriage and go home, now. I do not want you to see what will happen next."

His words frightened her more. "I am not leaving you or Djordi." Nothing and no one could make her run away now. "They will not go through with this," she added desperately, but she wasn't sure Tollman and his allies could be stopped. Why didn't Robert come forward and say or do something? Instead, he was watching her and Emilian with a speculation she instantly disliked.

"Can't you make her leave?" he demanded of Margery. "I want her gone!"

Margery was trembling, too. "We wish to support you, sir."

He turned away. "Robert, escort the ladies from the square."

Robert finally dropped his folded arms and came away from where he stood, behind the mayor and Tollman. "My cousin is correct. This is an improper venue for ladies."

She stared at him, wondering if he was a bungling fool.

"Will you help your cousin, sir? Will you stand up beside him as family should?"

"Emil seems to have a plan," he said with a shrug.

He didn't care what Emilian wanted, and he didn't wish to take Emilian's side, she realized.

Robert held out his arm. "Why don't we take some tea at the inn?"

Ariella turned her back on him. "I am not leaving," she told Emilian.

His look promised some future retribution. "Release Djordi," he said to Oswald and Tollman. He shrugged off his hunting coat and tossed it to the ground. He began unbuttoning the waistcoat. "I will be responsible for his punishment." He flung the waistcoat off. "I will take the flogging for him."

Horror made Ariella mute.

He could not think to do this!

Tollman smiled slowly, with real relish, while Oswald seemed stunned. "My lord, sir!"

Tollman laughed. "He's one of them. He's proved it since they came to town. He's a half-blood Gypsy, and to hell with his title."

Pale, Oswald said, "Tollman, the viscount has managed our affairs for years."

"It doesn't really matter who we whip, as long as the point is made," Tollman said savagely.

Aware that a terribly personal vendetta of some sort was being played out, Ariella turned to look at Robert, but clearly he was not planning an intervention. She gave up and rushed forward as Emilian threw his shirt into the ground. "Is he the mayor, or are you?" she cried to Oswald. "You cannot do this! He is the viscount St Xavier, a good citizen of this village, this country!"

"Release the boy," Tollman called to his men as if she hadn't spoken. He turned to her. "Miss de Warenne, it is your right to stay and watch the whipping. But I suggest you leave. Female hysterics will not help anyone."

"You cannot do this," Ariella said desperately, as two big men jumped up onto the wagon and untied Djordi's wrists. He leaped nimbly down, but his face was set. He strode to Emilian and a flurry of Roma followed. Emilian clasped his shoulder and spoke firmly and reassuringly. Ariella had not one doubt the boy wished to take the whipping and that Emilian would not allow it.

Then she saw everyone listening to Emilian speaking in the language of the Romany. Their stares were fascinated, even mesmerized. Tollman seemed satisfied and so did Robert. Her despair became complete. She went to him. "Don't do this," she begged in a soft whisper.

"You would have a boy flogged?"

"No," she managed. "I would have no one flogged."

His bare chest rippled as he breathed harshly. "Go home." He hesitated, his face tight. "Please."

She would never leave him, she thought, staring back. Tears had begun. She swatted at them.

A strong arm went around her. It was Djordi. "Come away," he said to her.

Emilian had turned. He walked over to the wagon. A big man followed, a carriage whip in hand. Emilian braced against the wagon's sides, head down, shoulders and back braced, biceps bulging.

Ariella pushed at Djordi. "Stop this, stop this now!" she cried, but Djordi wrapped her in his arms and she could not move. Then he started to drag her away, so she could not watch.

Tollman spoke to one of the younger men he was standing with, and the lad ran off. "Start it," he called.

The whip cracked, leaving a red mark on Emilian's back. He stood braced against the wagon as if made of stone. He hadn't even jerked.

The whip cracked again. She flinched, her heart exploding, but Emilian remained unmoving. It struck him a third time and she trembled, clinging to Djordi, overcome with panic, enraged at being helpless now. Emilian still did not make a sound. Dazed, she managed to control her tears. It would soon be over. Emilian would withstand the lashing.

Tollman stepped forward, a cat-o'-nine-tails in hand, his expression ruthless.

Realizing what he intended, Ariella screamed, struggling to get free of Djordi.

He cracked the dangerous whip. The crowd roared in approval as the barbed tail snaked across Emilian's back, savagely opening his flesh and leaving a trail of blood.

"Stop!" she screamed wildly, but Tollman struck Emilian viciously again. He flinched, almost going down to his knees. The crowd jeered. He fought to remain upright and clung to the wagon, panting audibly now.

Tollman flayed him mercilessly.

Ariella screamed, Djordi holding her so she could not interfere.

Emilian went down on his knees.

The crowd cheered.

Tollman wanted to kill him. As Tollman whipped Emilian another time, he finally fell facefirst to the ground. Ariella bit Djordi's hand and she was released. She ran toward Tollman, only to be seized by someone from behind. She was flung away, back into the crowd.

Margery screamed for her.

She went down. Briefly, panic blinded her, but she heard the whip cracking. *Tollman would kill him if he was not stopped.* She felt many hands on her, and she clawed at them, desperate to get up, to save Emilian. But they were steadying her, lifting her, not thwarting her, as the brutal whip cracked again. She surged to her feet, pushed past them, now running to the coach. Her coachman stood by the horses, his face a mask of horror.

"The gun, Jackson, the gun Father keeps beneath the seat!" she screamed.

He whirled, leaping onto his box. As he came off it, she took the gun. "Is it loaded?"

"Yes, Miss de Warenne," he began. She was already behind the excited mob. She fired into the air and the crowd parted like the Red Sea. Ariella ran through it and saw Tollman, whip in hand, and Emilian, who lay prone and bloody, facedown in the grass. She pointed the gun at Tollman's chest. "Enough," she warned. Dear God, she was ready to kill him for what he had done.

Tollman turned to her. His stare widened. "Don't shoot."

Her vision blurred and the gun danced uncontrollably in her hands. "Is he alive?" she managed. *If Emilian was dead, she was going to commit murder. She was going to gun this bastard down.*

"Put the gun down," Emilian said hoarsely, sitting up.

Stevan, Djordi and several other Romany men reached him, kneeling by him, supporting him as he sat. Jaelle appeared, crying and crouching beside him, taking his hand.

Tears gathering, Ariella stared at Tollman. *Emilian was alive.* But look at what they had done to him. She hated them—she hated Tollman.

Tollman stared back, his eyes filling with fear.

"Ariella, don't do it," Margery whispered, having come to stand directly behind her.

She blinked furiously at the tears. The gun wouldn't stay still. She looked at Emilian, into his gray eyes. Pain was etched into every line of his face. Although the wounds were on his back, blood was dripping down his chest, the cat having snaked over his left shoulder.

"Don't," he gasped.

Ariella felt her mind come to life. He was right. She could not murder anyone in cold blood. She lowered the gun.

Tollman strode past her, but as he did so, he hissed at her. It was a threat, but she couldn't distinguish his words. She dropped the gun and ran to Emilian.

Stevan held him up. He looked at her briefly, but his face was so weary and filled with pain, she could not decipher anything else. Then his eyes closed and he slumped backward, fainting in his uncle's arms.

She knelt, taking his hands. The horror vanished. There was only resolve.

Suddenly Robert stood over them. "I'll take him back to Woodland."

She looked up, enraged. "Get away from him!"

He stiffened and then, with a shrug, he walked away.

She fought for composure, looked up at Emilian's uncle. "Stevan, please carry him to my carriage."

Stevan looked at her in surprise. "We will take him now."

She stared back. "No. I will take care of him at Rose Hill."

ARIELLA STOOD BREATHLESSLY in the front hall as Stevan and another man helped Emilian inside. Jaelle stood beside her, trembling and trying not to cry. Ariella put her arm around her. Emilian was conscious and trying to walk, but he was in such pain that Ariella knew he wasn't aware of where he was or what was happening. He was still bleeding, and leaving a trail on the parquet floors. "Can you get him up the stairs and to the first bedroom on the right?" she asked, surprised at how calm she sounded.

She was so afraid for his life.

Neither man answered. As they started for the staircase, Ariella saw Emilian's eyes close, but she felt him fighting to stay conscious. Jaelle ran up the stairs behind them.

Light footsteps sounded. Ariella turned as her stepmother

rushed into the hall just in time to see the Romany men half-carrying Emilian up the stairs. Amanda's eyes widened, going from his mangled back to the bloody floors. "What happened?"

"St Xavier chose to take a flogging for a Romany boy," Ariella said, facing her stepmother grimly. "He has been flogged to within an inch of his life. I am taking care of him here."

Her stepmother stared. It was not a request and they both knew it. Nothing had ever been this important to Ariella.

Amanda nodded. "I'll send word to your father to fetch Dr. Finney and Rob Marriot, who is a fine surgeon."

"Thank you," Ariella said, relieved. The family doctor and the surgeon resided in London. "Can you send me a maid with soap, water, rags and whiskey?"

"Of course."

Ariella ran up the stairs to the closest bedroom, normally used by Alexi. Emilian lay on his stomach, breathing hard, his eyes screwed shut, his face damp with sweat. His back was raw. Ariella could not believe what had been done to him. Had Tollman deliberately tried to murder him?

Stevan said quietly, "His wounds need to be cleaned."

"I know. I will do it." She could not coddle herself now. She shoved her ill feelings aside.

"Do you know how to take care of man who has been whipped?" Stevan asked.

"You can tell me how." He was not going to interfere and neither would he take Emilian away.

He looked at her. "I will bring a potion for him to drink. It will help with the pain and the swelling. I will bring poultices for the wounds."

Ariella nodded, going to the bed and pulling up a chair. "We have sent for a surgeon and a doctor from town."

"They won't come."

Ariella gave him a dark look. That kind of thinking would

get them nowhere. She knew her family doctor, at least, would come to Rose Hill. She pushed Emilian's long hair away from his face and froze. A white brand was on his right ear, and there was no mistaking the letter *T.* "What is that?" she gasped.

"He was branded," Stevan said grimly. "I did not know. It must have happened long ago. He must have been caught stealing."

She was appalled. Another terrible injustice.... Would it ever end? She took Emilian's fisted hand in hers. "Can you send for Hoode?" she asked Stevan. "Not only does he serve Emilian well, I think he cares about him. He can help."

Stevan nodded but did not move.

"I'll ask Djordi to go," Jaelle whispered. She remained ashen, standing at the foot of the bed.

Ariella didn't care if Stevan wished to linger. The maid would arrive at any moment and Ariella would start wiping away the blood so she could inspect the extent of his wounds. She was afraid of what she would find. She was fairly certain some of his lacerations might need stitches. And she was so afraid of an infection.

It was three hours to town by rail. She desperately hoped both Finney and the surgeon would arrive by midnight.

She raised his fist to her mouth and kissed it. "You were so heroic…though I wish you hadn't been a hero today. But don't worry. You are safe now and I am taking care of you. My family will take care of you, Emilian." She realized she was starting to cry. She was in so much pain, too. He hadn't deserved this. She wished she could miraculously heal his every wound, even those in his heart.

His lashes moved.

"And don't you even think of going to Woodland," she choked. Then she leaned close to kiss his cheek. Her tears covered his face. "Today, I hate them, too."

His eyes opened and he looked at her.

She forced a smile.

He blanched; his eyes closed instantly. She heard him choke off a moan. She whirled to see Stevan still standing there. "Please, hurry. He is in so much pain."

Stevan said, "He is young and strong. It will take more than a whipping to kill him."

She trembled violently. "That is what Tollman wanted, isn't it? He wanted to kill him! There was no call for this kind of brutality."

"You were there," he said. He walked out and Ariella met Jaelle's gaze.

"This is because of me," she whispered. "The other day Emilian went after Tollman for what he tried to do. Tollman now hunts Emilian."

"It isn't your fault," Ariella said curtly. "Will you send for Hoode? You or Djordi can take the coach."

Jaelle nodded, rushing past Amanda as she hurried in, a maid with her, her arms loaded with the items Ariella had asked for. Amanda was grim as she paused beside Ariella. "I brought laudanum. It would be best to dose him thoroughly before you attempt to attend those lashes."

Ariella took the dropper, nodding. But even as she forced five drops into his mouth, her mind raced darkly. This had been more than a case of prejudice; this had been personal, too. Tollman had wanted to kill him.

She was afraid this wasn't the end, but a terrible beginning.

ARIELLA SAT in the chair beside Emilian's bed, watching him as he slept. She had left the draperies open, and the sky was studded with stars and a crescent moon. She guessed it was close to midnight. She had checked—the last trains would have arrived over an hour ago. It did not appear that either the doctor or the surgeon would arrive that night. She was beyond dismay.

She had thoroughly cleaned his wounds, Hoode arriving well before she was done, and a few hours ago, she had dosed him with more laudanum. Amanda, Margery, her aunt Lizzie and Dianna had been by time and again, to express their concern and see if they could help. Jaelle was asleep on the love seat in front of the fireplace.

He didn't appear to be in pain, but that was only because he was so heavily drugged. The skin that remained on his back was on fire, but he had yet to become feverish. Still, she desperately needed the doctor. She reminded herself that he was young and strong, as Stevan had said.

"Ariella?"

She turned at the sound of her father's voice. Cliff stood in the doorway, his attention going from her to Emilian. She ran into his arms.

He held her briefly. "Dr. Finney is in the hall, and so is Marriot."

Her relief brought tears. "Thank God."

"Apparently we all received your message simultaneously," he said, his focus returning to Emilian. "How seriously is he hurt?"

"He was viciously flogged. If I hadn't stopped it, I believe he would have been whipped until he was dead," she said in a harsh whisper.

Cliff put his arm around her. "I heard what you did. I am proud of you."

Ariella couldn't smile. "I am still in shock. It is unbelievable that men could act so violently and cruelly," she said tersely. "Jack Tollman did this while most of the village stood and watched—even the gentry."

"You have led a sheltered life," Cliff said. "I have always wanted to spare you this kind of hatred and tragedy."

"My mother was treated this way, wasn't she?"

Her father stared back at her. "Yes. She suffered the same kind of bigotry."

Ariella inhaled. "What will happen now?"

"Tollman broke the laws of this country," Cliff said seriously. "He assaulted an innocent man."

"He needs to be prosecuted for what he has done! What if Emilian dies?"

"I have every intention of seeing Tollman properly and lawfully punished for his actions."

Gladdened by this last bit of information, Ariella turned. Dr. Finney stood there with another gentleman, whom she assumed was the surgeon. Her brother was with them, too. She left Cliff and went into Alexi's arms.

He hugged her. "I leave for one day and there is a crisis," Alexi said tersely. He meant to tease, but he was sober.

"I am sure if you were here, none of this would have happened," she said, low.

Alexi looked piercingly at her for one more moment, but Ariella did not care if he guessed her secrets now. Jaelle had awoken. Cliff gestured and they all went into the hall. Ariella seized Finney's hand before he and Marriot went into the sickroom. "Thank you, Dr. Finney. Thank you!"

He smiled kindly at her. "How could I possibly refuse you, Ariella?" He had been treating the family for over twenty years. He entered the sickroom, closing the door behind him.

Cliff said to Alexi, "Why don't you find Miss St Xavier a guest room? I imagine she will wish to stay here while her brother recovers."

Ariella knew her father intended a private discussion. She tensed, certain he would begin to probe into the real, personal reasons for her defense of Emilian that day. When Alexi and Jaelle were gone, Ariella folded her arms, daring to look at Cliff.

He was staring very closely. "Are you in love with him?"

Her tension escalated. An honest answer could only lead to the truth of their affair, for her father was too astute. Cliff would be crushed and furious. Any compassion that he felt for Emilian would vanish. He might not even pursue justice. But how could she lie?

"You don't have to answer me, Ariella. It is obvious."

She wiped her tears. "I am in love with him."

He studied her. "I wouldn't have chosen him for you."

"Because he is Rom?"

"No, because he reminds me of a wounded lion, and wounded beasts strike out whenever they can, at whatever they can. Nothing is as dangerous."

She hugged herself. "He *is* wounded. He has had a difficult life, being scorned by the English as a Gypsy while living amongst them as an Englishman."

"I can imagine. I saw how he was received at the Simmonses'. You, of course, believe you will heal his wounds?"

"I intend to try." She swallowed. "You told me that when I came forward with the man of my choice, no matter whom it was, you would give me your blessing."

"I did. And I meant it. But I have grave reservations now."

Ariella knew she should stop. Emilian didn't love her, and she knew her father must never guess that his feelings were unequal to hers. There was no need for any blessing, but still she said, "So you disapprove? Or worse?"

"I will try to approve, Ariella." He pulled her close and kissed her forehead briefly. "I will give St Xavier the benefit of the doubt."

She was overcome with relief.

Then Cliff said, "Has he asked you to marry?"

Her relief vanished. Somehow she said, "We have only just met."

Cliff stared very closely at her. He finally said, "So he has no intentions to marry you."

Ariella tensed. "That isn't what I said."

"Darling, I am forty-six years old. I can read between the lines. I can arrange a marriage for you. I have little doubt I can persuade St Xavier to see the benefits of such a union."

Ariella stared. Of course there were benefits—her good name, her fortune. "I will marry for love," she said, "or I will not marry at all."

A look of resignation appeared in Cliff's eyes. "Of course you will. You are my daughter. Fine. For the moment, I will not intervene."

"Thank you," Ariella said.

CHAPTER FOURTEEN

"'FORE GOD, HIS GRACE IS BOLD to trust these traitors....
They shall be apprehended by and by.... How smooth and
even they do bear themselves!"

What was this, he wondered in confusion. Where was he?

"As if allegiance in their bosoms sat, Crowned with faith
and constant loyalty."

His back burned, as if on fire, And his head hurt explo-
sively. Worse, he was so dry he could not swallow. What had
happened?

"There are no innocent Gypsies."

His mind, groggy and dull, urged him to awaken, and an
odd horror began. His stomach felt dangerously sick. He
was going to vomit—which meant he had to get up. But his
body was so heavy that even though he ordered himself to
rise, nothing happened. He realized he lay on his stomach,
clutching a pillow.

"There are no innocent Gypsies."

"Stop! You will kill him!"

Ariella! He tensed, suddenly remembering why he was
prone on his belly in a bed he did not recognize. He had taken
the flogging for Djordi, and it had been vicious.... Ariella
had been there, screaming and weeping for him.

"The king hath note of all that they intend, by intercep-
tion which they dream not of."

He went still. *Ariella was reading to him.*

Her voice was soft, melodious, soothing. The horror eased

and the nausea faded. He had one cheek on the pillow, turned toward the sound of her voice. He must be at Woodland, and she was at his side.

He wanted to open his eyes but his lids seemed to weigh dozens of stones. He blinked, fiercely now, determined to have a glimpse of her. And finally he saw her.

She sat beside him in a chair she had pulled up, a book in her hands as she read from it, her tone changing with the dialogue but never rising loudly. She remained immersed in the novel; she was the most stirring sight he had ever seen.

She pointed the gun and it wavered frighteningly, her face a mask of rage, and he knew she was an instant from murdering Tollman.

No one had ever tried to defend him so wholeheartedly, not ever.

He suddenly thought he recalled her gentle touch on his feverish back, cool and wet against red-hot flames. He thought he recalled her bending over him, adjusting his pillows and pulling up the coverlets. Had she kept cold compresses on his forehead, too? Or were those all dreams?

Maybe this was a dream, he thought. She was so beautiful and kind, so brave, that this had to be a dream.

"Emilian! You are awake," she gasped, closing the book, her eyes trained upon him.

He wanted to smile, but he kept seeing her with the gun, an instant from murdering a man on his behalf.

Her expression was worried. "You will be fine," she whispered, closing her small hand over his larger one. "Don't try to move. You need to lie still for several days so you can heal properly."

His heart beat wildly. Why had this little woman behaved as she had? Why was she hovering over him now?

She stood, releasing his hand. "Are you thirsty? Let me help you drink. You must still be in pain. I have laudanum. Doctor Finney advised me to keep you dosed until the end of the week." She was already pouring water into a glass from the bedside pitcher.

She was an angel, he thought, an angel of mercy. She was *his* angel of mercy.

And his lids closed of their own volition and there was only darkness.

HE WOKE SLOWLY, in stages, daylight against his closed eyes. A nagging dread emerged as he rose up from the heavy, thick clouds of sleep. The feeling was familiar—it had been haunting him at moments like these. There was something he had to do, to face. And as he awoke, he knew something was very wrong.

Emilian tensed. He did not feel very well. In fact, his back was stiff and sore—no, he was stiff and sore all over, and he did not know why. He lay on his side, but when he began to move onto his back, the soreness increased. Fully awake at last, wondering at the slow, difficult process, he squinted against dull daylight, his temples pounding, his mouth unbearably dry. He realized he was in a strange bed. What the hell?

He glanced past the bed and saw Ariella.

She sat in a big upholstered chair, drawn so closely up to his bed that it touched the mattress. Asleep, she was clutching a book to her chest, her legs curled up beneath her skirts, a few stocking-clad toes visible. Her golden hair was loosely pinned up, with many tendrils escaping. His heart skipped.

I will take care of him at Rose Hill.

He slowly pushed himself to sit up. Now, he had vague, dreamlike recollections of Ariella hovering over him, nursing him, giving him water and laudanum. And she had been reading to him. He recalled that, too.

His angel of mercy.

Warmth unfurled in his chest. He did not understand it. He dared not contemplate her too closely now. He finally sat, his back sore but not terribly so, and that perplexed him, for he remembered being in the fires of hell when he had first been brought to Rose Hill. He was damned weak, and terribly hungry. He was also utterly naked beneath the sheets and blankets covering him.

He saw the pitcher of water and the glass on the bedstand carefully swung his legs over the side of the bed, keeping the sheets with him. When he reached for the pitcher, he saw his hand shaking. He cursed.

What was this? How long had he been in bed? Clearly, he had been dosed, probably with laudanum. He lifted the pitcher, sweating.

"Let me do that," Ariella cried, standing and taking the pitcher from him.

He sank back against the pillows, grimacing as his back came into contact with the cotton and down.

She was so beautiful, exactly the way an angel should look.

She poured the water and held the glass to his mouth.

He took the glass from her. "Ariella, stop. I am not an invalid."

She hesitated before allowing him to take the glass. As he drank, she stood there wringing her hands, as if uncertain whether he could even drink by himself.

How long had she been taking care of him?

He drained the glass and took the pitcher, refilled the glass, and then drank again. His hand still trembled, but not as badly as the first time.

"How do you feel?" she whispered, taking the empty glass from him and setting it aside.

"Like hell," he said. "I am sore, stiff and weak, obviously. How long have I been here?"

"Seven days."

His eyes widened. "Have you been dosing me the entire time?"

She nodded. "You needed stitches. Both the doctor and surgeon wanted you in bed, lying still, for as long as possible. You had a low fever for several days, too." She touched his forehead.

He did not move. He was grimly satisfied when he felt his pulse quicken and begin to thicken his loins. Obviously he was well on the mend.

"You have no fever now," she said quietly, and her hand strayed to his cheek.

She had been caring for him for seven days. She had been ready to murder Tollman for him. He caught her wrist reflexively. He might be weak, but he wanted to pull her down into the bed with him. He wanted to stroke her and hold her and slowly make love to her. He wanted to show his gratitude. "I could have told you I had no fever," he said softly. He slid his hand to hers and held it.

She smiled a little. "I am so happy to hear that seductive tone of voice!"

"Am I being seductive?" he murmured. Seduction was safe, he somehow thought. Anything else was far too dangerous.

"Your eyes are gleaming," she whispered.

"I am sitting here naked, Ariella, and I am not so sore as to be dead."

She pulled his hand to her mouth and quickly kissed it, flushing. Then she sat, reaching for the book on the floor.

When had anyone ever cared about him this way? In his entire life, he could not think of anyone, except his mother, who would have sat with him as she had and who would have threatened Tollman as she had. She was so different from all the other *gadji* women. But he had known that the first time their eyes had met.

"Are you in pain?" she asked.

He shook his head. "My back is sore, that is all, and no wonder, if I have been sleeping for a week. Thank you."

She stared breathlessly. "Emilian, you have nothing to thank me for."

"Was it my imagination, or did you hover over me the entire time I lay here?"

She smiled. "I hovered."

He smiled back at her. "Maybe your true calling is nursing."

She shook her head. "You needed aid. I was determined to be the one caring for you."

Her words were like a fist to his chest. Her eyes were still shining. In them, there was so much love and so much trust. But he did not deserve that trust, did he? He did not deserve so much love. He could not return her feelings—he did not even want to. But his heart felt so odd. There was that strange warmth inside it. He owed her so much now.

He reminded himself that she was a *gadji* princess. One day, there would be a *gadjo* prince.

Uncomfortable, he glanced at the book she clutched. His eyes widened when he saw Shakespeare on the spine. Relieved at the distraction, he said, "Have you been reading *Romeo and Juliet* to me?" He was amused.

"I have been reading *Henry V.*"

His smile vanished and he sat up straighter. "That is hardly a romance novel."

"I lied. I do not read romance novels," she said.

The "lie" was hard to comprehend. "Why *Henry V?*"

"I admire King Henry," she said. Her gaze was direct. "In spite of his shortcomings. He was proud—too proud, really— but so brave." She added, "He was so easily prodded into battle. A simple mockery made him wish to go to war."

He felt uncomfortable. "He was shortsighted."

"Perhaps, but he was a strong leader." Her regard did not waver. "His men trusted him. He had charisma and they would follow him anywhere."

"He was ruthless," Emilian said slowly.

"Yes, he was ruthless—when betrayed."

"He was betrayed and the English boys in his army were foully murdered," Emilian said, sitting even straighter. Were they talking about Henry or him?

"The tragedy has only made me even fonder of Henry," Ariella said firmly.

"Of course." She understood the parallels perfectly. "And do you approve of his vengeance? He made sure those boys were avenged."

"No, I do not approve, for Henry murdered all the French prisoners he had," Ariella said tersely. "Violence begets violence, Emilian. That is the moral here. Surely you know that. Surely you are not thinking of revenge!"

He looked past her, recalling Tollman's smirk and sneer. He glanced at her. "Henry married the French queen and became the King of France," Emilian said harshly. "That was the outcome of such violence."

"I cannot help but admire Henry's pride, his courage, his skill as a leader, but every time I read this, I cry when those children are unjustly murdered. And I cringe, knowing what Henry will do next!" she said. "I cry over the injustices the Romany have suffered and continue to suffer, and I have wept over what they did to you! I am cringing at the look in your eyes now."

He breathed hard, arms crossed now, thinking of how he would make Tollman pay. A flogging seemed appropriate— a brutal one. He trembled with anger and hatred. "You should have picked a different drama, Ariella."

"You are so proud—so courageous—but I pray that you will not allow your pride to dictate vengeance," she said harshly.

"I recall every single detail of what happened, Ariella," he said. "And while I thank God you did not murder Tollman, he must pay."

"He was arrested. There is an inquiry being launched. He will wind up in prison, Emilian."

The arrest surprised him, but then he thought she had somehow been behind it. Of course she had. "Will he be convicted?" He flung his legs over the side of the bed so quickly his back hurt and he grunted. He lost a great deal of the sheet and he seized it, uncaring that his navel was exposed.

She looked and flushed. "My father," she said, "is a fair man. Tollman broke the law when he decided to punish you for something you didn't even do. Punishment is reserved for judges and juries. We cannot take the law into our own hands."

He was certain she had pushed her father into seeking justice for him. "I don't need or want *gadjo* charity."

She inhaled. "That is unfair. My attending you wasn't charity."

"That I know. I am speaking of your father, going out of his way to please you, when he hardly cares about my fate."

"That is unfair and untrue." She left the chair and sat on the edge of the bed by his exposed hip. His pulse, already high with anger, responded instantly to her. She dared to caress his cheek again but the desire was welcome. He could not imagine not wanting her so badly, so urgently, even in the midst of a serious difference of opinion.

"He cares about justice. He cares about bigotry. And I was raised to have the same cares, the same values. Emilian, promise me you will leave Tollman alone."

It crossed his mind that she had become the extraordinarily generous and open-minded person she was because of her family. "I am not making any such promise," he said flatly. "How is Djordi?"

She tensed. "He did steal the horse, Emilian. He has been arrested, too."

He cried out, furious. "And Stevan and the *kumpa'nia?*"

"They remain at Woodland," she whispered, her eyes on his. "There have been no further incidents, not really."

"What does that mean?" He had to get out of the sickroom and return home.

"Tempers are high. The villagers want them gone. Father is trying to calm everyone."

"You are worried." He saw it in her eyes.

She grimaced. "Yes, I am."

"Allow me to worry. You have done enough." But her heart was simply too large and too accommodating to stop worrying about the Roma. He took her hand and looked up into her eyes. "You have spent a week of your life caring for me. I cannot repay you with an argument. Maybe you are right about your father. It has been my experience that most of society is intolerant, but not all of it. If he seeks to defuse the situation, I am grateful to him, as well as to you."

"If you want people to have an open mind about the Romany people, shouldn't you have an open mind about the *gadjos?* We are not all the same. I can't believe, in all your years at Woodland, you have not realized that."

He stared, thinking about how extraordinary she was.

She smiled at him. "You are too intelligent, Emilian, to be a bigot against all *gadjos.*"

She was right. And he did know some decent Englishmen. Something in his heart softened impossibly. "So I should walk into a salon and assume everyone is eager to be my acquaintance, and that the whispers I can just barely hear are not filled with condescension?"

"Yes," she whispered. "It can be an experiment." Her tone was rough. "It can be our experiment."

His heart lurched again. He let his eyes close and this time he kissed her palm slowly, tasting the soft skin in its center while his blood roared. There was one way in which he could pay this woman back, and it had nothing to do with social experiments.

She made a soft, throaty sound.

He pulled her closer, wrapping his hand around her nape. Her hair began to fall down. He pulled her other hand low onto his belly. She gasped, brushing the stiff folds in the sheet.

"I want to thank you, Ariella, for taking on Tollman—and for caring for me." He brushed her mouth once with his. He had never meant anything more.

Her eyes were wide, warm, loving.

He choked on an insane need to make love to her. "But don't ever interfere again, not in such violent matters," he said. He searched her face, their lips centimeters apart.

"How could I not interfere?" she whispered. "Emilian, I was so scared."

He almost told her, *So was I.* Instead, he brushed her mouth again, this time with more pressure. She whimpered and opened her lips. He let his tongue roam freely, slowly, sensually. Her hands moved to his shoulders, seizing him there, a sign he now knew well. It would be so easy to lay her down and move over her, into her, satisfying them both.

Damn it, he was at Rose Hill, and he owed his host so much. And he owed her now with his life.

He murmured, meaning to tease but too aroused to do so, "When am I allowed to resume normal activity?" And he did what an English gentleman would do: he released her.

She murmured, "I hope it is today."

HE WAS AWARE of his servant's intent regard as he wolfed down the bowl of stew. When he was done, he sighed.

"May I bring you more?" Hoode asked, smiling.

"No, thank you. You may help me finish dressing and you may tell me about Miss de Warenne." He stood, wearing only trousers. He had already checked his back in the mirror. It was crisscrossed with scabs and new pink skin. He felt certain there would be scars. That was good, as it would remind him to finish things with Tollman—and for the rest of his life, it would remind him that most *gadjos* deserved his hatred.

"Miss de Warenne, my lord, has proved herself the most loyal of friends."

Emilian crossed the bedroom to where a broadcloth shirt was hanging on a stand. "How so?"

"She only left your side when ordered to do so by her father, and then, for only an hour or two at a time."

He smiled at his reflection, oddly pleased, even satisfied, as he began to shrug on the shirt. He winced.

"Her entire family has been most accommodating. They are the highest people," Hoode continued. "Captain and Mrs. de Warenne checked on you, as did the earl's wife, Mr. Alexi de Warenne, the younger sister and Lady Margery. And they have given your sister a room, although I do not believe she has used it."

"My sister must have been worried. Can you send for her?"

"Of course, my lord." A knock sounded on the door. As Hoode went to answer it, he buttoned up the shirt. He tensed when his host stepped into the room.

Cliff de Warenne nodded at him politely. "I am pleased you are up and about," he said carefully.

Emilian faced his host. "I would like to thank you for your generosity and hospitality," he said. He meant it but he was wary, for de Warenne had probably come seeking information about his relationship with Ariella.

"You are welcome. The flogging was a travesty." De Warenne looked at Hoode. "I'd like a word with the viscount."

Hoode left instantly, closing the door behind him.

De Warenne regarded him with intensity. "Although we do not spend more than a month or two each year at Rose Hill, I feel an obligation to provide this community with leadership, and to set an example for others. Tollman is in a Manchester jail, but his family has hired solicitors, and I believe he will soon be released on bond. There is a controversy over whether any charges can be brought, as you volunteered to take the flogging."

He laughed. "Of course there is controversy. I am not worried about Tollman, even should he be freed."

Cliff shook his head. "I recognize the look in your eyes. I suggest you allow the legal system to manage this affair. Seeking vengeance will not help your case, and you have a responsibility to Woodland and the shire."

"Lately, I have come to believe my duties are to my Roma brothers and sisters," Emilian said. "What about Djordi?"

"I have arranged for him to leave with the Rom. He is young, and that is why he will be let off lightly, but he is to leave Derbyshire, St Xavier, and not come back."

"Of course not." He felt the hatred welling. Djordi was being banished, an age-old persecution.

"You might suggest that the next time he wishes to abscond with a horse, to choose one not so unusually marked," de Warenne said softly.

Emilian ignored that. At least Djordi could return to the caravan. But he was damned if he'd leave Tollman alone, not if he was released on bond.

"I want to discuss my daughter with you."

Emilian met his piercing blue gaze, tensing. "I owe your daughter a vast debt," he said flatly.

"Yes, you do. I believe she saved your life." His stare did not waver.

"I realize that."

"I asked you at the Simmonses what your intentions were. You said you had none."

Emilian did not respond.

"It is quite obvious that Ariella is very fond of you. Do

you return her feelings at all?" de Warenne said with growing heat.

Emilian turned from the other man, stunned by such a question. Surely de Warenne did not wish for him to step forth as a suitor. "Your daughter is an exceptional lady. I have never met a woman like her."

"Answer the question."

She was his angel of mercy. He breathed hard. "I am leaving, de Warenne. I am going north with the caravan."

De Warenne started. "Does Ariella know this?"

"Yes, she does."

"You are speaking as if you will not return."

"I may be gone for months, years. I do not know."

"What about your estate?"

"I have hired a manager."

"I fail to understand. You have been viscount for years. Why leave now?"

"That is my affair, de Warenne." He would not explain himself to anyone.

"Really? Because it seems to me that you have led my daughter on. In which case, your affairs become mine." De Warenne's eyes flashed.

Emilian prepared for battle, but with some reluctance. Not only did he owe Ariella and her brother, he owed this man, too. "I have never insinuated any false intentions to your daughter. To the contrary, I have been brutally honest with her." He thought he flushed. "I am half blood. I have never courted an Englishwoman, nor will I. Frankly, I have no plans to ever marry. I am going north. I do not know if I will return. Ariella knows all of this."

A tense moment ensued. "There is a family myth that has never been proved false. A de Warenne loves once—and it is forever."

He flushed. What the hell did that mean? "Surely I am misinterpreting your words. You cannot be implying that you wish for me to come forward as a suitor?" He steeled himself, for he expected de Warenne to laugh at him.

There was no laughter. Somberly, he said, "If that makes my daughter happy, yes."

He was stunned.

"Have no doubt, you are the last man I would have chosen for her. I have made an investigation this past week, St Xavier. You shun Derbyshire and London society, yet you manage Woodland magnificently. You have a keen intellect for business affairs, but you are a ladies' man—openly so. A man of business I can and do admire, but a recluse and a rogue? My daughter should do better and I fear for her heart."

He was reeling. His host actually wished for him to court Ariella? Was this a sick jest? "You seem to have forgotten that a great deal of society shuns *me* for my Gypsy blood," he said.

"You have been at Woodland since you were a boy. That makes you as English as myself. But you are entitled to your heritage—all of it—just as Ariella is entitled to hers. I do not object to your heritage. I object to your behavior."

Emilian recalled Ariella's admission that her mother had been a Jewess. But de Warenne taking that woman as a lover was very much like all the *gadjos* who took Romni women to their beds, wasn't it?

"I heard about your mother's murder in Edinburgh," he said suddenly. Emilian stiffened. "Is that why you are about to walk away from the life your father gave you?"

"I have a duty to her," he said, quietly furious now.

"I am sorry for your loss. But you have many duties, and not just to your dead mother."

He was not about to discuss Raiza with this *gadjo*. "Thank you," he managed to say, the words an utter pretense.

"I have had grave doubts about you from the moment we met," de Warenne said flatly. "I am an excellent judge of character, and my concerns are based on far more than the fact of your rakehell ways. You are angry, belligerent and somehow scarred—I do not mean physically. My daughter deserves a great and lasting love. Rakehells can be reformed, but a damaged man cannot give her the love she deserves."

He trembled, oddly dismayed, as well as angry now. "Ariella deserves a *gadjo* prince. I hope you find her one." He meant it.

De Warenne's eyes burned. "If you break her heart, I will be the one to personally make you pay."

He stiffened. De Warenne's reputation as a great friend and deadly enemy was well-known.

De Warenne stalked to the door. "The sooner you leave these premises, the better. I no longer feel very generous or hospitable. And the sooner your relationship with my daughter ends, the better. Make certain it remains platonic." De Warenne walked out.

THE MOMENT HE OPENED the bedroom door, he knew he had found Ariella's room. He could just barely detect her jasmine and tuberose scent, but every inch of the blue and beige decor was so simple and elegant that there could be no doubt. For one moment, his heart thrumming, he merely stood there and took in the serene interior.

He was leaving Rose Hill. Hoode was already downstairs, where his coach was waiting out front. He hadn't seen Ariella since that morning, and he felt certain she did not even know he was leaving. But that wasn't why he stood on the threshold of her private apartments.

He stepped inside and closed the door behind him, leaning against it. This was where she went to bed every night and woke up every morning; this was where, had he accepted her invitation, he would have made love to her. This was where she bathed, dressed, brushed her hair. This was her private, personal sanctuary.

A terrible need to know her completely, to fill in any lingering gaps, assailed him, and he could not deny that the prospect of leaving was distasteful.

A vase of white roses was on the table by the pin-striped sofa, undoubtedly from the gardens, and a book lay facedown beside it. He glanced from the sofa to the canopied bed, its covers and draperies the exact vivid blue color of her eyes. A book lay on the bed, too, as if she had left it there after reading.

He glanced around slowly, taking in every item: the two quietly elegant tea gowns hanging up on a stand in one corner of the room; the beautiful hand-painted jewelry box on the bureau, a collection of jewelry left out beside it; a hairbrush beside that; another book on the bedside table, along with a single yellow rose in a crystal bud vase. He glanced at the bookcase against one wall. No one he knew had a bookcase in the bedroom, and hers was full. It was odd. Or was it?

He went to the mantel first. Above it was a family portrait. He recognized her father and stepmother, perhaps as newly-weds, for from their dress and youth he surmised it had been painted two decades or so ago. The small golden girl seated beside them, a book in hand, was clearly Ariella. Her brother stood with them, grinning, his hand on a wolfhound. Ariella was solemn, intent.

She looked six or seven years old. He realized he was smiling. She had been raised in a close, loving family, he knew, and he was fiercely happy for her. All she needed now was a *gadjo* prince. He had not a doubt de Warenne would find her one.

He walked to the bedside table. A number of miniature portraits were there, including her brother's and her younger sister's. He could not imagine what it was like to have such a family.

He glanced at the bed, wishing he could ignore it. In spite of his recent conversation with de Warenne, he had a raging urgency to make love to Ariella. He did not think he could leave Derbyshire without doing so. It would be his way of saying thank-you—and goodbye.

He reached for the book on the bed and was surprised by the title. She was reading the latest political program espoused by the radical Francis Place.

I lied...I don't read romance novels.

He had already read parts of the People's Charter, and it was dry. Why would she attempt it?

He walked over to the bookcase and was very surprised to find novels by Baudelaire and Flaubert, in the original French. He saw histories of the Ottomans, Egypt, China, Russia and the Austro-Hungarian Empire. The last volumes were written in Russian and German. There were biographies on a dozen different kings and queens from a dozen different countries, as well as Suleiman, Genghis Khan, Cnut and Alexander the Great. And there was a treatise on the origins of the aborigines.

He realized his heart had slowed. Women did not read these kinds of works and studies. But she was so different....

He pulled an ottoman up to the bookcase and sat down, staring at the books and shelves. Ariella had read all of these books. He was certain of it.

She wasn't merely beautiful, kind and brave; she was intelligent and intellectual. To have a library like this one, she had to be as curious as an Oxford scholar, as curious as him. Did she agree with Place? Which history did she prefer?

How was he going to leave this woman behind?

The thought of leaving her seemed to be hurting his chest. But such feelings were unsuitable. He was Rom. She deserved a fine, honorable Englishman and a fine English world, one filled with privilege and luxury.

De Warenne had implied that he would be open to a suit.

It was impossible. He had misunderstood, or de Warenne hadn't thought it through and he would come to his senses and change his mind.

Maybe he could have given her such a life, before Raiza's murder. He could have given her pretty dresses, jewels and a handsome estate, but every time they went out, she would hear the whispers and feel the scorn. Her friends would desert her. There would only be false pretenses.

The door opened. He didn't move as she stepped inside the room.

Wide-eyed, she shut the door. "What are you doing in here?"

"I am looking at your books."

"I can see that."

He was leaving, as planned, but not without a very improper goodbye, one she would recall for a long, long time. "Afraid we will be discovered," he asked, standing, "and accused of being lovers?"

She breathed hard. "I am afraid that we will be discovered and *you* will be accused of being the worst scoundrel, a man who is preying upon me." But she stayed against the door, unmoving.

"I *am* the worst scoundrel. I have already preyed upon you." He started toward her.

She trembled. "You are in full form, I see."

"Yes, I am." He didn't move. "Why didn't you tell me you are an intellectual?"

Her high color increased. "It isn't fashionable. Intelligent women are scorned."

"But I despise stupid women," he said. "I am very impressed."

Her eyes widened. "You are?"

"Which is your favorite biography?"

She started. "I am taken with the King Cnut and Genghis Khan." Her lashes fluttered. "At least, until recently."

"Until recently," he murmured. "Dare you flirt now?"

She nodded. "Very much so."

He gave in. So much tension filled the room, it was impossible not to. He brushed the hair from her cheek. "And now?"

"I favor a Romany prince," she whispered.

He had thought so. He felt savagely elated, even if this was the prelude to a farewell. "You won't find a biography on any Rom. And I hate to disappoint you, but I am half blood and we do not have kings or princes."

"I don't need to read about my Roma prince, do I?" she said, arching a look at him.

He was her Roma prince. Lust exploded, mingling with something far more profound, something bottomless, something he must never analyze or identify. He pressed his bursting loins against her hips. Planting his forearms on the door on either side of her head, he kissed her, openmouthed and deep. *She was, beyond any doubt, the most extraordinary of women and he owed her his life.*

She kissed him back, her hand sliding low over his buttocks and lower still.

He thought about where he wanted them, and he shoved one thigh between hers, tearing his mouth from hers. "I want to make love to you, Ariella."

She nodded, clinging. "Yes."

He levered himself off her and the door. It was hard to do, when his body screamed at him for fulfillment. "I am on my way back to Woodland."

She paled. "So soon?"

"I am well enough—it is obvious." He knew his mouth curved.

She wet her lips, breathing hard. "I am glad you are recovered." She blushed. "And not for selfish reasons."

He smiled again, touching her cheek. "You do not have a selfish bone in your body."

She clasped his hand. "Should I call on you later, or tomorrow?"

He was deadly earnest now. He did not want her discovered and hurt, but there was no easy way to conduct an affair. He must either abuse his host's generosity and tryst with her at Rose Hill, late at night, or they must steal an afternoon together at Woodland. She deserved long nights with his undivided attention and long mornings with even more attention. She deserved champagne at midnight and strawberries and cream in the morning. But she was neither a bride nor a wife and he could not give her anything other than an hour or two of passion.

A night at Rose Hill was slightly less sordid than an afternoon at Woodland, but it was far more dangerous. He was well enough to travel now; the *kumpa'nia* would probably be leaving the following morning. "Call on me later today," he said. He added, "Promise."

She smiled. "I promise."

CHAPTER FIFTEEN

EVERYTHING HAD CHANGED between them.

Ariella slowly came downstairs. Emilian had left an hour or so ago. Something wonderful had come out of the terrible flogging. She saw it the way he looked at her now, his eyes gentle. A warmth she had never before seen shimmered there.

In another hour or so, she would meet him at Woodland. She could barely wait. She already knew that this time, when he took her in his arms, that warmth would be reflected in his eyes. This time, he would make love to her. She had no doubt that afterward she would receive the kind of smiles she had garnered that afternoon in her bedroom.

Her hand strayed to her abdomen. They had only slept together twice, but she had realized during the time she nursed him that she had missed her last monthly time. She was rarely late, but there had been so much duress recently. That likely accounted for the lateness. She had far graver matters to brood upon.

The county was like a keg of dynamite, the long fuse lit. as long as the Roma remained in the parish, it burned. It would not take much for that keg to ignite. The hostility between the English and the Roma was a terrible blight on her newfound happiness. She was afraid of what might happen next. Emilian wanted to go after Jack Tollman for revenge. She thanked God that Tollman remained in the Manchester prison. She couldn't begin to imagine what Emilian would do otherwise.

She heard voices coming from the receiving room and recognized Mayor Oswald. Ariella hurried forward. What was he doing here? She remained furious with him and everyone else for allowing Emilian to be beaten.

The mayor was seated with a cup of tea, as were two other gentlemen she recognized. Her father and Amanda were seated with them. The three men had all been present when Emilian had been flogged. She trembled with outrage as the mayor spoke. "We are so pleased that the viscount has recovered and has returned to Woodland, Captain. What happened was a terrible travesty and I cannot even begin to express the extent of my regrets."

Ariella faltered.

Her father saw her and smiled, but a look of caution was in his eyes. "Mayor Oswald has come to call on St Xavier and tender his respects, as have Squire Liddy and Mr. Hawkes. They called a few days ago, as well, but you were preoccupied."

"I hadn't realized." Her mind was spinning as the gentlemen rose to their feet. Were they sincere in their regrets? "Unfortunately, Tollman should have been stopped at the time. The viscount should have never been so abused."

Oswald flushed. "I agree with you, Miss de Warenne. The viscount has been a leading member of Derbyshire society since his father's death. We all look up to him. I still cannot believe what happened. I am very sorry and I look forward to the viscount's continued participation in our affairs. We all do."

Ariella realized that the mayor was sincere.

Oswald shook Cliff's hands. "We will call on St Xavier at Woodland, if he will receive us."

"I am sure he will," Cliff said. He escorted the gentlemen out, Ariella walking to the threshold to watch. When they were gone, he returned to her.

"That is quite the change of heart," she said.

"He has made a mistake. It is no insignificant thing that he has admitted it."

"How could he and the others stand by as they did and watch Emilian being flogged, almost to death?" she cried. "I will never understand it!"

"I have never been able to understand the psychology of a mob, Ariella. I have seen good men and women become vicious and cruel, entirely transformed by the emotions of a crowd," he said. "The mayor is horrified over what Tollman did to him."

"Better late than never, I suppose," Ariella grumbled. "Frankly, I am not in a forgiving mood, and I doubt Emilian is, either."

"St Xavier has been viscount for over eight years. While he has been very reclusive, and there has been gossip about him, he has been respected, almost feared. There has never been an incident like the one with Tollman. But since the Roma came, he has taken their side in this conflict. It has not helped matters."

"He lives with prejudice every single day of his life. He could hardly remain neutral, not when confronted with even more bigotry. *I* cannot remain neutral."

"I understand and admire your passion, Ariella. You would not be my daughter if you did not feel as you do." He was grim. "But as independent and as radical as you are, you cannot change people's minds and you cannot change the world."

Ariella smiled at him. "But I can try."

Her father stared. "You do not seem upset. Your spirits seem very high."

"Why would I be upset? Emilian has recovered. I am thrilled!" As she spoke, she thought of how much she loved him and blushed. She said quickly, "I feel as if the arrival of the Roma has set off a terrible chain of events. Their arrival has certainly intensified the conflict Emilian feels. I almost wish they hadn't come, but then, maybe we wouldn't have met."

"It was his uncle's duty to tell him of the tragedy, Ariella," Cliff said seriously. "Life is entirely unpredictable, and one event can change someone forever."

"What tragedy are you talking about?" He wasn't referring to the flogging, but that was the only tragedy she knew of.

"He did not tell you that his mother was recently murdered by a mob in Edinburgh?"

Ariella was shocked. Emilian had not said a word.

"That would be enough to make a man think of walking away from everything he has dedicated his life to."

I hate them all.

"No wonder he is so angry with us. No wonder their arrival has imploded his life. He must be grieving. Why didn't he tell me?"

Cliff touched her. "He is a dark, angry man, Ariella, and I suspect he was dark and angry before the Roma came."

"But now I fully understand him!" she cried. He needed her comfort even more than before.

"I know you disagree, but I do not think you can heal his wounds. I don't think he will let you, Ariella."

"You are wrong. Even if I can't entirely heal him, I can be his friend."

Cliff made a harsh sound. "Until he leaves with the Rom, and then what will you do?"

Her heart lurched. "What are you talking of? Emilian will not leave now."

Cliff's eyes widened and then narrowed. "Ariella, we had a distinctly unpleasant conversation earlier today. He claimed he has told you everything—including his plans to leave with the Rom."

She breathed deeply. "He did tell me everything, but that was before the events of this past week. Emilian isn't leaving.

We have reached a new understanding, Father. He cares about me now."

"Ariella, he has told me, in no uncertain terms, he is leaving. He is hard and determined. He is not going to give an inch. He has no serious intentions toward you. Even if he does care, his mother's murder has changed the course of his life."

"No. You misunderstood, or he hasn't really thought clearly—he has been so ill. He won't leave *me*. Not now, not after what has happened." She breathed hard. "This has to be our beginning."

Cliff stared. "I am afraid for you," he finally said. "And I do not trust St Xavier."

"Father, *I* trust him. I trust him completely."

WHEN EMILIAN ENTERED the house, Hoode was there to greet him, beaming. "Welcome home, sir."

Emilian smiled at him. He was acutely aware that this would be one of his last nights at Woodland for a long time. It might even be his final night there. He knew that his choice to go north with the *kumpa'nia* was the right one—the only one. He glanced at his father's portrait on the wall in the entryhall as he passed by it. Edmund was undoubtedly spinning in his grave with distress over his plans. Edmund had given him so much, but he must ignore their past now. What his father had wanted no longer mattered.

He went through the house, his thoughts veering to Ariella. The beautiful smile he saw in his mind's eye changed, and her countenance became hurt and accusing. One thing was very clear. He might miss her when he left, but it was for the best. She was the brightest light in his life, but he was the darkest shadow in hers.

"Emilian?"

He turned and saw his uncle approaching. He quickly

backtracked and they embraced. "How are you, Stevan? How is Simcha, the new child, and all the brothers?"

Stevan smiled. "We are fine, now that you have come back to us. How do you feel, Emilian?"

He hesitated. "I am ready to travel."

"Are you?" Stevan stared closely.

"I am more than ready to go. Can the caravan depart tomorrow?"

"We have been ready to leave for a week. We have only been waiting for you." Stevan clasped his shoulder. "What about the de Warenne woman?"

He tensed. "What about her?"

"Will she come with us?"

He stared, shocked. He would never, not in a hundred thousand years, push Ariella into the Roma way of life. "No, she will not come with us."

"So then you will be returning to her?"

His tension grew. "I don't know what I am doing." He spoke harshly. "If I return, I hope she will be with an Englishman." Even as he spoke, his heart lurched. *He would hate her* gadjo *husband.*

"I can see your confusion." Stevan clasped his shoulder. "Emilian, why don't you stay here at Woodland? You can go north at any time—you are a free man and your own master. But we must leave. Things are bad now between the Roma people and the *gadjos*. There is too much tension, name-calling, ugly looks, threats. Even the children fistfight. I am not sure how this has happened. Maybe in the north, they are used to us. They expect us to come in the summer and harvest their fields. They expect us to leave in the winter and they know where to find us to have their wagon wheels and chairs mended, their clothes and socks sewn. I do not like the southern *gadjos*."

He stared coldly. "Northern *gadjos* murdered Raiza."

He shrugged. "And Edinburgh is a dangerous place for the Roma, too."

"God willed the Rom to be Travellers. Yet in all of history, the Roma have never been able to travel freely," Emilian said. His frustration seemed to grow. "You should be able to travel freely."

"There have always been laws against us," Stevan said resignedly. "If you insist on leaving with us, so be it. You are always welcome." Stevan reached into his pocket and handed him a folded linen handkerchief. "I was going to give this to you if you stayed behind after all, but I will give it to you anyway."

Emilian took the square. "What is this?"

"It was your mother's. Your father gave it to her." Stevan turned to go, but then paused. "She is a good woman and she loves you. You will never find such a wife again. I would not leave her for too long and I would not wish her on another Englishman." He smiled and walked out.

Emilian was disbelieving. Ariella would be the perfect wife...but not for him.

Then he opened the handkerchief and saw a small string of gleaming pearls. A tiny gold heart pendant was attached to it.

His heart exploded in grief and pain.

He went to his desk and stared at the pearls. His father had given Raiza this necklace. It was no silly trinket. Had Edmund cared for her?

He was still grieving—and, maybe, he was grieving for them both.

He laid the pearls on his desk, then looked at the miniature by his inkwell. Edmund had worn a suitably severe expression for the portrait, one painted a few years before Emilian had ever come to Woodland. Emilian pulled the miniature closer and stared at it.

They had both wanted him to be Woodland's lord and

master. But while he owed Edmund for almost everything, he owed Raiza even more.

A light knock sounded; he had left the library door open. He looked up and saw Robert standing on the threshold of his library. He went still, recalling Robert standing with Tollman and the mayor after the first few lashes. Emilian had seen the malice smoldering in his eyes.

He had banned Robert from the estate, but he had dared come back now? Emilian slowly stood, feeling very, very mean.

Robert hurried forward, smiling. "I am so pleased you have recovered and that you are home!"

"Really?" A quiet, deep rage consumed him. "Are you as pleased to see me back at Woodland as you were to see me flogged?"

Robert tensed. "I wanted to stop it, but I am a stranger here. I have no authority."

"How many times have I supported you financially since I have become viscount?"

Robert flushed. "I don't know, two or three times—"

He cut him off. "You have come to me at least once a year every year for eight years, Robert. But you repay me with mockery and an utter lack of loyalty. What do you think you are doing here?"

Robert paled. "I am very loyal, Emilian. You must let me prove it."

"We are done."

Robert gasped. "You jest! We are all that is left of the once great St Xavier family!"

"As far as I am concerned, I have no cousin." He had never meant anything more. "Now get out. Get off my premises. Do not come back or I will throw you off bodily, myself."

Robert breathed hard. "You have always treated me like

scum, when we both know *you* are the scum—a dirty, lying *Gypsy*, nothing more!"

Emilian's fury exploded. "Get out," he said quietly, a breath away from assaulting his cousin and causing severe bodily damage.

Robert flushed, clearly aware of having gone too far. He whirled and crashed into Ariella as she stepped into the room. As they grasped each other to straighten, he did not even greet her, much less apologize. He tore free and stormed from the room.

Ariella turned to him, her eyes wide. "Do you wish to go after him?"

He was still furious. "I wish," he said slowly, "to never lay eyes upon him again."

She nodded grimly. "Good. He failed to defend you from Tollman, and he did not come to Rose Hill once to inquire after you."

He stared at her. She was so serious, so determined and so lovely. The rage faded. It wasn't important—*she* was important.

You will never find such a wife again.

He wished Stevan hadn't spoken of her that way. Stevan didn't understand that she was too good for him, and that he couldn't give her the future she deserved. After he was gone, she would eventually come to her senses. He was an infatuation, that was all. Besides, he knew in the end that her family wouldn't allow a marriage, no matter what de Warenne had suggested. The notion of a union between them was truly absurd.

This wasn't about marriage. This was about sensual pleasure; this was about lovemaking.

He was about to make love to her, slowly, sensually, until she begged him to stop. He wanted nothing for himself. He wanted to pleasure her, to show her how grateful he was, and that he had come to admire her, respect her.

Did he care for her, too?

She seemed to sense his desire, her eyes changing. "I know I have arrived on your very heels. Do you mind?"

He must not allow himself any affection. Hadn't he thought earlier that seduction was safe, while everything else was not?

"I will never mind you being close on my heels," he murmured, reaching for her. He pulled her slowly forward, until she brushed his heavy loins.

Her color heightened. "Is it possible that you are even more passionately inclined?"

"It is my gratitude that I wish to express," he whispered.

Her eyes brightened. "Maybe you must become ill again, if such gratitude will follow."

"Maybe," he said thickly. She was his angel. How could he not have come to care? Was that why he was so aroused? Was that why he wanted her this way?

He slid his hand up her waist, over her breast, and heard her breath catch. He stroked his fingers up her throat. Eyes locked, he slid his hand over her nape. Then he leaned forward. He intended a barely teasing kiss, but in the instant before their lips met, his stomach seemed to vanish. So much desire arouse, hollow and acute, that he froze.

She was so entirely different from every lover he had ever had. She deserved so much more than a Rom lover. She deserved so much more than this.

What was happening to him? He did not want a conscience now.

"Emilian?"

She deserved to be cherished, sheltered in an ivory tower somewhere. He could never give her that. He wheeled away from her. "Is this really what you want?"

Her color deepened. "I want nothing more," she said simply, "than to be in your arms. It is our natural progression."

He stared at her.

"You don't have to be afraid of me," she added.

He folded his arms, feeling defensive. "I am not afraid." Damn it, was she right? Had she achieved her natural progression? Were they now friends, on the brink of being lovers? "You want so much from me."

A huge silence fell. She whispered, "Why are you about to reject me again?"

"Ariella, I owe you more than I can repay—far more than this."

She inhaled. "You do not owe me anything. I have come to you out of love and friendship, and I am certain you wish to give me some love and friendship in return."

"You want more than I am ready to give. I will only disappoint you and hurt you. You need to go."

She hurried to him. "You won't disappoint me. You won't hurt me. I love you too much—and you need me too much."

He needed her so badly it hurt, but the pressure wasn't just sexual; it was his heart that ached. "I am afraid I have conceived a conscience. Ariella, I am only a passing fancy."

She shook her head. "You are my first fancy, but you are also my last."

She would not give in, not on this topic. "I do need you," he said roughly. "I need you in my bed, and I need you to look at me with love and hope. But there is simply no point to go on this way. It isn't fair, not to you."

"How can you say there is no point after all that has happened, when we are growing close?" She tried to caress his cheek.

He jerked away and caught her wrist, so she couldn't touch him. They were growing close, but he must not concede to her not on that point or the other.

"You are scaring me," she cried, riveted to his face.

"I may be scaring myself," he murmured, but as he spoke,

his voice was drowned out by Hoode, calling for him. Alarmed, he rushed to the door, jerking it open.

"Sir," Hoode cried, pale. "There is a fire at the Roma encampment."

EVEN RUNNING as fast as she possibly could, with her skirts hiked up to her knees, she remained meters behind Emilian, Hoode and a handful of other servants. The women and children had gathered apart from the camped wagons, every face stricken, but men were running back and forth from the brook with buckets of water, determined to stop the blaze. She halted, panting so hard that she was dizzy, as Emilian raced into the inferno. Several wagons were engulfed in flames. The buckets of water being thrown on them were useless, like throwing a glass of water on a holiday bonfire. Fear began. She did not like Emilian being so close to the flames, but he was speaking rapidly with Stevan, who was covered in ashes and soot.

Emilian dashed back to Hoode and the others. "Get every shovel from the stables and woodshed. Hoode, get farmers Brown and Cowper, have them bring all the bodies and shovels that they can. We'll have to dig to contain this. Hurry!"

As the men raced off, he turned his hard eyes on her. "You stay with the women and children or go home." He ran back to where the men were fighting the fire.

Ariella looked past them at the burning wagons again. She counted five aflame and knew they were lost, even if the flames could be doused, which she felt certain they could not. Emilian appeared on the other side of the burning wagons with a number of men and they began pushing the closest untouched wagon away. It was clear that the fire could easily leap to more wagons and beyond, to the stand of woods that sheltered the brook. She knew the blaze would rage out of control if the woods caught on fire, too. The entire estate could be endangered.

She glanced around anxiously. The horses had run off. That made moving all the wagons that much harder and slower. Then she hurried to the women and children. "Is anyone hurt?"

Jaelle stood. She had been cradling a baby in her lap and she handed the infant to another woman. "No one is hurt. But five families have lost everything, Ariella, every single thing."

Ariella touched her. They moved away. "How did this happen? Did someone neglect a cooking fire?"

"It is the middle of a spring afternoon. No one was cooking."

"What is it?" Ariella cried, not liking the look in her eyes.

Jaelle wet her lips. "I think I saw Tollman, running into the woods with another man."

Ariella went still. Then she glanced toward Emilian, trembling. He now had every man moving wagons, in an attempt to put a safe distance between them and the inferno. No one was trying to throw buckets of water on the flames anymore, as it was clearly useless. "Tollman is in jail," she said, staring at Jaelle. "You are mistaken. This is an accident."

"Is it?" Jaelle cried. "You have been at Rose Hill with Emilian all week. We have been here, afraid to leave the camp. Every time we do, we are threatened and told to go back to where we came from!" She added, "We are leaving in the morning, and it is not soon enough!"

Ariella didn't think twice. "Why don't you stay here at Woodland with Emilian and me. Your brother needs you, and I want to show you that all *gadjos* aren't cruel and hateful." She hesitated. "I want to be friends."

Jaelle stared. "We are friends. I like your family. And I know all *gadjos* aren't cruel. Mrs. Cowper brought us a turkey and another farmer brought us fish from the river."

"And I will bring you more food and supplies," Ariella said firmly.

"You had better be quick about it," Jaelle said tersely. "Because we will be gone by noon tomorrow."

Ariella stiffened, but before she could think clearly, hoofbeats sounded. She turned and saw her brother galloping to them, three horses on leads with him. He dismounted and handed the reins of his stallion to Jaelle. "Are you all right?" he demanded.

"I am fine. Alexi, if the fire reaches the forest, Woodland could be destroyed." She stopped. Emilian's servants had returned with additional men, obviously farmers, and everyone was carrying shovels and picks.

"I know." He glanced at the arriving horde. "We'll need to dig wide and fast to stop this monster. Ariella, why don't you take the women and children up to the house? They will only be in the way."

Before Ariella could even nod, he had flung off his jacket and joined the men. Emilian appeared on the other side of the burning wagons. He gestured at Alexi and then at the wagons, as if drawing an imaginary line. He shouted something at him. Her brother had taken a shovel and he shouted back, gesturing, as well. And suddenly twenty men were on one side of the fire, the rest on the other, and the digging frantically began.

SMOKE FILLED the early evening sky, but the fire had been extinguished. Ariella hugged herself, standing apart from the camp. Women were rushing up to and embracing weary husbands, brothers or sons. The Roma women had been joined by the wives of Woodland's servants and the neighboring farmers who had participated in the firefighting effort. The men were blackened from soot. Partial skeletons remained of six wagons, and several trees beyond the camp had been badly burned. Ariella did not see Emilian, but she saw

Alexi emerging from the far side of the destroyed camp, as tired and dirty as everyone. Where was Emilian, she wondered, trying not to become alarmed.

A violin moaned.

Ariella tensed, turning, to see a dark young man seated on a stool near one wagon, playing the violin. The melody was haunting and mournful. It spoke of a vast, consuming loss.

She trembled. No one had been hurt. The Roma were poor, but wagons could be rebuilt and possessions replaced. She knew that the kitchens at Woodland were in full swing, for she had asked Hoode to cook up whatever was at hand and have the staff bring it down to the tired men. As for the personal items lost in the fire, tomorrow she would enlist Margery and Dianna, and they would purchase bedding, linens, clothing and other necessary items. Surely the caravan was not leaving tomorrow. There would have to be repairs, at least.

Movement caught her eye. She saw Emilian trudging up to the house, his usually erect posture slightly bowed, as if he felt defeat.

She had already begged Jaelle not to mention to Emilian what she thought she had seen. She hurried after him. "Emilian."

His strides faltered.

"Emilian!" She broke into a run.

He paused and turned.

She could not make out his expression until she reached his side, because there were no lights this far from the house, and all illumination came from the stars and the moon. His expression was hard and tight. "Are you all right?" she asked breathlessly.

"I am fine." He folded his arms across his chest. His once-white shirt was gray. Black smudged his face, and his hair was pushed behind his ears, revealing his scar.

"Was anyone hurt?"

"No. No one was hurt."

It felt as if they had gone back in time to the days of their first meeting. He was acting like a stranger. She plucked his sleeve. "I have your kitchen staff working on a meal for all the men. You must be exhausted and hungry."

His cold gray eyes met hers.

"I know you are angry." She bit her lip. "This was an accident, wasn't it?"

He trembled. "Djordi and two others saw Tollman in the woods before the fire started, with another man."

She inhaled. "Tollman is in jail."

He gave her a look. "He was released this morning on bond."

"Promise me you won't go after him."

His smile was mirthless. "I have never made any promises to you, have I?"

She did not like the sound of that. "You cannot take the law into your own hands."

"Why not? Because I have responsibilities of leadership, like your father? Because I should set an example for the community, like de Warenne?"

"Yes!" she cried, afraid. "And because you are better than they are!"

He made a disparaging sound. "I have never understood what you have seen in me, other than my rather pleasing features and body."

She recoiled.

"It is over, Ariella."

She felt the world still. *"What?"*

"It is *over*," he cried.

Shock began. "We are over? Just like that? Because of a bastard like Tollman?"

"We are over because you are a *gadji* princess and I am Rom," he roared.

She backed away from him.

But he seized her wrist and towered over her, not allowing her to retreat. "What? No pretty pleas? Afraid of the savage half blood?"

She felt the tears trickle. "I hate it when you are this way."

"Good, because I hate everyone, every *gadjo*, every damned one." He released her.

She wiped the tears. "You know you don't hate everyone. You know you don't hate every *gadjo*. You know you don't hate *me*."

He shook his head furiously. "Right now I do."

She cried out.

"I am setting myself free," he said harshly. "Here and now, I am *free*."

"Emilian!"

He strode away.

CHAPTER SIXTEEN

SHE STARED at the housemaid who was removing her clothing from the closet. Her bags were on the bed, being filled with her smaller items and possessions; her gowns would be transported on hangers, carefully wrapped. She was returning to London. It was over.

Ariella felt her heart lurch with pain. Two weeks had passed. At first, she had told herself that he would not go through with his departure and then, when it had become clear that the Roma were gone, that he would realize his mistake and return. She had prayed, paced, stared out the window and hoped. But with every passing hour and every passing day, her hope had dwindled. Finally, there was none left.

He wasn't coming back.

She was staring out the window, past the grounds where the Roma had first camped, toward the north, where they were headed. How many times had he told her that he could not return her feelings—that he *would* not? She hugged herself. She had fallen deeply in love with a dark, tormented, very complicated man. The question now was how to forget he ever existed.

That was going to be impossible.

The truth was, her stubborn heart didn't want to ever forget; her stubborn heart was certain this wasn't over and it never would be. Her heart intended to love him from afar and cherish every memory. Her heart meant to wait for him to come back to her, even if it took years.

However, she must not allow her heart to rule her mind or her life. She hadn't been able to sleep or eat. She was truly exhausted and becoming ill. That morning, she had been light-headed and nauseous, a cause for more concern. Ariella hoped it was the flu. For her own sanity, her own health and happiness, she must leave Rose Hill and try to recover her old life. The alternative was to wait for him to come back, to wallow in despair and grief and endanger her health, when it might be years before he returned. Even then, he would not necessarily be returning for her; even then, he might be as set against their future as ever.

Her door was open. She turned when she realized she had company. Her stepmother smiled briefly at her, her green eyes questioning, and Dianna was tearful. "I heard you are leaving this afternoon," Amanda said quietly.

Ariella knew that the entire household had realized she was in love with Emilian and now suffered a broken heart over his departure. Hiding her grief had been impossible. "I am returning to London," she said, not bothering to even attempt a smile. "I can't stay here, like this."

Amanda hugged her, which only made Ariella wish that she could be entirely honest. It also made tears imminent. "I am worried about you going on to town alone. It is so hot in the summer!" Amanda said. "Why don't you stay with us at Rose Hill? The ball is next week and we are leaving two days later. You can come home to Windsong with us afterward," she said, referring to their home in the southwest of Ireland.

She would do nothing at Windsong except wander the grounds, thinking of Emilian, the way she had done at Rose Hill. "I am going to London, where my friends are. There, I can immerse myself in my studies, in public debates, and spend days in the library and museum. I will be happy." Even as she spoke, her words rang hollow.

I am setting myself free.

At first, she had thought he wished to be free of her. She had quickly realized he wished to be free of the torment of living in a world where he was scorned every single day behind his back and where he was powerless to protect the Roma from hatred, bigotry and violence.

She would never be free. Even running away to London wouldn't change the past, erase her memories or vanquish the love in her heart.

"I am so worried about you," Amanda said. "But there is one bit of good news."

Ariella doubted that.

"Tollman has confessed to starting the fire and he has been arrested. This time, there is no gray area. He broke the law and he will be going to trial."

"What happened?"

"Alexi," Amanda said, smiling. "Apparently he induced Tollman to confess."

"Good."

"Please think about what it means to leave the family right now," Amanda said. Then she squeezed her hand and left.

Ariella glanced at her sister. Dianna cried, "I hate him for what he did to you! I hate him for stealing your heart and so callously abandoning it. I hate seeing you like this. Oh, Ariella, he is not worth it. There will be someone else."

Ariella grimaced. "The one thing I am sure of is that there will never be anyone else. It doesn't matter," she lied. "Until I met Emilian, I had no interest in men. Now I am returning to my old life, where I will resume my intellectual pursuits. I am not going to forget Emilian, but I hope that, in time, my memories won't be so painful."

Dianna hugged her, hard. "I know it sounds trite now, when you are so hurt, but time does heal all wounds. I love you—we all love you. Please, think about coming to Windsong this summer."

Ariella surrendered. "I will think about it, but I feel I must go to London now."

Dianna smiled sadly and left. Ariella was relieved, as it was so hard to say no to her little sister and she did not want to stay on the subject. But then Margery stepped into the room, her expression stern. Ariella immediately knew that more pressure would be forthcoming.

"You are so pale!" Margery exclaimed. She held a tray in her hands with covered plates. "I know you haven't had breakfast. I have brought you eggs and sausages. Can you sit down and eat?"

She wasn't hungry but she knew she must eat. She sat down. "You remind me more and more of Aunt Lizzie every single day."

Margery smiled briefly and set the tray down. "Well, as my mother is renowned as being one of the kindest and most generous of ladies, I hope I can be half the lady that she is." Her smile vanished. "I wish I could comfort you."

Ariella took a dutiful sip of juice. "No one can comfort me. But perhaps, in time, I will find a way to navigate through my memories without so much pain. Being in town should help."

Margery sat across from her. "We are going to Adare for the summer. Please, Ariella, please come with us."

Adare was the seat of the earldom, located not far from Windsong, the river Shannon running through it. She shook her head. "I am going to London. I know you think I will be alone, but I will immerse myself in so many studies and pursuits that I won't be lonely at all."

Margery said swiftly, "I have a wonderful idea! Why don't we travel? We can tour Greece and Italy—you know how lovely those places are in the summer!" And from the way she spoke, Ariella knew this was a plan she had conceived previously.

Ariella stabbed her eggs with a fork. And instantly, she felt sick.

When she didn't answer, Margery said, "If you don't want to travel, then I am coming to London with you, and that is that."

Ariella fought the nausea, gave in, and ran to a chamber pot and heaved. Margery rushed to kneel beside her. The heaves were awful, as they had been for the past two days. Ariella clung to the pot, thinking about the fact that she wasn't sick except when the nausea began and she had missed her last monthly time. Which meant she wasn't ill, not exactly...

Finally she sat on her heels and looked at her cousin, who stared back, eyes wide with shock.

Ariella whispered, "Margery, what if I am carrying his child?"

SHE WAS DANCING FOR HIM.

It was late and the stars were out. Many fires burned, and the smell of roasting chicken pervaded the camp. Most of the children were abed and Nicu was playing his violin, another man his guitar. The music was deep and mournful; no one had forgotten the fire or the whipping. He hadn't forgotten.

Stevan had prevented him from seeking out Tollman and making him pay, begging him to forgo more violence. As they were ready to depart, he had agreed, but with a vast reluctance.

Now he watched her, vaguely appreciative of her beauty and grace, but his observations felt clinical. The way she moved her hips told him that she would be a passionate, fierce and pleasing lover. As she whirled, she lifted her skirts daringly high on her thighs. He didn't smile. He didn't really care.

He sat apart from the others. Once, he would have enjoyed her performance and sharing his passion with her. But he had no real interest in her now. Ariella's image burst into his mind. His heart seemed to ache and his loins finally stirred. He hated the damned feelings.

He was determined to put the past behind him. But during the long, idle days on the road, her image slowly invaded his thoughts, as did memories of all the moments they had shared. To get his errant mind onto another subject, he would think of Woodland and wonder if the estate manager, Richards, was getting on. The state of the estate continued to worry him. His duty to it seemed an inescapable part of him now, as ingrained as his handprint. And inevitably he would wonder if Ariella was getting on. He hated himself, because he had betrayed her trust yet again.

He knew her too well now. She was hurt because he had left, but damn it, he had never promised her anything except a night of pleasure.

If he ever saw her again, would her eyes still shine with trust and love?

Jaelle suddenly sat down beside him, appearing somber. He smiled at her, but it felt forced. Jaelle nodded at the dancer. "She wants you. They all do, all the women who do not have husbands, and even some who do."

His loins had begun to fill, but not because of the dancer. He needed release. It had been weeks since the Simmonses' ball. When did he ever go weeks without a lover? Why hadn't he made love to Ariella before he left? Ah, yes, he had suddenly sprouted a conscience.

He hadn't been in the mood to make love to anyone since leaving Derbyshire. It was insane.

"You aren't happy here."

He looked at his sister. He was about to deny it, but that wasn't fair. He put his arm around her. "I have lived with the *gadjos* for eighteen years. It isn't simple for a man to walk away from one life and start another, all in a single day." In fact, it was damned difficult and maybe impossible.

"You are more *gadjo* than Rom."

Her words felt like the truth and that disturbed him, because if she was right, what did that mean? But then he thought of Raiza, who had died in Stevan's arms, not his own. "I am a half blood," he said firmly.

"So what? So am I. But my father didn't want me—he doesn't even know me—and I am Romni. Your father wanted you. You are fortunate, Emilian, and you are *gadjo* because of it. Why are you here?"

"You know why I am here. It is because of our mother. I owe her this, Jaelle."

Jaelle seemed bewildered. "She is dead, Emilian, and your being here won't bring her back to life."

He stared past her into the firelight. He believed he owed Raiza this attempt to reclaim his Roma heritage. But Jaelle's words felt like the truth.

The dancer had stopped and was sipping wine, glancing at Emilian through her dark lashes. Jaelle stood. "Will you take her?"

He hesitated. He needed a woman; of that there was no doubt. But she wasn't the woman he wanted.

"I thought so. Go back to your woman, Emilian. She is good and beautiful and if you wait too long, another man will take her."

His eyes widened.

She shrugged and sauntered off.

He wanted another man to take her, he thought. He wanted her to forget him. Or did he? His heart accelerated wildly. The truth was that he *hated* the idea. Even more importantly, he *missed* her.

Missing her had implications he must not consider. Missing her was dangerous.

But he didn't want the beautiful Romni woman who was so eager to warm his bed. He wanted Ariella, because they had never finished what they had begun. Because he hadn't shown her his gratitude. He had only hurt her with his anger, and she didn't have her English prince yet.

He had to go back, just for a night. Nothing had changed. Even if Jaelle was right, even if the English part of him was stronger than the Rom, he had made a promise to Raiza and to himself. He was going to her grave. He would find his Roma heritage, and nothing could stop him. But the caravan moved slowly and he had his prized stallion with him.

He stood, a terrible excitement filling him.

In four or five days, he could be at Rose Hill.

IT WAS HALF PAST TEN in the evening. Supper had long since ended. Ariella sat in bed, holding her still-flat belly, thinking about the child she was probably carrying. The shock was wearing off. She had started becoming sick in the mornings a few days ago, and her breasts seemed to be swelling, too. If she had conceived the first night they had spent together, that made her almost six weeks along.

A pregnancy seemed very likely and she was afraid. Not once in her life had she ever dreamed she would have a child out of wedlock. She couldn't even begin to imagine what she would do or how she would manage. Her family would be in an uproar. And then there was Emilian. He had to be told, didn't he?

She couldn't think of all the issues now. *She was carrying Emilian's child.*

From the ashes of grief and despair, joy began unfurling.

She stroked her flat belly, crying. There were no regrets. How could she regret carrying Emilian's child, even if he didn't love her? For she loved him and she always would. Even if she never saw him again, she would have this part of him—this part of them. The child was a wonderful gift, a blessing. For the first time since he had left her, she felt her heart stir and beat, becoming alive again, and suddenly the future loomed, filled with bright light. She realized she couldn't wait to hold their child in her arms. *She loved this baby.*

But it was bittersweet, because as she imagined holding their tiny infant daughter or son, she saw Emilian standing over her, smiling at them. She wasn't sure if that would ever happen—she wasn't sure of anything just then, except that she had been given a miracle.

"Ariella?" Margery whispered. She poked her head into the room, clad in her nightclothes.

Ariella smiled at her. "Come in."

Margery did so, closing the door. She hurried to the bed and climbed into it. "I have been thinking about you all day. Are you crying?"

"No." Ariella touched her hand, smiling. "Don't worry. I am happy, Margery, so very happy. I am having his child!"

Margery stared in dismay. "You must send Emilian a letter. He will come back and marry you if he knows the truth."

Ariella's joy gave way to foreboding. "No. That isn't a good idea."

Margery gasped. "You will tell him, won't you? You will marry him?"

Ariella grimaced. "I will always love him. And I believe he cares for me, I do. But I will not force him into marriage, and certainly not with our child."

Margery paled. "He seduced you. He has an obligation to take care of you and this child."

"I wanted to be seduced. He did not take advantage of me. And I have the means to give this child a very good life."

Margery was wide-eyed. "Ariella, your father will force Emilian to the altar, no matter what you wish."

Ariella feared Margery was right. "That would be a mistake. Emilian will see it as an attack or a trap, and he will be furious. No. My father won't do any such thing, because he won't know about the child."

Margery cried out.

Ariella bit her lip hard, some of her euphoria vanishing. This was going to have to be a secret. She could barely believe that she could not share her joy with her family. "I am going to have to go away and have this child alone."

"You are as independent and as eccentric as ever! How can you intend to be an unwed mother?" Margery cried. "You will be scorned and ostracized! You cannot keep such a secret forever, anyway!"

Ariella looked at her. "I may have to go away for some time."

Margery paled. "Eventually you will have to come home, and the secret will be out," she pointed out. "They will hunt him down then, you know that, even if it is a year from now—even if it is *years* from now. The moment they realize you have had his child, he is doomed."

Ariella tensed. "I will talk them out of it. In any case, I am beginning to realize going to London now is not the best idea. The city is unhealthful in the summer months."

"Ariella, it is Emilian's right to know," Margery persisted.

"Yes, it is. And I will tell him, but I haven't decided when." She simply couldn't think of that issue now.

"You are determined to go this alone," Margery finally said.

"Right now, it is my only choice."

Margery inhaled. "Bloody hell," she said, surprising Ariella. "Please know that I think you are making the wrong decision. I think he should be told the truth and that he should marry you, no matter what he wants to do, for your sake and the baby's."

"Then we are in disagreement," Ariella said.

They stared at each other. Margery took her hand firmly. "If you really plan to have this baby in secret, you know I am staying with you."

Ariella looked into her worried eyes and felt her own

tears rise. They were tears of gratitude and relief. "You are the most loyal friend I have. I am afraid, Margery," she admitted, trembling. "I am afraid of being alone during the next few months, I am afraid of being alone during childbirth and I am even afraid of being alone after the baby is born!"

Margery hugged her. "You aren't alone. You won't be alone. I will be with you for as long as necessary." She wiped her own moist eyes and her tone became brusque. "Let's start to think of where you wish to live for a good year. We will claim we wish to tour, and in a few months we will set out. Maybe we can lease a villa in the south of France. The climate is good, you speak the language well and I can get on."

Ariella nodded, a new excitement beginning. "I like that," she said slowly. "The south of France is beautiful. It will be a wonderful place to have this baby."

THE NEXT WEEK PASSED in a flurry of plans. Trying not to arouse suspicion, Ariella and Margery took long walks in Amanda's gardens, with Margery carrying her sketch pad and charcoal. She was, fortunately, an adept artist, and she claimed she intended to do a watercolor study of one of Amanda's famous coral roses after leaving Rose Hill, which required a vast number of sketches and long hours in the gardens. To all appearances, Ariella was now immersed in the history of the Mongols, and it was simple enough to read in the gardens while Margery "sketched."

The sketch pad was filled with notes. Letters had been sent to several London agents, and replies had just been received. There was more than one pleasant villa on the outskirts of Nice available for a long lease. Margery had just sent her personal secretary off to the south of France to inspect the various accommodations. Within a month or so, they would be able to determine which villa to let.

Ariella had begun to hint to her family that she wished to

travel. Her father seemed pleased, and she knew he was relieved that she was getting over Emilian. If only he knew the truth. But there was no guilt. She had to protect Emilian from his wrath and that meant going forward in absolute secrecy.

Margery's father, the Earl of Adare, had arrived the other day for the ball, with his heir, Ned, and his younger sons. Margery would soon sit down with him and ask him for permission to tour. Ariella knew her uncle would never refuse such a request.

They were actually about to pull off their charade. If all went as planned, she and Margery would soon be on their way to France, with no one the wiser.

ARIELLA HAD NO WISH to attend Amanda's ball, but there was no choice. While everyone knew she did not like such fêtes, it was her habit to grumble and then dutifully attend. She intended to behave as usual.

As she slowly approached the ballroom, the house was already alive with laughter, conversation and the strains of the orchestra. Ahead, she saw the ballroom, filled with ladies in their colorful evening gowns and glittering jewels, the men in their black tailcoats, white-coated waiters passing out flutes of champagne. She saw her father and Amanda standing not far from the ballroom's entrance, surrounded by a handful of guests whom they were obviously greeting. Cliff was golden and handsome, Amanda stunningly beautiful, her small gloved hand on his arm. Ariella smiled to herself. On a night like this, it was so clear that they remained deeply in love.

She paused, not going any farther into the room. Impossibly, she saw herself waltzing in Emilian's arms.

She did not want to be swept back to that May night. She had been immersed in making plans and there had been little time to mourn what she'd had and lost. She had become adept at instantly changing her thoughts. The moment she missed him, the moment it hurt, she would think of the tiny life growing inside her and imagine holding her newborn for the very first time.

Her heart lurched. Emilian felt so close. If she dared, it would be easy to remember every moment they had shared. It would be easy to recall every detail of that one night. She saw him staring at her from across the room, she saw him smiling down at her as they danced, while she trod on his toes. She saw the warm, passionate look in his eyes, and she could almost feel his strong hard body as he held her far too closely.

Ariella breathed. She still missed him terribly, and yearned for his return. Having his child could not ease that.

She must not allow herself to indulge in such fantasies and such memories now. Emilian was gone. It might be years before she saw him again. She was determined to have a healthy child. Dwelling on the past would not help her health. It would not help the baby. She decided she would stay a mere hour, and then plead a headache and leave.

"Would you like to dance, Miss de Warenne?"

Ariella tensed at the sound of Robert St Xavier's voice. She faced him, disbelieving. She had not forgotten his utter treachery the day Emilian had been flogged. Now, she recalled the insults he had shouted at Emilian when he had been banished from Woodland. She stiffened impossibly and stared coldly at him. She put all the condescension she could into her tone. "I'm afraid not."

He seemed incredulous and he flushed.

"There is only one St Xavier with whom I would ever dance, and the viscount is not here," she added as imperiously.

He was crimson now. "You might change your tune," he said angrily. "Emilian has gone Gypsy. I always knew the day would come. He won't come back, and that hurts you, doesn't it?" He shrugged and insolently looked at her low-cut dress. "You are welcome at Woodland any day, Miss de Warenne."

"What does that mean?" she demanded, aghast. Did he dare insinuate that he wished for a liaison with her?

His eyes widened with mock innocence. "You misunder-stand me." He laughed coldly. "No estate can be without its master for very long, and Woodland is no exception."

Ariella instantly understood the innuendo. Surely, surely, Robert did not think to be lord of Woodland in Emilian's absence! "Woodland has a master—and it also has an estate agent."

He laughed. "I am Emilian's next of kin, his heir. If he forfeits the estate by a prolonged absence, I am next in line. In any case, I have taken up residence there. I have no inten-tion of letting some agent steal me blind."

"Nothing is yours to steal," she cried, stunned. "Woodland is Emilian's. He is viscount, and I have no doubt the estate manager is a stellar man!"

Robert smiled at her. "Then why don't we say that I am looking after my beloved cousin's interests while he is gone?" He bowed. "Please call, Miss de Warenne. You have been interested in the wrong St Xavier, and I feel certain I can persuade you of that."

She trembled with outrage as Robert walked away. He hated Emilian and Emilian despised him. They were rivals. Did he know of her illicit affair and think to encourage a liaison in order to take her from Emilian? Or were his inten-tions acceptable? Perhaps he wished to court her. He might hope for marriage and her fortune.

Margery tugged on her arm. "Is he a suitor?" she asked, incredulous.

"No, he is not." She remained distressed. Did Robert truly think to somehow possess Woodland, taking it from Emilian? But that was impossible, wasn't it? She glanced at Margery.

"If Emilian never returns, what will happen to his estate?" But even as she spoke, she knew.

Her child was Emilian's heir. Her child, if a son, was the next viscount.

Margery gave her a long look. "For your child to inherit the title you would have to come forward very publicly. But I don't know if you could succeed, Ariella, not without Emilian's support. And you would have to marry."

Ariella tensed. Did she have to tell Emilian about their child after all? *Her child had every right to Woodland.* Robert's treachery might make it necessary for her to tell Emilian the truth after all, sooner than she had intended. "I am certain of very few things, but one of them is that Emilian will claim this child when I ask him to do so. Let us hope he isn't staying away forever. Not for my sake, but for this baby's sake—for his or her future."

Margery leaned close. "I still believe you should tell Emilian the truth now. His cousin is a scoundrel, and I fear he thinks to cause trouble."

Ariella hoped Margery was wrong, and that St Xavier was harmless, a man of bluffs. They squeezed hands and separated, sharing silent looks. Ariella saw Robert standing some distance away now. Although he was with several gentlemen, he was regarding her unwaveringly. He lifted his flute in a salute when their eyes met.

She turned away, flustered. Margery was right. Robert was up to no good. She could let his behavior pass, but only for the moment. She needed to carefully think the situation through.

"Will you dance with your father?" Cliff appeared at her side, smiling at her, but his eyes were filled with speculation.

She failed to smile. "You know I detest dancing," she said. "Father, Emilian's cousin has moved into Woodland and seems to think he is master there, in Emilian's absence."

Cliff glanced at Robert. "I have heard."

"You have heard!" she cried. "Emilian would never allow this. He despises Robert. Can he simply move in and take over the estate?"

"I have heard he has done just that, and that the estate manager, a good enough man, is incapable of standing up to him. Ariella, I thought you were over St Xavier."

She knew it behooved her to be honest now. "I will never be over him. But I am not going to mourn for something that will not be."

Her father started.

"I will always love him, but I realize I made a mistake." She dared to add, "The tour I am planning has lifted my spirits." She quickly kissed his cheek. "I know you will approve of the plans Margery and I have made."

"I sense a conspiracy," he said, but he smiled.

"It is vast," she said lightly. "I am going to step outside for some air," she added. She slipped away, and as she moved through the crowd, she avoided eye contact, not wanting to be waylaid. But she was almost certain that Robert was watching her again.

She shivered. She did not trust him and he had become a threat to her child's future. She must decide what to do—and soon.

She slipped outside onto a flagstone terrace, one lit with gaslights. Although it was a beautiful July evening, she was alone, and that relieved her. She touched her belly. *Don't you worry,* she thought. *I will never let anyone jeopardize your future, and neither will your father.*

And suddenly she felt his presence.

CHAPTER SEVENTEEN

EMILIAN.

Her heart skipped wildly. She whirled, searching the shadows frantically, wondering if her instincts were playing cruel tricks on her. And then her heart stopped.

Emilian stood on the other side of the terrace, staring at her.

She could not move. She could not even cry out. *He had come back.*

He advanced, his strides hard and long, his eyes on her. Ariella began to shake. *He had come back and everything would be all right now.*

He paused abruptly before her, his gaze searching, his smile hesitant, uncertain. She somehow breathed; she somehow smiled. His eyes flashed silver in the dark and his hands closed on her shoulders. "I have missed you."

She flung her arms around him and held on, hard, burying her face against the vast, solid wall of his chest.

He stroked down her back. "Ariella, do not misunderstand," he said.

She looked up. "What is there to misunderstand? I have missed you, too, terribly." She clasped his rough, unshaven jaw.

His eyes blazed. "Will you ever hate me? Condemn me? Judge me and find me lacking?"

"Never," she cried.

He turned his face and kissed her hand, his mouth hard

and demanding on her palm. As Ariella felt the tremor in his body, he wrapped one arm around her, pulling her closer; she felt his manhood, hard and massive against her hip. His silver gaze was molten as it locked with hers. She trembled, the desire acute.

"There has been no one since you," he said.

She felt more tears. He was telling her that he had been faithful to her. She leaned up, urgently seeking his mouth.

Their lips fused. His mouth was hard and frantic. The fervor of his kiss shocked her, and then she thrilled, returning it. She clawed his shoulders and his teeth grated hers. She began to spin. She needed him desperately; she loved him desperately. *Thank God he had come home.*

They stumbled down the terrace steps, lips locked. Ariella wanted him to pull her down in the grass, move his big, hard body over hers, into hers. She needed to be joined with him now. She needed to weep in rapture. She didn't care that the ballroom was a terrace length away.

But he tore his mouth from hers and pulled her across the lawns, away from the terrace. He turned her against a wall, one cast in shadows, finding her mouth again, claiming it. Her back pressed against the wall, he started lifting her skirts. She sucked on his mouth and his hands tore at the slit in her drawers. He made a harsh sexual sound, sliding his fingers over her wet, throbbing flesh. She tore her mouth from his to cry out.

He dropped to his knees and his tongue thrust against her. She flung her head back, no longer capable of thought, reveling in the pleasure. Clasping his head, she wept in a fierce, sudden release.

Still in the throes of rapture, her knees gave way. She felt the wall scraping her bare back as she sank to the damp grass. He moved over her, his mouth covering hers, and she felt him unfastening his breeches. Then his lips moved to her throat, causing the delicious sensations to start fluttering all over her again. His mouth moved lower. Something hot, hard and huge caressed her inner thighs.

She managed to look at him. His eyes were blazing. "I came back to make love to you," he said roughly. "I want to make love to you all night."

She wasn't certain she could respond, for he stroked over her again, making her seize his bulging arms, clawing him to restrain him. "Good," she gasped.

His silver eyes blazed. He moved, thrusting deep.

Ariella held on to him and wept with love and need. He groaned, moving hard and fast, his urgency inescapable, nipping her throat, embedding himself in her, and as she spasmed around him, he whispered in her ear, Romany words she could not understand—but their meaning was inescapable. *I love you.*

She shattered another time, into a thousand rapturous pieces.

He cried out, collapsing on top of her, and as she held him, floating in joy and the aftermath of release, he spasmed, his face against her neck, again and again.

Neither one saw the man standing in the shadows of the terrace, watching them.

ROBERT ST XAVIER SAUNTERED into the ballroom, intent. He scanned the crowd, looking for his host. A terrible impatience began. Cliff de Warenne was nowhere to be seen. His next choice would be Cliff's brother, the Earl of Adare, but he did not see Tyrell de Warenne, either. He was suddenly furious. His Gypsy cousin might be done with his little lover by the time he got to the business at hand.

And then Alexi de Warenne appeared, a beautiful blond woman on his arm. They were immersed in a flirtation, but Robert did not care. He hurried after Alexi, rudely tapping his shoulder from behind. The other man whirled, his expression cool and incredulous.

"I beg your pardon," Robert said swiftly. "But I believe you should step outside. You will be interested in what is happening on the terrace, at the north end."

"What the hell are you talking about?" Alexi asked, annoyed.

"Your sister is there, and she is hardly alone." He refrained from smirking, barely.

Brilliant blue eyes widened. Then Alexi looked at the woman. "Excuse me," he said, and, his strides swift, he left them.

Robert smiled, very pleased with himself.

THEY REMAINED ENTWINED, Emilian's big body within hers. Ariella sighed, touching his rough jaw. He lifted his head and smiled at her. He had never looked at her so tenderly and openly before. His eyes were shining.

She touched his face again. "You have a beautiful smile. I hope I will see it more often."

"Have I ever told you that your eyes are my obsession?" She started.

"You have the most amazing eyes. I often wish I could deserve the trust I see in them." He brushed her mouth and began moving within her.

She stroked his back through his jacket and shirt. "You do deserve my trust," she began. Then she sighed, shivering with growing pleasure, for he was huge now, pulsing deep within her. She moaned and he feathered kisses down her throat and to the low vee of her bodice.

"I need you," he whispered, "so very much." He moved deeper and paused.

Her body clenched at his fiercely, making it hard to think much less speak. She scraped her nails across his wool-clad shoulders. "Don't stop."

She felt him smile and he moved. "Take your pleasure, darling," he murmured.

Ariella gave in to the growing pressure and let the pleasure become her life. As he moved, her love overcame her and she wept softly as she climaxed in a maelstrom of love and surrender.

She floated, half-conscious, back to him, aware of him kissing her gently, pulsing within, yet holding back. She smiled to herself. *I am so happy.*

"Get off of her!"

Ariella held on to Emilian, vaguely aware that she should be alarmed. Surely she hadn't heard her brother shouting at them.

"You bastard!" Alexi roared.

And sanity returned as Emilian was flung from her to the grass. Ariella sat up in time to see Alexi tackling Emilian, fists slamming into him, his rage a murderous frenzy.

They had been discovered.

Jerking her clothes down, she screamed, "Alexi, stop! Alexi, stop right now!" She jumped to her feet.

But Alexi was pummeling Emilian, who merely braced against the blows with his forearm, protecting his head from the other man.

Ariella seized Alexi from behind, screaming at him. Emilian instantly scrambled away and to his feet. He lifted his hand to his mouth, which was bleeding. Ariella held on to one of her brother's arms, refusing to let go, but Alexi shook her off anyway.

"Don't," she shouted as Alexi ran at Emilian again. "I love him—stop it, right now!"

But Alexi hit him again. This time, Emilian used his arm as a shield, blocking the blow.

Three men ran past her, toward Alexi and Emilian. Her horror knew no bounds now, for a crowd had gathered on the terrace behind them—and the three men rushing at Alexi and Emilian were her father, her uncle and Margery's older brother, Ned.

Ned and the Earl of Adare seized Alexi, restraining him. Alexi remained furious, breathing hard. Her father paused before Emilian, incredulous. "Is this what I think it is?"

"Yes," Emilian said softly.

Cliff hit him.

Emilian went down.

Ariella was frozen, horrified.

THEY HAD GATHERED in the library. Ariella trembled, hugging herself. She had never seen her father so enraged. She wasn't sure she had ever been this afraid, either. She could not begin to imagine what he might do to Emilian. She glanced at him. He stood on the other side of the room, and she knew better than to go to him, when that was what she desperately wished to do.

Emilian was dangerously angry, too. In fact, she knew that stance well—it was belligerent, for he had been cornered and he was waiting for an attack. His stare was cold and hard and directed back at Cliff.

No good was going to come of this confrontation and she knew it. She trembled, feeling violently ill, dizzy and weak. She hoped she was not about to succumb to a late-night version of morning sickness. Margery and Amanda had quickly presented themselves, word of the tryst obviously spreading like wildfire. Her cousin now held her hand, squeezing it reassuringly, but Ariella was not reassured.

The Earl of Adare laid his hand on her shoulder. "Are you hurt, Ariella?" he asked. His tone was grim, but his blue gaze was kind.

"No," Ariella cried. "Uncle Ty, I am fine!"

Cliff whirled to face her, incredulous. "He has seduced you!"

Ariella did not even try to deny it. She was frankly tired of so many secrets and lies.

Cliff looked at Emilian murderously, but before he could

erupt, Amanda reached his side. "She is in love with him," she said softly.

Cliff breathed hard. "And that is all that is saving him from the bullet I wish to put between his eyes."

Ariella gasped. "Father, please be calm and rational."

"How can I be calm? And I am very rational. I asked him if he had intentions and he said he had none. I knew he wished to seduce you—I knew he was no good, a man of no honor! I knew it the moment I saw him with you, when they were camped at Rose Hill. But I allowed myself to be persuaded to keep him under this roof when he was seriously injured. And this is how my generosity and hospitality is repaid!"

"It is not his fault," Ariella said, desperate to defend and protect him from Cliff's wrath. "If anyone is at fault, it is me."

Emilian finally spoke. His face hard, he said, "I take full blame. You are right, de Warenne. I seduced your daughter, very intentionally."

Ariella cringed.

Cliff launched himself at him. Neither the earl or Alexi moved to stop him and Ariella cried out as Cliff slammed his fist into Emilian's face. Emilian reeled but did not stagger backward. Amanda seized Cliff from behind. "Battery will solve nothing," she cried. "Why don't you think about what is best for Ariella now?"

"That is precisely what I am doing!" Cliff shouted.

"It is not his fault," Ariella cried, aghast. "I knew what would happen if I allowed him liberties and I did so anyway. I wished to be seduced!"

Alexi turned a disbelieving look upon her. "You are the most trusting person I know. It is obvious you were the easiest prey a man like this could have. I feel certain he took advantage of your naiveté in every possible way." He glared at Emilian. "My sister is too good for you."

"I happen to agree with you," Emilian said. "She did not deserve any of this."

Cliff was breathing hard. "I indicated I would accept a suit from you. Now there is no choice. The gossips will make certain the entire country knows of my daughter's ruin. You, sir, will marry her."

Emilian stared, his face expressionless and tight.

Ariella felt tears gathering. This was not how she wished for them to proceed! He had come back because he missed her. In time, he might have even come forth as a suitor. Had they not been discovered, she might have told him about the child. But now Emilian was ready to explode, and that would make matters even worse. She did not want him forced to the altar! Margery touched her, but she ignored it. "Father, no."

Cliff whirled. "What the hell does that mean? How could you do this, Ariella? How? Is this how I have raised you? To steal around behind my back like some East End trollop?"

Ariella gasped.

Emilian stepped forward. "I took advantage of your daughter. She is hardly a trollop."

"You defend her?" Cliff cried.

"I am the one who should be called names."

Cliff's mouth curled. "Your father may have been an honorable Englishman, but you are despicable—a man with no honor whatsoever."

She was ready to retch now. Margery steadied her, as if she knew.

The Earl of Adare stepped between Cliff and Emilian. "You do realize we insist upon marriage?"

Emilian shrugged but his gaze slid to Ariella. For one moment, Ariella saw so much regret in Emilian's eyes, and she did not want him to regret one single moment that they had shared. "In spite of what the noble captain thinks, I am not entirely without honor. If she agrees, I will do the deed."

Ariella jerked in dismay at his choice of words and his cold, scathing tone.

"We will have to marry immediately, though, because I am rejoining my people and traveling north. She can stay behind and wait for my return." He shrugged again, as if beyond indifference.

She went still, staring at him. He hadn't come back to stay?

Cliff exploded. "You would marry her and abandon her? Over my dead body!"

"You cold bastard," Alexi hissed. "Can't you see how you are hurting her?"

"She will be well cared for, with my entire staff at her disposal. Call it abandonment if you will."

Cliff started for him. Amanda seized him, begging, "Please, control your temper. We will solve this, somehow!"

He hadn't come back to stay, Ariella thought, stunned. He had come back to make love to her. But he had missed her— he had said so. And now he would marry her out of a sense of honor, duty and even regret, but not out of love or affection? Now he would let her family force him to the altar? She stared at him. How could she reconcile the man standing in the library with the man whose arms she had just been in? She desperately reminded herself that cornering Emilian was always the worst tack.

"My daughter will *never* be abandoned at the altar," Cliff ground out. "There will be a marriage, and the two of you will return to Woodland when the vows have been made."

"I left Woodland," Emilian said, "for my own reasons. I am not your slave. You cannot force me to remain at Woodland. I said I would make amends, but I will also say this. Your daughter deserves far more than I can give her, de Warenne. Maybe you should think carefully about the life she will live as a half blood's wife. Maybe you should consider finding her a proper blue blood for a husband."

"You are not getting out of this. You ruined her—you will marry her," Cliff said furiously.

Adare stepped between them again.

Ariella realized she was dizzy and weak. She had never seen her father as hateful and she could not bear the enmity between him and Emilian, not now. She hurried to a chair. Margery bent over her. "Are you all right?"

She blinked back tears. "No." She looked at Emilian, wishing he would give her some small sign of his affection.

Cliff turned away, shaking. The earl spoke. "You are the viscount of Woodland. From what I have heard, you can give her exactly the kind of life she deserves. You do not want to go up against me and mine. You will do what is right— and walking away from her on the paltry excuse that you are deficient somehow, a half blood, is not what is right. I am certain you and I can come to terms as far as the living arrangements go."

Now her uncle would buy Emilian for her. She covered her face with her hands. How had their joyous reunion been turned into something so ugly and distasteful?

Emilian finally looked at Ariella. "I am going north—even if it means going up against the great de Warenne dynasty."

Ariella told herself not to cry as she stared back at him. His expression was too hard, too cold. "I can't marry Emilian," she whispered. "Not this way."

All eyes went to her. She only looked at Emilian, but his face was an impassive mask. She wet her lips and said, "May I have a word alone with him?"

Cliff laughed coldly. "When hell is frozen over."

Adare touched him. "He won't run away, Cliff. Let's give them a moment."

Cliff shook his head. "I don't want him alone with my daughter."

The earl said, "Did you wait to exchange vows before carrying on with Amanda? Did I wait before taking Lizzie to wife? We do not know that this is the end of your daughter's world. It might be the beginning. Let us hope so."

"You would not be so calm if this was Margery!" Cliff exclaimed, but he turned. "Five minutes. And St Xavier? I am close to committing murder, so I suggest you keep your hands to yourself and that you remain in this room until I return." He left.

When everyone was gone, Ariella sat back down, aware of being utterly distraught again. It was the child, she thought helplessly. "You didn't come back to stay with me."

"I didn't come back to stay," he said quietly. He walked over to her and knelt, taking her hands. Ariella pulled them away and clasped them tightly together in her lap. He instantly stood. "But I did come back for you," he said. "I came back to see you. I owe you so much…and this is how you have been repaid."

She stared into his eyes, looking for the truth in his heart.

"I am so sorry," he said, his regard unwavering. "I never meant for any of this to occur."

"Then what did you mean?"

"I am not good with words," he finally said. "I came back, hoping I could show you how grateful I am to you for all you have done for me, and for Djordi, Nicu, Jaelle and the others. I never expected discovery, Ariella. I wanted to make love to you. I wanted to smile at you afterward, and perhaps, even laugh together."

She almost cried. "Do you care for me, Emilian?"

Their gazes locked. He finally said, grimly, "I do care."

She had not been delusional after all. Some small comfort was to be had.

"I will marry you, Ariella, if that is what you truly want."

She sat up straighter. "But that isn't what you want."

His eyes blazed. "I have never considered marriage! Not to you, not to anyone. As my wife, you will live with whispers and scorn. It will not be pleasant. But if we do not marry, it will be even worse for you."

She wet her lips and said, low, "I want more than marriage from you."

He breathed. "I know. But I am not a man like your father, capable of a grand, undying passion for a woman. I will never be that man."

Was he telling her that he somehow knew he would never love her? "I don't care about my reputation. I never have."

"You may feel differently the next time you are out in society."

"Are you trying to encourage this forced union, when you have blatantly said you have no wish to marry anyone?" she cried.

"I am English enough to do what is right," he exclaimed, flushing. "If you tell me you want marriage, I will step up. But I am going north," he warned. "You can live in luxury at Woodland or you can stay here."

If ever there was a moment to tell him about their child, it was now. A part of her wanted to tell him the truth, but it would muddy the waters. He would insist on marriage for all the wrong reasons. He might even change his plans to travel. The effect was the same as holding a revolver to his head. He had to come to her of his own free will. She would never give up hope that one day he would do so.

She covered her aching heart with her hand and prayed she was making the right choice, especially for their child. "I will never marry you this way, under such dreadful circumstances," she finally said.

A long pause ensued. "I think, in time, your father can repair the damage done this night. He is powerful enough to find you the nobleman you deserve. I know you will forget me, Ariella, eventually. There will be someone else, a proper Englishman, who will give you a perfect and very English life. You will be happy," he said. He shrugged. "You may even decide that you hate me for all I have done."

"I will never hate you," she said, brushing at a tear. "And there will never be anyone else."

He inhaled.

But he was leaving, perhaps for years. She stood. "Have you glimpsed the freedom you are looking for, Emilian? Have you found happiness?"

"No, I have not." His face hardened. "I am glad you have refused to marry me. You deserve more than the life of a half blood's wife."

She stared at him, finally realizing that he thought to protect her from the torment he was afflicted with. "You underestimate me," she said, surprised.

"You are a de Warenne!" he exclaimed, as if that explained everything.

"And you are both the viscount St Xavier and the son of a proud Romni."

He breathed hard. "No—it is one or the other. Am I English or am I Rom?"

And the freedom he was seeking suddenly became clear. It wasn't simply about escaping condescension and scorn. "Emilian, if you are going north to become a Rom, you will never be free. You are too English. You belong to two worlds, not one."

"No man belongs to two worlds," he cried, his eyes blazing.

She stared, the conflict and torment visible on his face and in his eyes. Until he realized who and what he was, he would never be at peace. He could not discover who he truly was without learning about his lost heritage. And no matter how she wished to heal him, she could not do so.

He had to go.

Her heart lurched in anguish. She felt the tears rise. "I will always love you," she whispered. "I will always miss you."

His eyes widened. "Are you telling me goodbye?"

She couldn't speak; she nodded.

He crossed the space between them, taking her by her shoulders. "I am hurting you again. I didn't come back to hurt you, Ariella."

"I know," she whispered. She wrapped her arms around him and held on hard.

He held her back as tightly.

Then she stepped away. "Go. Go north, with your mother's people. I am going to pray that you find what you are seeking—and that you will decide to come home. I will be here, Emilian, when you do—when you are ready to allow yourself happiness."

"I may never find what I am seeking."

She thought about their child, who would one day need his or her father. "Yes, you will. I have no doubt. I think the answers to your questions are much closer than you realize."

His eyes widened. "Ariella, don't wait for me."

"There isn't going to be anyone else, Emilian." She clasped his rough cheek, suddenly exhausted. "Go now, before they return," she said. "And Emilian? I love you."

He stiffened, his face strained, his silver eyes blinding. Then he nodded and was gone.

WHEN SHE FINALLY RETURNED to her bedroom, she leaned against the door, beyond exhaustion. Cliff, still intent on a forced marriage, had threatened to go after Emilian and drag him back to Rose Hill, but in the end, Amanda had convinced Cliff to let him go, as that was what Ariella wished. She hugged herself. Her father was furious and she didn't trust him not to get on a mount and set chase after Emilian.

She tried not to cry. He had only left an hour or so ago, and while she desperately needed a respite from her family, which was in turmoil, she missed him so much that the pain was consuming. Had she done the right thing? He had been prepared to go through with a forced marriage—and he did care for her. He had finally admitted it.

Ariella went still. What was she doing, allowing him to leave her this way, to face his future alone?

He had to go north. She understood that now. But she could go with him.

She had to go north with him.

Stunned, Ariella let her mind turn over the notion. Everything had happened so quickly, there had been no time to really think. Of course she had to go north with him, as a lover, as a friend, and eventually, as the mother of his child. Marriage didn't matter, not now. Being together in this terrible time was what mattered!

Ariella turned to the armoire but did not open it. He would object, at first. She had not a doubt. He didn't want her to suffer by being at his side, and he didn't want her to live the difficult Romany life. But he was not going to send her away when she caught up with him. Her mind was made up. She loved him enough to fight for them both.

She ran from the room. It was only a few hours before dawn, and she banged on Alexi's door. He opened it instantly, fully dressed, and she realized he hadn't gone to sleep yet. She knew he was distressed for her and had been brooding. The glass of whiskey she saw on the table before the fireplace confirmed it.

He was alarmed upon seeing her. "You need to go to bed," he said sharply.

She walked past him and then closed his door so they would have privacy. "I need your help," she said. "And I will do anything to get it."

His eyes narrowed.

"I am going after Emilian," Ariella said.

"Like hell!" he exclaimed.

"I need you to help me catch up to him and the caravan, Alexi. If you do not help me, I will go by myself."

His eyes widened. "So you think to marry him after all, and become a Gypsy? Father won't allow it."

She tensed and avoided the question. "Father isn't going to know, because we are going to sneak away in the middle of the night. Alexi! I am deeply in love. You know what that means for a de Warenne."

He stared furiously at her.

"It means nothing and no one can stop me."

CHAPTER EIGHTEEN

"THERE THEY ARE," Alexi said, his expression grim.

Ariella's heart leaped as she followed his gaze. They were on a road winding along a ridge in a gig they had rented in York. Even by rail, it had taken them three long, endless days to reach the Roma caravan. Alexi had known the caravan was at York, for Jaelle had told him they would pause there before going on to Carlisle. Now, she stared down into the meadow where their colorful wagons were camped, the horses loose and grazing, the evening's cook fires already blazing.

There had been no goodbyes at Rose Hill. She hadn't been brave enough to tell Cliff what she had intended. Instead, she had written him a long letter, being as candid as she dared. He would be angry, but she prayed Amanda would eventually calm him. She had begged him not to come after her and Emilian.

Every bone in her body ached, not from sitting for so long, but from the tension of daring to pursue Emilian and her awareness that he might be furious when he saw her.

"Let's go," Alexi said.

Before he could lift the reins, she restrained him. "I know I have not convinced you that Emilian is worth my efforts, because I see your doubt every time I look into your eyes. Alexi, I will go on alone."

He exploded. "Why? Let me guess! He will be furious that you have had the gall to chase him!"

Her tension increased. "He will be angry with me at first.

But this is best for him—and it is best for me. In any case, I want to go on alone. You won't help matters."

"No." He gave her a dark look. "I know you are madly in love. I have decided to give you a chance to win his love, because I never dreamed I would see you like this. As furious as I am with St Xavier, he must have some redeeming qualities. But I am not leaving you here on the road by yourself. I am leaving when I am certain you are safely ensconced in the camp. And, Ariella? The day will come where I will force him to the altar."

She had been fortunate enough to get him to aid her in her pursuit. She accepted that he wasn't going to let her go on this final leg alone. She chose to ignore his last remark—one he had made many times. She would worry about marriage when the time came.

She nodded and he cracked the reins. The gig began to descend toward the caravan. Her heart thundered now. All she had to do was get past Emilian's initial anger, somehow. And there was one simple, ancient means of doing so, one every woman instinctively understood. But the stakes were so high and she was afraid of failure. She could not imagine going back to Rose Hill now.

Barefoot children were playing hide-and-seek, their scrawny dogs yapping at their heels. She saw Nicu, Djordi and the other young men erecting the last of a dozen large canvas tents. A few women were beginning to prepare the evening meals. She surveyed the far side of the camp. Shirtless, Emilian had a wagon wheel on a stump and was repairing it. He was so beautiful her mouth went dry, but from the way he was beating the rim, she knew he was frustrated and angry.

Alexi had halted the gig. Ariella jumped out as the noisy camp fell silent. Even the children stopped shouting and laughing, turning to look at her. One of the youngest boys smiled, then a little girl. An older girl, Katya, waved.

She somehow smiled back, but she was so nervous she felt sick. However, she must not let him see that she was uncertain and anxious. She had to be bold; she had to be coy and confident; she had to be impossibly alluring.

Jaelle straightened from a cook fire, her eyes wide.

Stevan walked away from a bright green tent. He waved at her.

Ariella wanted to wave back, carelessly if at all possible, but Emilian had straightened. He saw her and froze.

Her heart thundered so loudly now that she was sure he could hear it, even with the many meters separating them. She realized she was crossing the distance between them, slowly, steadily. She could not smile, but this was so right. He had to know it, too.

The light in his gray eyes flared and the anger she had expected covered his face. He dropped the hammer but didn't move.

She paused before him. "I have decided to come with you after all."

His broad chest heaved. "I don't think so."

She smiled. "You miss me and you care. You cannot take back such a confession."

His face seemed in danger of cracking. "A man says many things in the heat of the moment."

She trembled and told herself not to give in. She squared her shoulders and gave him a long, intent look through her lashes. "You did not tell me you cared in the heat of any passionate moment. In *that* moment you told me you needed me—desperately."

He flushed. "You should be too proud," he said, "to chase after a man who does not want you!"

His words didn't hurt because she knew the last part of his statement wasn't true. She smiled and laid her palm on his bare, wet chest. She felt his heart racing very swiftly and she experienced a flare of satisfaction. *Her touch had a powerful effect on him.* "Emilian, we both know you do want me—in many ways. I am not going back. I am staying with you."

He was disbelieving. He seized her hand, but for one moment didn't remove it. Then he flung it aside. He tore his attention from her to Alexi, who remained seated in the gig, watching them like a hawk. "So you have decided on marriage after all?" he demanded of her.

"No. I am not marrying you, not until you ask me to do so with love in your heart."

His eyes widened.

"I am here as your friend and lover," she added softly.

His color returned. "And your brother has agreed to let you be my mistress?"

"You know I would never tell him such a thing." She laid her hand on his bare arm. He shuddered as she slid her hand over his bicep. His silver gaze smoldered and she realized she had more power over him than she had realized. "You missed me and returned to Rose Hill. I missed you the moment you left. My place is with you, Emilian," she stressed. "Even here, in the *kumpa'nia.*"

"Damn it, your place is at Rose Hill, or in London or even at Woodland!" He shook her hand off but her touch and words had done their work, for she noted that there was some doubt now in his eyes.

She was about to triumph, she thought in abject relief. "Let me spend the night," she said. "I am too tired to go back tonight. We can argue tomorrow, if you wish."

His gray eyes hot, he leaned close and murmured, "This is a dangerous game, if you think to have me so smitten by dawn that I will not send you back!"

Her heart raced. She could seduce him to her will, couldn't she? She wet her lips and whispered, "You won't be able to send me back at dawn."

He stared and she stared back. He said, "That is a challenge I accept."

She trembled, aware that her efforts were double-edged, for her own body was far too warm. "Good," she said.

He folded his arms across his chest, causing the pectoral muscles to bulge above them.

Her tension heightened. "Where is your tent? I would like to freshen up."

His eyes blazed, partly with anger and partly with heat, and he pointed at a dark green canvas structure. Ariella smiled at him, then went to bid Alexi goodbye.

ARIELLA WONDERED if everyone's tent was as pleasant as Emilian's. A beautifully carved chest contained his clothes and personal items. He had a small, portable desk and a chair, as well as an elegant Chinese rug. The bed consisted of a large mattress, covered with blue silk sheets beneath a navy-and-gold paisley comforter. The candlesticks by the bed were sterling silver.

She found a hand mirror in the chest and was pleased to see that her eyes were bright and her cheeks flushed. She looked rather sultry, but not sultry enough.

Her body hollowed. She was with Emilian now, and they were finally going to spend the entire night together. It would be the first of many. She was not going to let him send her away in the morning. She must make certain he was so smitten with her that he couldn't bear to part with her.

She smiled uncertainly at her reflection. She did not have much experience, but in his arms, she became a very different woman, one entirely shameless, without any inhibition. She must recall that fact now and use it to boost her confidence. She was going to seduce him; she was going to make love to *him*. He thought this a game and a challenge, but it was neither.

"May I come in?" Jaelle asked.

Ariella turned, pleased to see her. Jaelle came in, leaving the tent open behind her. Ariella noted her pretty pale green blouse, which bared her shoulders, and the dark purple skirt she wore, which encased her narrow hips before flaring seductively out. The brown embroidered sash showcased her tiny waist, and her hair was loose.

Ariella was wearing an ivory and brown long-sleeved gown with a round neckline and small collar, her hair pulled tightly back into a chignon. There was no question that her ensemble was not going to serve her well.

Ariella embraced her briefly. "I hope you don't think I was wrong to pursue your brother."

"If he did not love you, he would not have gone back to Rose Hill to see you—and he would not be refusing all the pretty women in the camp."

He had told her there was no one else, but still, Ariella was thrilled.

"It is good that you came for him, because another woman would steal him away sooner or later," Jaelle said. She shrugged. "You love him. So chase him if he thinks to run. I would."

Ariella took her hand. "He intends to send me home tomorrow."

Jaelle laughed. "Really? Then you must change his mind. That should be easy enough."

She breathed and thought of the night to come. "Yes, I intend to change his mind tonight. Can you help me?"

EMILIAN CUPPED his glass of wine, staring at his tent. Then he realized what he was doing and instantly turned away. But he wasn't interested in anything or anyone else. His attention returned to the tent. The flap had been closed at least an hour ago. What was taking her so long?

He knew what she was doing—she was washing, doing her hair, adding rouge, perhaps, and touching the pulse points of her body with perfume. She was preparing for the night she would spend with him.

Tension stiffened his body impossibly. The sun was now setting. Nicu was playing his violin, but the tune was jaunty, which annoyed him. Most of the children had finished eating and the younger ones had been put to bed. One of the women who had been trying to bed him for days was dancing with another man. As if she knew he was lost to her now, she had eyes only for her partner. He ignored them, staring intently at his tent. He almost thought he saw her shadow within, but that was impossible through the thick canvas.

He remained disbelieving. Not only had she followed him across half of England, she intended to stay with him. And she didn't even wish for marriage. Of course she didn't—she was too damned independent for her own good. He did not want her there with him, not under any circumstance. She was not a Romni and she would never be one.

He cursed and flung the wine aside. How had one act of revenge turned into so much anxiety, anguish and passion? Why did she have to be so different from other young ladies? Any other *gadji* would have demanded marriage, rather hysterically. She thought to be his lover and friend and she would travel like a Romni with him.

Well, that was fine with him. He would make love to her all night, but in the morning, he was putting her on the next train bound south.

The flap moved, and he watched an angel of desire step into the night.

She smiled at him.

He breathed hard, stunned. Her glance was arch and inviting. Her long, dark golden hair was loose and flowed in wild waves over her shoulders, which were bare. She wore a yellow blouse and gold sash, the effect as revealing as a corset. He saw that she was naked beneath the blouse and he felt his mouth turn dry. The purple skirt she wore was iridescent and it flowed over her hips and thighs like fine silk. His pulse drummed with urgency now, making it hard for him to recall why he did not want her there after all.

She started forward, and her hips seemed to sway, her breasts seemed to float. He realized she was barefoot.

"What do you think?" she asked, and she pirouetted for him.

He seized her wrist and pulled her up against his hard, hurting body. "I think we should go inside my tent."

Her eyes were wide, but then they warmed and her lashes lowered. She laughed, the sound husky. "But you are never in a rush," she murmured.

- "I am always in a rush," he murmured back, "when I am with you. I just manage to control myself."

He felt her breasts heaving against his chest, her nipples hard and tight.

She laid her hands on his chest, over his loose lawn shirt, and shifted, brushing her hip against his bulging loins. "I wish for a glass of wine," she said. "And I want to dance."

He released her, stepping back.

She tossed her hair and sauntered into the firelight. He watched her for a moment and when she turned, lifting her arms, it drew her blouse impossibly tight. Arms high, she swayed to the music.

Although his lust blazed, he felt himself still as she rotated her pelvis and hips in an ancient sensual rhythm. She turned slowly, so he could watch her back again, and when she faced him, she used her hands to fan out her hair, her eyes on him. His heart exploded. She smiled at him again, lashes low.

He strode into the circle of light and caught her; she laughed. As he covered her mouth with his, forcefully, it crossed his mind that the sound he had just heard had been a bit triumphant. He forced his tongue deep, and when she was clinging, he pulled back and said, "You haven't won yet."

She somehow slipped from his arms, surprising him and darting ahead. He filled impossibly as she ran lightly toward the tent. Then, savagely intent, so aroused he could not think coherently, he followed her. She vanished inside.

He stepped inside, as well, dropping the flap behind him.

Candles burned in glass lanterns. She loosened the sash, dropping it by her feet.

He went still, realizing what she was doing.

She began to tug the yellow blouse over her head, very slowly, and she tossed it aside. Then she paused. He stared, his pulse drumming. The tips of her breasts were engorged and entangled with her hair. He couldn't seem to breathe. She smiled and turned her back.

She loosened the skirt and began sliding it down her hips. The moment he realized she was naked beneath the skirt, he went still, mesmerized, impossibly rigid. She slowly slid the skirt down her high buttocks and then lower, down her thighs. She let it go and it pooled on the floor.

He gave in, reaching her from behind, clasping her waist. He pulled her against his pounding loins. "Are you enjoying yourself?" he asked thickly.

She leaned against him, trembling. "Very much," she said as thickly.

"I am master here," he murmured, meaning it. But he moved his mouth over the side of her neck.

She shuddered and gasped, arching fully against him. He turned her swiftly and their gazes met; he caught the hair at her nape, wrapped it around his hand and kissed her, deeply.

He knew he should go slowly, but he could not. He tore his mouth from hers. A moment later he had pushed her down onto his bed, and he was already reaching for the flap on his breeches. She had his hair in her hands and their eyes remained locked.

Her blue eyes shimmered with far more than lust. There was so much love there. He moaned, slowly moving into her.

In that moment, he knew that her being there with him in the *kumpa'nia* was so terribly right.

She gasped, beginning to cry. She touched his cheek, his back, wrapping her legs around him. He somehow moved slowly, savoring every long stroke, wondering at the stunning pleasure, the bursting joy, a chaos in his heart.

She would give up everything to be with him, just like this. But wouldn't he give up everything for her, too?

"Emilian, yes." She wept in pleasure and he gave in, crying out in his own release, joining her in the wonder of pleasure and love.

He held her tightly when they were both through, his face wet from tears. He did not want to let go.

HE LOOKED AT HER as she lay asleep, while dawn's pale light filtered into the tent. She had fallen asleep perhaps a half an hour ago, snuggled against his chest. He had one arm around her, and her beautiful, perfect face was turned toward him, so he could study her every stunning feature. His heart beat hard as he stared at her. They had made love all night, but he could do so again easily.

He tore his gaze from her face and stared up at the dark ceiling of the tent. He had never known a woman like this one. Now it was time to admit that he had never wanted any woman as he did Ariella. He had never cared this way before.

He almost laughed. Ariella had gotten her way, hadn't she? They had become friends and he could no longer deny it. She had achieved her natural progression.

He gently disengaged and put his hands beneath his head. She deserved better than him and more than this. They might be friends and lovers now, but he was a half blood and she was too good to be any man's mistress, much less a Rom's. She deserved a proper marriage and her Englishman.

The thought crept into his head that he could return to Woodland and marry her.

He was not quite shocked and he slowly sat up and stared down at her.

He wasn't returning to Woodland. But she had to go back, even if he wanted her with him. That was another stunning admission. *He wouldn't mind her staying with him, like this. He had come to care for her that much.*

But it was impossible. What he wanted did not matter. He simply could not allow her to be a part of the ugly world the Roma lived in, and he wouldn't allow her to be his mistress.

But all of Derbyshire already knew of their affair from the Rose Hill ball. Her pursuit of him to York might even be out, as well. Servants eavesdropped and gossiped. Sooner or later, Ariella's latest escapade would be the rage among the rumor-mongers. They would call her a Gypsy whore—if they weren't doing so already. But only behind her back and never to her face.

De Warenne would have his hands full finding her a proper husband. It wouldn't have been that easy before—now, it would be even more difficult.

He would buy her a husband, Emilian thought. But he had already known that. He knew de Warenne would choose with great care.

He hated the idea of her being shackled to someone she did not love.

He hated the idea of her marrying someone else.

He exploded. She was tainted by association with him. He hadn't intended any of this. If he had let the de Warenne family force marriage upon them, she would be living with the scorn of being his wife, but it was far better than the scorn of being his lover. He could not allow her to stay with him and live the hard life of a Rom and he couldn't send her back ruined. His mind was made up.

Her hand covered his. "Aren't you going to sleep at all?" she asked.

Startled, he looked down at her. "I am enjoying looking at you."

Her smile faded and she searched his eyes. "What is wrong?"

He somehow smiled. "Nothing."

She surprised him by taking his large hand to her mouth and kissing it. "You are sad! How can you be sad now, after the night we have shared?"

He hesitated. "You cannot stay here, Ariella."

She sat up. "I will not leave."

He sat, too, surprised. "I mean it."

"Too bad! And don't try to claim that you do not want me. That is bunk."

He almost smiled. "I will always want you."

"Good." She cupped his cheek. "Then that subject is ended."

"No, it is not. You pursued me here against my wishes. I am sending you back. But I will not allow you to be my Gypsy whore."

Her eyes widened and she flushed.

"That is what they will call you, behind your back. Loud enough for you to hear, by the way," he said darkly.

She lifted her chin. "Fine. Then I am a whore." She shrugged. "I suppose the slur will hurt, but I will manage and it will pass. I am *not* leaving you."

He smiled. Her eyes widened, but he knew when to be seductive. "That isn't the subject I wish to discuss...darling." And he pulled her into his arms.

"Why am I getting the distinct feeling that this is not about making love?"

"But I am going to make love to you very shortly." He cradled her in his arms. "We should have been married at Rose Hill."

"What?" she gasped.

He searched her beautiful eyes.

"But you don't want to marry me," she finally said, her eyes wide.

"I don't like being forced into anything. No one is forcing me now. I wish to make an honest woman of you." He pulled her down, beneath him.

"Stop! This is so important!"

"I don't want to see you hurt. I don't want to see you scorned. You should have never come, Ariella. But you did, and we are very entangled," he murmured, repositioning himself for more effect.

"So you wish to marry me to protect me?" she asked huskily.

"Something like that," he said roughly.

"When you can tell me that you love me, I will accept," she gasped.

"I care about you—I need you—and I miss you when we are apart. Isn't that enough?" *If he said the words, she would agree. And would they really be a lie?*

"You are coming very close," she breathed. "But not close enough."

She sighed as he began brushing her mouth and her lips. "Impossible man," she murmured.

He spent the next five minutes readying them both. When she was moaning in pleasure and he was pushing deep, he whispered, "I do love you."

She gasped, her eyes flying wide open.

And he wasn't certain he did not mean it.

"Sit with me," Emilian said the next day, his expression very difficult to read. It was so impassive, he could have been seated at a table, gaming with cards.

But he was on the driver's seat of a wagon pulled by a pair of sorrel mares. The caravan was departing. The first few wagons were already on the road. She was too happy to be tired, despite having had only a few minutes of sleep, and raised her skirts to climb up onto the driver's seat with him. He lifted the reins and the two mares walked forward.

She remained impossibly aware of him. He smelled like fresh mown grass, pine and something far more exotic, perhaps an Eastern spice. She smiled, admiring his beautiful profile, thinking of his heated confession. Her heart soared. "How far does the caravan usually travel in a day?"

"Ten or fifteen miles." His gray eyes swept her face. They seemed to linger on her mouth. "There is no rush."

She thought of his declaration again and her heart raced. Would it be forgotten in the light of day? "It is such a beautiful morning," she exclaimed. She wasn't sure the sky had ever been as blue, the sun as bright, the birds as cheerful. She wasn't sure Emilian had ever been as handsome.

He glanced ahead. "Perhaps in a day or two the nomadic life will become boring."

"I haven't been this far north in years," she said swiftly, thinking that as long as they were together, she would never be bored. "Besides, it is a part of my heritage, too, even if I have never done more than study it in the history books."

"You were raised as an Englishwoman," he said slowly. "Have you ever wondered about your mother's life?"

"Of course I have. It was a life of bigotry and exodus, of ghettos and hatred. I wish I had known her and her family, or at least whether they suffered or lived well."

"You have no desire to find them?"

"When she was with my father, she told him her father had died in Tripoli, and there was no one else. So no, I have had no desire to try to trace that side of my ancestry."

"Will you ever consider returning to Rose Hill?" he asked seriously.

She faced him fully, and laid her hand on his thigh. "You know you don't want me to go."

He flushed. "You think you are an enchantress now?"

Ariella decided she did not even have to bother to reply. He knew that answer.

He finally said, "I am waiting for a reply to my proposal."

"Emilian, surely you did not mean it!"

He said softly, "I did mean it. And do not demand another confession."

Was she so foolish? She was deliriously happy because he had finally told her he loved her, and she was carrying his child. She beamed. "I will wait for another confession," she said. She leaned toward him and brushed her mouth over his cheek. "I am an independent woman, a strong one. I will not be broken by the Romany life."

"What does that mean?" he demanded.

"It means yes, I will marry you."

"WILL YOU, Emilian St Xavier, take this woman to be your lawful wedded wife?" the rector asked, smiling.

It was only a few hours later. Ariella stood in a small village chapel, almost disbelieving, clad in an ivory lace dress that had belonged to Jaelle's grandmother. She wore her own pearls. Emilian wore a dark frock coat, silk shirt and dark cravat, with pale trousers and his boots. The entire *kumpa'nia* was crowded into the old church, which had been strewn with wildflowers, pinecones and wreaths woven with daisies.

He had insisted they marry that very day. Ariella had wondered at the urgency, but he had refused to discuss either a proper wedding or any postponement. It hadn't really mattered, for marrying Emilian was her wildest dream come true. She only regretted the fact that her family was not present. The preparations had been made in such a whirlwind that her head was spinning, even now as Emilian said, very firmly, "Yes, I do."

The rector, a young man whose buxom wife was wide-eyed with excitement in the first pew, turned to Ariella. "And do you, Ariella de Warenne, take this man to be your lawful wedded husband, in sickness and in health, in good times and bad, until death do you part?"

She met Emilian's eyes. His demeanor was partly sober and partly grim. She had never seen a man as determined, and certainly not at his own wedding. Was he having doubts about her? Did it matter? Their journey had definitely begun and nothing and no one could stop them now.

"Ariella?" Emilian asked.

She smiled at him. "I do take this man to be my lawful, wedded husband, until death do us part."

Relief flared in his eyes.

Had he really thought she would change her mind and stand him up at the altar? Didn't he know how much she loved him and that she would never stop loving him? Or was something else worrying him?

"You may exchange rings," the rector said.

Ariella wasn't terribly surprised when Stevan produced two simple gold rings, perhaps locally purchased, perhaps borrowed. Emilian gave her a look and murmured, "I will buy you the diamond of your choice when we return to Woodland."

Were they returning to Woodland? As he slipped the wedding band on her fourth finger, she stared at it, breathing hard. Tears of happiness began.

Stevan handed her his ring, and she slipped it onto Emilian's finger. She looked up, her vision thoroughly blurred.

"I now pronounce you man and wife," the rector cried. His wife started to weep and the Roma clapped and cheered.

"You may kiss the bride," the rector said warmly.

Ariella couldn't quite smile, but Emilian smiled at her, his eyes oddly soft. He leaned toward her and brushed her mouth once, and then just stood there, looking at her. She felt him tremble.

Emilian didn't move, his hands tightening on her shoulders. She sensed he wanted to say something but simply couldn't. And then they were surrounded by their friends, the men pulling him away, the women hugging her enthusiastically. Someone started playing a flute.

Ariella wiped her eyes. My God, she thought, dazed, watching the men pounding Emilian on the back—they were married, at last.

CHAPTER NINETEEN

ARIELLA PAUSED on a hill, staring down into the valley below. A small, quaint Border village was nestled just below the ridge. It consisted mostly of stone farmhouses, framed by lush fields of hay and oats. Smoke came from the stone chimneys and birds flocked on the thatched roofs. Sheep were grazing in the fields with a few cows scattered about. Ariella saw a pair of furry gray donkeys. It was charming and picturesque and her impossibly happy heart leaped.

She had been traveling with Emilian as his bride for over a week now, and she was more deeply in love than she had ever dreamed possible. They rode together as he drove the wagon by day, discussing the works of Shakespeare, Chaucer and Keats, the radical thoughts and programs of Owens, Shaftsbury and Place, the history of the Romany, the Vikings and the Jews. They debated the efficacy of Peel's police and the continuing reform of the penal codes. They argued over the extent and content of parliamentary reform. He was well educated and as intelligent and as well-read as she. And he was a progressive thinker. She could not be more thrilled.

He did not condemn her for her independent manner or thinking. Every debate brought the light of admiration to his eyes. In fact, he frequently conceded to her when they were in disagreement. Many times she had heard him say, softly and seductively, "Point taken."

Ariella hugged herself, and then danced a few steps forward, feeling as light and buoyant as the clouds. It was late afternoon. They had stopped for the evening a bit earlier than usual. Behind her was a stand of woods and beyond that, the encampment. She should go back and help Jaelle with their supper.

She heard an odd whinny.

It was high-pitched, the sound of a young animal in distress.

Ariella glanced around. It took her a moment to see a young horse, perhaps a yearling, caught up in a thicket. It snorted again, showing the whites of its eyes. It was frightened, trapped in the brush.

She would need a rope. She briefly debated going to get Emilian. Then she saw that the colt was bleeding on its forelegs, undoubtedly having panicked and hurt itself. She hurried down the slope.

The young animal went still as she approached. Ariella undid her sash, crooning to the colt. He started backing up, thrashing in the thorny brush, when she tried to put the sash around its neck. She soothed it again and eventually had the colt lassoed. A moment later she was leading it out of the thicket.

She was about to let the horse go when she saw two men heading rapidly her way, obviously coming from the closest farm. The men were very angry and she was instantly alarmed.

She released the colt. Her every instinct told her to flee, but that was absurd. "Good afternoon," she began, smiling, but the younger man did not stop. She was shocked when he seized her arm, so hard she cried out.

"We seem to have a Gypsy horse thief," he said. "A pretty one, at that."

She was so surprised that for one moment, she did not speak. *What had he said?*

He leered at her, looking directly down her low-cut blouse.

"You misunderstand," she cried, trying to jerk the bodice up. Her cheeks flamed "Let me go!"

He jerked her against his body. "Shut up."

For one moment she was so stunned that she was incapable of thought, as well as speech. *No one had ever spoken to her in such a manner before.*

"We brand Gypsy thieves in Skirwith, but we screw their whores." He grinned at her.

Real fear seized her.

They thought she was a Gypsy—this was how they treated Gypsies—look at what had happened to Jaelle and Raiza!

Horror began, melding with the fear. "Let me go, this instant! How dare you speak to me in such a way," she cried. This could not be happening. She was Ariella de Warenne and she was the viscountess St Xavier!

"She sounds like a high-an'-mighty lady," the older man said. He slapped the colt's rump and sent it running off.

Ariella was now still, acutely, horrifically aware of the man's body pressed against hers. His intentions were terrible—she had to get away. "Let me go," she said again, firmly. "I am the viscountess St Xavier."

"God, she thinks she's a countess! Are you a Gypsy countess, sweetheart?" He laughed. "I'll tell you what. Trick for trade. You do me and we'll leave your pretty ears alone."

She closed her eyes against her fear. Then she said, "Let me go or you will pay."

"Johnnie, she sounds English," the older man said with some uncertainty.

"Must be an English Gypsy." He slid his hand over her breast.

Ariella struggled, red exploding in her brain. He laughed, pulling her blouse down, revealing her breasts. Ariella didn't think—she reacted. She bit his arm as hard as she could. He howled, releasing her.

She ran.

She lifted her skirts and ran up the slope, as hard as she could, in full-blown terror. She heard him cursing, heard his footsteps, his heavy breathing. *He was so close behind her.* She forced her legs to pump harder, gulping air, mindless with the fear. *She had to escape him.* She stumbled onto the hilltop but didn't pause. Her lungs exploding, she ran toward the stand of trees. Branches tore at her hands, arms, her cheeks, and he grabbed her skirt from behind.

She went down hard on her face and belly.

"Gotcha," he snarled.

Ariella screamed for Emilian. As he crawled to her, she rolled over and went for his eyes with her nails.

He jerked back and she raked his face instead. Then she seized a stone. Rearing up, she smashed it against his jaw. She was stunned when his eyes widened and rolled back in his head. He collapsed a moment later.

She fell to her hands and knees, shaking, shocked, breathless. And then she heard Emilian. Somehow she stood, pulling up her blouse, and staggered through the woods toward him.

I AM SORRY, Emilian, but Emma was the wife of both Cnut and Aethelred. You have your facts wrong.

He smiled to himself, for she was probably right, and then thought of their recent debate on the subject of Catholic Emancipation. Ariella had pointed out that the universities still excluded dissenters, while he had tried to explain that sometimes gradual reform was for the best. She had begun to refute that—until he had kissed her.

He laid the load of firewood down, his mind now transported to the night before and the night to come. Images tumbled through his mind of his beautiful princess bride, naked and flushed, moving over him, riding him, demanding so much. His pulse was hard to ignore. She had become a very bold and adept lover, and he did not mind, not at all.

He had meant to send her back to Woodland right after their wedding night. But that had been the best night of his life, filled with desire, explosive passions and simple smiles. He had told himself he would send her back the following day—but that day had been as pleasant, as uplifting, as had the days afterward. He knew that she had to go back eventually. She could not live with him as a Gypsy. This interlude must end—sooner, not later. He knew she would argue and that he would miss her. But he was simply delaying the inevitable.

He glanced at the sun, which would not set for an hour or so yet. Not an evening came that he was not as impatient as a raw boy to be with her.

And he heard her scream.

For one heartbeat, he was in disbelief. He whirled, heading for the woods, his heart exploding in alarm. "Ariella!" There was no reply.

He ran harder, faster. But before he reached the woods, she emerged from them, stumbling. She was dirty, bedraggled, her blouse torn. He froze in horror.

What had they done to her?

She staggered, holding out her arms. He rushed forward, catching her. "Are you all right?" he gasped hoarsely.

She shivered in his arms. "Now I know what it is like to be Romni," she said brokenly.

The world went still. He felt the cold, savage and ruthless part of himself take over. "Were you raped?" he asked quietly. He would kill the *gadjos* who had done this.

"No," she said. "I am fine, Emilian," she began, but then her expression froze. Eyes wide, she gasped, doubling over, clutching her abdomen.

He held her, going down to his knees with her, terrified. "Ariella! What is it?"

She didn't speak—clearly she couldn't. He tore her hands from her stomach, expecting to find a terrible wound there, but her clothes were intact. He thrust up her skirt, but her belly wasn't even bruised. She cried out again, striking his hands away, folding over in pain.

He held her while she fought a torment he could not identify. There was so much fear. "What is it? What is wrong? Ariella, answer me!"

Panting, she looked up at him, her cheeks as white as sheets, her eyes bright with pain. "The baby..." she gasped. "I can't lose our baby!"

EMILIAN SAT outside his tent, holding his head in his hands. His aunt had ordered him away hours ago, when he had become paralyzed by the sight of Ariella holding her belly in pain. Her moans had followed him outside. They had ceased a while ago.

She was carrying his child. Why hadn't she told him? Had he gotten her pregnant the first night they had been together, a night of *budjo* and revenge, or the next time, when he had used her in almost as much anger? He was sick over her pain and at the thought that their child might have been conceived from such ruthless, savage acts.

He kept seeing her shining eyes, her joyous smile. She deserved happiness. She could not lose their child!

The silence was heavy, stunning. What was happening? He shuddered, finding it hard to breathe. He had selfishly delayed sending her back to Woodland and now she was suffering a miscarriage.

He felt someone clasp his shoulder firmly.

It was Stevan. He hadn't realized his uncle had come out of the tent and he rose to his feet. The moment he met his uncle's sober eyes, he knew. *No,* he thought, panicking.

"She lost the child, Emilian."

He pulled away, shaking his head, so undone, he felt near tears. "Ariella?"

"She is resting. She will be fine."

Would she? He wiped at a stray tear. *They had lost their child because he hadn't sent her back to Woodland.*

"It was still early in the pregnancy. She said she was only ten weeks along," Stevan said, trying to console him.

He covered his face with his hands. She had conceived that first night at Woodland. *Do you believe in love at first sight?*

Ariella believed she had fallen in love with him at first sight.

Do you believe in fate?

Was this loss fated? Ariella did not deserve this. Look at what he had done to her!

His aunt approached, wiping her hands on a damp cloth. Simcha smiled kindly. "She is young and strong. There will be more children and you must tell her so."

He trembled, filled with self-loathing. "Of course. How is she?"

Simcha gave him a look. "She is grieving. It is usual."

He steeled himself. She would hate him now, too. But he deserved the hatred.

He ducked into the tent. He thought he was prepared for the worst, but when he saw her lying there, tears streaming, not making a sound, he was undone. His heart broke in half.

As she wept soundlessly, he became aware of the extent of his own devastation. He hadn't known of her pregnancy, but she had been carrying his child. *They would never know this child. They would never even know if it had been a boy or a girl.*

Somehow, for her sake, he pushed through the black waves of anguish, grief and guilt. He knelt beside her, taking her hand. He did not know what to say.

She had been accosted in the woods—because of him. She had lost their child—because of him. She was in pain and sorrow—because of him.

"Ariella?" When she didn't respond, he touched her cheek. "I am sorry."

Her face tightened. Then, finally, her lashes lifted, and more tears poured down her face. "I lost our baby," she choked.

There was a chance that she might not have been pregnant at all. Yet Simcha had said she was certain. "Are you sure?"

She nodded. "I have never missed a time. I missed two times and my body was different...." She closed her eyes, bit her fist and sobbed against it.

He pulled her fist to his chest, and then it was simply not enough. He pulled her stiff, resistant body into his arms. She wept against his chest and he held her helplessly. And his tears finally mingled with hers.

ARIELLA STARED up at the dark green ceiling of the tent. *The baby was gone.*

The feeling of emptiness intensified, the sense of loss became consuming. She had no tears left to shed, and the grief had become a black, bottomless hole in her heart. She kept picturing what their child would have looked like. She imagined it had been a boy with Emilian's gray eyes. How could this have happened?

She hugged herself. The Romany lived in a world of bigotry and hatred, a world filled with injustice. Even though she knew, rationally, that she could have had a miscarriage at Rose Hill or Woodland, ignorant, hateful *gadjos* had done this to her. They had accused her of horse stealing, and they had assaulted her in a cruel and brutal way. Because of the two farmers, she had lost her baby. And this was how the Roma lived. How did anyone stand it?

She closed her eyes tightly, trembling. She had understood how difficult the Roma way of life was before arriving at their camp to be with Emilian, but somehow, the entire truth had escaped her until this tragedy. Just then, she hated the *gadjos* and understood Emilian's hatred well.

She trembled and was surprised when a tear leaked down her cheek.

"You are awake," Emilian said, sounding relieved.

He was the father of her child, the man she loved, the man she had given up everything for. He was her husband and he shared her loss. She needed him now, but her heart didn't stir. There was too much grief.

He sat down beside her, took her hand and held it tightly. "Ariella, can I please bring you something to eat?" he asked quietly, but she recognized the uncertainty in his tone.

"How can I eat?" she managed.

"You must eat, even though you have no appetite," he said.

She noted that he looked tired, as if he hadn't slept. He looked older—there were lines on his forehead and his face seemed drawn.

"You've been sleeping for two entire days," he continued, unsmiling.

"I am so ill," Ariella whispered. "My heart hurts so much. I don't know what to do, Emilian. I don't know how to get through this."

"I know." He reached for her. "But you will get through this, I promise."

She went into his arms, but his embrace didn't chase the grief away. She wept again, surprised she had more tears to shed.

He held her until she was done.

He stood up. "I am going to get you some soup Simcha made," he said, his tone thick.

She did not have the strength to argue. She looked up at him and found him staring intensely at her again. He was visibly distressed. Had he loved their child, too, after the fact?

"Emilian?" she whispered. "I should have told you.... I was going to. I was waiting for the right time."

He nodded, and he seemed incapable of speech.

He was grieving, too, she thought. "We will have other children...eventually."

His face tightened. "Ariella." He stopped, as if he thought the better of what he must say. He inhaled and said, "I am sorry."

She nodded at him. "I know."

His eyes blazed with anguish and he left.

It crossed her numb mind that something else was wrong with him—terribly so—but she simply didn't have the strength or will to try to comprehend it now. She moved onto her back and stared up at the ceiling.

THEY HAD CROSSED the Borders several days ago. The caravan had halted for the night. They were two days from the town where he had been born—the town where Raiza was buried. Yet the significance of that was somehow lost in the trauma of Ariella's miscarriage.

He had set up their tent, and Ariella was making their bed. He stood beside his wagon, watching her through the open tent flap. She had lost weight. She ate very little, and didn't sleep well. She woke up in the middle of every night, crying. He held her, feeling helpless, consumed with his guilt.

She moved slowly now, without enthusiasm, tucking the sheets beneath the mattress. Once, she had been like quicksilver. Once, she had been impossibly, adorably talkative. He understood that she was grieving. She had every right to her sorrow. He mourned, too.

He had done this to his healthy, happy bride.

It was too late for regrets, but he knew he should have never married her. He should have never returned to Rose Hill to see her. He should have sent her away the moment she had found him in York.

He watched her finishing the bed, shaking out the heavy comforter. She was strong enough to go back to Woodland, he thought.

She caught him staring and smiled wanly at him. Suddenly tears filled her eyes and she turned away so he wouldn't see.

He caught her in such moments of grief every single day and every single night.

His self-hatred had grown.

He moved to their tent but did not enter it. "I'll cook tonight," he said. That wasn't what he wanted to say. He had to tell her that she was going back to the life of an Englishwoman. He was certain she would not argue with him.

He should be relieved. He was not.

"Emilian?" She faced him, wiping her eyes. "Can you come here?"

He was surprised, uncertain of what she wanted, as he stepped inside the tent. She began untying her gold sash. "What are you doing?" he exclaimed, but he instantly knew.

She let it fall and smiled wanly again. "We haven't been together since…in a week. Make love to me." She reached for her blouse.

He stilled her hand. For the first time in his life, he knew he was incapable of making love to a woman. "Why?"

She forced the fragile smile again. "Don't you need me?" she whispered.

She thought to see to his needs? He was incredulous. "I'm fine," he said swiftly, an utter lie. He was never going to be fine again. He had done far more than ruin this woman.

She touched his cheek. "You're not fine. Neither one of us is fine. I am never going to forget what happened, but sooner or later, we will have to try to put the past behind us. I thought lovemaking might help us both."

"Ariella, you are clearly not in a passionate mood."

She put her arms around him. "Then hold me, please."

He did, trembling.

"I don't want to disappoint you," she said.

He choked and could no longer stand his pretense. He clasped her shoulders, set her back and looked down at her. "I knew that no good would come of your being pulled down into the filth with me."

She blinked. "What are you talking about?"

"How many times have I said that you deserve a Prince Charming?"

Her eyes widened. Then she cried, "I can't debate this now!"

He released her. "I have no intention of debating you, Ariella. Once, you were the brightest light I could see—as bright as the North Star. Once, your every other expression was a smile, and laughter trailed in your wake. Your eyes used to smile at me!"

"I have lost our child. I am sorry, Emilian, but I am struggling with my grief."

"I know. Damn it, do not apologize to me!" he roared.

She flinched.

"I seduced you for *budjo*—and you have been with us long enough to know what that means."

She paled impossibly and he knew she hadn't realized.

"I started this. I hunted a beautiful, perfect English princess and I brought her down."

"No," she whispered. "Stop! Why are you doing this?" She began to cry. "I am hurting, Emilian." She held out her hand. "Please, don't do this now."

He shook his head, refusing to take her hand. "I started this and I am ending it. This marriage was a terrible mistake."

She sat down, as if her legs had given way, gasping.

"Look at what I have done to you!" he cried. Then he realized his face was wet. He swatted at the tears.

"You didn't do this," she begged hoarsely.

"You are living like a Gypsy because of me! Can you

honestly tell me that you like living like this? Did you like being called a Gypsy whore? Did you like having those strange men grope you? Did you like being assaulted?" he shouted.

"I don't know how anyone can live this way," she sobbed. "I hate this life. I hate it here!"

Finally, he had the truth from her. She couldn't live like a Gypsy. And in a way, he was relieved. Hadn't he been expecting such condemnation ever since they had first met?

She covered her face with her hands. "I can't fight for us now. I can't."

"There is nothing to fight for. I am ending this marriage," he said.

She dropped her hands and stared up at him, horrified.

His heart screamed at him, but he did not want to hear its protest. He could not give her the life she deserved. He had given her pain, sorrow and loss. Worse, he had failed to protect her, his own wife.

He found his voice. "The marriage is a mistake. It should have never happened. I will give you a divorce."

"How can you do this to me now?"

"You will thank me sooner than you think."

Her eyes widened. He felt his heart harden and shrivel up into nothingness. Then he turned and left.

She stumbled after him and clung to the tent flap. "You bastard. Damn you! Damn you for doing this to me!"

He gasped, not looking back, but her words felt like a knife in his back. He had turned her against him, at last.

He walked away, never faltering, into the woods. And then the rage arose, like a howling beast, and it was black with despair. The woman he loved had vanished with the loss of their child. Now, too late, he knew he loved Ariella de Warenne.

CHAPTER TWENTY

THE GRAVE WAS in the family cemetery at Adare.

Ariella slowly walked past marble headstones, raised tombs with stone effigies and several magnificent mausoleums. It was quiet in the cemetery, where her ancestors had been buried since the end of Queen Elizabeth's reign. She shivered. It was October now. The sky was overcast, threatening rain. Even clad in a heavy wool gown and an even heavier mantle with a hood, she was too thin and always cold.

Not a day had gone by since Emilian had left her in Windsong's front hall almost two months ago that she did not visit the monument that commemorated her child. But this morning she'd realized that she had not come to the cemetery yesterday. She had been busy with callers from town. She frowned, disturbed. For the first time in ages she had enjoyed a lively debate on the upcoming parliamentary elections.

She realized she missed London.

Ariella faltered. She had a sacred duty to her child, but instead she was reminiscing over a pleasant afternoon and yearning for town. She looked up at the sky. The sun was behind the thick gray clouds, as if determined to come out.

I am feeling better, she thought.

She smiled a little as she drifted past the mausoleum where the previous Earl and Countess of Adare were entombed. She had loved her grandparents dearly. They had passed away comfortably in their sleep within months of each other. She was always comforted as she passed their tomb. Now she could almost feel them walking with her, as if content and pleased.

I am becoming romantic, she decided.

But behind the stone edifice was a glaringly empty section of land, the plot her father had reserved for his immediate family. Ariella's smile faded. Amidst all the green grass and oak trees there was one small white marker.

Two months ago, the sight had brought fresh tears. Now, Ariella simply knelt solemnly before the stone, laying a bouquet of white roses there.

Beloved child of Ariella and Emilian St Xavier
July 27, 1838.
Forever rest in peace

"How are you?" she whispered. She was no longer able to envision her infant as clearly as she once had. In her mind's eyes, the infant had become vague in feature, except for the stunning gray eyes she imagined. The eyes she saw belonged to Emilian.

She tensed. She could not go to the cemetery without thinking of her child's father. It had been impossible, as if Emilian was with her when she went to visit.

She breathed hard and focused on their child, because oddly, she was almost ready to think about her husband. "Your mother is feeling better, but that doesn't mean I love you any less."

She sighed. "I think I am going to London," she said. "I think it is time I got back to living." Her smile wavered. "But I will come see you before I go, and I will be back for Christmas."

Emilian's gray eyes blazed at her—with anger.

I started this and I am ending it. This marriage was a terrible mistake.

Ariella stood. She hated remembering their last moments

together in the *kumpa'nia*. She had been so sick with grief that their terrible argument was shadowy and vague in her mind, which relieved her. But that didn't mean she failed to understand how ruthless he had been. He had decided to end their marriage when she was so incapacitated with grief that she had been incapable of fighting back. That night he had driven her to the closest railhead, refusing to speak with her. She had been too overwhelmed with hopelessness to even try to talk him out of it. He had added an insurmountable weight to her grief and mourning.

I am sorry, but this is for the best. You will realize that when you can think clearly.

They had traveled by rail across the Lowlands, then taken a ferry to Ireland. Ariella had been consumed with hurt, but she had been furious, too, almost hating him for choosing that moment to destroy their marriage, when she should be allowed her grief. She would never forget the hard and set look he had worn on his face, day after day. She had huddled against the train window, trying to keep herself as far from him as possible, grieving and raging silently, while he sat rigidly beside her, staring purposefully ahead. The tension had been impossible.

"I am going directly to London to petition for a divorce."

"How can you do this to me? How can you do this to us?"

He hadn't spent more than a moment or two in the house. It had been raining, a downpour.

We both know this is my fault.

He had climbed into the rented carriage and driven away, not looking back.

Ariella vaguely recalled collapsing in the drive and being carried back into the house by her brother. She recalled Alexi volunteering to kill him, but she had begged him not to interfere, not to make things worse. She was so sick with grief and exhaustion, she had tried to turn her back on Emilian and her memories, her thoughts of him and their marriage. She had been too overwhelmed to fight him. And in a way she had been glad—and relieved—to be home. Windsong was the safest haven she knew. Her private apartments were an even safer sanctuary, where she could crawl into bed whenever she wished and heal her wounds.

But his image slipped into her mind unannounced, with stealth, every day, several times. Instantly she would be awash with hurt and anger and so much confusion. Then she would dismiss her thoughts. She had enough pain. She did not need any more.

She had tried, very hard, to avoid thinking about the divorce. Now, for the first time, Ariella wondered if a deed for a separation had been granted to Emilian in the ecclesiastical courts.

Hurt consumed her and she sank back down beside her child's grave. Why was he doing this? They had been so happy for a while.

Poignant memories assailed her. She saw him smiling at her as their wagon rolled down a country road, while she chatted merrily away. She saw him dancing in the firelight, his smoldering gaze upon her, a prelude to the passion they would share in his tent. She remembered how he had looked at her after their exchange of vows, as the entire *kumpa'nia* surrounded them, the men congratulating him. His eyes had been so warm.

I will always want you.

She stood, shaken. Image after image of Emilian came—looking up from a cook fire where he knelt; moving over her, seductive, intent; at the Simmonses' ball, watching her from afar like a hawk. She saw him clad only in a shirt and breeches and his high boots, that very first time they had met. She saw him welding the smith's tool, bare chested, muscles rippling. She saw him seated at his desk in Woodland, the epitome of the lord of the manor.

I love you.

Were they still married? Had he received the deed of separation? To attain it, he would have to accuse her of adultery. *She could fight this divorce if she wanted to.*

Ariella lifted her skirts and ran through the cemetery to her waiting coach. For suddenly, she was ready to fight for their marriage and their future.

SHE RAN BREATHLESSLY into Windsong's grand entry hall.

"Ariella, have you been to the cemetery?" Dianna asked pleasantly, coming from the hall. She faltered, her eyes widening. "Oh! Something has happened. You look ready to ferociously debate someone—you look like yourself!"

"Dianna!" Ariella cried. "Do we know if Emilian has attained a deed for a separation, or worse, if a bill for our divorce has reached parliament?"

Dianna looked at her closely. "I know nothing."

Ariella searched her face, well aware that her family might wish to hold such profoundly unpleasant news from her. "Where is Father?" Cliff had returned from London several days ago with Amanda.

"He is in the library, intent on catching up after being away."

Ariella turned to go, but then whirled. She hugged her smaller sister as hard as she could, leaving her gasping and breathless.

"What was that for?" Dianna cried to her back.

Ariella glanced over her shoulder. "You have hovered over me for two endless months as if I were an invalid. I hope I never have to return the favor…. I love you!"

The library door was open and Cliff was seated at his desk, clearly immersed in his accounts and ledgers. Ariella knocked. As he looked up, she smiled and walked in. His eyebrows lifted.

"I hope I am not interrupting. I have decided it is time I went to Woodland."

"I see." He stood and came out from behind his desk. "Emilian is not there."

"I assumed as much. But as his wife, it is my home, too. Am I still his wife?"

Cliff put his arm around her. "He has yet to file with the courts for a separation, Ariella."

Ariella was stunned. "What could that possibly mean?" A filing with the courts always came first, before parliament would consider the divorce proceeding.

"I do not know, but a man who wishes to jettison his wife does not drag his feet. Emilian is certainly dragging his."

Ariella cried out, her mind racing swiftly. Had Emilian changed his mind?

I love you.

"So you will now fight for your marriage?"

The shroud had lifted—suddenly, there was hope. She breathed hard. "I will always miss the child I was never given a chance to know. But I also miss Emilian." In that moment, she realized she had never missed anyone more.

When Cliff studied her, she cried, "I know you do not care for him, but we are married. I need your support and your blessing."

"I have already given my blessing, Ariella, to both of you."

She stared closely. "Please don't blame him for what he has done. He has suffered enough."

"Blame is a dangerous game. I could blame your brother for taking you to him, couldn't I? I could blame Emilian for letting you stay with the Roma. I could also blame myself, Ariella, for not watching Emilian more closely, for allowing him under my roof, for not watching you carefully," he said. "I could blame myself for not tracking you down and bringing you home the moment you ran away to him."

She hugged him again, aware that Cliff held himself responsible for the loss of her child. "This isn't anyone's fault, including yours."

"I am trying not to blame myself, but it is very difficult." He smiled at her, tears in his eyes. "You are young and the doctors say there is no reason there won't be more children."

"I must win Emilian back, first, and he is *not* an easy man. I don't even know where he is, and I cannot force him back to Woodland."

Cliff put his arm around her. "The man was distraught when he brought you here. You were too distressed to be aware of it, but I saw how much he cares. When he left I saw his anguish, although he tried to hide it. I have changed my opinion of him, Ariella. I believe Emilian is in love with you."

Her heart soared. "I also believe that he loves me, but that doesn't mean he will wish to reconcile. I intend to give him some time, but if he doesn't return to Woodland, I will go to him."

"You, my dear, are up to the many challenges he represents." He walked back to his desk and removed several letters from a drawer. "Word of your marriage apparently got out upon your return here. These are from Woodland's estate manager."

Ariella was surprised. "He is writing me?"

"You are mistress of Woodland." Cliff hesitated. "Robert has taken the estate into his possession. He now calls himself viscount. My solicitors have advised me that if years go by without Emilian's return, there are laws of adverse possession which might enable Robert to successfully claim that the estate is now legally his."

Ariella stared, outraged. "I am going to Woodland immediately."

ARIELLA PERCHED on the edge of her seat as her carriage entered Woodland's front gates. It was painful to be returning this way, without Emilian and with no clue as to his whereabouts. As the coach traveled up the graveled drive, she almost expected Emilian to saunter out of the house. There were so many bittersweet memories and she was assailed by each and every one of them. She had never missed him more.

Margery reached for her hand and squeezed it. "We will confront that scoundrel together," she said.

Ariella was too tense to smile. She would fight for her marriage, but first, she must fight for their home. When Ariella had first arrived at Windsong, Margery had been in London. But she had rushed to Adare immediately to comfort Ariella, as most of the family had. She had insisted upon going with her to Derbyshire.

In truth, Ariella had wanted her cousin's company, and she had accepted her offer. Her father had wanted to come, too, but Ariella had told him she would send for him if she could not manage Robert herself. Alexi was in Hong Kong, and that was fortunate, because he would have insisted on joining her and he would have undoubtedly taken Robert St Xavier's head off.

Ariella now said briskly, to hide her agitation, "The estate looks well. The grounds seem immaculate and the outbuildings are in good condition. I see that Richards has been allowed to do a part of what Emilian hired him to do."

Richards's letters had been ominous in content. Robert was doing more than claim he was viscount. He had managed to get access to the estate's bank accounts. According to Richards, the man was hell-bent on refurbishing Woodland to his liking, while throwing one lavish party after another. He was devouring the estate's funds. Soon, there would be no profits and no reserve. Richards had begged her to summon Emilian to rectify the situation. Barring that, he had asked her to come herself and take action.

"This is your home now, too," Margery reminded her, sensing her distress. "You must fight this interloper for it!"

"I know. I have to confess, I have never been drawn into

a battle like this before." She stared at Margery. "If only Emilian would come home. He would boot Robert on his backside."

"Don't worry about Emilian now," Margery advised. "Let us first get past his despicable cousin."

"You are the best friend I have ever had." Ariella hugged her.

"I feel the same way," Margery whispered.

The coach halted. Ariella tensed as her door was opened. She thanked the coachman and stepped down, her heart racing, her cousin following. Then, shoulders squared, she went up to the pair of front doors and knocked, expecting to see Hoode. He, at least, was an ally, and she had no doubt he would quickly fill her in on the sordid state of affairs at Woodland.

But a tall, white-haired manservant whom she did not know opened the front doors. "Yes?"

Ariella could not imagine who this servant was. She glanced past the servant and froze. The ancestral portraits that had once adorned the front hall were gone. In their place were paintings she had never seen before. Some were frankly erotic; others were simply bizarre. None of the beautiful, centuries' old furniture that had once adorned the hall was present. Instead, new furniture, all costly, cluttered the room. Expensive rugs now covered the marble floors. Margery, who was standing behind her, inhaled. "He has spent a small fortune."

"Where is Hoode?" Ariella demanded in outrage. Clearly, Robert was hell-bent on spending Emilian's money as he chose. She saw that the candles on another new table had been allowed to melt onto the marble top. She also noticed a stain on the marble floor and that the new red velvet upholstery on a settee was ripped. The room had been redecorated, but it had also suffered from negligence and abuse.

"I am afraid that Hoode is no longer employed by the viscount."

She drew herself up. "Hoode is most certainly employed by the viscount," she said fiercely. "Where is Robert?"

"The viscount is not to be disturbed."

She fought her temper and lost. "Your name?"

"Barnes."

"Barnes, my husband is the viscount. I ask you again, where is Robert?"

He paled. "In the library, my lady."

She started aggressively down the hall, then whirled. "Find Hoode and bring him to me!"

"Yes, my lady," he said, bowing.

Ariella rushed down the hall, Margery behind her. She glanced into the salon as she passed and was dismayed to see several gentlemen there, playing cards and drinking wine. Not one was correctly attired. Worse, the room had the peculiar odor of stale ale, tobacco and unwashed bodies.

The library door was closed. Ariella didn't even consider knocking. She thrust it open and froze.

Margery crashed against her back and gasped.

Robert St Xavier had a woman on Emilian's desk and he was busily fornicating with her.

Ariella turned abruptly, pushing Margery into the hall and away from the vile and disgusting scene. Her cousin's eyes were popping. "You do not have to see that," she said firmly.

"What are you going to do?" Margery whispered, her eyes huge. "I think you should have your father handle Robert!"

"Stay here," Ariella said. She whirled and strode back to the library. She had left the door open. Nothing had changed. "I beg your pardon," Ariella said furiously.

Robert jumped away from the woman, his eyes widening with surprise. The woman squealed and dove behind the desk.

Ariella knew she was flushed, but she kept her eyes on his face. "Get out of my house," she said hoarsely.

He smiled, the light in his eyes changing as he adjusted his clothes. "Well...well...it is Miss de Warenne, my cousin's lover. You are intruding, Miss de Warenne." He faced her squarely now, hands on his hips.

Ariella shook with rage. "I do not care to repeat myself. I want you out of this house now. I will not have Woodland turned into a bordello."

He laughed at her. "Are you sure that is what you want? I feel certain there is more."

She seethed at the lewd innuendo. "I do want more. I want every penny which you have stolen from us repaid."

He blinked. "I am viscount now, and unless you wish to join me this afternoon, I want *you* gone."

She trembled and turned. A pair of ceremonial swords hung over the fireplace. She leaped onto an ottoman and took one down, even though she had never been taught to fence. Robert began to laugh, which only fueled her determination. She jumped nimbly back to the floor. Robert's expression changed as she strode to him, becoming alarmed as she aimed the sword at his chest.

"You do not know what you are doing!" he cried, turning white.

"You are wrong. I know exactly what I am doing. I have watched my father and brother on the decks of their ships, murdering pirate swine as they attempted to board!" That last was a bit of an exaggeration. She struck the blade against his chest, right through his lawn shirt. She hadn't meant to cut so deep but she didn't bloody care.

He blanched and reached for her hand.

She pressed the blade deeper and he cried out, releasing her. "You have cut me," he gasped, backing away.

She followed him. "Emilian is viscount here and I am his wife. This is my room—this is my house. I said get out. I am losing patience." He hit the wall. She pressed the blade into his chest again.

"You're mad," he cried, ducking away, his shirt ripping another time as he did so.

"I am the Viscountess of Woodland," she said furiously. "I married Emilian and I have the certificate to prove it. You, sir, are nothing but a rogue and a scoundrel who seeks to steal our home—our life! *Get out!*"

He ran.

When he was through the door, she turned and stared at the woman. Half-clad, she gathered up her shoes and rushed out, as well. Ariella began to shake. There was blood on the tip of the sword, and the blade did not look particularly dull. She felt sick, but not because of what she had done. She looked at Emilian's beautiful desk. It had been defiled.

She glanced around the room and saw tears in the brocade sofa. Food and drink were everywhere; a tray of leftovers was even on the floor. The entire house had been defiled, she thought.

"Are you all right?" Margery asked from the doorway.

Ariella nodded. "There is one more thing I must do." She went past her cousin, sword in hand. As she approached the salon, the stench from within accosted her. She paused on the threshold, but the five men within were drunk and raptly attentive to their game. If they knew she stood there, they did not care.

"Madam? My lady?" Barnes corrected himself, appearing behind her. "May I rouse these rascals?"

"Yes, you may," Ariella said in relief.

She watched him interrupt the game and inform the gentlemen that they must gather up their things and leave Woodland immediately. "The viscountess has returned and she insists," he said firmly, ignoring their drunken protests.

When they were finally gone, Ariella walked into the salon and simply stood there. She had done it. She had rid

Woodland of Robert, at least for now, until Emilian returned—if he ever did. She trembled.

Then, realizing she still held the sword, she turned. "Barnes, clean this and replace it where it belongs. Assemble the entire household at five o'clock. I wish a word with everyone. And, Barnes? I will have this house returned to the exact state it was in before Robert thought to depose my husband and rearrange it. I expect everything to be in proper order by the time the viscount returns."

Barnes took the sword and nodded. "And when is the viscount expected?"

Ariella tensed. "I do not know. But he will come back, of that there is no doubt."

Barnes bowed and left.

Ariella hugged herself. He had to return sooner or later, didn't he?

The truth was that she simply did not know.

HE SLOWLY WALKED down the grassy hill in the dull autumn twilight. The cemetery where Raiza was buried was ahead. He could barely recall the night he had spent there two and half months ago, seated on the wet earth in the rain before the small whitewashed wooden cross that marked the spot where she had been buried. He had just returned from leaving Ariella at Windsong. He hadn't been back to his mother's grave since.

He had spent the past two months traveling with the Rom, as far north as Inverness. They had only just returned to the Borders a day ago, for they would winter there, as they did every year. Stevan was taking orders for the chairs, tables and desks he would mend; Emilian was taking orders for the wagon wheels he would repair and the ones he would make. A long dark winter lay ahead.

He still had not filed for divorce.

He would see to it soon.

He was very resolved now, for he had learned how to survive the loss of what felt like his entire life by becoming adept at self-control and emotional detachment. His thoughts did not wander; they stayed firmly in the present. His heart was iron-clad. He must not think about the only time he had come to this grave, his mind and heart consumed with Ariella. He must not recall the grief he'd been consumed with. That night he had come to mourn Raiza, but he had mourned for his wife.

He tried to think of the common labor he would begin on the morrow. He was becoming renowned as an extraordinary wheel maker.

He laughed bitterly, an image of Woodland flashing through his mind. He avoided all thoughts of the estate, too. It was too dangerous. He must not care about Woodland. He would never be the viscount again.

From viscount to wheel maker, from Englishman to Rom....

His heart stirred again unpleasantly in his chest, an unhappy feeling he was instantly wary of. He had deliberately buried his heart the day he left Ariella at Windsong, with all the memories they shared, and he had no intention of rediscovering it. She had brought so much light and joy into his life. Now he lived in shadows. Now, he knew the difference. He deserved a living hell.

Feeling sorry for himself was out of the question. He focused as he walked past the first few modest grave markers. He stood before the marble marker he had ordered for Raiza. He must mourn her properly now. He must say goodbye.

But his heart was thundering and he could not seem to control it. For the first time in months, he saw his mother as he had as a boy, smiling and content, darning his socks before a nighttime fire while he sat at her feet. The boy picked up a violin and began to play; the boy was a Rom, and he was content with his simple life.

He closed his eyes and suddenly, vividly, recalled his last moments at Rose Hill, when he had been recuperating from the flogging. Ariella was with him, her eyes flashing as she discussed Henry V with him. In that instant, he knew that was the precise moment he had fallen in love with her.

You belong to two worlds, not one.

How could anyone belong to two worlds? How was it remotely possible?

His heart hurt him now. Hadn't he spent the past six months living like a Rom? And hadn't he spent the previous eighteen years living like an Englishman?

The night before, a young Rom and a local girl had gotten married. It had been a night of music, song, laughter and dancing. The girl had been Scot, the daughter of a nobleman's houndmaster. The young groom was going to stay with his bride in Glasgow, and he was going to work for an honest wage in town. She did not want to travel; she did not want to leave her family. No one was surprised, except for Emilian. There were so many Rom venturing away from the life, and so many half bloods, with one foot in each world.

The pain filled him completely, his temples throbbing, and he feared his head might actually explode.

"No man belongs to two worlds," he roared, and to his surprise, he felt tears on his face. "I am Rom!"

The *gadjos* had killed Raiza—and they had killed his and Ariella's child.

Your father is a good man, Emilian. He can give you a life I cannot.

He heard his mother as clear as day, saw her imploring expression as she begged him to understand, just before she sent him away with the runner to his new English life and family.

I can give you so many opportunities, Emil. Let me do so!

Edmund had loved him, he suddenly realized, and not just because he was his heir. He had loved him in that careful, polite and very English way, never showing open affection but allowing him to explore every avenue he wished to, encouraging him to do so. Edmund had loved him because he was his son, and he had been so proud of his achievements.

And Stevan had said Raiza had been filled with pride, too.

He sank to his knees. He no longer grieved for Raiza. He regretted choosing one life so completely over the other one, but he wasn't sure there could have been any compromise. Both of his parents had chosen the English way for him and, finally, he understood why.

What was he doing, mending wagon wheels? He hated the mindless, mundane labor. The long, idle days on the road bored him. He missed his accounts, his artwork, his books. He missed his luxurious home.

He saw Woodland now in all its splendor and glory—splendor and glory that was a monument to his efforts and duties and cares. He thought of his beautiful library, of the hundreds of books he had personally chosen and read and reread; he thought of his English gardens, thoughtfully and carefully designed by him; he thought of his stable of pure-blooded broodmares, all in foal to his prized stallion. He thought of his efficient staff, his business affairs and relationships, his tenants and their farms. He cared about his tenants—he even knew the names of their children! *What was he doing?*

He reached out to touch the marble headstone, Raiza's loving image coming to mind again. "I am not Rom," he heard himself whisper. "I am *didikoi.* I am a half blood."

Her smile never faltered.

In that stunning moment, he almost felt as if she had reached down to him from heaven to give him her silent blessing. He felt a caress upon his shoulder, but surely, it was the twilight wind.

He stood, remaining shaken. He had gone north to grieve for her and to find his Roma heritage. Instead, he had married and lost a wife and a child, while finding a truth he had never expected. He could not fit into the Roma way, not for a lifetime. He missed Woodland and the challenges of maintaining a profitable estate. He missed a great deal of his English life. But the Rom part of him was strong, too.

There was no more doubt now. He belonged to two worlds, not one.

And for one instant, he had a vision so strong, he thought Ariella had materialized before him. Then her face changed and he saw that it was Raiza standing there in the moonlight.

He blinked and realized he had seen her in his mind.

He had stayed with the Roma this long not because his mother had been murdered, but because he was running from the pain of losing Ariella. He would never get over losing her, he realized, but he couldn't keep running. Duties and responsibilities awaited him at Woodland. People awaited him at Woodland.

There would always be whispers—but not from everyone. Some *gadjos* were good, kind and fair, like the de Warennes. Like Ariella.

I am going to pray that you find what you are seeking and that you will decide to come home. When you do, I will be here....

He stiffened, amazed at his memory now. Ariella had meant those words, after their discovery at Rose Hill, but everything had changed since then. By now, Ariella was in London, debating her radical friends, having moved past the loss of their child. He hoped that was the case. She so loved to debate, and she was good at it. By now, she was indifferent to him.

Woodland was waiting.

He was going home.

She wouldn't be there, but that was what was best. And maybe, when he next saw her, she would have forgiven him for all that he had done to her. Knowing her, he was certain there would be no blame and no grudge. She might even be with her Prince Charming, but he intended to accept it and be glad for her. He only hoped that they could finally be friends.

He would settle for her friendship now.

HIS HEART THUNDERED with excitement as he stepped down from the hired coach in front of Woodland's great doors. He stood very still for a brief moment, in the chill of the early December day, noting that the grounds and buildings all seemed in perfect order. Richards had done well. He was very pleased.

A passing groom saw him and faltered, then grinned and doffed his cap. "My lord! Good to have ye back!"

Emilian smiled at him, surprised to realize that he felt rather happy. "How does it go, Billy?"

"Very well, my lord. Ye've got some fine new colts, sir."

His excitement increased. As he turned, the gardeners on the lawns by the water fountain were also doffing their caps. His pleasure increased. He nodded at them, smiling. Beyond the fountain, behind his stables, he saw last spring's crop of foals, gangling weanlings now. They were racing the wind, and more pleasure crested as he saw that they all were in fine form.

God, it was good to be home.

He approached the house and bounded up the front steps. He did not knock, and as he entered his great hall he was pleased to note that all was exactly as he had left it. Hoode came charging from the corridor beyond, eyes wide in his pale face. "My lord, you've come home!" He beamed.

"Hello, Hoode," he said, tossing his top hat at him, which Hoode caught. "Yes, I have come home, and I am very pleased by what I am seeing."

"My God, sir, you must thank your wife for that! She marched in here and forced your cousin from these premises, sir, at the point of a sword. And just in time, too, as he was running this estate into the ground!" Hoode said, smiling.

The day went still—the world went still. He wasn't even certain that his heart continued to beat.

He had misheard. Ariella was here? Surely she was in London with her eccentric friends!

It was a moment before he could speak. "I beg your pardon?"

Hoode was enthusiastic. "Lord Robert attempted to take over the estate and the title, my lord. He gave me the boot, and then began recklessly spending your fortune on whatever pleased him. Her ladyship returned in the nick of time, I must say! You are a fortunate man, sir."

His heart thundered. Incredulous, afraid he was in the midst of a dream, he now looked past Hoode. And she stood there on the threshold of his salon, his angel of mercy, the most beautiful vision he had ever beheld. She was crying and he instantly knew they were tears of happiness.

She was waiting for him, as she had promised.

"Ariella?" He still could not believe it.

"You have come home," she whispered, visibly trembling.

"I have come home," he managed, the shock fading. The joy tried to surge forth but he contained it. "And you are here? You are waiting for me?"

"Where else would I be?"

He started toward her, hope and love flooding him. "You could be at Windsong—you could be in London—you could be anywhere else!" He reached her but was afraid to touch her. He was afraid this was a dream and she was an illusion that would instantly vanish.

But she touched his cheek, the gesture tender and familiar, and her caress caused his heart to explode in the kind of joy he had never thought to feel again. "I'm your wife. My place is here. I told you I would be here, waiting for you, or have you forgotten?"

He cried out, crushing her in his embrace. She clung and he held her tightly, still trying to understand that this woman believed in him enough to have returned to him and that she truly loved him.

He looked down at her. "I haven't forgotten," he said hoarsely, overcome by the small woman in his arms. "But how can you forgive me for the child we lost? It was my fault."

"It was an accident, Emilian. It was not your fault. Have you ever considered that I have blamed myself for pursuing you in the first place?"

His eyes widened in alarm. "I don't want you to blame yourself for anything, ever!"

She clasped his face. "I don't want you to blame yourself for anything, either."

He inhaled, his heart pounding. Carefully, he said, "So we are at an impasse?"

"No." She smiled at him. "You must forgive yourself so we can have the future we deserve."

He crushed her in his arms again, afraid to ever let go.

In his embrace, she murmured, "You never started divorce proceedings."

She was so warm and soft in his arms, and his body began to respond with shocking hunger and need. "I put it off."

She pulled back and grinned at him. "I wonder why?"

"I think you know why," he said roughly.

She batted her eyelashes at him.

"I am more than happy to confess, I have remained so completely and desperately in love with you that I could not even speak with an attorney."

She laughed, a bright, happy and expectant sound he hadn't ever anticipated hearing again. "A confession in the bright light of your hall?" she teased. "What new aspect of your character is this?"

The joy bursting from deep within him was the kind of happiness he had never experienced, not even during their first days of wedlock. "I thought that giving you up was best, Ariella," he said seriously. "Not for me, but for you. But then, I meant to stay with the Rom. Instead I have returned to Woodland. You were right. I belong to two worlds, not one."

Her eyes were wide. "Oh, Emilian! I have never seen your eyes so light and bright. I have never seen you smile so openly. The dark shadows are gone!"

With trembling fingers, he stroked her cheekbone, her temple, her face. "I will never be entirely Rom, just as I will never be a proper, blue-blooded Englishman. Can you manage, darling?" He was stunned that he was with his wife.

She laughed. "Thank God for that! I am not in love with a proper blue-blooded Englishman—I am in love with my half-blood prince."

She meant it and he flushed in even more pleasure. He knew her well enough now to realize she could never love a proper Englishman—she was too original and too independent. "There are no Roma princes," he murmured, "as you well know."

"Of course there are. You are standing right before me. You have told me many times that one day I would find my English Prince Charming, but you were wrong. For you are my prince, Emilian. You have been my prince from the moment we first met and nothing will ever change that."

He was so undone he could not speak. She had always looked at him with those shining eyes, and he now realized the expression had been more than love and trust. She looked at him with a vast and utter admiration.

And hadn't he always looked at her with the same respect? She was a great lady, the kind of woman a man like him could only dream about previously. Yet she had somehow become his lover, his friend and his wife and once again, she was declaring her undying love. This time, for the first time, he believed her.

Ariella de Warenne loved him, with the deep, undying, once-in-a-lifetime love the de Warenne men and women were notorious for.

He even believed it was their fate.

He doubted he could speak properly, so he lifted and kissed her hand. Then he cleared his throat. "I do not deserve you." When she began to protest, he silenced her by tipping up her chin. "Shh. I do not deserve you, of that, there is no doubt. But…I am never again giving you up. I have made a choice, Ariella. I am going to try to be the prince that you think me to be. I love you, Ariella. I intend to spend the rest of my life proving just how much." He added, "You must prepare yourself. There will be many more such declarations."

She wrapped her arms around his neck. "You have nothing to prove, Emilian. I know how much you love me."

He pulled her close, overcome by so much feeling, so much happiness, so much love. The future loomed brightly before them. "No, darling, you have no idea."

She whispered, trembling, her body warming for his, "Then do show me."

He brushed his mouth over hers, gently, sensually. He began to think of some very creative ways to profess his love. "Come upstairs with me, darling," he murmured in his most seductive tone. "I am going to start that proof right now."

And his beautiful, eccentric *gadji* princess grinned up at him, her eyes shining.

Emilian St Xavier's heart soared high and free.

* * * * *

Turn the page to read an excerpt from
DARK EMBRACE
the third book in Brenda Joyce's highly acclaimed
bestselling paranormal romance series
THE MASTERS OF TIME

HE WAS A MAN, NOT A WOLF, and he was bleeding from his gunshot wounds. His blue eyes blazed with rage and fury... and he was utterly naked.

Brie cried out, pressing her back harder into her door. This man bore no resemblance to the Master she'd met last year. She couldn't breathe, choking on fear. She looked from his beautiful, furious and ravaged face to his bloody body and then at the gold chain he wore, with the fang hanging on it. She inhaled. He was all hard, rippling muscle and his entire body throbbed with tension.

She tore her gaze upward. "You're alive," she gasped. "You're hurt!"

His blue eyes were livid. "*Never* summon me again."

His anger enveloped her. It was terrifying, for there was so much hatred in it. Brie shuddered. The power of his hatred made her begin to feel sick. She tried to shake her head. She hadn't summoned him!

He was the Wolf of Awe.

What had happened to him?

The Wolf wanted blood and death. Brie felt the bloodlust. And she had seen the evil.

She could barely think. "You've been shot." She realized she was whispering. "Let me help you...Aidan."

He snarled at her. "Come closer an' see how ye can really help me, Brianna."

He remembered her.

His mouth curled unpleasantly.

She exhaled harshly and didn't move, uncertain that he wouldn't turn into that wolf and rip her to death. But he had saved her from the gang. If he was going to hurt her, wouldn't he have done so already?

Her temples pounding with the pain of taking in so much of his rage and hatred, feeling faint, she met his glittering blue gaze. His hard stare was unwavering. It was cold, menacing. *How could a man change so much in a single year?*

She was terrified of him, but she was supposed to help him, wasn't she? "You're bleeding," she whispered. "You could bleed to death."

He barked at her, a dark, bitter laugh. "I willna die, not yet."

She tried to feel past the hatred and anger, the lust for more blood, but if he was in pain, it eluded her. If he had been weakened, she couldn't feel it. He was probably too angry and filled with adrenaline just then.

She pushed the fear aside. She could not let him die. Her heart exploding, she turned and opened the linen closet, not far from the kitchen. She took several towels out and faced him. His gaze moved from the towels in her hands to her face.

The distance of a small kitchenette separated them. She started forward slowly, in case he tried to seize her—or worse, turned into the Wolf and leaped at her.

"Dinna!"

She faltered by the kitchen counter. "Here." She held out the largest towel.

He looked even angrier.

Brie tossed it at him.

She thought he meant to catch it. Instead, he batted it away with one hand. Her gaze dropped of its own accord and she knew she flushed. "You need clothes—and medical attention," she whispered, dragging her eyes upward.

"I need power," he said dangerously.

Demons lusted for power. All evil did. Brie felt tears of fear and despair well. She somehow shook her head. "No." *What had happened to him?* That Wolf had been evil. That Wolf had destroyed those teenagers. He was shrouded in darkness; there was no white light. How could this be *her* Aidan?

He suddenly turned and picked up the towel, his every movement filled with raw fury. He wrapped it around his waist. When he looked at her with his blazing eyes, he said, "They were lost."

She trembled. He had read her thoughts. "You don't know that their souls couldn't be reclaimed."

He snarled at her.

"Are they all dead?"

"Every last one," he said savagely, as if triumphant.

She wiped at her tears.

"Ye cry for the deamhan boys?"

She was crying for him. "No. I'm sorry. You saved me, and I'm judging you."

It was a moment before he spoke. "I hardly saved ye, Brianna," he said, so softly that her heart skipped and then thundered.

Brie found her gaze fixed on his. In that instant her tension changed. Desire charged through her body in response to his blatantly seductive tone.

He knew. He smiled. "Ye ran. I hunted ye here," he said as softly.

She became still, her body tight now, quivering, while fear surged. She began shaking her head, refusing to believe him capable of hurting *her.*

She prayed that he had not fallen so far into black evil that he could do such a thing.

But dear God, she was standing face-to-face with the man she had just spent the past year dreaming of. In the circumstances, her body should not be reacting to his very male and obviously virile presence, but it was.

Brie wet her lips and backed up.

His lust escalated dangerously, changing. It overshadowed the anger, the hatred. The need to draw blood vanished. She began to feel dizzy, hollow and faint. Her heart was pounding so hard it hurt. His gaze was on her face and the tension that throbbed between them seemed so charged, Brie thought the air might blaze.

Brie closed her eyes. So much emotion was swirling in the room, she was becoming confused. She had to keep a grip on her mind. She had to fight her empathy. She couldn't desire him now! He was simply too dangerous.

She fought for control. When she opened her eyes, he looked oddly satisfied—as if he sensed her internal struggles. "Aidan, please sit down." She swallowed, knowing she sounded like Tabby with her first-graders. "I can stop the bleeding until the medics get here." Keeping up the pretense, she nodded at the sofa.

He laughed at her. "Dinna speak as if I'm a small boy. Three bullets can't kill the son of deamhan."

She went rigid. *He could not be the son of a demon.* Was this a bad, bad joke?

"Aye," he said, growling. "The greatest deamhan to ever walk Alba spawned me."

Brie began shaking her head. More tears rose. How could this be happening? "You're a Master!"

"Damn the gods!" he roared.

She cringed, shocked. "They'll hear you!"

"I dinna care!"

Brie did not move, searching his furious gaze. *He hated the gods.* She trembled, afraid for him.

His blue eyes changed, becoming brilliant now, blinding. "Ah, Brianna," he murmured. "Ye care so much," he purred.

His lust for power and sex made her reel. But she was also

sickened, in her heart, as well as her stomach, because the rage and hatred, the lust, the frenzy of it all, were too much for her to bear. "What happened to you?"

"Come here," he said softly.

She tensed, instantly aware of what he intended.

"Ye want to come to me, Brianna."

She wanted nothing more. And suddenly she wasn't sure why she was hesitating.

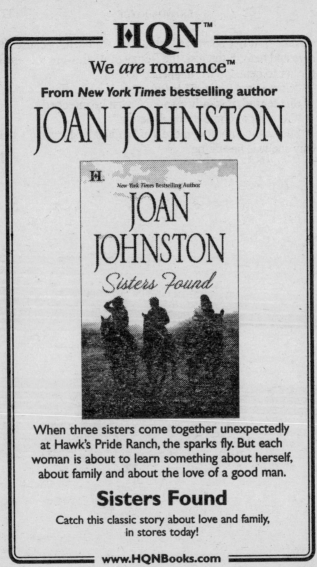

REQUEST YOUR
FREE BOOKS!

2 FREE NOVELS
FROM THE ROMANCE/SUSPENSE
COLLECTION PLUS 2 FREE GIFTS!

YES! Please send me 2 FREE novels from the Romance/Suspense Collection and my 2 FREE gifts (gifts are worth about $10). After receiving them, if I don't wish to receive any more books, I can return the shipping statement marked "cancel." If I don't cancel, I will receive 4 brand-new novels every month and be billed just $5.49 per book in the U.S. or $5.99 per book in Canada, plus 25¢ shipping and handling per book plus applicable taxes, if any*. That's a savings of at least 20% off the cover price! I understand that accepting the 2 free books and gifts places me under no obligation to buy anything. I can always return a shipment and cancel at any time. Even if I never buy another book from the Reader Service, the two free books and gifts are mine to keep forever.

185 MDN EF5Y   385 MDN EF6C

Name _____ (PLEASE PRINT) _____

Address _____ Apt. # _____

City _____ State/Prov. _____ Zip/Postal Code _____

Signature (if under 18, a parent or guardian must sign)

Mail to **The Reader Service:**
IN U.S.A.: P.O. Box 1867, Buffalo, NY 14240-1867
IN CANADA: P.O. Box 609, Fort Erie, Ontario L2A 5X3

Not valid to current subscribers to the Romance Collection,
the Suspense Collection or the Romance/Suspense Collection.

Want to try two free books from another line?
Call 1-800-873-8635 or visit www.morefreebooks.com.

* Terms and prices subject to change without notice. N.Y. residents add applicable sales tax. Canadian residents will be charged applicable provinaal taxes and GST. This offer is limited to one order per household. All orders subject to approval. Credit or debit balances in a customer's account(s) may be offset by any other outstanding balance owed by or to the customer. Please allow 4 to 6 weeks for delivery. Offer available while quantities last.

Your Privacy: Harlequin is committed to protecting your privacy. Our Privacy Policy is available online at www.eHarlequin.com or upon request from the Reader Service. From time to time we make our lists of customers available to reputable third parties who may have a product or service of interest to you. If you would prefer we not share your name and address, please check here. ☐

BOB08

HARLEQUIN
More Than Words

"Jeanne proves that one woman can change the world, with vision, compassion and hard work."

—**Linda Lael Miller**, author

*Linda wrote "Queen of the Rodeo," inspired by Jeanne Greenberg, founder of **SARI Therapeutic Riding**. Since 1978 Jeanne has devoted her life to enriching the lives of disabled children and their families through innovative and exciting therapies on horseback.*

Look for "*Queen of the Rodeo*" in
More Than Words, Vol. 4,
available in April 2008 at eHarlequin.com
or wherever books are sold.

SUPPORTING CAUSES OF CONCERN TO WOMEN   **HARLEQUIN**
WWW.HARLEQUINMORETHANWORDS.COM

MTW07JG2

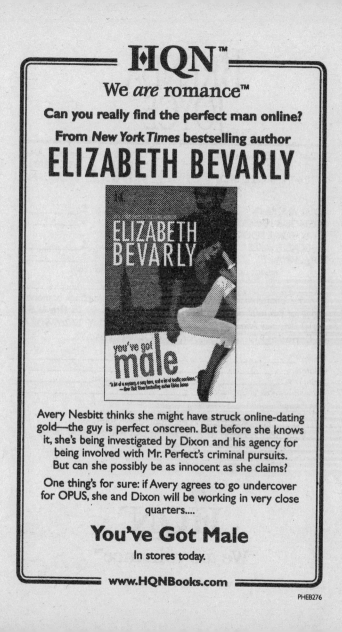

BRENDA JOYCE

77244 THE PERFECT BRIDE	___ $7.99 U.S.	___ $9.50 CAN.
77137 A LADY AT LAST	___ $6.99 U.S.	___ $8.50 CAN.
77184 THE STOLEN BRIDE	___ $6.99 U.S.	___ $8.50 CAN.

(limited quantities available)

TOTAL AMOUNT	$ _____
POSTAGE & HANDLING	$ _____
($1.00 FOR 1 BOOK, 50¢ for each additional)	
APPLICABLE TAXES*	$ _____
TOTAL PAYABLE	$ _____

(check or money order—please do not send cash)

To order, complete this form and send it, along with a check or money order for the total above, payable to HQN Books, to: **In the U.S.:** 3010 Walden Avenue, P.O. Box 9077, Buffalo, NY 14269-9077; **In Canada:** P.O. Box 636, Fort Erie, Ontario, L2A 5X3.

Name: _____

Address: _____ City: _____

State/Prov.: _____ Zip/Postal Code: _____

Account Number (if applicable): _____

075 CSAS

*New York residents remit applicable sales taxes.
*Canadian residents remit applicable GST and provincial taxes.

HQN™

We *are* romance™

www.HQNBooks.com

PHBJ0408BL